≈≈≈≈≈≈≈

Jewell crawled to her purse on all fours. She didn't know Daniel was following until she felt his hands on her hips as she dug through her bag. She looked back and saw that he already had his boxers off.

"What are you doing?"

"Nothing, baby. Take your call."

He penetrated from behind just as she pulled the cellular from her purse. Jewell gasped and dropped to her elbows. She pushed the answer button on the seventh ring.

"Oh, uh, *uh*, hello?"

"Vanessa! How you doing, girl?" Percy sounded like he was in a good mood. Jewell definitely was.

"I'm, uh, I'm fine."

Daniel was digging for gold. Jewell looked back at him with a worried expression, but he smiled and kept on plowing.

"Did you talk to your friends?" Percy asked.

"Yeah."

"Do they want to play ball?"

"Yeah. They, they do."

"Good," Percy said. "So they still got my slab?"

"Yeah."

"*And* my eggs?"

"Yuh, yeah."

"*Great*," Percy said. "You're a smart girl. I knew you'd make the right decision. Can we meet tomorrow night? Just me and you; *leave your boys at home*."

"Yeah," Jewell said. "Where?"

Percy gave her directions to a location Jewell knew very well. That was a good thing because she wouldn't have remembered anything complicated. With the liquor in her system and Daniel knocking against her walls, it was hard enough to keep from moaning into the phone.

Jewell hung up with the heroin king and looked back at her butt naked boyfriend.

"You a freak," she whispered.

He grinned and blew her a kiss. "That's what you like about me."

≈≈≈≈≈≈≈

JEWELL AND THE DAPPER DAN

KEITH THOMAS WALKER

KEITHWALKERBOOKS, INC
This is a UMS production

JEWELL AND THE DAPPER DAN

KEITHWALKERBOOKS

Publishing Company
KeithWalkerBooks, Inc.
P.O. Box 331585
Fort Worth, TX 76163

For information write
KeithWalkerBooks, Inc.
P.O. Box 331585
Fort Worth, TX 76163

ISBN-13 DIGIT: 978-0-9850500-0-9
ISBN-10 DIGIT: 0985050004
Manufactured in the United States of America

First Edition

Visit us at www.keithwalkerbooks.com

KEITH THOMAS WALKER

5

This book is for Keisha Mennefee, author of Blue Interlude

MORE BOOKS BY
KEITH THOMAS WALKER

Fixin' Tyrone
How to Kill Your Husband
A Good Dude
Riding the Corporate Ladder
The Finley Sisters' Oath of Romance
Blow by Blow
Harlot
Plan C (And More KWB Shorts)
Dripping Chocolate
The Realest Ever
Jackson Memorial

Visit keithwalkerbooks.com for information about these and upcoming titles from KeithWalkerBooks.

ACKNOWLEDGEMENTS

Of course I would like to thank God, first and foremost, for giving me the creativity and drive to pursue my dreams and the understanding that I am nothing without Him. I would like to thank my wife for being my first and most important critic, and I would like to thank my mother for always pushing me to be the best I can be. I would like to thank Janae Hampton for being the best advisor, supporter and little sister a brother could ever have. I would also like to thank (in no particular order) Brandy Rees, Denise Bolds, Sabrina Scott, Dianne Guinn, Kierra Pease, Anna Garza, Anthony Douglas, Jarvis Howard and Uncle Steven Thomas, one love. I'd like to thank everyone who purchased and enjoyed one of my books. Everything I do has always been to please you. I know there are folks who mean the world to me that I'm failing to mention. I apologize ahead of time. Rest assured I'm grateful for everything you've done for me!

CHAPTER ONE
LOVE IN THE CLUB

There were over 700 sweaty bodies in attendance at Club Destiny, but no one garnished as much attention as Daniel Curry. He was a tall man, teetering over six feet, three inches. He was brown-skinned; the color of an unpeeled almond. His suit was from the Versace collection. The slacks and vest were charcoal colored. His jacket was dark as well, but it had a plaid design with lavender stripes that matched his tie perfectly. His shirt was a darker purple. His cufflinks were solid gold. His eyes were low and serious.

Daniel removed his wool fedora like a gentleman as he approached the bar, but his progress was impeded by a massive crowd of party-people who were just as thirsty as he was. There was never enough room at this club, but a couple of tipsy patrons moved aside to let the well-dressed man by.

Daniel stepped slowly and leaned on the bar's exquisite marble finish. A voluptuous bopper caught his eye, and she quickly approached him. Daniel leaned forward and made his drink request very close to the barmaid's ear.

Club Destiny always did pretty good business, but the occupancy was unusually high tonight, and MC Freeze was in rare form. The bony deejay flipped records and cut melodies so flawlessly you'd think they were recorded that way. Kanye's *Niggas in Paris* belted from speakers so large only one of them could fit in the bed of an F-150. If your ears weren't ringing when you left this establishment, MC Freeze would feel like he'd done you a huge disservice.

The barmaid stared at the crowd over Daniel's shoulder and smiled delightfully, as if he was whispering sweet nothings in her ear. She wore dark red lipstick with a generous coat of candy gloss. Her eyes were brown and wistful, almost fully closed. Her breasts were huge. Leaning over, she exposed nearly six inches of cleavage. She licked her lips seductively and giggled, and then she backed away from Jewell's man.

The waitress turned to retrieve the required liquors, and Daniel's reaction to her physique was not lost on his girlfriend - who watched from a considerable distance. Rather than back away from the bar, Daniel remained with his elbows bent on the counter. He flipped the fedora casually in his hands. His bald head glistened under the lamp light. His eyes followed the waitress' sashaying tail, and he pursed his lips and grinned – *not a lot*, but very little went on that Jewell wasn't aware of.

Clarissa Hunt, nicknamed *Jewell* because of her exquisite taste for diamonds and rare gemstones, leaned back in her seat and crossed her long legs. The move was enough to light a dozen horny eyes in her direction, but none of these timid men approached her table. They ogled from a distance, as if she was an exotic creature or a fragile museum exhibit.

Most of these club goers weren't really *men* anyway, in Jewell's opinion, regardless of their age or what they had between their legs. A *man* does not wear tube socks with Dockers, for example. A man does not throw up gang signs and grab his crotch when his favorite song comes on. And a man is not intimidated by a beautiful woman with no ring on her finger. A real man does not look you dead in the eyes and then look away nervously when you smile at him.

Jewell snickered and rolled her eyes at the deadbeats two-stepping around her. She looked back to the bar and was not surprised to see Daniel still working on their drink order. The waitress was in his mug again; grinning alluringly as she mixed the intoxicants. Their faces were close enough to kiss.

But even these indiscretions were mild, and Jewell knew she shouldn't expect much better of her boyfriend: When she met him, Daniel didn't even want a relationship in the classical sense. He told her straight up; he was looking for another *bitch* to add to his stable. Anyone who'd been a pimp at one time or another couldn't be faulted for grinning at a couple of stray asses here and there, could they?

And it wasn't like Jewell was totally without sin herself. She looked away from Daniel and scanned the club for a man she could hook up with tonight. And her encounter would go much further than the casual flirting Daniel was involved in. Jewell wanted a guy she could leave the club with; a special gentleman who would take her all the way to his house, if she played her cards right.

"A rum and coke, for the lady..."

Jewell looked up and saw that her boyfriend had finally made it back with their drinks. Daniel had his fedora back on. He held both drinks in one hand with a stylish cane crooked in the other. Jewell tried to get him to leave the cane at home, but that was like asking Rosie O'Donnell to do a few sit ups: Some things were simply not meant to be.

Daniel was not meant to be anything less than the best dresser in the room; any and every room he's ever been in. Dapper Dan wore turquoise Easter sweaters with long-sleeved button downs to football games. He donned slacks and suspenders at the grocery store. When it was *really* time to get decked out, he wore tuxedos and sported *real* top hats; big enough to pull a rabbit from. When he undressed for the day, Daniel put on five-hundred dollar smoking jackets and satin pajamas with designer house shoes.

In addition to his stunning sense of style, Daniel was also a very handsome man. He had no hair on his head other than his thin eyebrows. His eyelashes were long; almost feminine. His eyes were a beautiful bronze. He had a strong jaw line and thin, pink lips. Daniel had a smile that could melt the panties off any dame. And if the smile didn't work, his voice was as smooth as Billy D's in a Colt 45 commercial.

Works every time.

Jewell took her glass and eyed him curiously. She wouldn't mention the flirting she observed because things like that were petty considering the depths of their relationship. It was his cane that had her attention.

"That's not the same one you had earlier, is it?" she asked. Her words were barely audible over MC Freeze's tunes.

Daniel squinted and leaned towards her mouth. "What?"

Jewell stood and met him halfway. She had to pull her dress down immediately because the one-piece slid up to ridiculous heights when she sat down.

For her evening at Club Destiny, Jewell wore a pink Chanel that was sleeveless, backless, and damned near *dress*-less. She stood five feet even. At 123 pounds, she was considered overweight by whatever scientific community came up with those height/weight charts, but *fat* was the last thing on the mind of anyone who saw her in that dress.

Jewell was fair-skinned; slightly darker than a walnut shell. She had large eyes, full lips, and sexy legs that were always her best attribute. Her hair was jet black, long and straight; flowing halfway down her back. The Chanel clung to her like honey, putting to shame all the other floosies who thought they looked special in their freakum dresses.

Jewell had thick thighs, a video vixen ass, and a small waist. She always thought her breasts were her weakest feature, but any man who got a chance to fondle her 32-B's was damned happy for the opportunity.

Growing up, Jewell was often told she was pretty enough to model. That was a dream she planned on seriously pursuing one day, but there were so many other things going on during her teens and twenties. She was thirty-four now, and Jewell knew that her *modeling window* had officially closed.

She stretched the dress over her butt and put a hand on Daniel's chest to brace herself. He didn't budge at all. Daniel was the hardest, strongest, and most beautiful man Jewell had ever met. In a hurricane, she would run past ten light poles and grab onto his rugged arm instead.

"That's a different cane!" Jewell spoke loudly, directly into his ear. Daniel's scent was Boss cologne. "What happened to the one with the gold handle?"

Daniel toted an alpaca walking stick with a silver dog head. At home Jewell thought he had the golden crook.

"I was gonna bring the other one," he said. "But–"

Jewell giggled as a memory came back to her. "That's the one that has the dent?" she guessed.

"From that fool's head," Daniel confirmed.

The recollection brought a sneer to his face, but it affected Jewell differently. She loved it when her man got violent with people. She downed her rum and coke in three hefty swallows and dropped the glass on the table. She grabbed Daniel's arm and pulled him in the direction of the dance floor.

"Come on."

"Where?"

"I wanna dance," Jewell said, smiling like a debutante.

Daniel took only one sip of his drink before setting the glass next to hers. He wasn't worried about anyone slipping him a mickey, because he didn't plan on returning to the table. And since he never paid for anything at Club Destiny, the eight dollar martini meant nothing to him.

Jewell held his hand and led him to a spot on the floor where she could shake her tail feather. The club was so dense you couldn't stretch out your arms without punching someone, but gangsters and hoochies parted for Jewell like she had Moses with her. Everyone paid attention to them. Even faithful boyfriends couldn't keep their eyes off her body.

Only a stallion like Jewell could start arguments simply by walking through a crowd. Jealous females hissed at her and rolled their eyes. They made mental notes of what they should wear next weekend, but getting a dress like Jewell's was only half the battle. These hateful women could never have Jewell's looks. They couldn't duplicate her style or her attitude, and they'd have to take out a loan to compete with her accessories.

Jewell wore three rings on her right hand. The most expensive had a 5.77 ct yellow diamond valued at over twenty-thousand dollars. The bracelet on her left hand glistened with 14k white gold and thirty-six mounted diamonds weighing 6.8 carats apiece. At $3,000, her pearl diamond pendant was the cheapest piece of jewelry she had on.

She found a spot away from the DJ booth and let go of Daniel's hand. She turned and stared at him longingly. Jewell began to bounce energetically with the music, but her boyfriend teetered indecisively. Daniel wasn't much of a dancer, and Club Destiny's premier deejay was well aware of his short-comings. MC Freeze brought his Kanye West mix to a swift end. The fast tunes were replaced by Aaliyah's *Rock the Boat,* which was Jewell's favorite song. Daniel was the only man she knew who could request a jam without even looking at the man in charge.

"Why you way over there?" she asked.

"Huh?" Daniel came closer.

Jewell stood on her toes and sucked his earlobe.

"Why you way over there?" she asked again; her hot breath making the hair stand on the back of his neck.

"What about the mark?" Daniel said.

"He's not here."

Daniel put his hands on her waist, then on her hips. His cane was cold against her leg, but his hands were warm. Jewell rocked her hips to the beat of Aaliyah's sultry ballad. Daniel sighed. He took a deep breath and his nostrils flared.

"What's wrong?" she asked.

"I ain't never cool with this," he said.

"It's worth it," Jewell promised. She turned her back to him. Her body undulated like an anaconda.

Daniel dropped his four hundred dollar cane like it came from Walmart. He put both hands on his woman's hips, and slid them up her sides. He pulled her closer and traced his fingers down her stomach. Jewell laid her head on his chest oblivious to the morons watching them. She reached up and rubbed Daniel's cheek with delicate fingers. He grinded more persistently.

"Ooh, baby. What you doing?" she whispered.

Daniel kissed the side of her face. "You know I don't like to dance," he breathed against her neck.

Jewell was quite the opposite. She shimmied like a belly dancer; grinding her ass in Daniel's lap. Aaliyah's breathy lyrics seemed to come from her very soul.

Boy you know you make me float

Daniel's stomach pressed hard against her back. His hands were insatiable. One snaked up towards her breasts. The other slid unabated in the direction of her panties.

Before we drift any deeper

Jewell didn't think he'd go any further, but Daniel was not a man who believed in limitations. Both hands struck gold simultaneously. His left cupped her breast; his right clutched the moistness between her legs.

Jewell gasped and inhaled sharply. A jolt of electricity bounced between Daniel's hand and her pubic hairs. Her eyes flashed open, and Jewell saw that she wasn't the only one getting a rise out of Daniel's antics. A couple of goons dancing in front of them stared in wide-eyed amazement. Jewell pulled her skirt down and turned to face her man. Her smile was like Marilyn Monroe's when she sang for the president. Daniel's hands slid to her ass as soon as their bellies touched. Jewell stood on her toes to get close to his ear.

"Where's your cane?" she asked.

"I dropped it."

"Someone's gonna steal it."

"Nobody's gonna steal *my* cane."

She looked down and saw the silver dog head twinkling between her legs.

"I'd get it," she said, "but you can see my panties when I bend over. Those guys behind me have been looking too much as it is."

Daniel looked over her shoulder and his whole expression changed. Jewell knew that look well.

"Don't start," she said, but her man wouldn't look at her.

"Which one?" he asked.

Jewell reached between his legs and groped his growing soldier. He was almost at a full salute.

"Can we get in the office?" she asked.

Daniel didn't answer; his eyes were still on the squares. Jewell stroked him more insistently, and finally she got his attention. He stared into her eyes and the color drained from his face.

"Whatchoo doing?" he said.

"You wanna mess it all up?" she asked. "This is *business*, remember?"

Daniel smiled. "You sho right."

"You a little high strung," Jewell noticed, her hand still on his stiffy. "You want me to get that out of you?"

"You wanna go to the office?" he asked.

"Damn, baby. You read my mind."

Daniel bent to collect his cane. Jewell stood in front of him; keeping her ample hips between his eyes and the losers he was mad at. Daniel turned and led the way to the manager's room upstairs. Aaliyah's sultry tunes followed them all the way.

Oooh, baby I love your stroke

≈ ≈ ≈ ≈ ≈ ≈ ≈

JEWELL AND THE DAPPER DAN

Club Destiny was managed by a shrewd drug dealer/entrepreneur known as *Boon*. Boon was an imposing figure; toting 240 pounds on his six foot frame. He always carried a pistol in one jacket pocket, and he was known to keep a Ziploc baggie full of ecstasy pills in the other. Boon was not related nor was he close friends with Jewell's boyfriend, but Daniel walked into the manager's 2nd floor office without knocking, like he had legitimate business there.

The room was small. There was one table, one file cabinet, and two monitors transmitting images from the club's eight security cameras. There was a large window in the wall directly ahead of them. This window extended from corner to corner, ceiling to floor. Through the glass, Daniel and Jewell had an excellent view of the club's activities. They were in no danger of missing the black businessman from up there.

But there were two waitresses currently occupying the office. They were chopping up a monster line of what appeared to be coke, or maybe speed. They looked up at Daniel and his woman with anxious eyes.

The room was dimly lit. The only light came from a bathroom tucked around the corner.

"Y'all need to move around," Daniel said.

The girls gathered their paraphernalia quickly and exited without a word. Jewell pressed up against her man when they were gone. The music was just as loud up there as it was downstairs. With Daniel off the floor, MC Freeze sped up the tempo again. A gangster rapper energized the crowd with lyrics supremely important to the black existence: a nice ride with an equally nice interior:

I'm in my cool whip
Inside's Jello

"I'da been alright if you didn't wear that dress," Daniel said. He propped his cane against a chair and then went after his girlfriend like a grizzly bear. He put his arms around her waist and hefted her with little effort. Jewell didn't know what his plans were until he turned and placed her butt gingerly on the table. Her feet dangled two feet off the floor. Sitting up so high, she and

Daniel were roughly the same height. He stepped into her, and Jewell opened her legs to allow him access.

Daniel took of his hat, like a proper gentle, and sat it on the table next to her.

He kissed her softly. She darted her tongue between his lips. Daniel grunted and then backed away and took off his jacket. Jewell's heart raced. She leaned back on the table; supporting herself with shaky arms. She was so eager, she thought she might leave a puddle on the table. Daniel draped his coat neatly over the back of one of the chairs. When he stepped to her again, the bulge in his slacks was visibly throbbing.

Jewell sat up to meet him, and Daniel put his hands on her hips. He stared into her eyes with an almost vacant expression and slid his hands under her dress. He hooked her panties, and Jewell lifted her tailbone from the table to facilitate their removal. Rather than toss the thong aside, Daniel slipped the underwear over his neck, taking a healthy sniff when the crotch passed over his nose.

"You a freak," Jewell said with a wicked grin.

"You the one trying to get booty at the club," Daniel noted. He kissed her again. Jewell could smell herself on the nifty collar he wore, and that turned her on more for some reason.

"No, *you* did," she mumbled around a mouthful of his bottom lip.

"*I* wanted to beat those niggas up," Daniel reminded.

"So, why'd you grab me like that?" she teased.

"I was just dancing," he said. "You know I can't dance."

"I like the way you dance just fine," Jewell said. She reached between his legs to undue his zipper. Daniel backed away.

"Don't tease," she said.

"This is your special night," he said. "I'm gonna hook you up."

Jewell didn't think she heard him right. "Huh?"

Daniel dropped to his knees and cleared up any doubt. "You heard me."

"But you don't like doing that."

"But you like it."

"I don't want you... *Oh*...."

His tongue darted between her legs like a cobra tasting the air. Daniel hated to eat at the Y, but at the same time he was so *good* at it. It was a cruel twist of fate. It usually took a whole lot of persuading and even more reciprocating to get him down there, but Jewell's eyes and clitoris were not deceiving her. Daniel really had stepped up to the plate and initiated her favorite of all past times.

Jewell exhaled slowly. She knew it was too good to be true, and it was. Before she could get her hips working, something flashed in the corner of her eye. She sat up and squinted at the security monitors. Daniel started sucking a certain spot that made her want to keep her mouth closed.

But she couldn't.

"Is, is that him?" she asked and pointed.

Daniel's head jerked up. He stared up the length of her body, and then followed her finger to the monitor.

"Yeah. That's him." He stood quickly and wiped his mouth with the back of his hand. He pulled the panties off his neck and tossed them to her.

"Come on. Let's go."

"You owe me one," Jewell said, but Daniel was all about business now. He slid into his jacket and scooped up his hat and cane.

"Get yo shit together. Let's go," he said, and walked out of the office before she was done getting dressed.

CHAPTER TWO
THE BLACK BUSINESSMAN

Percy Hamilton was not born with a silver spoon in his mouth. Despite the relative success of his grandfather's business, Hamilton Furniture, Percy endured a rather average upbringing. His father was insistent that Percy not grow up like so many other spoiled sophisticates in Overbrook Meadows, so he made the young heir attend public schools rather than private. As an adolescent, Percy wore Wayless shoes most of the time. He got one dollar every morning to buy a lunch tray like any other south side kid.

When he got to high school, Percy didn't get a car until the second semester of his senior year. And when he graduated, he had to earn his own academic scholarship. By then his parents had enough loot to put him through Harvard, but there was a lesson to be learned. Percy's father wanted his son to know what it was like to be a *regular* black man. He often told him, "*The money in your bank account may gain you privileges, but never lose sight of how this country really feels about you.*"

Percy didn't obtain his grandfather's inheritance until he was twenty-one. By then he understood his position in American society, but he made another revelation at that time: Percy decided his father was stone cold crazy. Money was to be spent and *enjoyed*, not horded in banks, stocks and mutual funds. His grandfather did good to make the family business what it was, but what's the sense of working hard if you never get to play?

Plus Percy understood that you have to spend money to make money. When he got behind the reigns of his family's legacy at the age of 31, Percy was the first Hamilton to advertise on a mass media scale. For a while you couldn't go a day without seeing him on television. His ads were goofy and obviously low-budget, but they served their purpose. Due largely to Percy's efforts, Hamilton Furniture was now the largest African-American-owned business in Overbrook Meadows.

Percy Hamilton was one of only twelve black millionaires in the city.

He was also young and flashy and very well known at the party scenes. Percy wasn't a good looking guy, but looks are so unimportant when you hit the strip club with thousands of dollars stuffed in your pockets. When he frequented one of the city's night spots, Percy would have a few women on each arm the minute he walked through the door – and this was the case tonight at Club Destiny. By the time Jewell made it downstairs, she knew she had her work cut out for her.

Daniel was already out of sight and long gone. Jewell didn't look for her boyfriend. Instead she boogied her way to the V.I.P. section and eyed her prey. She didn't initially like what she saw, but that was immaterial.

Percy Hamilton was the color of a used tire. Jewell knew a few Mexicans who insulted blacks by calling them *llantas,* and she figured whoever came up with that slur had someone like Percy in mind. The furniture king had small, beady eyes and full cheeks with protruding lips. He was a short man; only an inch or so taller than Jewell, and he was moderately overweight. Jewell thought he might look a little better if his fat was distributed properly, but most of it hung out around his belly and waist. Percy Hamilton had a big gut, a big booty, and hips that would only look appealing on a woman.

For his evening at Club Destiny, Percy wore a canary yellow suit with a white shirt and black tie. His shoes were expensive and shiny, but his suit had a visible stain on the lapel, and his tie was too short. None of this took away from his allure, however. Percy Hamilton lounged in the V.I.P. section with a bottle of Cristal on his table and two girls holstered on each of his womanly hips.

His entourage consisted of just one burly brother, but this guy was about the size of an adolescent Kodiak. The bodyguard stood at the entrance of the V.I.P. room with his arms crossed over his massive chest. He had big eyes and flabby jowls, and he had news for Jewell as soon as she got within earshot.

"Mr. Percy don't want no more company." His voice rumbled like an eighteen-wheeler.

Undaunted, Jewell stumbled up to the big man as if she was drunk. She wobbled on her stilettos and placed a hand on his arm for support when she reached him.

"Huh?"

The bodyguard rolled his eyes. "I said Mr. Percy don't want no more company."

"*Percy*? Who's Percy?" Jewell cackled.

The big man politely removed her hand from his forearm. "You need to move around, lady."

Jewell looked past him and tried to make eye contact with the mark. "Nuh uhn. I wanna go in *there*." She pointed and wavered like she might fall over any minute. The guard was unimpressed.

"I said Mr. Percy don't want no—"

"Who is that?" someone called from inside. Percy spoke quickly and softly.

Bingo.

Jewell looked past the big guy and locked eyes with Mr. Hamilton. He was as ugly as she remembered from his television commercials, but this wasn't a casual encounter. He could look like Beetlejuice from the Howard Stern show for all she cared.

"Hey!" Jewell drawled. "How come I can't come in there with y'all?"

Mr. Hamilton's eyes grew very large. The four skanks in the V.I.P. with him were fairly attractive, Jewell would give them that, but she had a distinct advantage over them: Those women would go through gallons of Crystal to reach Jewell's supposed level of intoxication. Plus none of them looked as good as she did in that Chanel. It was really a no-brainer.

"Hey man," Percy chastised his bodyguard. "She can come in here. We got plenty room. Let her in, Daryl."

Jewell smiled inwardly and stepped smoothly. She shot the cockblocker a big, "*Hmph*!" as she passed.

The V.I.P. section at Club Destiny wasn't all that special. Instead of the tacky, metal chairs they had in the main area, big-spenders got to sit on a large, leather sofa. The sofa was a one-piece, and it was U-shaped. It wrapped around a lone table topped with liquor, glasses, roses and confetti. Percy sat in the middle with two boppers on either side.

There really was plenty of room for Jewell, but she didn't want to be too far away from the mark. She walked in and spoke to Percy directly; ignoring the four women.

"What y'all got going on in here?" She sounded as country as a pot of possum stew. She almost brought bubblegum, but that might have been a little *too* much.

Percy stared at her curves and flashed all thirty-two choppers.

"We just in here having a little champagne," he said. He hefted the bottle and looked around for another glass. "You like Cristal?"

One of the girls on his left rolled her eyes. "*Hmph*! Don't look like she need nothing else to drink." The others seemed to agree.

Jewell stared down at the one who spoke up. "For your information; I can handle my alcohol *just fine*!" She hiccupped loudly to prove her point. "Excuse me."

"Yeah, yeah, she fine," Percy said. He licked his lips and winked at her. "*She just fine*." He grabbed one of the other girl's empty glass and poured Jewell a drink.

At that moment she knew she had him.

"I don't like *her*," Jewell said, pointing at the woman who spoke against her. "I'm not staying if *she's* gonna be in here, too. She don't like me." Jewell spoke innocently, like a gassed grade-schooler.

Percy fixed an evil eye on the girl Jewell pointed to. "Hey baby," he said, "I'ma come find you later."

The woman was dumbfounded. "You kicking *me* out?" She puffed out her chest to make the real question evident: *You kicking these titties out?*

"I'll come find you later," Percy promised.

The dame shot fire from her eyes at Jewell. "But I was here first!" she said to Percy.

"I'll holler at you *later*," he said again. His smile was warm and sincere; probably the same one he used to move all of those sofas and bedroom sets. Jewell made a mental note to be wary of that smile. Percy might be as good at lying as she was.

The rejected bopper stood and gathered her belongings roughly. She snatched up her glass and downed one last swig of champagne before turning to leave. She sneered at Jewell. Jewell smiled back, thinking to herself, *One down.*

Before she exited, the woman turned to the last girl on Percy's left side.

"Come on, bitch!"

"Huh?"

"You rode with *me*, Tracy. And *I'm* finna go."

Tracy looked to Percy for help. Percy threw up his hands. "I can't take you home, baby."

Jewell couldn't believe her luck. *Damn, two for one!*

Both girls left the V.I.P. with a whole lot of attitude, and Jewell took their vacated spot. She immediately grabbed the drink Percy made for her and downed it all in one swallow. She burped pleasantly.

"*Oops.* Excuse me." She smiled nervously, and Percy smiled back.

Jewell looked down at her empty glass. "That stuff is good. What'd you say that was?"

Percy looked up to the skies and thanked sweet Jesus, and then he turned to face Jewell; totally giving his back to the other two bimbos. He looked Jewell up and down and actually rubbed his hands together.

"That's Cristal, baby."

Sitting so close, Jewell found that his breath was rather tart. She sighed, but her intoxicated grin remained intact. "*Cristal*? You mean like what those rappers be drinking?"

Percy nodded, grinning like the Cheshire cat. He poured her another glass. "You like it?"

Jewell swallowed only half this time. "Yeah. It's good. We don't drink this stuff at my house."

"What you drink?" Percy asked. He expected her to say Boones Farm, or something of the malt liquor variety, but that wouldn't work with the character Jewell was portraying that night.

"My boyfriend likes Château Mouton, Bollinger..." she said.

Percy studied her jewelry instead of her thighs this time. "You, your boyfriend?"

"He play for the Mavericks," Jewell explained placidly. "He think he's *all that.*"

Mr. Hamilton looked around, nervous for the first time. He stared past his bodyguard at the people dancing in the club. "Your boyfriend, he's *here*?"

Jewell laughed and placed her small hand over his. "No he's not here! You think I'd be all up on you if he was here?"

Percy smiled uneasily.

"Fuck him anyway," Jewell drawled. "That motherfucker ain't about shit. He got two other bitches." She held up three fingers. "He think I don't know, but I do," she whispered conspiratorially. "He can't *never* fuck. A thirty-two year old man who can't fuck? What kind of shit is that? Am I ugly? You think I'm ugly?"

Percy shook his head. "No way."

"You'd fuck me, right? If you was my boyfriend?"

Percy nodded. "Twice a day."

"Huh?"

"I said, yes. Uh, yes ma'am."

"Don't call me *ma'am*," Jewell said. "Do I look old to you?"

"No ma'am – I mean, *no*. No you don't. I'm sorry. It's just a habit. The way I was raised. What's your name?"

"Stacy," Jewell aka Sheila aka Monique aka Vanessa aka Clarissa Hunt said.

"Well, if *I* was your man, you wouldn't never have that problem with me, Stacy."

"You talking about *fucking*?" Jewell asked.

The mark nodded hesitantly. "Um, yeah. That's what I'm talking about. I would keep you *very* happy, in those regards."

"Really?" Jewell said. She moved her hand under the table and stroked his thigh.

Percy flinched. "Um, yes, uh, Stacy. I would definitely take care of you."

He smiled and Jewell smiled back at him.

"You'd take care of me *and* them two?" She nodded in the direction of the other girls.

Percy didn't even look back at the hoochies. "No, just you," he said, staring into her eyes like he wanted to propose.

"So, why are they here?" Jewell asked.

Percy spun around like he heard a rattlesnake behind him. "Hey, y'all, y'all need to go," he told the holdouts. They immediately began to protest, but it was much ado about nothing.

"Gone now. Here." He offered them the whole bottle of champagne. "Take this with you. No hard feelings, ladies. Alright? I'll catch up with you some other time."

The women took the two hundred dollar bottle and called Jewell a *bitch* on their way out. Jewell smiled at them and thought to herself, *Two more down...*

Percy turned back to her and grinned like the fool he was. "Now, where was we?"

Jewell grinned back at him.

And one to go...

≈ ≈ ≈ ≈ ≈ ≈

Percy Hamilton had the means to live anywhere in the city, but he chose to build his fortress on Overbrook Meadow's south side because this is where his factory was. He built his three story home right next door to the furniture store, as a matter of fact. And while this made for a quick commute to work, it also left him vulnerable to the many hoodlums and dopeheads on that side of town.

To combat this, Percy installed a multitude of security features to make people like Jewell's job a lot harder. Completely encircling the property was a ten foot wrought iron gate with pointy spikes at the top. Anyone who made it past that had to deal with the two hulking Rottweilers that roamed the front yard freely. If you managed to get over the gate *and* past the dogs, Percy had surveillance cameras pointed at each entrance and an alarm system inside the house. Mr. Hamilton also had a stout bodyguard named Daryl who lived at the residence and was within earshot of his boss at all times.

Jewell knew about all of these security features already. Her task was daunting, but she was only worried about one thing when they reached their destination: Jewell didn't want the cameras to get a good look at her face as she entered the furniture king's home. To combat this, Jewell let her bangs fall over her eyes when she got out of the car. She kept her head down under the porch light; studying the fresh polish on her toenails.

If Percy didn't have such a raging boner, he might have noticed his date's demeanor, but he was too busy trying to get under her dress. He stood behind Jewell and fondled her buttocks as his bodyguard unlocked the front door. Jewell gritted her teeth and tolerated this groping.

When they got inside, Percy lifted the back of her dress altogether so he could get a good look at her posterior – something he'd wanted to do since they left the club. Jewell tolerated this as well while she watched big Daryl disable the alarm.

These people are amateurs, she thought.

"Ooh, *goodnight*!" Percy catcalled from behind. "That's a lot of ass!"

Jewell pulled her dress down coyly and turned to face him. "Calm down *Casanova*. I gotta tinkle. Where's the ladies room?"

"Right this way," Percy said, still grinning like a 13 year old with a Hustler magazine. He led her through his spacious home, and Jewell took a mental inventory as they walked. She turned to see if the bodyguard was coming with them. The bull moose disappeared down a different hallway.

When they got to the restroom, Jewell went fishing rather than close the door right away.

"Where's that big guy?"

Percy was hopelessly lost in lust. "Who, Daryl? He in there."

"In there *where*?" Jewell asked. "I don't get down with that freaky stuff. None of that tag-team shit's gonna happen."

Percy chuckled. "No ma'am, I mean Stacy. I would never do anything like that to you."

"It's just gonna be *you*, right?" she asked.

"Yeah. Just me. I promise."

"So where's that big dude gonna be?"

"He likes to sleep in the living room," Percy said. "Big Daryl wears out sofas as fast as I can make them."

Jewell smiled and put her hand on the doorknob. She pulled it slowly, and Percy moved his head so he could stare at her until the last possible second.

"You sho is fine," he said.

"I'll be with you in a second," Jewell told him. She closed the door and sighed quietly. Thank God there was a lock.

Alone in the bathroom, Jewell quickly got down to business. She removed her cellphone from her purse and sent a text message that was brief and to the point.

2 dogs, cams on doors, brinks 209641, 1 guard in l.r.

She sat on the toilet and waited. Fifty seconds later her phone vibrated, indicating she had an incoming message. It was from Daniel.

ten min

She texted him back.

hurry up

Daniel sent her another message.

i luv u

Jewell took a deep breath and fixed her makeup before she left the bathroom. She immediately wished she'd stayed in there. Percy was waiting for her in the hallway, and instead of the canary yellow suit, he donned only a robe now. The robe was clean at least, but his bare legs were ashy. Jewell hoped he still had underwear on under there, but no way was she that lucky.

"What kind of music you like?" he asked. The furniture king had nice teeth, but his smile made Jewell nauseous.

"I don't know," she said. "What you got?"

"Come on." He put an arm around her waist and led her down the hallway; presumably to his bedroom. Halfway there his hand was on her ass again. A sneer flashed on Jewell's face, but Percy didn't notice. He slid his paw under her dress and gave her right cheek a squeeze.

"*Damn* you got a nice ass!" He slowed so he could get behind her and look at it some more. Jewell kept walking. Percy lifted her dress and smacked his lips.

This was not the *worst* for Jewell, but it was pretty bad. At least he couldn't see the expression on her face from back there.

"*Lawdy, Lawdy!*" Percy cackled.

"Which way, *Mr. Man?*" Jewell asked. There were at least six doors in the corridor.

"Baby, I don't care which way you go, just *keep walking*," Percy said; holding her dress in both hands like reins.

"Ooh, my booty's getting cold," Jewell said, but the ruse backfired immediately. Percy took that to mean she wanted some body heat.

"I can get you warmed up."

Oh, please don't, Jewell thought, but his hands were already on her. They were smooth at least, but they weren't Daniel's so they weren't right.

Percy rubbed her fanny and giggled maniacally. Jewell started to count the minutes in her head after that: It took thirty-two seconds to get from the bathroom to the bedroom. Once there, it took her two and a half minutes to find a C.D. she wanted to listen to. Then she played sick and got him for another three minutes in the bathroom. After that Jewell did a sexy dance for him that took a whopping five minutes.

By the time Percy complained that she was giving him blue balls, his time was up. A commotion in the living room made him forget about sex altogether. It sounded like big Daryl might be having it out with someone.

"What was that?"

Percy lay flat on his back with his feet and penis pointing skywards. Jewell stood at the foot of the bed dancing seductively.

"What was what?"

The furniture king sat up; his eyes wide. "You didn't hear nothing?"

"Hear what?"

But Percy Hamilton never rode the short bus to school. He rolled over quickly and reached for the drawer in the nightstand next to his bed. Always game for a fight, Jewell jumped onto his back and snaked an arm under his chin. She almost locked in a decent choke hold, but the pudgy bastard was stronger than he looked. Percy gagged and flipped over onto his back, pinning Jewell beneath him. He then wrestled out of her grasp and rolled over again until they were face to face; her on bottom, him on top.

"What the fuck you doing?" he asked. His breaths were quick. His face was set in a deep scowl. Gravity pulled and stretched his features out of proportion. His cheeks got even flabbier. His lips hung dumbly.

Jewell looked up at him with her teeth bared. She was about to send a David Beckham kick to his raging boner, but a wonderful noise came from the doorway. It was the sound of a weapon being cocked.

CUHCHIK!

"Get the fuck off her!"

Jewell looked up and sighed out loud this time. The interloper was dressed completely in black. He wore leather gloves, a ski mask and tinted goggles to hide his eyes. He toted a

Smith & Wesson 20 gauge shotgun with a charcoal-colored barrel and a walnut stock.

Jewell had never been happier to see her man.

"*I said get off her!*"

Percy looked over his shoulder and then back down at Jewell. The cocky, sex-starved furniture king was gone now. Mr. Hamilton looked like he'd seen Satan himself, and depending on how he played his cards, that might very well be the case.

"I'ma, I'm – alright. I'm getting off, see..." Percy's eyes were big like boiled eggs. He held his hands in the air and crawled off of Jewell gingerly. His still stiff penis brushed her leg, and Jewell cringed, but luckily this was as close as she would ever get to that thing.

"Okay, okay man. Everything's cool," Percy said when their bodies were separate. He pleaded with the masked intruder: "Don't, don't, don't point that thing at me man. Please."

Jewell quickly made it to her feet. She pulled her skirt down and brushed the hair from her face. Percy watched her and the reality of his situation slowly dawned. His expression changed. He looked like a child watching dogs mate for the first time.

"It, it was *you!*" he hissed.

"Shut the fuck up!" Daniel barked.

"Fucking bitch!" Percy burned holes in Jewell with his eyes.

Daniel closed the distance between them with four quick steps. He thumped Percy on the side of the head with the butt of his shotgun. Percy let out a sharp, girlish squeal and clutched his throbbing temple.

"*Aw!* Man, *please*! I'm sorry! *I'm sorry*"

"Go wait outside," Daniel told his girlfriend.

Jewell didn't like that, but her participation in this crime was no longer needed. Daniel didn't want her hanging around after the crew got there, and Jewell was obedient to her man. Dapper Dan never led her astray before.

On the way out, Jewell passed a few more guys dressed all in black like her boyfriend. One toted two duffle bags full of shiny equipment; drills, torches, borescopes, ultraviolet lights and inks – all things essential to safecracking wizardry. In the living room two similarly dressed goons had Percy's burly bodyguard roughed up and hogtied. Jewell walked past them without a word, and soon she was in the moonlight again.

The summer evening was warm and humid.

Jewell stepped quickly on Percy's cobbled sidewalk, and she didn't stumble in her stilettos. In the lawn she encountered two humongous Rottweilers in the midst of an unnatural sleep. They lay close to each other, like two beached whales on a desolate coastline. Their big chests rose and fell almost in tandem. One farted loudly as Jewell slipped through a wrought iron gate that wasn't as secure as it appeared to be.

Thirty-six seconds later Jewell climbed into the backseat of their getaway car; a 1982 Suburban parked indiscreetly in the driveway of one of their safe houses. Before relaxing or sending Daniel a text about the loose floorboards in Percy's bedroom, Jewell took that damned wig off and gave her head a good scratching. Her real hair was short, styled in an auburn-colored bob.

In the scant moonlight, Jewell looked even more beautiful without the synthetic mane.

CHAPTER THREE
MISS EVELINE

Jewell turned down her stereo as she pulled into the driveway at 3613 Forbes Avenue. Her music wasn't too loud to begin with, but the occupant of this domicile had very sensitive ears. And contrary to last night's activities, Jewell was generally respectful of her elders.

She stepped out of her champagne colored Navigator wearing an outfit strikingly different than the one she donned for the job at Club Destiny. Today Jewell wore a black pants suit that made her look like a high-powered attorney. The slacks were form-fitting, but not too tight around her hips and thighs. Her patent leather pumps weren't as cute as her stilettos, but Jewell looked sexy in anything she put on.

She had the sleeves of her jacket rolled up with the cuffs of her blouse protruding fashionably. She had only two rings on her right hand this evening; one princess cut and one baguette. Her left hand was naked, say a modest tennis bracelet dangling from her wrist. Jewell's hair was short on the sides and layered on top. She toted a leather hobo bag made by Prada.

Instead of approaching the front door of the three bedroom flat, Jewell stepped from the driveway onto the manicured lawn. She walked along side the house, taking care to avoid the large ant mounds scattered across the greenery. Twice already Jewell tried to get rid of the bitey insects herself, but so far these fire ants were immune to everything Home Depot had to offer. Jewell made a mental note to call in the professionals tomorrow. When all else failed, white people could get the job done.

When she got to the back of the house, Jewell saw that her rose bush was as bad off as she envisioned. The struggling buds caught direct sunlight everyday at high noon. Jewell used the water hose to saturate her ailing flowers, but she knew it was all for naught. Unless you've got the time to attend to them everyday, you're not going to grow pretty roses in Texas.

When she was done with the hose, Jewell wrapped it neatly on the reel mounted next to the back steps without getting a drop of water on her suit. No dirt on her hands either.

Jewell headed for the backdoor, and then stopped suddenly with a strong feeling that she was being watched. She looked right, then left, and there she was. There were plenty nosey neighbors in this area, but Mrs. Gaffney had to be the absolute worst.

Its one thing to be aware of your surroundings, but this woman wholeheartedly sought out trouble. Like now, for instance: She stood at the fence separating her backyard from the one Jewell occupied. Her upper body was totally concealed behind high-growing shrubs, but the leaves were sparse at the bottom of the bush.

Jewell could see Mrs. Gaffney's pants and shoes clearly. It was actually quite comical; like someone trying to hide behind a stop sign.

"Can I help you?" Jewell asked loudly.

Mrs. Gaffney stepped from behind the bush. She was a dark-haired woman, forty-years old or so, as pale as skim milk. She wore gardening gloves but hefted no hedge clippers. She wasn't at all embarrassed about getting caught snooping yet again.

"Hello," she said.

"Why are you hiding behind the bushes?" Jewell asked. The animosity between them had aged like a fine wine.

"I wasn't *hiding*," Mrs. Gaffney said. "I heard someone back there and–"

"And you wanted to be nosey," Jewell said.

"If there was a burglar back here, you'd thank me," the older woman quipped.

"If a burglar wants to come and water these roses, he's welcome to it," Jewell said. She rolled her eyes and Mrs. Gaffney stuck up her nose up, and they both turned and carried on with their business.

Jewell shook her head as she fished the correct set of keys from her purse. She had six separate key rings in this bag. In her line of work, there were always a lot of cars and motel rooms and safe houses, but Jewell kept track of it all. She couldn't remember the last time she selected the wrong key. She unlocked the backdoor and kicked the grass from her pumps before entering the house.

She heard her mother calling as soon as she closed the door behind herself.

"Tonya! *Tonya?*"

Jewell followed the voice, walking briskly. She knew it was coming from her mother's bedroom, but there was no guesswork needed to figure that out: Eveline Hunt was an invalid, only leaving her bed for meals, church, and trips to her bedside commode. Diabetes robbed her of her sight and fitness long ago. Breast cancer was currently devouring what was left of her.

Jewell reached Miss Eveline's room and gasped inwardly. Her mother weighed a mere eighty-six pounds nowadays. Blue-haired and foggy-eyed, Eveline struggled to rise from her portable toilet. She wore her best Sunday dress, but it looked ugly hiked up over her pencil legs and bony knees. Her hands were like claws. They clutched the metal handles on her toilet in what looked like a death grip. Her scrawny elbows trembled from the effort.

Jewell's mother was a few shades lighter than her daughter. A hundred years ago she could have passed for white in the midst of stern segregation. She was still beautiful now; even with her sightless eyes and gaunt features.

The ailing woman quit her struggles and turned her cloudy eyes in the direction of the doorway when Jewell entered.

"Clarissa?"

This was the only person who referred to Jewell by her birth name.

Despite the scene and the pungent smell of death, Jewell smiled. "How do you always know?"

Eveline smiled too and relaxed in her seat. "I heard you out there watering the roses. I was trying to get that girl in here before you came in."

"Where is she?" Jewell asked. She approached her mother and kissed her softly on the forehead. She put her arms under Miss Eveline's armpits and hefted the thin woman from the seat.

"She's in there," Eveline said. "She's alright, baby. Don't go in there yelling at her. She just falls asleep sometimes. She's got that *sleep apnea.*"

Jewell wiped her mother and pulled up her panties. She straightened her mother's dress and pulled her stockings up too, but there was hardly any meat for them to cling to. They started sliding again as soon as she let them go.

"I thought I got you some new panty hose," Jewell said.

"You did," the older woman said. "This is them."

Jewell stood and led her mom to the bed. Eveline had a stiff gait, like the Tin Man after a few nights of rain.

"You gonna have to put some weight on, Mama," Jewell said, "before you go and disappear on us. What happened? Your knees bothering you today?"

Eveline sat on the bed gingerly and sighed. Jewell sat next to her.

"Yeah. I made it over there pretty good," the older woman said, "but they lock up on me when I tried to get up."

In addition to the diabetes and cancer, Jewell's 69 year old mother suffered from occasional dementia and osteoarthritis. This woman never drank or smoked. She attended church every Sunday and never lied or stole. Eveline compared her current sufferings to the story of Job, but Jewell wasn't as strong spiritually. Jewell thought her mom got a bad deal; maybe God let her slip through His fingers like He did with all of the starving babies in the world.

"Who was you arguing with out there?" Eveline asked.

Jewell rolled her eyes. "You already know."

Her mother smiled. There was still a lot of sunshine in that smile. "You need to leave that lady alone," she said. "She's just doing what she see fit."

"How many people did she call the police on last year?" Jewell asked.

Her mother chuckled.

"And did anybody ever get arrested?" Jewell asked.

Again this cracked her mother up.

Jewell was surprised the police still responded to Mrs. Gaffney's calls. The middle-aged busy-body reported everything from strange sounds to Jehovah Witnesses. Never had Jewell met someone so eager to put somebody in jail.

"I'm gonna go talk to Tonya," Jewell said.

Her mother's smile fell. "It's alright, Clarissa. I like this one."

"What's sleep apnea?" Jewell asked.

"It's a condition," her mother said. She stared at her daughter's face with those filmy, unseeing eyes. It would have been a little creepy if Jewell didn't love her so much.

"That's not a condition," Jewell countered. "That just something fat people say when they eat too much and want to take a nap."

Eveline smiled, but she knew this wasn't a laughing matter. "It *is* a condition, Clarissa. You can look it up. Hand me my medical dictionary."

The frail woman pointed, but her daughter didn't even look that way.

"Did she help you get dressed?" Jewell asked.

"No. But I can do that by myself, mostly."

"When was the last time you saw her?"

Her mother thought about it. "It was about, about an hour ago."

"What was she doing?"

"When?"

"When you saw her?"

"She was..." Eveline smiled and shook her head.

"I know she was eating," Jewell said. "I can still smell it."

"It's a *condition*."

"Well she needs to get some other job," Jewell said. She stood and headed out of the room.

"I like her," Eveline called. "She's a nice lady. And she's strong. She helps me out a lot."

But all of that went in one ear and out the other. Jewell's nostrils flared as she stepped through the darkened hallways. How dare that heifer leave her mother struggling on the toilet? Jewell deposited her purse on the dining room table and cracked her knuckles when she got to the living room.

She found her mother's nurse fully stretched out on the couch. Ms. Tonya Tomlinson, LVN of more than six years, snored loudly with her mouth open. The remote control for Eveline's floor model television rose and fell on her belly with each healthy breath. In the background, Judge Judy berated a defendant for wearing a tee shirt to court.

Jewell wanted to kick the nurse, but she kicked the pillow Tonya's head was on instead. The chubby woman sat up with a start and looked around frantically.

"Huh?"

Jewell stared down at her with her hands on her hips. "What the fuck you doing in here sleep?"

"I'm, uh, I..." The nurse blinked hard and wiped spittle from the corner of her mouth. She looked from Jewell to the wall clock and then back to her employer's hateful eyes. "I *just* fell asleep," she said. "For a *second*. What happened, Ms. Hunt? Is something wrong?"

"Yeah. *You* wrong," Jewell said. "You need to get your shit and get out of here."

Tonya's mouth fell open. "What? *For what*? It was just for a *second*, Ms. Hunt. I *promise*. I like it here. I've been doing a good job. Ask your mom. She likes me."

"What's this crap you've been telling her about sleep apnea?"

"Oh that's true," the nurse said quickly. "I do have that."

"What *is* it?" Jewell asked.

"I have trouble sleeping at night," Tonya said woefully. "Sometimes I get sleepy in the daytime, but it's not my fault. I'm usually okay. *Please* give me another chance."

Jewell couldn't believe the woman's nerve. "You need to stay home with that mess," she said coldly. "If it's something wrong with you – making you fall asleep – you should get some other kind of job. How you gonna take care of somebody if you can't stay awake? You're damned sure not gonna be sleeping in *my* mama's house."

"It was just one time."

"For real, lady. You need to get somewhere."

The nurse thought about it for a second and decided to stand her ground. She looked Jewell dead in the eyes. "You can't fire me."

Jewell cocked her head to the side. "What?"

"I said you *can't* fire me." Tonya spoke more defiantly this time. "I have a disability. And it's *protected*. You can call the agency if you don't believe me. They'll tell you."

"They can't tell me nothing."

"They'll tell you I got rights–"

"You got the right to get the fuck out of here before I kick your ass." The nurse was nearly twice her size, but Jewell feared only death these days.

Tonya looked up at her and grinned. "You'll what?" Apparently this wasn't the first time she'd been threatened with physical violence.

Hot blood flowed through Jewell's veins. The hair stood on her forearms. On the outside, her adrenaline rush created only a subtle shift in demeanor, but it changed everything about her inwardly. Jewell saw fire in the corner of her eyes, but there was still time to backtrack and deal with this rationally.

"My mom's sick," she said. "She only has about a year left, probably not even that long. All I wanted was for you to make her *comfortable*. I don't need to come in here and see her struggling to get off the toilet 'cause your fat ass is in here sleep." Jewell immediately regretted calling the portly woman *fat*, but the damage was done.

The nurse flinched, and Jewell's words ignited anger rather than remorse.

"What was that you said though?" Tonya asked. "About how you gonna kick my ass?"

Jewell would never threaten to do something she wasn't prepared to follow through with, so she stepped forward and delivered a blistering open-hand slap to the nurse's jaw. The blow sounded off in the quiet house like a balloon popping.

SMACK!

Instead of backing away and allowing the woman to stand and possibly gain the momentum, Jewell stood over the nurse; ready to jump on her if the LVN wanted to rumble.

But Tonya wanted no parts of that. She stared up at Jewell with a look of total shock. She brought a hand to her face and caressed her stinging cheek. She dabbed at a trickle of blood in the corner of her mouth with her pinkie finger, and then she stared at it queerly. She looked up at Jewell with tears in her eyes.

"Why you, why you hit me?"

Jewell expected a multitude of responses, but that wasn't one of them. She took a couple of steps back when it was clear the big girl didn't want to be combative.

"I told you to leave," she said. "If you stay in somebody's house after they tell you to leave, that makes you an intruder. I can hit you if I want to."

"But, but I was just trying to tell you..." The nurse trailed off, both of her eyes leaking now.

Jewell felt a sting of regret, but she only had to think of her mother laboring on the toilet to re-energize her animosity. "So, you ready to leave now?"

Tonya nodded. She stood slowly and looked around for her purse. Jewell planted her back foot in preparation for a sneak attack, but the nurse simply collected her belongings and headed for the front door. Jewell followed her out.

Tonya turned to face her former-employer when they got to the porch. "You're gonna tell them I was sleep?"

Jewell was taken aback. "Why?"

"They'll fire me," the nurse said. "If I fall asleep again, they said they would."

Jewell shook her head. "You said they were cool with your – *whatever you say you got.*"

Tonya lowered her head. "No. They don't like it either."

"Sounds like you need to find another job," Jewell advised.

"I know," Tonya said. "But this is what I went to school for. I got three kids. I need to work."

Jewell sighed.

"You could tell them I was late," Tonya offered. "I never got in trouble for that before."

Jewell said she'd tell the agency whatever Tonya wanted her to. The nurse smiled gratefully and Jewell closed the door on her. She went back to her mother's room and found Eveline sitting on the corner of her bed listening intently.

"You gotta stop doing that," the older woman said.

Jewell sat next to her and held her mother's hand.

"Did you hit her?" Eveline asked.

"That was the TV," Jewell said.

Eveline frowned.

"She was gonna hit me first, Mama."

"No she wasn't. Tonya wouldn't hurt a fly."

"I know that *now*," Jewell said. "But she was acting like she wanted to fight."

Eveline shook her head. "You need to cut out that foolishness, baby. You're too old to still be getting into fights with people. Ain't nothing happened so bad you can't use your *words*. Nothing's *ever* that bad."

Jewell's mom would have taken a brick to the head marching next to Martin Luther King. Jewell, on the other hand, would have been in a storefront loading shotguns with Huey Newton.

"I'm getting better, Mama."

"Is Daniel coming to church with us?"

Just the thought of him brought a smile to Jewell's face. "Yes. He's meeting us here. Should've been here by now."

Eveline reached up and touched her daughter's lips. Jewell's smile made her mother smile too. "When y'all gonna get married and have a baby?" she asked. She inquired about that almost every time they talked, and Jewell grew excited whenever she thought about it.

"Pretty soon," she said.

"I was hoping I'd get to hold my grandbaby before I had to go home, but if you still not pregnant yet, I don't think I'm gon' make it."

The elder Hunt referred to her inevitable death as *going home*. According to her doctors, she should have *gone home* two years ago. Jewell knew her mother was living on borrowed time now. Everyday and any day might be *the* day.

"If I have a baby, you'd better still be here," Jewell said.

"I'll be with you, even if I'm not here," Eveline promised.

Jewell kissed her mother's sunken jaw. "I know you will."

"I want you to do something for me," Eveline said.

"Anything, Mama. What is it?"

"This is *serious*," Eveline said. "Tell me you'll do it."

"You know I'll do anything for you."

"I want you to help Cedric."

A brief hopelessness washed over Jewell's face, and she was glad her mother couldn't see it. Cedric Hunt aka *Slim* was Jewell's 42 year old brother. He'd been locked up more times than he had fingers; even more so as of late because of a devastating heroin addiction.

Slim got released again four months ago. He swore he would stay clean and do right this time, but Jewell had long ago stopped believing and stopped trying to help her big brother. Some people were destined to be fuck ups their entire lives. It's a sad realization, but it makes sense mathematically: Where would the world be with no rich and no poor? No winners and no losers? Tragically, you have to have them all.

"I know what you're thinking," Eveline said.

"How do you know?" Jewell asked.

"'Cause we're just the same," Eveline said.

That was news to Jewell.

"You don't see it 'cause we act so different," Eveline went on. "But we *think* alike. You're a good woman, Clarissa. You got a good heart."

Jewell thought about last night's caper and felt sick to her stomach.

"If you could get him a job down there at your company, I'd feel a lot better," Eveline continued. "It ain't got to be nothing big. Even if it's in the mailroom, at least it's *something*, you know?"

Miss Eveline thought her daughter was a manager at a telemarketing firm.

"I don't think he can work with me," Jewell said honestly. "If I get him in, and he messes up, it's gonna come back on me."

"Could you at least try?" Eveline asked. "If he messes up, that'll be on him. But he says he's doing right this time. I talk to him sometimes, and I believe him, Clarissa. He says he doesn't want to go to jail no more. He wants to get a regular job, but no one will hire him. I know you can help him, baby. This'll just be one less thing I have to worry about when I go home. I pray for that boy all the time."

Jewell hated that her mom put her in this position, but how do you turn down what might be a *last* wish? "I'll see what I can do, Mama."

Eveline squeezed her daughter's hand as tightly as she could. "You make me so proud..."

Jewell put an arm around her mother and they rocked in silence for awhile until someone rang the doorbell.

"That's Daniel," Jewell said.

"How do you know?" her mom asked.

"I can feel him," Jewell said, and that was true. Even after six years, her boyfriend still gave her goose bumps.

CHAPTER FOUR
A LITTLE BIRD TOLD ME

When she met him, Daniel drove a 1974 Coupe de Ville with whitewall tires and fuzzy blue dice hanging from the rear-view mirror. In 2002 it was odd to see a Cadillac that old still on the road, and Daniel turned out to be full of oddities.

Jewell was running one of her boyfriend's dope houses when she met Dapper Dan. Her beau, a lanky thug known as *Low Dawg*, got popped with a trunk full of marijuana and a pistol under his seat. Jewell didn't like selling drugs and she certainly didn't like working out of a crack house, but even back then she was a die hard hustler.

Low Dawg's clientele was already established, and the junkies were going to come whether he was locked up or not. If Jewell didn't get their money someone else would, so for three months she was an avid pusherman.

One of Jewell's favorite customers was a skinny fiend known on the streets as *Bird*. Bird was twenty four years old, but she looked 16. She was also blonde and blue-eyed, so her prostitution profession was off to a smashing start. Bird charged a hundred dollars for a lay, averaging 15 tricks a day during the summertime. She came to see Jewell every few hours to get her fix of crack and mainly heroin. If she made two hundred dollars, Jewell got half, but Bird never left the dope house *totally* broke. She constantly told Jewell that she couldn't go home to her *daddy* empty-handed.

Jewell liked Bird, so she let the addict shoot up and smoke out at the trap whenever she wanted. Bird was very grateful for this because the Overbrook Meadows Police Department was cracking down on prostitutes back then. It was damned near impossible to get loaded in public.

Bird never skitzed too much when she got high, and she always had fascinating stories to tell. After a few months Jewell considered her more of a friend than customer, but money was always Jewell's foremost concern. Even letting Bird hang out at the dope house was merely a means to get more *ends*.

Their set up was perfect, but everything fell apart when Bird took too long to get back on the streets one day. Her *daddy* had to go looking for her, and the last thing he wanted was to find his hoe getting high with *her* own money that was rightfully *his*.

Daniel pulled up to Jewell's crack house one foggy Saturday morning and hammered on the front door like he was the police. Jewell grabbed her .44, itching to bust a cap in his ass if he didn't cut out the foolishness, but Bird implored her to be civil.

"*Don't shoot*! That's my boyfriend!" she hissed.

Jewell had her gun pointed at the center of the door, ready to put a hole in it and whoever was on the other side.

"What?"

Bird's eyes were wide like saucers. She was plenty high, but Jewell saw stone cold terror in her features too.

"It's my boyfriend! That's *Daddy*."

"What the hell is he doing over *here*?" Jewell wanted to know.

"He's looking for me. I was supposed to be out there already."

"He can't be starting no mess over here," Jewell warned. She lowered her pistol, but she didn't un-cock it or put it away.

Daniel continued to pound on the door. "Open up, Bird! I know yo ass is in there!"

"Quit banging on my door, nigga!" Jewell shouted through the wood. "This *my* house!"

"Who is *you*?" Daniel demanded.

"None of your business!"

Bird bit her nails and squirmed like she had to pee.

"Listen," Daniel said, lowering his tone to a respectable volume, "I *know* Bird is in there. Three people done already told me. This ain't got nothing to do with you. I just want my girl."

But Jewell wanted her too. Bird was her biggest spender and most loyal customer.

"You gonna have to catch up with her some other time!" she yelled through the door. "This is *my* house. Anybody who comes here is *my* company, and you can't come over here messing with my company."

"Alright," Daniel said. "I can respect that. Just do one thing for me: Can you get her close to the door so I can tell her something before I go?"

Bird shook her head, but Jewell said, "She right here. Talk, fool."

"Check this out, Bird," Daniel said, his voice changing again, "if you don't get yo fonky ass out here *right motherfucking now*, I'ma mess you up so bad they won't know if you a dead dog or what. I'll kill you, bitch. You know I will."

"*Alright!*" Jewell yelled through the wood. "She heard you. Now gone."

But Bird suddenly had a change of heart. "I'ma go out there," she whispered.

Jewell's jaw dropped. "What? *Why?*"

"He'll do it," she said plainly. "He ain't playing."

"You can stay here with me," Jewell offered. "You can still do whatever you want to get your money, but it'll be *all yours*. You can score from me, and you can sleep here too."

Bird shook her head. "No. I better go."

Jewell sighed and Bird opened the front door. As soon as there was sufficient space, Daniel's arm burst through like a lunging snake. He grabbed a handful of blonde hair and yanked Bird out with hardly any effort. She stumbled down the concrete steps and fell to her knees in the front yard.

"*Get yo stanky ass in the car!*" Daniel barked. He delivered a swift kick to her rump to get her going, and Bird did the most amazing thing Jewell had ever seen. The skinny prostitute wobbled to her feet, apologized for her foolishness, and then climbed into the Cadillac's passenger seat.

Jewell was both dumbfounded and infuriated. She turned to sneer at the asshole who probably just cost her a few hundred dollars a day. But as mad as she was, Jewell couldn't help but admire the bald-headed stranger.

Daniel wore a full zoot suit that day. The slacks and vest were mustard-colored. His jacket was plaid with patterns that matched his pants. Daniel had two long chains that hung from a front belt loop, dangled all the way down past his knees, and then disappeared in his back pocket. His shoes were snakeskin's and square-toed. His hat had a large, white feather protruding from the band.

"What are you, a pimp or something?" Jewell asked sarcastically.

Daniel stared into her eyes and smiled eagerly. "Yeah, baby. I'm a pimp. And that's my bitch. How much of my money she been spending in here?"

"That was *your* money?" Jewell asked. She looked the flashy interloper up and down. "How many dicks did *you* suck this morning?"

Daniel chuckled.

Jewell stepped inside and tried to close the door, but he stopped her.

"Hey. Can I talk to you for a second?"

"If you don't want to make a buy, we don't have nothing to talk about."

Daniel pulled out a thick roll of greenbacks. "I'll buy from you," he said. "As you already know; my snow bunny got herself a substance abuse problem."

Jewell studied his features and didn't see any tricks up his sleeve. Plus he did have a lot of money. She invited him in and locked the door behind him.

"Sit down," she instructed.

Daniel took a seat on her couch and crossed his legs. He leaned back and stretched his arms over the back of the sofa.

Jewell went into the kitchen to retrieve the merchandise. Daniel watched her every move.

"What you got that thing for?" he asked.

"What thing?" Jewell called over the bar.

"That *pistol*," he said. "You know how to use that?"

"Bang on my door like that again," she said. "You'll find out."

"You was gonna shoot me?" he asked with a big smile.

Jewell took her baggies and scales from the cupboard. "What do you want?"

"What you got?"

"I got brown and white. Hard and soft."

"What does Bird usually get?"

"Half and half."

"Alright. That's what I want then."

"Two fifties?"

"Yeah."

Jewell weighed and packaged his narcotics. When she took it to him, Daniel closed his hand around hers rather than accept his purchase. Startled, Jewell jerked back, but his grip was true. She was suddenly sorry that she left her gun in the kitchen.

"Ain't this Low Dawg's spot?" he asked.

"Let go of my hand."

But he wouldn't, not right away. "You ain't scared to work in here all by yourself?"

Daniel was handsome and confident. Jewell stared into his eyes and nearly got lost in them.

"I can take care of myself," she said.

"You Low Dawg's woman?"

"Something like that."

"You making good money?"

"That's not your business. Let go of my hand."

He released her and Jewell tossed the drugs in his lap. "That's a hundred dollars."

He slid two fifties from his roll, staring at her the whole time. "You a good-looking gal," he said. "Is Low Dawg getting out?"

Jewell took the money and stuffed it in her back pocket. "Why?"

"'Cause I like you," Daniel said. "I was wondering if you want to come with me."

Jewell smirked. "And do what? Be one of your bitches, like Bird? I would *never* let you talk to me like that. I damned sure wouldn't let you put your hands on me."

Daniel smiled. "That's not for everybody."

"So what you want with me?" she asked.

He pursed his lips. "I like your attitude," he said. "I like your hustle. You look like you're down for whatever. You don't meet too many broads like that."

"I'm doing fine by myself," Jewell said, but she couldn't hide her interest. "What I need you for?"

"You need some *guidance*," Daniel noticed. "You out here *renegading*. See, like this place..." He waved his arm across the room. "This here is pretty lame. You finna go to the penitentiary, and you don't even know it."

He had her full attention now.

"Everybody wants to get paid," he went on, "but some hustles are dumber than others. Look around, girl. Right now you're stuck. If the laws come in through the front and back, where you gonna go? You can flush all you want, but if you sold to an informant, they got you anyway."

"I don't sell to informants," Jewell said.

"How you know?" Daniel asked. "If they catch Bird with that needle she got in her purse, what do you think she'll do to get loose? You don't think she'll tell who she scores from? You don't think she'll come up in here and make a buy with marked money if they tell her to?"

Jewell never considered that. "That's *your* girl," she said. "You don't trust her?"

Daniel sneered. "I don't even trust my *brother*," he said. "My *blood* brother; I don't trust his ass no more than I trust you or anybody else out here. You got a nice little hustle, shorty, but you not gon' make it like this.

"They call this place a *trap*, but it ain't just a trap for the crackheads. It's a trap for your ass too. You can't post up and wait for The Man to come get you. You gotta stay mobile. I made a hundred thousand last year. Never stayed in the same house more than three months."

"You still haven't said what you want with me..."

≈≈≈≈≈≈≈

What Daniel wanted was to rob a PACE check cashing facility.

Secured behind bullet-proof glass and reinforced doors, the cashiers there handled tens of thousands of dollars each day with virtually no fears. But after extensive research, Daniel found one rather large kink in their system: The two-to-ten o'clock clerk was recently divorced. He was lonely, and he was a big time freak. Rumor had it he once let a prostitute in through the back door for some quickie fellatio during his lunch break.

Daniel had been trying for months to duplicate the urban legend, but so far none of his whores were seductive enough to get invited inside.

46

Jewell proved to be just what the clerk was looking for. She and Daniel pulled off the robbery one week after they met at her dope house. They made forty-two thousand dollars from the job, and Daniel split it with her right down the middle even though she never pointed a gun at anyone.

With twenty thousand in her pocket, Jewell left the dope game for good and began to hustle *smarter*, rather than harder. She and Daniel started off as crime partners, but a sultry relationship soon blossomed. When she realized she was in love with him, Jewell asked Daniel to give up his hoes and hang up the pimp hat for good, and he did.

By the time Low Dawg got out of jail eight months later, he had no chance of getting his woman back. Jewell and the Dapper Dan were more than a couple then: They were the most successful Bonnie and Clyde duo Overbrook Meadows had ever known.

≈≈≈≈≈≈

Jewell left her mother's side and went to answer the door. Her boyfriend greeted her with a full body hug. He had large hands that were hard and strong, but also gentle when he wanted to be. He caressed her back from bra-line to panty-line and buried his face in her neck, kissing lightly. He smelled like Fendi cologne.

"Hey," he said.

"Hey. Feeling a little amorous?" Jewell purred.

He removed his hat and stared into her eyes with one arm still around her waist.

"You look beautiful," he said. "And everything went perfect with the–"

Jewell put a finger to his lips.

"Everything went well," he whispered. "We moved most of it already."

"How much?" Jewell asked. Her bright eyes glistened like diamonds.

"We're going to meet tonight," Daniel said. "It's good though. Real good."

"Who dropped you off?"

"Davis."

Jewell left Daniel in the living room and went to retrieve her mother. Eveline had already managed to get into her wheelchair by herself.

"What are you doing?" Jewell rushed to help her.

"I'm alright," Eveline said. "Girl, I'm not as helpless as you think I am." She sounded confident, but her paper-thin chest rose and fell rapidly from the effort involved in walking to her wheelchair. Beads of sweat blossomed on the dying woman's forehead.

"Mama, why do you keep doing this? Who are you trying to impress?"

"I'm not trying to impress anyone, child. I'm just living my life."

"But Mama—"

"Hush now. I ain't dead yet, Clarissa. As long as I got strength to walk, I'm gonna walk just like God meant me to. I'm in that bed too much as it is. Doctor said it's good for me to exercise."

"That doctor doesn't know what he's talking about."

"I'm not dying on my back," Eveline said adamantly. "I'ma die on my feet, so I can fall over and bust my head like everybody else."

Jewell was aghast, but her mother grinned.

"That was Daniel?" the older woman asked.

"Yeah."

"Well, come on," Eveline said. "Take me in there so I can see what he got on."

Next to Daniel himself, no one was more interested in his costumes than Eveline Hunt. Jewell wheeled her to the living room, and Daniel behaved like a knight in shining armor. He dropped to one knee and spoke to the matriarch at eye level. He held and kissed her aged hand and told her she looked beautiful. Then he stood for what was always Eveline's favorite part of the encounter.

"What is that, Calvin Klein?" Jewell asked.

"No," Daniel said. "This is Italian. Handmade."

"Oh, *excuse me*," Jewell said with a smirk. She stood behind her mother's chair with her hands on Miss Eveline's shoulders. "Okay, Mama, today Daniel's wearing a three-piece, vested suit that was *handmade* in Italy."

"Ooh, let me feel," Eveline said. She reached for him, and Daniel stepped closer and held out his arm. Eveline caressed the fabric delicately. "Nice," she said. "What color?"

"It's black," Jewell said, "with red pinstripes on the coat, the slacks too. The vest is solid black. It's nice. Everything fits *perfectly*."

"What else?" Eveline asked eagerly.

Jewell smiled at her man, and Daniel winked at her. "Well, you know everything's coordinated," she said. "His shirt is solid red. The sleeves are a little longer than the coat, so you can almost see his cufflinks. He got a red handkerchief in his breast pocket and a red tie with black stripes."

"He doesn't have a hat?" Eveline asked, almost disappointed.

"He does," Jewell said, "but he's not wearing it inside."

Daniel scooped his hat from the couch. "It's red, Ms Hunt. Same as my shirt."

"Call me Eveline," she said. "Does it have a feather?"

"No, Miss Eveline," Daniel said. "Not today."

"Oh, well," the old woman said. "It all sounds so nice. I'm sure you look as sharp as ever. Even without the feather."

"He does," Jewell confirmed. "Daniel looks *very* handsome tonight."

≈≈≈≈≈≈≈

They left together and made it to Ebenezer Baptist Church in time for praise and worship. When they got inside, a perky woman with an infant boy on each hip met them in the foyer.

"Hey *family*! Hey Mama!" She bent and gave Miss Eveline a hug and a kiss on the cheek.

Eveline Hunt had three children in all. She loved them equally, but Yolanda was the only one who *really* made her mama proud. Slim never did well in school, and his life continued to spiral out of control when he dropped out. Jewell garnished a lot of ill-gotten praise from her mother, but it was all based on lies. Eveline would have a stroke if she knew her daughter was involved with a ruthless crime syndicate.

But Yolanda gave the Hunt family a breath of fresh air. Always on the straight and narrow, Yolanda did moderately well all the way through high school. She actually got her diploma, which was more than Slim and Jewell ever did.

Yolanda didn't go to college or try to accomplish anything spectacular after graduating, but her life turned out picture-perfect anyway: She gave herself to the Lord and to her church, married an up and coming deacon, and was now the proud mother of five beautiful, well-mannered boys. Her husband was an assistant pastor, only a year or two away from buying his own church.

Jewell gave her sister a hug and plucked one of the twins from her arms. She held the boy aloft and grinned at his pudgy face. "Which one is this?"

"That's Matthew," Yolanda said. "This is Jacob."

"You need to get some name tags," Jewell said.

"I ordered some bibs with their names on them," Yolanda said. "They'll be here in time for the reunion."

"That's cute," Jewell said.

"Are you staying for the whole service?" her sister asked.

Jewell said she was, but that turned out not to be the case.

Midway through the sermon Daniel got a text message. He leaned over and put his lips close to Jewell's ear. "Come on," he said. "We gotta go."

On the way out, Jewell found her sister in the children's chapel.

"Hey girl, I'm sorry, but we have to go. Can you take Mama home with you?"

"Take her *home with me*?" All five of Yolanda's children were under the age of eight. Jewell knew she was already overwhelmed.

"Yeah. I fired Tonya today."

"Why you keep firing those girls?"

"Cause they sorry," Jewell said.

"Well *you* need to start keeping her, if you don't like her nurses."

"I'm sorry Yolanda," Jewell said. "I'll get her another one tomorrow. Thanks."

She and Daniel turned left the church arm in arm.

≈≈≈≈≈≈≈

Forty minutes later Jewell pulled her Navigator into the garage of Safe House #3. Located on the north side of town, this two story domicile was clean, spacious, and nondescript. The gang paid twelve-hundred dollars a month to rent the place, but so far none of them ever spent the night there.

A large Hispanic family lived next door to the safe house. They had huge parties in the backyard sometimes, but they paid little attention to the usually vacant brick house on their right. On the other side of Safe House #3 was an elderly black couple. These old timers hardly ever ventured past their porch, and they didn't care to meet their seldom seen next door neighbor either.

The lawn at the safe house got mowed every week, and Miles rigged a few lights and a television to come on by themselves every night at seven p.m. sharp. The rent was never late, and they never let the mail pile up either.

Jewell and Daniel entered through the back door with big smiles on their faces. Jesse and Miles were already there and so was Davis. Jesse had a bottle of champagne in hand, but no one was ready to pop bottles just yet.

"Did you see the paper?" he asked with a worried expression.

"They covered it in the morning," Daniel said. "It was nothing. No leads."

"I saw it too," Jewell said. "It was just like with Zales. They didn't have nothing. No suspects, no pictures."

"Well, they got a picture now," Miles called from the dining room. He held up the Metro section from the *Overbrook Meadows Gazette*. The glaring headline made the contents of Jewell's belly flip.

MILLINAIRE ROBBED IN HOME INVASION

Daniel stepped quickly to study the paper with Jewell right behind him.

The article was pretty basic. It had a little more information than the early edition, but still not enough facts to cause worry for the gang. The problem was the two pictures included with the article. The first was a photograph of Percy Hamilton. It was a studio shot; cropped and professional.

The second picture was a composite drawing of one of the bandits. Rather than attempt to describe any of the masked men, Percy gave a description of the one person he could readily identify. And though the composite was black and white, and the long hair threw things off a little, it was still a pretty good match.

Jewell studied it, almost in a daze. Her heart jumped up her esophagus and rattled in her throat. Those were definitely her large eyes and full lips. The nose was right on too. Even the physical description was tragically accurate: The police were looking for a short woman; no more than five foot two. Their suspect was light-skinned and curvaceous. She wore expensive jewelry and may be going by the name *Stacy*.

Jewell showed her face during a lot of capers, but never had someone remembered so much about her afterwards.

"That don't look like you," Daniel said, but if he really believed that, he was in the minority.

CHAPTER FIVE
THE SYNDICATE

Miles Sandifer was 29 years old, married with two children, and an expert in all things electronic. Miles disabled Percy Hamilton's security system from a Suburban parked four blocks away using only a laptop. For a job a few months ago, he hacked into the mainframe at a Mercedes dealership and reserved two E Class models for Daniel and Jewell to pick up. Having him around was a necessity, but Miles was more nerd than gangster. He had a fondness for pistols; revolvers in particular, but Jewell knew he'd surrender before firing his weapon.

Fortunately their group worked more with stealth than violence. You don't need to run in with guns blazing when you have people like Jesse Fuentes on your payroll. The 30 year old Laredo native started off hot-wiring Impalas when he was in middle school, and he graduated to home invasions by the twelfth grade. Jesse could disable most alarms as well as Miles, but safecracking was his bread and butter. Watching him work was breathtaking, like watching open heart surgery.

Both Jesse and Miles were indispensable, but a healthy mix of brain and brawn is never a bad thing. Some people absolutely will not part with their valuables unless they've been hogtied and pummeled, or unless their wife and daughter have been missing for a few days. For jobs like this, the gang had Daniel and Davis. Davis could have been a first or last name. He didn't want to say, and no one in the syndicate was going to make him.

The 43 year old Desert Storm vet toted two pistols most of the time (a police model .357 and a PX4 Storm manufactured by Baretta). Davis had no particular burglary skills, but he was down for all things evil, and whether he would actually kill someone was never up for debate. Whether he could *stop* shooting once the first body hit the floor is what Jewell often wondered about.

Either way, whenever Davis went on a job with them, Jewell knew for sure she was going home that day. She might have to run through the enemy's blood and flee the state afterwards, but she was definitely getting away.

So far the gang was 32-0, but Daniel didn't like to refer to them as a mere *gang*. He said their band of merry thieves was more of a *syndicate*; defined by Webster's as *a group of persons or concerns who combine to carry out a particular transaction or project.*

The closest their syndicate had ever come to prosecution was the composite of Jewell in this evening's paper. They sat around a dining table topped with jewelry, documents, and cash money and tried to come to a consensus.

"That's not you," Jesse said. He tossed the newspaper to the table and looked around anxiously.

Jewell stared at him and thought he was full of shit.

Jesse was a very attractive burglar. He kept his dark hair shaved short on the sides, and he usually had a bang hanging over his forehead. He was dark-skinned, with large eyes and pink lips. He reminded Jewell of a young Mark Consuelos.

Miles picked up the paper and stared down his glasses. "I don't know," he said, nibbling on his bottom lip. Miles had short, blonde hair; the same length on top and on the sides. He was clean-shaven and eccentric; sporting wire-rimmed glasses with his pants pulled up too high most of the time. Miles had a nervousness about him Jewell didn't like, but it never interfered with his work.

"I think it's pretty dead on," he said.

"Dead on for her and a million other girls," Daniel said. He sat next to his woman with his chair pushed close to hers. He had an arm around Jewell's shoulder, and that was probably the only thing keeping her in the chair. Everyone thought she was handling this well, but the real reason Jewell remained quiet was because she didn't want them to hear her voice quaver.

"He's right," Jesse said. "That picture looks like every girl at Stilettos on a Friday night." Jesse was addicted to strip clubs, preferring the ones with ebony entertainers.

"That's what I'm telling y'all," Daniel said. "Even if it *is* right for her, it's right for a lot of bitches. They can't say that's my baby based on *that* picture." He gestured to the newspaper like it was something disgusting.

"Cool," Jesse said. "So, so we cool?" He wore a white button-down with black slacks and polished loafers. He eyed the loot on the table fervently.

"Tell me what you think," Jewell said to Miles. Daniel exhaled audibly. But his opinion was clearly biased, and Jesse was too anxious to get paid.

Miles looked over the paper again and then studied Jewell's face. He put a finger to his lips and clicked his tongue.

"Your short hair definitely helps," he said. "With this drawing, your attention is drawn to all that hair. Looking at you now, I'd have to say it wasn't you."

Relief washed over Jewell like a cold shower. In her opinion, Miles' green eyes and pale skin put him right on par with the prosecutor and the jurors. His decision was of utmost importance.

"But it's..." He trailed off, reading the paper again.

That *but* was like a dagger in Jewell's heart.

Daniel felt her body grow tense. "But what?" he said, his words laced with enmity. "You always want to come with that negativity, Miles. Just 'cause *you* got a dark cloud following your ass around don't mean—"

"You want the truth or not?" Miles asked. "I'm not gonna argue with you."

If this wasn't her freedom in jeopardy, Jewell might have laughed at that. Arguing is what these two did best.

"Yeah, nigga. I want the truth," Daniel said. "But we ain't got time for you to keep going back and forth. You said it don't look like her. Everybody said that."

"*I* think it looks like me," Jewell said.

Daniel gave her a look but didn't say anything.

"I didn't say it doesn't look like her," Jesse said. "I said it looks like her and every other black girl..."

Daniel rolled his eyes. "This nigga..."

"What do you think, Miles?" Jewell asked again.

"I think it does look like you," he said and threw his hands up in a *My bad* gesture. "But I'm more worried about the other stuff they got in here."

Jewell subconsciously bounced her knee.

"This some bullshit," Daniel muttered.

"Why is it bullshit?" Miles asked. "'Cause you don't want to hear what I've got to say?"

"'Cause you don't give a fuck about her!" Daniel shouted. "You sitting over there with that smug ass look on your face."

"Fuck you, Daniel," Miles said, his ears growing red.

The average Joe would have caught a quick beat down for speaking to Dapper Dan that way, but Daniel tolerated quite a bit from Miles to avoid in-fighting.

"Watch your mouth," he said.

"If she gets arrested, we might all go down," Miles said. "She knows everything about us. You think I don't care about that?"

"Baby ain't no snitch," Daniel said, his nostrils flaring.

"Just chill," Jesse said. He took the paper from Miles. "Jewell's not going to jail."

"I'll bail you out, baby," Daniel told his woman. "I will. And we'll run."

Jewell nodded but almost started crying too.

"What about you, Davis?" Jesse asked.

Davis sat at the head of the table with a stern look on his face. Like many men of action, he rarely spoke. Jewell thought he went a little crazy in the war, but Daniel said he was just a serious person. Davis never argued, never begged, and he never said he was going to do something he wasn't prepared to do.

Miles slid the newspaper across the table, but Davis wouldn't take it. "I already seen it."

"What do you think?" Jewell asked.

Growing up in the south, she never thought she'd be in cahoots with a redneck, but Daniel trusted this man more than any other. Davis had long brown hair that brushed his shoulders and was usually oily. He had a thick moustache and leathery skin indicative of a heavy smoker. His teeth were lightly tarnished, and his breath was never without an odor.

And despite the tens of thousands of dollars he made with the group just this year, Davis didn't dress like a man with money. He usually wore jeans and a tee-shirt with white sneakers or cowboy boots. He had baby blue eyes that were dead and piercing at the same time.

Davis leaned forward on his elbows and stared at Jewell without expression. It was so quiet you could hear a roach fart.

"Yeah it looks like her," he said with a Texas twang. "But Jesse's right. It looks like a bunch of other black girls too."

Daniel squeezed Jewell's shoulder, but she didn't feel better.

"What you got to worry about is that *description*," Davis went on. "Miles is right: A cop's not gon' arrest you for just the picture. If they get you, it'll be because someone recognizes them descriptions. Ask yourself: Who knows you wear a wig sometimes? Who knows about your jewelry? Who knows you do set ups like this? That's the person you need to worry about."

Jewell felt hopeful for the first time. "Y'all the only ones who know all of that."

"Then you're alright," Davis said definitively. "If you wanna pack it up, that's your choice. But I think you'll be okay."

"That's what I'm saying," Daniel chipped in.

"Me too," Jesse said. "So we're through?" He watched his cronies with hungry eyes. "Everybody cool? Can we get down to business? I got somewhere I need to be."

Business was all of the loot scattered across the table. Everyone definitely wanted to get down to that.

"I'm cool," Miles said. "We'll give it a few days, see what happens."

"Alright," Jewell said with a sigh. "I'm cool too."

"You sure?" Daniel asked her.

"Yeah," she said, and she meant it. "I'm alright."

"*Good*," Miles said. He stood to orchestrate things as he usually did. The syndicate did not have an official leader, but Miles had a degree in accounting, so they let him manage the financial side of things. "So, that picture's dead, right? Y'all want your money?"

"I want my money," Davis said.

Jesse chuckled

Miles grinned. "Now, most of this shit's useless," he said, scooping a stack of papers from the table. "We've got foreign bonds, T-Bills, stocks and shit–"

"Fuck that," Daniel said. The last time they tried to move financial documents a good accountant friend got a lot of heat from the feds and later got himself murdered.

"I can get rid of them if y'all want," Miles said. "I've got a few more contacts, but it will take a while."

"Naw, man," Jesse said.

Miles tossed the papers to the table. "Then we'll burn those."

There were a lot of other goodies on the table, so no one was too upset.

"*This*," Miles hefted a black duffle bag half-full of clinky things, "this is some good stuff right here. Dude had a lot of bling; cufflinks, bracelets. That bastard had four Rolexes."

Jewell saw a lot of goodies in the brief time she was in there. She knew it was going to be a nice score.

"I got rid of most of it," Miles said, "but this other stuff..." He reached into the bag and produced a thick handkerchief. He unfolded it carefully, revealing a diamond and gold encrusted globule shaped like an egg. It was the most beautiful thing Jewell had ever seen.

"I mean, who keeps shit like this?" Miles asked. "Y'all ever seen one of these?"

"That's Faberge," Jewell said.

"I know *that*," Miles said. "I'm just saying; who still collects these? We've got half a dozen of them. My guy wouldn't touch it."

"I know some people," Daniel said.

"I know," Miles said. "I left the good stuff for you."

He handed the bag over. Daniel peered inside and whistled. He leaned over to show Jewell what was inside, and she grinned like a much younger girl. There were definitely a few items in there that she would keep for herself.

"I knew you'd like that," Miles said and winked at her.

"How much you gonna get for that?" Jesse asked.

Daniel pawed through the glittering treasures briefly. "Fifty easy," he said. "Maybe a little less. I'll know for sure by tomorrow."

"That's good," Miles said. Jesse thought so too.

"So, I guess that brings us to these," Miles said, lifting an envelope from the table. There were five in all; one for everyone. "I don't know if that guy has something against banks or what, but between the safe and the floor, we walked out of there with sixty-two; *cash*."

Davis grinned; the most emotion he would ever show.

"I got eight for the stuff I got rid of," Miles went on, "so altogether this wasn't too bad. A hundred and twenty once Daniel gets rid of that."

"I'll have it in a couple days," Daniel said.

"I've already divided this," Miles said, "So we're good to go." The envelopes were bulging but not sealed. He slid them across the table, and everything suddenly seemed worth it again. Fourteen thousand apiece would have made this score rather mediocre, but everyone still had ten more coming from Daniel. Twenty-four thousand for one night's work wasn't too shabby at all.

Jewell squeezed Daniel's hand, and he turned to kiss her. Jesse popped his bottle and poured everyone a drink. The atmosphere became more festive, but Daniel had something he wanted to get off his chest before the meeting dispersed. He stood and waved his glass for quiet.

"Check it out, y'all: We did a good job, like we always do, but I think we need to look at my airport job again."

Jesse's smile faded. Miles sighed and rolled his eyes.

"Y'all keep stalling me out," Daniel went on. "Like y'all don't want to get paid. Now baby's face is all in the news. I ain't tripping though. But I want y'all to get down with me on this. Everything I plan is *tight*."

That was true, but Daniel's airport job had been a source of contention for many months already. Usually when the gang declined a job, that was the end of it. But Daniel wouldn't let this one go.

The mood dropped a few decibels and everyone looked around with uncertainty. Miles was the first to speak up.

"Come on, Daniel. We're having a good time."

"Yeah man," Jesse said, checking his watch. "I gotta go in—"

"You got a minute to talk," Daniel said.

"It's not happening," Miles said. "That's like, what? A *ninety-percent* fail rate? Nobody's doing that, Daniel. You shouldn't ask us to."

"It's not *ninety-percent*," Daniel snarled. "I talk to my inside guy everyday. It can be done."

"A mother can lift a car off her kid," Miles said. "But I wouldn't put money on it."

"Those airports, that's crazy," Jesse agreed. "You can't hardly get on a plane without getting searched."

"We're not even going in the *terminal*," Daniel argued. "That's what I can't understand about y'all." His face wrinkled with disgust. "You won't even let me lay it out. Soon as you hear the word *'airport,'* your tail shoots up between your legs."

"No Daniel, we heard you just fine," Miles said. "We heard you last time, and we heard you the time before that: You want to walk into a *highly secured* part of the airport, pull guns on armed guards and walk out with 50 million in cash and diamonds. That's your plan, right? I miss anything?"

Jewell saw the veins on her boyfriend's neck bulge, but there was no other change in his demeanor.

"We might not have to pull any guns," he said calmly.

"But *they're* gonna have guns. And you said we're gonna pack heat, right?"

Miles could be an asshole, but even Jewell wasn't totally on her boyfriend's side this time.

"You know what, Miles," Daniel said. "You got a wife. You got kids in the city. I can understand why you got a little bitch in you."

"*Bitch*?" Miles put a hand to his chest. "*Me*? You know damned well I take just as many chances as anyone in here! This has nothing to do with whether I have balls or not. This is *common sense*. Your job is *flawed*, Daniel. It can't be done. No one in this room wants to get killed with you."

"Davis said he'll go," Daniel announced.

The room grew quiet, and once again all eyes fell on the gringo. Davis shrugged.

"What the fuck?" he said. "We're doing good, Miles, but I don't want to be doing this shit for the rest of my life, either."

Daniel nodded.

"Either way we're taking risks," Davis said. "He says I only have to take one more risk and I'm through. I'm set for life. That sounds like a nice arrangement."

"That's right," Daniel said.

Miles was stupefied.

"Baby with me too, if we need her," Daniel tacked on.

Jewell nodded though she had no idea what she was getting herself into.

"What about you, Jesse?" Daniel asked. "You wanna get rich, or you wanna live job to job – like them squares out there living check to check? You wanna visit the islands, or rent one of them motherfuckers?"

Miles stared at his friend, almost *willing* him to decline, and Jesse did not disappoint. He shook his head and shrugged.

"I just don't like it, man. It's a shit job, Daniel. I think we'll get killed."

Daniel sighed, realizing he was once again thwarted. He got further this time, but his job required at least four men. It was either get Miles and Jesse on board, or shop around for a new syndicate.

The meeting lasted another thirty minutes and a few more bottles of champagne were passed around, but Daniel remained in a somber mood. He reminded Jewell of a Langston Hughes poem she remembered from high school.

What happens to a dream deferred?

CHAPTER SIX
DEALING WITH THE DEVIL

When the meeting dispersed, Jewell clung to her boyfriend in the garage of Safe House #3 – still not sure what she should do.

"You wanna get something to eat?" Daniel asked.

"You know I do," she said, smiling up at him with her breasts pressed against his torso. "But what about that picture?"

"I thought you said you wasn't worried about it."

"I'm not. Not really."

"Everybody said you're cool."

"I know."

"Then let's go somewhere crowded," Daniel suggested. "So you can see for yourself. If everybody starts looking at you, then *you're* right. If they don't, then *I'm* right."

Jewell frowned. "But if I'm right, we won't be able to finish our dinner. I bet the police won't let us take it to jail with us."

Daniel gave her a serious look. "Baby, if you really scared, we can split. We can go to San Bernardino tonight. We'll be straight."

"No, I'm alright," Jewell said.

"You sure?"

"Yeah. You're with me no matter what, right?"

Daniel smiled again. "For sure." His lips were nice. They reminded Jewell of Tupac's.

She blew him a kiss, and he leaned down to smooch her properly.

"*Get a room!*"

Jewell looked up and saw Davis grinning at them. Jesse and Miles were already gone, and it was just the three of them in the garage. Davis drove an '82 Corvette. It was candy apple red and bad to the bone. It was about the only thing he put any real money into. He climbed inside and then rolled down his window when Daniel waved at him.

"Hey, you wanna get something to eat with us?"

"Where you going?" Davis asked.

"I don't know. What you like?"

"I was on my way to Joe T's," Davis said.

"You were going to eat by yourself?" Daniel asked.

"Yeah. What's wrong with that?"

"Uh, nothing," Daniel said. "Well, can we go eat with you then?"

"If you can keep up," Davis said and rolled up his window.

≈≈≈≈≈≈≈

Davis bounced his Corvette through traffic, doing at least twenty miles over the speed limit the whole time, but keeping up with him was no problem for Jewell's man. Before the syndicate, before pimping, and before graduating high school, Daniel was the wheelman for a fearless thug named Fredrick *Bumpy* Marlowe.

Bumpy was a stick up man, but he didn't rob banks or liquor stores, "where the white man got all dem camera machines." Instead Bumpy preyed on the drug dealers of Overbrook Meadows' south side. A speedy getaway was crucial, and Daniel never let his boss down.

The setup was perfect, the money was good, and the victims wouldn't even call the police. Bumpy raked in five thousand every weekend, and his sixteen-year-old driver made eight-fifty.

Things went south when the drug dealers banded together to protect their livelihood. When Bumpy went into that last dope house, ten armed goons were waiting for him. They shot him in the kneecaps, tied him to a chair, and beat him to death with the butts of their pistols. They cut off his penis, put it in his mouth, and slit his throat for good measures.

A similar fate might have befallen Daniel, but the hooligans never checked the back alley to see if there was a driver waiting. When Bumpy didn't come out after fifteen minutes, Daniel simply drove home with a valuable lesson learned: If you're going to rob, make sure you *over*-plan. And never rob the same 7-11 more than once.

Hustle smarter, not harder.

JEWELL AND THE DAPPER DAN

≈ ≈ ≈ ≈ ≈ ≈ ≈

Davis pulled into Joe T Garcia's with Daniel right on his bumper. They parked on the same row and got a dimly lit booth together once inside. Jewell had never been there before, and she was immediately impressed with the authentic Mexican atmosphere and cuisine. They ordered beef fajitas, *chile rellenos*, and tortilla soup – and Coronas, of course.

At nine p.m. the restaurant was almost filled to capacity, but no one stared at Jewell or their oddly mismatched threesome. Towards the end of the meal, Davis put down his fork and stared at Daniel.

"What?"

"So you gonna tell me about this cockamamie job of yours or not?"

Jewell laughed. Daniel did too.

"I thought you said you was down with me," Daniel said.

"Yeah. I'm willing to do the job with you," Davis said, "but that don't mean I understand it."

"See this, baby," Daniel said to Jewell. "You're in the midst of *true loyalty*. You'll probably never see anything like this again."

"I followed that fool ass president to Iraq," Davis quipped. "I can follow you to the airport."

Daniel put his elbows on the table and held his hands together as if praying. Jewell liked it when her man schemed. Nothing was sexier.

"This is the perfect job," Daniel said. "See, I got a guy..."

Jewell grinned. All of Daniel's proposals started off like that. He must have known every *guy* out there.

"He works security down at the DOM," Daniel said. "In the cargo area."

The *DOM* was the Dallas/Overbrook Meadows airport. It was the biggest and most secured airport in the state; as grand as the JFK. Thinking about taking *anything* from there gave Jewell goose bumps.

Davis nodded, listening intently.

"There's a plane that comes," Daniel went on, "all the way from Germany. It comes in, usually four times a year."

"Your guy knows exactly when it's coming?" Davis asked.

64

"My guy oversees the crew that unloads the plane," Daniel said with a chuckle.

"And there's diamonds on the plane?" Davis guessed.

Daniel nodded. "More than you've ever seen. We got four Herzberg stores in Overbrook Meadows, two in Arlington, one in Grand Prairie, six in Dallas. The plane I'm talking about supplies all of 'em."

Jewell's heart skipped a beat. Herzberg was one of the largest diamond retailers in the world. Only DeBeers exploited more Africans.

"So you wanna stick up the cargo area?" Davis asked. He didn't seem at all worried about the carnage that would ensue.

"No," Daniel said. "The cargo area is like Fort Knox. The guards are armed, you got locks and gates everywhere, and you can't even get in the safe without inserting two keys at the same time – these keys just happen to be on chains around the wrists of two assholes we can't compromise."

Davis nodded.

"There's absolutely no way to stick up the cargo area," Daniel said.

Jewell let out a pent up breath.

"When the diamonds come in," Daniel went on, "they'll stay in the safe for about nine hours. The next morning an armored truck will come and pick them up for distribution to the stores."

"So how do we get 'em?" Davis asked.

Daniel grinned. "We take 'em off the truck."

Jewell shook her head. Davis did too.

"The armored truck?" he asked.

Daniel nodded.

"You can't stick up no armored truck," Davis said knowingly. "They'll radio it in. They'll start shooting out of those *fucking* holes. Hell, they won't even stop. They got LoJack–"

"They're only going to get panicky if you try to stop them on *streets*," Daniel said. "But we're robbing that truck *in the airport*, before it leaves the cargo area."

"What about the guards?" Davis asked. "You said there were guards over there."

"Yeah, but we're going to be dressed just like them," Daniel said. "That's why the truck is going to stop for us, and that's why they won't be suspicious. If you get pulled over by the guys who just loaded your truck, what are you gonna think?"

"I would think they forgot something," Jewell said, getting it for the first time.

"You're not gonna think you're getting robbed," Daniel said.

"But the other guards," Davis said, "aren't they gonna be a little suspicious when they see us stopping the truck?"

"They're not gonna see us," Daniel said. "There's a blind spot. I call it my *window of opportunity:* Once the truck gets loaded, it has to take a particular path to get out of the airport. There's only one way it can go, and it has to turn a corner. The guards at the cargo area won't be able to see the truck once it turns that corner."

"And that's when we rob it?" Jewell asked. "Between that corner and the exit?"

"That's right," Daniel said.

Davis still looked confused.

Daniel patted his coat. "You got a pen, baby?" Jewell found one in her purse, and Daniel drew a diagram of the airport on the back of a receipt. When he was done drawing and talking, everyone at the table felt like the job really could be done.

"Miles still won't go for it," Davis said intuitively.

"I know," Daniel said. "But I figure if I let him be the pick up man, he won't have so much of a problem with it."

Davis rubbed his chin. "Yeah. He'd go for that. Not too much risk."

"Just pick up us and the diamonds," Jewell thought out loud.

Daniel turned to look at her. His brow was furrowed. "Baby, I didn't say you were coming."

"You said you needed four guys to go in," she said.

"Maybe we can do it with three," Daniel said and turned back to Davis. "You think you can talk to Jesse?"

Davis nodded. "Yeah. I'll talk to him. That boy spends it as fast as he gets it. I can make the money sound real good to him."

"If you can get Jesse," Daniel said, "Miles will get down with us." He leaned back and sucked his teeth. "This is gonna be sweet. You'll see..."

≈ ≈ ≈ ≈ ≈ ≈

When their waitress brought the check, both men were drinking and laughing pleasantly. Jewell sat back in her seat pouting; wondering why the hell she couldn't participate in the airport job.

On the way out of the restaurant, a policeman in the lobby looked them over *a little long*, Jewell thought. But that was probably because of the strange threesome they made; Jewell and Daniel were still in church clothes. Davis was dressed for the honky tonk.

≈ ≈ ≈ ≈ ≈ ≈

Forty minutes later they were home at last. Jewell disrobed quickly and slipped into the shower with Daniel right behind her. Their pad was what Daniel considered a *throwaway*, but you'd never know that from looking at it.

The two bedroom condo was plush; they had custom-made draperies, a solid oak bedroom set, and an original Georgia O'Keefe hanging in the living room. In the den there was a 50 gallon saltwater aquarium where fluorescent green lemon butterflies danced with fire-bellied angelfish. They had a 65 inch plasma television and a superb view of downtown from their balcony, twelve stories high.

"When are you going to look at that bag?" Jewell asked as Daniel cuddled with her in the tub. The steam was thick and soothing. Daniel was the only man Jewell ever met who could tolerate a shower as hot as she liked it. She stood with her back to him; facing the soft spray. Daniel kissed the top of her ear and put his hands on her hips. The bathroom smelled like honeydew and mulberries from Jewell's scented soaps.

"What's the rush?" Daniel asked. He reached under her arm and took the bath sponge from her hands. He rubbed it down her spine, and Jewell sighed.

"You're not gonna sell *all* of it, are you?" she asked.

"Why not?" Daniel said. "Where's the soap?"

"In my hands."

Daniel reached around her again, with both arms this time. He cupped his hands over hers and worked the sponge slowly until he had enough lather. Everything was wet and slippery. Jewell felt like they were making pottery together.

"Did you see something in there you like?" Daniel asked. He pressed his body close to hers and worked the sponge between her breasts and down her belly. His lips brushed the back of her head, and Jewell felt him growing against her backside.

"Yeah, I did."

"What was it?" Daniel asked. The sponge dipped between her legs. He lathered her pubic hairs and then abandoned the sponge altogether in favor of his smooth, curious fingers. Jewell leaned back and laid her head on his chest. She closed her eyes. A rivulet loosened, and the hot water blended with her own currents.

"It was a necklace," she said. "Three strands; yellow diamonds on the bottom. I think the gold was two-toned."

"I saw that," Daniel said. He moved his hands to her hips and pulled her closer. He was fully erect now; poking the small of her back. Jewell wished she was taller, or maybe she'd bathe with her stilettos on next time.

"You saw it?" she asked.

"That's worth more than one of them eggs," Daniel said. "That necklace probably retails for eighteen thousand."

"Can't you still get fifty without it?" Jewell asked.

"Maybe."

She turned to face him. Daniel's eyes were half closed. He looked intoxicated. Beads of sweat twinkled on his bald head. His lips were glistening. Jewell wanted to gnaw on them, a little. She retrieved the sponge and rubbed his stomach and chest.

Daniel only went to prison once, but the effects of his stay were still apparent some ten years later: His thick neck exploded into bulging traps, big shoulders and strong arms. His pecs were nothing less than *delightful*. Jewell liked to run her tongue down the crease in the middle. His nipples deserved ample sucking as well. Daniel didn't have a six-pack, but his stomach was flat and hairless. His erection throbbed between them like an excited missile.

Jewell stood on her toes to kiss him. Daniel's hands immediately made their way to her ass. He pulled her even closer, squeezing hard. Jewell sucked his tongue eagerly.

"Can I have it?" she asked between kisses. She knew it was unfair to force a decision from him while so much of the blood meant for his brain was diverted elsewhere, but Jewell really wanted that necklace. She had a lot of jewelry, but that chain was unique. One of a kind trinkets turned her on more than money.

"You can have it," Daniel said. "I think I can still get fifty without it."

Jewell grinned from ear to ear. "Turn around," she said.

Daniel presented his back, and Jewell scrubbed every inch of it. He stretched his arms out and leaned on the tiles in front of him. His back was broad, fanning like a cobra, and it was smooth. There were no blemishes; no bumps to pick at. Daniel had a nice bubble-butt too.

"How come you don't want me to do the airport job with you?" Jewell asked.

"I didn't say I don't want you," he said. "I just don't need you to go *in the airport*. There's a lot more stuff we gotta do."

"Like what?"

"I haven't worked it all out yet," Daniel said. "I know we gon' need ID cards, security uniforms. We need to do a test run and steal one of their patrol cars."

"What part do you need me for?" Jewell asked.

"I don't know. We'll see."

"I can't believe we're going to do this," she said, smiling wickedly. "*Fifty million dollars...* I knew one day you'd lead me to big things, but I never expected nothing like this."

"When?" Daniel asked.

"When what?"

"When did you know I would lead you to big things?"

"When I first me you," Jewell reminisced. "When you came to my dope house to get that bitch."

Daniel chuckled. "Damn, I forgot all about that ho."

"I can already imagine myself as a millionaire," Jewell said. "Everybody gets ten, right? Miles gets it just for picking y'all up?"

"Hell naw," Daniel said. "I ain't giving that motherfucker *shit*."

The soap squirted from Jewell's fingers.

"What?"

"You heard me."

She pulled his arm, and Daniel turned to face her. He wasn't smiling at all.

"You're gonna *burn* Miles?" she asked.

Honor among thieves was an antiquated notion, but it still held true for the syndicate. Everything always got split five ways. No one held out, and no one ever got burned.

"Even if Miles wants to go *in* the airport, he ain't getting *shit*," Daniel said. "Jesse either."

Jewell stared at him, waiting for the punch line. There wasn't one.

"This is gonna be our last job together anyway," Daniel said. "And *I'm* the only one who can move those diamonds. Everybody's gonna be waiting on me to get in touch with them after I make the sale, only we ain't never coming back this time. We'll be gone, forever. Just me and you, baby. Fifty million; all ours."

Jewell's heart thumped. Daniel's words excited her, but she was also fearful. She felt an undeniable sense of foreboding, but more than that Jewell had never been more turned on. She dropped the sponge and wrapped her fingers around his stiff member.

"Are you serious?"

"Why not, baby? Miles don't want to do it anyway. I been *begging* that fool to get rich. I'm through begging. Fuck him. Why should he get paid?"

"What about Jesse?"

"Fuck him, too."

Jewell was light-headed. She squeezed the warm flesh in her hands, and Daniel emitted a soft moan. She stared into his eyes and caressed more delicately, until he pulsated beneath her fingers.

"What are you thinking?" he asked.

"I don't know," Jewell said.

"You down or what?"

"You know I'm down."

"You don't want me to stiff them lames, do you?" he asked.

Jewell thought about how long she'd known those men and how much money they'd made together. They were good guys, even Miles, but crime is crime. It wouldn't be the first time she backstabbed someone close to her.

"What about Davis?"

"That's the only thing," Daniel said. "That's my boy. I can't do him like that. I'd make sure he got his ten, maybe a little more. Me and you staying together, so we don't need *all* of it."

Jewell leaned against him, and Daniel wrapped his arms around her. They kissed like newlyweds, and the night took on an abstract quality. At some point Daniel clutched her hips and lifted her into the air. Jewell wrapped her legs around him, and Daniel stepped out of the shower – not at all hindered by her weight. He headed for the bedroom, sucking her lips along the way, but his libido got the better of him midway down the hallway.

Daniel leaned Jewell against the wall and penetrated her with minimum friction. He supported her with two strong hands on her back. Jewell held onto his neck and shoulders. She stared into his eyes, breathing raggedly. Daniel stared back at her, pumping slow, but hard. Jewell felt him in her belly. She felt him in her toes and fingertips as well. Daniel was always a great lover, but tonight it was an all-encompassing experience.

By the time they got to the bedroom, he was spent but not drained. He sat on the bed with Jewell still on his lap. She pushed him to a lying position and coerced another erection with the sensual movements of her hips. Within seconds he was like a petrified log again.

He pulled her shoulders down so that her hair brushed his forehead. Daniel liked to feel her breasts and her belly and her breaths on him when they made love. Jewell liked the same things. She licked his neck and sucked his Adam's apple.

Daniel's hands were everywhere. He caressed her shoulders and her ass and all places in between.

Before he climaxed again, Jewell abruptly stopped all motions. She sat up so she could look him in the eyes.

"What's wrong?"

"I stopped taking my pill."

"Why?"

"I'm ready to have your little boy," she said. "Mama wants to see her grandbaby before she, before she goes."

Daniel watched her for what felt like a long time. "What about you?"

"I believe in you," Jewell said. "I believe this job is gonna work. We'll be together, and we can go anywhere we want. We can get regular jobs. We'll be *good* parents."

Daniel smiled. "How long ago did you stop taking them?"

"It's been a while," Jewell said. "I think I'm ready. I feel like I can get pregnant."

"Alright," he said and rolled her into missionary.

As they made love that night, Jewell believed something tragic yet beautiful was occurring. She loved Daniel more than any man she ever had or ever would love again. She trusted him fully. She would follow him through the gates of paradise or into the fiery depths of hell. In the back of her mind, she knew it would probably be the latter.

CHAPTER SEVEN
HUSTLING A HUSTLER

Jewell stood over the kitchen sink with her cell phone in the crook of her shoulder. She was in the process of peeling what had to be the juiciest grapefruit ever. It was huge too, almost the size of a cantaloupe. Daniel knew a guy who grew them in his own garden; right in the city.

Jewell wore a blue camisole with gray jogging pants. She was barefoot and had no bra or panties on. The kitchen floor was cold, so she stood on one leg; switching feet ever so often like a flamingo. From the window in the dining room, she could see the sun, bright and orange, barely visible over the horizon.

The smell of fresh coffee and pastries titillated her nasal cavity. Daniel loved his morning java as much as she did. He usually woke up a few minutes after she poured her first cup.

Jewell rolled her eyes as she listened to the nonsense coming from the other end of the phone.

"... and Ms. Hunt, we've already spoken with you about this. I spoke to you *myself* as a matter of fact. You said you would call me and notify us of *any* problems you might be having with our staff. After that last one, you said you wouldn't confront them yourself – unless it was some sort of emergency."

"It *was* an emergency," Jewell said.

"Ms. Hunt, I hardly think tardiness qualifies as an emergency. The fact is–"

"That's not why I fired her," Jewell said.

"Really? I spoke with Tonya last night and she said–"

"I know what *she said*," Jewell interrupted, "'cause she tried to get me to tell that same lie." Jewell thought briefly about the sob story her mother's last nurse gave her. Tonya said she was suffering from a medical condition. Supposedly she was doing her best to stay awake, and Miss Eveline certainly liked her. Plus Tonya said she had three children to provide for.

Oh well, Jewell decided. *Fuck her.*

"Excuse me?"

"She says she's got some kind of disorder," Jewell said. "She said she can't stay awake when she wants to. *And* she said y'all knew about it, and *still* sent her out to my house."

There was a pause. When the secretary spoke again, Jewell knew she had the upper hand.

"We, um, we were aware of that situation with Tonya. But we were led to believe she had it taken care of."

"Well, she don't," Jewell said. "When I came home, my mama was in her room screaming for that damned nurse. She was stuck on the toilet – she could have had a heart attack *right then*."

"I'm terribly sorry."

"I go looking for your nurse, and I find her fat ass on the couch; *stretched out*. If you know you have a problem sleeping, why would you lay on your back while you're supposed to be at work? She probably got her a little nap in everyday. She didn't expect me home that early."

"Ms. Hunt, I, I would like to apologize on behalf of Tonya and our company. You are a valued client, and I'm sure we can find a nurse who meets your standards."

"I don't know," Jewell said. "I like you guys, but I don't want to take anymore chances like this with my mama. When Tonya said y'all knew about her condition, that made me feel real bad. Like, what kind of people are you sending to my house?"

"Ms. Hunt, I can assure you this will *never* happen again. If you'll give us another chance, I'd like to offer you two days – no, *one week's* services for free. I can have a different nurse out there this morning, by eight a.m. You won't owe us anything until the nineteenth."

"Um, okay," Jewell said. So far she'd cursed out three nurses from this agency, but they were still willing to give her the benefit of the doubt. Jewell jotted down the name of her new LVN and checked the time on the microwave before she called her sister. It was a quarter after seven. Yolanda would be up because one of her boys was old enough to go to school. Maybe two of them were, Jewell couldn't remember.

Yolanda's husband, Deacon Chauncey Worthy, answered almost immediately.

"Hello?"

"Hey," Jewell said. "How you doing, Chauncey?"

"Blessed and highly favored," he said, and Jewell felt like gagging. She couldn't stand the overly-religious types. It's one thing to love the Lord, but some people throw it in your face every chance they get.

"Yeah, me too," she said. "Is my sister there?"

"Yeah, baby. Just a minute."

That was another thing Jewell didn't like about Chauncey: He referred to all women as *baby*, *darling*, or *sugar*. Jewell hated when any man did that, but Chauncey was supposed to be a man of God. She suspected a scandal or two in his future.

Yolanda came to the phone panting. "Huh, hello?"

"Hey, girl. What you doing?"

"Trying to get these boys dressed," she said. "Everyday there's a shoe missing, or their socks, or *something*."

"What about mama? How's she doing?"

"She's fine," Yolanda said. "'Cept every time I go in there she's trying to get up again. She hates that bed."

"She hates the one at her house too," Jewell said. "She's determined to die on her feet."

Yolanda didn't say anything, and Jewell regretted her words. She knew her sister coped with things differently.

"Hey, I got her a new nurse," Jewell said. "She'll be there at eight. Can you take Mama home and wait with her until the new lady comes?"

Her sister sighed loudly. "I'm already trying to get these boys ready. Mama's not dressed or nothing. And Peter got to be at school at *eight*. How am I supposed to get them and Mama ready too?"

"Can't your husband take Pete to school?"

"He's busy studying. He's giving the word tonight."

"He can stop for a minute to watch his kids. What does he think; all he had to do was drop off the sperm and that was it for him?"

"Why can't *you* come get Mama?" Yolanda asked.

"'Cause I'm halfway across the city," Jewell said. "It'll be eight o'clock by the time I get there."

"*Ooh*, I'm *sick* of this," Yolanda groaned.

Jewell's temper was worse than a cornered rattler. "Sick of what? You only had her for *one day*, Yolanda. Every time you have to do something for Mama, you get this little attitude."

"I got five—"

"I don't want to hear that. You got a grown man over there who can help with them kids. Mama says she asked you to get her a new comforter last month. You couldn't even do that."

"I was short last month."

"That's 'cause your husband doesn't have a job."

"He do have a job."

"He'd make more sweeping than preaching," Jewell said, then she stopped herself before any more venom could come out. She took a couple slow breaths. "I didn't mean that."

"He *will* make more money," Yolanda said. "When he gets his own church—"

"I know," Jewell said. "He's going to be a good pastor."

"Then we'll be able to pay *all* of Mama's bills," Yolanda said.

She'll be dead by then, Jewell thought, but she would never say such things. She got off the phone with her sister much like she always did; in the middle of a never-ending argument.

Jewell sat down at the kitchen table with her grapefruit. As she nibbled, it struck her that it wasn't even seven-thirty, and so far she got into it with everyone she talked to. Daniel shuffled into the kitchen sleepy-eyed but still beautiful, and Jewell girded herself for argument number three.

"Hey baby," she said.

"Hey." He walked up behind her and kissed the top of her head. He put his hands on her shoulders and jerked on the spaghetti straps of her camisole. The thin fabric rubbed her nipples and the friction gradually put them in a state of excitement – which was what Daniel wanted. He sat across from her with a dopey grin and stared at the beauty he created.

"I wish women didn't wear bras," he said. "Nipples are so underrated."

For breakfast, Daniel wore a silk pajama suit designed by Ralph Lauren. The dark red blended well with his skin tone.

Jewell got up and poured him a cup of coffee; black, with no sugar or cream. She set the microwave for thirty seconds to re-heat the sausage patties she made for him, and she opened the oven to retrieve his biscuits and cinnamon rolls. Everything looked and smelled wonderful, just as she planned it. Jewell never ate breakfast herself, but she always made sure Daniel's first meal was restaurant quality, especially today.

With the food in front of him, Daniel was a happy camper, but it was hard to hustle a hustler.

"What's with the cinnamon rolls?" he asked. They were his favorite breakfast treat, but supposedly Jewell had him on a diet.

"I don't know," she said. "What's wrong with them?" She sat across from him and bit into the pink meat of her grapefruit. When she looked up, Daniel was still staring at her.

"What?"

"You tell me."

Jewell sighed. "Okay. There *is* something I wanted to ask you..." She batted her eyes, but her womanly wiles were all but lost on Daniel. Dapper Dan was definitely no Percy Hamilton.

"I already gave you that necklace," he said, not smiling anymore. He stuffed a whole sausage patty in his mouth and gobbled roughly.

"I thought you forgot all about that necklace," she said with a slutty smile. Once again Daniel became more guarded than amorous.

"I don't forget *shit*," he said. "'Specially something like that. That necklace retails for eighteen thousand."

Damn, Jewell thought. She started to wake him with oral stimulation this morning, but *noooo*; she decided to make some funky cinnamon rolls instead. *Always go with your first thought.*

"You in a bad mood?" she asked.

"You getting me there."

"Why? What I do?"

"You got something to ask me, and you know I'm gon' say no. You might as well spit it out so I can say '*Hell naw*,' and we can get on with the rest of our day."

"I want to bring my brother in on the job," Jewell blurted.

Daniel stared at her like she suggested they turn themselves in.

"*Hell* naw," he said; his eyebrows scrunched together.

"Baby, why not?"

"You *know* why not."

"He's different now," Jewell said. She had no idea if this was really the case, but her mom said he was. Eveline was blind and senile, and she would bring a sick raccoon in out of the cold, but still...

"Slim ain't different," Daniel said. "You don't get off heroin till you *die*. That's the only way to shake them needles."

"Some people get clean."

"Name *one*."

"Just 'cause I don't know them *personally* don't mean it doesn't happen."

"I ain't never seen it," Daniel said. He bit into one of his cinnamon rolls and grinned. "Damn, baby. These good."

"Mama asked me to help him out," Jewell said.

Daniel took a deep breath and blew it out of his nostrils. "How come you always gotta put *her* in it?"

"I'm not putting her in it; I'm just telling you what she said."

"Why *you* gotta look after him? He's damned near ten years older than you. What the fuck kind of sense does that make?"

"Just *one last time*," Jewell pleaded. "You said you need another guy for the job. If you use my brother, then we won't have to worry about him anymore. He'll have his own money."

"Enough to blowout his fucking heart," Daniel said.

"If he does that, then it's on him," Jewell said. "I just want to try. You don't even know if he's still getting high. You haven't seen him in two years."

"You telling me Slim ain't getting high?" Daniel asked. He stared hard at her, daring her to lie.

"I, uh, I—"

"Just what I thought."

"I don't know if he is or not, Daniel. I haven't seen him that much since he got out this last time. But I can tell you this," she maintained eye contact so he'd know she wasn't fibbing, "I haven't seen or heard *anything* about him getting high, from *anybody*. So, as far as I know, he's been sober at least four months."

Daniel shook his head. "You wanna fuck up my job," he said. "We get *this* close to retiring, and you wanna fuck it up."

"I'm not gonna mess it up, Daniel. I want it just as bad as you. If Slim's still like he was, then we won't use him. At least we can find out."

"Alright," Daniel said. "Go find out then."

Jewell's eyes brightened. "For real?"

"Yeah," he said. "Go ahead and check on him if you want. If he's fucked up though, baby, you'd better not lie to me."

"I won't," Jewell said, her heart light in her chest.

"I'm for real, girl. If he looks even *kind of* high, you'd better tell me. This is some real shit, baby. I'm not letting him fuck off my money. I know that's your brother, but I'll kill him like any other nigga."

Jewell didn't doubt her man at all. If they had a different kind of relationship, she would have cursed him out for threatening such a thing, but they were both gangsters before anything else.

"I'll check on him today."

"Go *early*," Daniel suggested. "Catch him when he wakes up. And don't call and tell him you're on your way either."

"Alright," Jewell said. She stood and gave her boyfriend a kiss and then went to the bedroom to change for the day.

Daniel had already made the bed, which was odd, but that wasn't the only surprise he left for her. Right in the middle of the mattress was a large jewelry box, about the size of a Bible. There were no markings on it, but Jewell knew it was for her. She sat on the corner of the bed and opened it in her lap. Sitting on a black bed of felt was her new necklace.

She already knew what it looked like, plus they lived in the same house; Daniel could have simply handed it to her. But it was things like this that kept Jewell in love with her man. It's always the little things.

CHAPTER EIGHT
GOING DOWNTOWN

Jewell's first solid memory of her big brother was from an incident that occurred when she was four years old. She was a big fan of the Punky Brewster sitcom back then, and her favorite episode got interrupted one afternoon because of a frantic call from Cedric's middle school. Cedric was fourteen at the time; giving the 8th a second go-round after an abysmal effort the previous year.

Jewell's mom was a good deal healthier in those days, but she already had a slight limp from the arthritis that would decimate her decades later. Eveline had no man and no car, so she had to get her little girls dressed for the eight block hike to Dunbar Middle. Jewell didn't want to miss her program, and she cried most of the way there. And when they got to the school, life gave her something totally different to cry about.

Her big brother was in the principal's office bloodied and bruised. His tee-shirt was soiled and ripped in several places; hanging from his scrawny frame only by the collar and one sleeve. Cedric's lip was busted, his eye blackened, and his nose was pudgy and tender. The wounds aside, Jewell would never forget how *emaciated* he looked.

Cedric had always been a small kid. He was tall and noticeably thinner than most of the boys his age. He had long arms and legs; the result of a recent growth-spurt that made all of his school pants high-water. Jewell thought he got into a fight about his clothes again, but the principal said this latest altercation had nothing to do with schoolyard bullying. Much to Eveline's surprise, Cedric initiated his latest altercation, and the principal said it was *gang-related*.

Jewell had no idea what any of that meant, but she studied Cedric's demeanor and knew that her brother was different somehow. The brooding and bloodied misfit sitting in that office didn't seem like the same guy who helped her get cookies off the high counters and played dolls with her sometimes.

As if to reinforce this change, Cedric suddenly stood in the middle of the meeting. Before anyone could stop him, he snatched a bronze apple from the principal's desk and chucked it across the hallway. It flew into an adjacent office where one of his assailants sat with his parents and the assistant principal.

The apple hit the other kid right on the temple, and the fact that Cedric would do such a thing right in front of the principal and his own mother was enough grounds for expulsion. Cedric completed the eighth grade at an alternative school. He made it all the way to his sophomore year at Dunbar High before getting kicked out again. This time it was for drug possession, but Cedric was a pusher back then, not a user.

By the time Jewell got to high school, people called her brother *Slim*, and he was a well known dealer and gang member in the city. He always had a new car, always had a big booty stallion on his arm, and he always had a pistol on his person for the numerous enemies he was accumulating. He snorted heroin recreationally, but most of the city's premier thugs and players did that. Only about one in fifty went on to develop serious addiction problems that left them dysfunctional. Slim just happened to be one of those unlucky few.

Jewell dropped out of high school in the tenth grade. By then Slim had graduated to sticking needles between his toes. Two years later he did his first bid in prison for what's known as a *dopefiend move*: He broke into a closed convenience store for an ill-fated smash and grab.

He got out of jail six months later, but the revolving door scenario became a reality for him. Altogether Slim spent time in the penitentiary and state jail on eleven separate occasions. His latest release was four months ago.

≈≈≈≈≈≈≈

Jewell pulled into her brother's apartment complex and parked in a restricted spot close to his building. Security was known to be lax there, but she took a handicapped placard from her glove compartment and hung it on her rearview mirror just in case.

It was only eight thirty a.m., but there were already a few goons and ghouls about. Slim's complex had a dozen well known crack spots, and, like the marines, junkies never sleep. One of them approached Jewell as soon as she exited her vehicle.

Jewell wore tight bell-bottom jeans with a long-sleeved blouse and open-toed sandals. The crackhead wore a tan tee-shirt that was probably white some time ago, a pair of equally soiled jeans, and *open-toed sneakers*. Most people replace their shoes once the toe cap detaches from the soles, but not crackheads.

"Hey, excuse me, ma'am," the doper said.

Jewell kept walking, and the stranger followed.

"Um, excuse me, ma'am."

Jewell gripped her purse strap a little tighter and turned to face the stranger. "I ain't got no money," she snapped.

But the junkie knew better. Her Lincoln Navigator, Coach bag, tennis bracelet and diamond solitaire told him something different.

"Ma'am, if you–"

"I ain't got *nothing*," Jewell said more forcibly. "No *dollar*, no *quarter*, no *nothing*. Now gone! Go on, now."

The bum didn't move, so Jewell turned her back on him. She started walking, and she heard his shuffling feet following close behind. But Jewell felt no trepidation as she slipped into a deserted corridor leading to her brother's apartment.

She waited, and when they couldn't be seen from the main street, the addict made his move. Jewell heard his footsteps increase speed, and she glanced over her shoulder. The vagrant was within ten feet already, reaching into his front pocket. Jewell was pretty sure whatever he had in there was no match for what she had in her purse, so she turned for a face off.

"Nigga, why you following me?"

He stopped and pulled a bright orange box cutter from his pocket. He extended the blade with a trembling thumb.

"I, I didn't want it to go like this," he said.

"Like what?" Jewell asked.

He scratched his head with his free hand. "Huh?"

"Huh?" Jewell said.

He sneered at her. "Gimme yo purse. And that bracelet. And, and, and, and that necklace too."

"Are you *robbing* me?"

"I, I didn't want it to go like this."

"Can I get my ID out of here?" Jewell asked. "You don't need it. You just want the money, right?"

Before the lummox could respond, she reached into her purse and wrapped her hand around a chrome .44 magnum. It was cold but comforting. Jewell drew the pistol and pointed it, no more than eight feet away from his head.

Much to her surprise, the dopefiend promptly pissed his pants. The stain blossomed on his crotch and worked its way down both legs slowly. It was disgusting to watch, but kind of funny too. His eyes were huge like the jiggaboos in old Bugs Bunny cartoons.

"I'm, I'm, I'm, I'ma, I'm, *I'm sorry*!" he pleaded. "Don't shoot me. *Please!*" He trembled with both hands in the air. Jewell let him squirm for a few seconds.

"What's wrong with you?" she finally asked. "Why you out here messing with people? You steal from *women*?"

"Ma'am, I don't. *I swear.* I, I didn't, I, it was a accident. *I swear. Please* don't shoot me."

"You know Slim?" Jewell asked.

"I didn't, I don't, who?"

"Slim. He stay right up there." Jewell pointed with her free hand. "In apartment 94."

"I, I, I mighta seen him. He, he skinny? Old dude?"

"Yeah," Jewell said. Slim was only forty-four, but his junkie-lifestyle added at least ten years to his features.

"I don't know him. I seen him a few times. Please put that gun down, lady. Don't shoot me."

Jewell kept her pistol trained on his forehead. "He get high?" she asked.

"Me?"

"Naw, *fool*! I know *you* get high. I'm talking about *Slim;* the man who stay up there."

"That dude? Naw. No ma'am. He don't get high. I smoke every day. I know everybody over here who smokes. He don't smoke with us."

"What about heroin?" Jewell asked.

"What?"

"*Heroin*! Does he use heroin?"

"Lady I don't know. Please get that gun off me. I done pissed ma pants…"

"Gimme that box cutter," Jewell said.

"Here." The addict held it out to her and took a step forward.

"Drop it!"

He did.

"Gimme them shoes too," Jewell said.

His face became a mess of anguish and confusion. "Muh, mah shoes?"

"You never got jacked before?" Jewell asked.

He looked down at his tattered sneakers. "But, but I need these. These all I got."

"You didn't care about taking all *I* got," Jewell said. She pulled the hammer back on her weapon. "Run them shoes!"

He kicked them off awkwardly, almost falling in the process.

"That shirt too," she said.

"Lady *please*!" He was on the verge of tears.

"You wanna die for that shit?"

He didn't. He pulled it over his head and dropped it next to his tennis.

"*Please*. Please don't kill me."

"Go on," Jewell said. "Start running. That way." She gestured with the gun, and the dopefiend didn't need to be told twice. He turned and sprinted with all the grace of a three-legged salamander.

Jewell watched until he was out of sight, and then she turned; leaving his belongings on the sidewalk. She climbed the stairs and put her gun away when she reached her brother's breezeway. It took a lot of knocking, but Slim finally answered his door wearing only a pair of boxer shorts. He squinted at the sunlight and then beamed brightly at his visitor.

"*Lil sis*!" Slim threw his arms around her like they hadn't seen each other in years. He was a little funky, but he didn't have the stench of death that usually clung to him.

"Hey Cedric."

He backed away and held her at arms length. "Damn you look good, girl! What you doing over here so early?"

"I came to talk to you about something," Jewell said. "Can I come in?"

"Yeah, yeah! Come on." He stepped aside and Jewell entered his dank apartment. He closed the door and locked it behind her.

Slim's digs were rather subpar compared to Jewell's condo. In the front room he had a couch, a loveseat and a television – and that was it. There were no coffee or end tables and no shelves. The TV sat on the floor rather than inside an entertainment center. There was nothing in the dining room either, just empty space and clean carpet. Jewell suspected the bedroom might look the same way, because there was a pillow and a blanket on Slim's couch. She didn't need a CSI team to know he'd been sleeping there.

Jewell quickly scanned the room, looking for drugs or drug paraphernalia. There was a lighter on the floor, but no needles, no cotton balls and no spoon with a burnt-black bottom. That didn't mean a whole lot, but it was a good sign. The apartment had the smell of stale cigarettes and bachelorhood.

Jewell sat in the loveseat, and Slim took a seat on his couch. There was a pair of jeans on the floor next to his foot. He grabbed them and slid them on shamelessly.

"Why you over here so early?" he asked again with a bright grin.

Slim wasn't an unattractive man, but he would never win a beauty pageant. He kept his hair shaved short, the same length all around, and he had no moustache or goatee. Slim was the darkest member of the Hunt family with skin the color of cherry wood. He had large eyes and a flat nose. He always looked tired to Jewell. Even if you caught him after a full eight hours of sleep, he would have the same worn down expression. Slim had long arms and legs, a flat stomach and a caved-in chest. He was a couple inches taller than Daniel.

"I came to see you," Jewell said. "I haven't seen you in a few weeks. I told Mama I would check on you."

"How Mama doing?"

"She's, she's fine," Jewell said. "It's day by day, though. Doctors don't know how she managed to make it this long."

"She strong," Slim said. "She always been strong."

"You talked to her?"

"Yeah." Slim grinned. "I talk to her all the time. I wanna go over there, but I don't have a ride. The buses stop running by the time I get off."

"What kind of work you doing?" Jewell asked.

"Janitor," Slim said with defeat in his eyes.

"How's that going?"

Slim held his arms out. "Look around. This all I got. I make enough to pay the bills and eat and that's it. And if they find out about my record, they'll fire me from that job. White man don't want a nigga to have shit."

Blaming *whitey* was Slim's favorite thing to do. Jewell was a little disheartened to see he still wasn't taking responsibility for his crummy life.

"You seen Yolanda?" he asked.

"Yeah. I saw her at church yesterday. Talked to her this morning."

"What she doing?"

"Popping out babies fast as she can," Jewell said. "She'll get pregnant again this year, watch."

Slim smiled.

"How about you?" she asked. "You still not ready to settle down and have a little girl – or a big-headed boy?"

Slim grinned and shook his head. "I'm a *janitor*," he reminded her. "A janitor and a ten-time loser. The only women who'll come in here is hookers, and they leave soon as they get their money."

"You got money for hookers?" Jewell asked.

Slim gave her a look. "These crackheads out here only want ten dollars. Everybody got ten dollars."

"They never want to get high in here?" Jewell asked.

Slim cocked his head. "What you trying to say, girl? Why don't you just spit it out?"

"Daniel might need some help."

Slim's disposition immediately improved. They only used him for two jobs in the past, but he got *major* paid each time.

"Daniel wants me to help with a job?"

"He *might*," Jewell said. "Let me see your arms."

Slim jumped up and displayed the crooks of his arms. "I'm clean, Jewell. Look. *Nothing*. No tracks."

He was moving around so much she had to grab his arm and hold it still. There were no fresh needle marks. She checked the other one too.

"See. I'm clean," Slim said. He returned to the sofa and sat on the edge of his seat with his elbows on his knees. "What's the job? When is it?"

"We're still planning it right now, Cedric. But I can tell you this: Daniel don't trust you. He thinks you still messing with that stuff."

"*I'm not*," Slim said emphatically. "Where he at? Let me talk to him. I go to work everyday. I come home to this shit hole and go my ass to sleep. I don't do nothing bad – smoke cigarettes, that's about it."

He sounded good, but Jewell only half-believed him. "You been using for a long time, Cedric. How you know you're alright this time?"

"I been out four months," Slim said. "I had the same job ever-since. When was the last time I had a job this long?"

Jewell shrugged. It had been a while.

"And this apartment," Slim said, "It ain't shit, but I pay my rent every month. They *never* put a notice on my door. *Oh!* And check this out!" He stood and dug in his pockets. He came out with a wad of bills and receipts. "Look," he said, handing her a piece of paper.

Jewell unfolded it and saw that it was a check stub.

"I just got paid yesterday," Slim said. "Look how much I made."

Jewell didn't know why he was so happy about two hundred and thirty dollars, but then he started to count out his money. He had two hundred and twenty-five dollars, cash.

"If I was getting high, would I have got paid yesterday and only spent *five* dollars?"

That was the best evidence he could have given her. "No," Jewell said. "You woulda spent all of that." She handed his stub back.

"I know!" Slim said. "So you gon' tell Daniel I'm cool? I need this, lil sis. I'm sick of living like this. Did he say what kind of job it is; how much it'll make?"

Jewell smiled. "If we do this job, it'll be our *last* job."

Slim looked confused. "Why?"

"This is big," she said. "The biggest one ever."

"Big like..."

"Like *millions*," Jewell said. "Ten apiece."

Slim's jaw dropped, and she saw that he still had nice teeth. If crack or speed was his drug of choice, he'd look like a jack-o-lantern by now.

"For real?"

"Yeah," Jewell said. "But that's all I can tell you about it right now. If you stay clean, I can get you in. If you wanna get high, we can't use you."

He nodded. "I'm clean. I swear."

"I believe you," Jewell said, and she really did. "But you gotta *stay* clean, Cedric. This may not go down for a month. You can't mess up at all before then. Hopefully you won't mess up afterwards either."

"I won't, sis. I swear. I'ma do right."

"We'll see," Jewell said. She stood and stretched her back. "I'm finna go check on Mama. You wanna come?"

"I can't," Slim said. "I'm working a double today."

"Well, I'll keep in touch," she said. "I'll talk to Daniel and let you know what he says."

"Tell him I'm not gon' let him down," Slim said. "I don't even like getting high no more."

"Alright," Jewell said with a smile. She gave him a hug and let herself out of the apartment. Slim stepped out onto the breezeway and watched her march down the stairs.

"A *million*?" he said. "For real?"

"Bye Cedric." Jewell rounded the corner and was out of sight.

≈≈≈≈≈≈≈

The crackhead's clothes were not on the sidewalk where she last saw them, and the junkie was similarly nowhere to be found. Jewell got into her Navigator with a big grin on her face. Seeing her brother sober was only half the reason for her euphoria.

It's really gonna happen, she thought to herself as she started the car. She closed her eyes and could almost see those diamonds.

≈≈≈≈≈≈≈

Jewell turned her car stereo down as she came to a stop at 3613 Forbes Ave. There was another car already in the driveway. Jewell parked next to a late model Honda Prelude she'd never seen before. She was eager to meet her mom's new nurse, but she went to the back of the house first to check on her roses.

She wasn't expecting any improvement after only one day, but the suffering buds looked a lot better. Encouraged, Jewell unraveled the hose and gave them another generous dousing. When you broke as many laws as she did, city-imposed watering bans meant nothing.

Her mom's backdoor swung open, and a dog-faced blonde wearing blue scrubs appeared behind the screen. She had nice hair, but that was her only flattering feature. Her eyes were too close together, her bunny rabbit teeth poked out too much, and she had no chin; after her bottom lip, her face just sloped down and became a neck.

But she did hear someone in the backyard, even though Jewell didn't make much noise. If she could hear that, she could hear Miss Eveline calling to get off the toilet, so Jewell liked her right away.

"Hi," she said. "I'm Miss Eveline's daughter."

"Oh," the nurse said. Her cold features lapsed into a warm smile. She opened the door and stepped down the porch to meet her new boss. Jewell was stunned to see that the new LVN had an awesome figure. Her boobs were big and perky, her stomach was flat, and her hips were nice and slim. Jewell met a few but-her-face's in her lifetime, but this woman needed to be in some kind of record book.

"Hi. I'm Priscilla." She stuck a hand out and Jewell shook it.

"Hey, Priscilla. I'm Clarissa. I guess you're our new nurse..."

"Either that or I'm a very nice intruder," Priscilla said and laughed amiably.

Jewell gave her a cordial chuckle. "How's my mom doing?"

"Oh, she's a peach," the nurse said. "She gets up a lot though. I'm used to them still being in the bed when I check on them, but your mom is never in the same place twice!"

Jewell nodded. "Yeah. I can't get her to stay in bed either."

"Here, let me get that for you," Priscilla said. She took the hose from Jewell and wrapped it around the reel.

"Thanks," Jewell said. "Is my mama awake?"

"Yeah. She's in there looking at her photo album."

Jewell headed up the steps. She stopped in the doorway and gave the new nurse a look.

Priscilla smiled. "Yes, I know she's blind."

Jewell entered the house with the confused look still on her face. In her mother's room, she found Miss Eveline sitting up in bed with her favorite photo album open on her lap. Jewell paused in the doorway, but there was no surprising this woman.

"Clarissa?"

"Yeah, Mama. It's me." Jewell went over and gave the old woman a kiss on the forehead. She sat on the bed and held her hand. "What you doing, Mama?"

"Looking at my photos," Eveline said.

Jewell stared at the woman's eyes. They were as cloudy as ever.

Miss Eveline laughed. "You don't think I can still see these pictures, do you?"

"How, Mama?"

The old woman tapped her temple with a crooked finger. "I still got it all up here." She closed the album and reopened it to the first page. "There are four pictures over here," she said, running her hand across the plastic cover. "This is your uncle Ray," she said, pointing to the correct photo. "He's standing in front of that old Grand Am he used to have. He's wearing a white tee shirt with khaki pants. And he's not smiling. Uncle Ray never smiled in his pictures."

Eveline stared straight ahead into nothingness, but her observations were dead on.

"This is Juanita," she said, pointing at her youngest sister. "She's wearing a, uh, a *red* dress, with a black belt." Eveline smiled. "She's got that belt pulled all the way up – right under her boobs!"

Jewell laughed. "I think it's her boobs that sank down to that belt."

"I thought you were going to have a chest like her," Miss Eveline said.

Jewell used to wish for bigger boobs, but at least her average-sized ones were perky. "No, I'm happy with what I got."

"Here's Juanita's boys," Eveline said, pointing at a different photo. "And here's your uncle Paul."

"How do you remember that?" Jewell asked.

"Child, I've looked through this book more times than any book I ever had. More times than the Bible – forgive me Jesus."

"Isn't there a picture of my daddy in there?" Jewell asked.

"Page twenty-three," Eveline said immediately. The pages weren't numbered, but she flipped through them quickly and stopped assuredly. She caressed the whole page and then pointed at a black and white photo of a man in a white suit. "Right here," she said.

Jewell leaned down and stared at the picture. She'd seen the snapshot before, but not in at least ten years. Her father was handsome and well dressed. He was a thin man, but he had the swagger of a big nigga. He was killed in prison when Jewell was seven years old. She got a couple of letters from him before he died but never saw him face to face. If not for the picture, she would have no idea what he looked like.

"Tell me about my daddy," she said. This request was as old as time, but Miss Eveline loved to reminisce. Her memory was all she had left. That's where all of the colors were, all of the laughter and the tears.

Jewell rested her head on her mother's shoulder as the old woman spun her yarn. They talked about Cedric's father and Yolanda's daddy too. After an hour or so, Jewell found herself nodding. Miss Eveline wasn't talking anymore. Jewell looked up at her and grinned. The old woman was completely knocked out. Her mouth hung open, and she sucked air softly.

Jewell carefully positioned her in a lying position and gave her mom a soft kiss before leaving the room. In the kitchen she found the new nurse sitting at the table doing a crossword puzzle. All of her predecessors would watch television or *take a nap* during their downtime, but not this freak of nature. Jewell wished Priscilla a good day and exited her mother's house through the front door.

The first thing she noticed when she got outside was a police car parked behind her Navigator. Jewell inhaled sharply, and the hair stood on her arms. Her heart knocked, and a frosty chill enveloped her.

A million thoughts ran through her mind, but before she could sort them out or scream or duck back inside, a uniformed police officer appeared from the side of the house. He was brown-haired and handsome, short and stocky. The gold tag on his chest read, "**OREILLY**." He saw Jewell and made a B line in her direction.

"Hello."

Jewell stood frozen. Visions of the Hamilton caper flashed before her eyes; the pink Chanel, the club, Percy's living room... She didn't want to believe her luck finally ran out, but the cop gave her a bad vibe right away. He stared at her like he recognized her, or wanted to recognize her.

"Hi," she said. "Can I help you?"

"Um, maybe so." The officer stepped onto the porch and stood in front of her. He looked her up and down. "I'm officer O'Reilly; Overbrook Meadows Police Department."

It's nothing personal, Jewell told herself. *One of the neighbors got robbed. There was a hit and run down the street.* "Okay..." she said.

The policeman sighed and put a hand on his hip. "Look, I really don't mean to bother you, ma'am. I'm here because we got a report of a suspicious person at this residence."

Jewell inwardly breathed a sigh of relief. She smiled and shook her head. "There's no suspicious people here. Just my sick mama and her nurse."

The policemen nodded and smiled back at her. "Yeah, uh. Look, I know this is gonna sound crazy, but I think you're the suspicious person I'm here for. Your description matches – unless there's another black woman in there with a white blouse, bell bottom pants and short hair..." He waited, but Jewell didn't have anyone to pin that on.

"What's this about?" she asked. "I just came to visit my mama."

Again Mr. O'Reilly looked pained to have to bear this news: "Someone thinks you look like a fugitive they saw in the newspaper."

His words were like bullets. Jewell took a shot in the chest; her sternum caved in and forced the air from the lungs. The world swam around her, but she remained focused long enough to look over at the neighbor's house. Mrs. Gaffney's living room curtains were parted. The busybody stood behind them watching intently.

Fucking bitch! Jewell thought, but she didn't let her face register the animosity she felt. Instead she smiled.

"I'm not a fugitive," she said with a chuckle. "And I already know who called you. You're talking about that lady right there." Jewell pointed, Mrs. Gaffney stepped away from her curtains, and the cop shrugged.

"She calls the police all the time," Jewell said. "On *everybody*. Y'all should know she's crazy."

The cop grinned. "Every time we put a sketch in the paper, we get calls from loonies all over the city. But, to be honest with you, you do look a lot like the composite we have."

"What composite?" Jewell barely managed to keep her lips from quivering.

"There was a burglary a few days ago—"

"A *burglary*? I never stole from nobody!"

"I understand, ma'am. I really hate to put you through this, but this is a pretty big deal. We're covering all leads, which means people like you might get inconvenienced."

Inconvenienced?

"Do you have a driver's license I can take a look at?"

Jewell finally allowed her face to show some of the horror she felt. "Why do you want my license? I didn't do nothing. I don't want to be involved in no investigation." She was capable of becoming fully hysterical but figured it wouldn't play well.

"Ma'am, I didn't come here to harass you, and I certainly don't want you to go through anything uncomfortable, but we have to get to the bottom of this. You're probably not the girl we're looking for – as a matter of fact I'm pretty sure you're not, but this isn't going away until we know for sure."

"How do you *know for sure*?" Jewell asked, although she really didn't want to know.

"I need you to come downtown with me," the cop said. "We'll do a line up. Once the guy says it's not you, you're free to go. We'll never bother you with this again."

Jewell thought she might be the one to piss her pants now.

"This is *bullshit*. I don't want to be in a line up."

"It's not as bad as you think."

"No. I have things to do. I don't have time for that. This is crazy."

"I understand your unease," the cop said. "But this is something that has to be done. Like it or not, you're a suspect until we can prove otherwise. The easiest way to do that is let this guy take a look at you."

Jewell wanted to respond like an innocent person, but she couldn't find the words.

"May I see your driver's license, ma'am?"

She sighed and reached into her purse, glad she left her .44 in the car. Jewell had three identities in her wallet; all were official driver's licenses, coming straight from the DMV. She decided to be Vanessa G. Hardgraves for this encounter.

"Here."

The officer took the plastic and compared the image to the woman standing before him. He smiled and put the card in his breast pocket.

"Okay Vanessa. You are not under arrest. You can follow me in your own vehicle if you want."

"I really have to go downtown?"

"It won't take that long. I promise. We'll have you in and out." His smile was warm and disarming.

Another squad car pulled in front of the house as they stepped off the porch.

"I'm following both of y'all?" Jewell asked.

"No," O'Reilly said with a grin. "You're still going to follow me. My partner is going to follow you."

CHAPTER NINE
THE LINE UP

Jewell had a Sync system installed in her car, so she was able to make a call without the cop in front or the one in back knowing she was on the phone. She merely turned off her radio and said, "Call Daniel." Her voice trembled more than she thought it would. A moment later her boyfriend's ringing cell phone played through all fourteen speakers in her Navigator.

The hardest part was holding her tears in while waiting for him to answer. She knew the policemen were watching her every move. Crying wouldn't play well with her assertion of innocence. Making a dash for the closet freeway and heading for Mexico probably wouldn't play too well either.

After five long rings Daniel answered his phone.

"Hello?"

"Baby, we got trouble." Jewell checked her rearview mirror, but the cop behind her had on shades; she couldn't tell if he was watching her mouth or not. The one in front made eye contact with her every ten seconds or so.

"Trouble like what?"

"I'm on my way downtown," Jewell said with a hitch in her throat. Her lips wrinkled up and her eyes watered. Through the blur, the drive took on the distorted quality of a carnival ride.

"Downtown for what?"

"I got a cop in front of me and another one behind me. They came to Mama's house. Somebody called them on me; said I look like that lady in the paper."

"Oh shit, baby. You serious?"

"Ye, *yeah*." Her voice skipped. She swallowed hard, but there was no saliva. "They got me."

"Don't say that, baby. Calm down."

Jewell took a few quick breaths. "Oh, okay."

"Where you at?"

"On Beach," she said. "I think we're about to get on 30."

"Can you run?"

"Not from both of them. Plus they got my ID."

"Which one?"

"Vanessa Hardgraves."

"Aw, man, baby. What the fuck? They arrested you?"

"No. I'm in my own car. But they said I had to go with them. I think they're going to put me in a line up."

"They told you that?"

"Yeah."

"Oh shit. This is crazy."

"You said that picture didn't look like me," Jewell said. The first tear snaked down the side of her face. It itched, but she didn't wipe it.

"Baby, it doesn't. They can't do noth–"

"*Yes it does!*"

"They can't do nothing *either way*," Daniel said. "You didn't do nothing. They can't prove nothing."

"You talked to me."

"What?"

"You talked to me; at his house."

"No I didn't."

"*Yes you did.* In his bedroom."

"What'd I say?"

"You told him to get off me."

"That don't mean nothing."

"You told me to wait outside."

"That don't mean nothing either."

"It means you know me."

"That's not enough," Daniel said. "They can't arrest you for that."

"What if they do?"

"You already know, baby. Just deny everything. Don't even admit to being at his house."

"What if he picks me out in the line up?"

"They can't arrest you just 'cause he say you was at his house."

"*But what if they do, Daniel?*"

"Then we'll go to Plan B," Daniel said.

Plan B meant he'd bail her out and they'd skip town that very night. They'd go to San Bernardino and start over. Jewell would never see her mother again. She wouldn't even come back for the old woman's funeral. They would get new identities, prey on new lames and hopefully build a new syndicate one day.

"Okay," Jewell said, knowing that no matter what they charged her with, they would have to offer a bail. No one got killed or even injured, so it shouldn't be that high.

"Do you know who called the police?" Daniel asked.

"My mama's *neighbor*," Jewell said with no uncertainties. "Why?"

"We don't get along. She real nosey. She calls the police all the time."

"Do you have jewelry on?"

The feeling of hopelessness rushed back. "*Yes.* A, a bracelet. And a necklace."

"Damn, girl. Why you got that shit on?"

"You saw me when I left the house! *Why didn't you say something then?*" Another tear fell. This time she smothered it with her shoulder unconsciously.

"Alright, baby. Calm down. It's cool."

"*No it's not!*"

"Yes it is. You trust me, right? I never told you wrong before, have I?"

You said that picture didn't look like me, Jewell thought but said nothing.

"Listen: They can't get you for the burglary," Daniel said. "They're gonna sweat you. If they got it in their mind that you were the set up girl, they'll fuck with your head. They'll lie. They'll say you're taking the wrap. They'll say you can go home if you help 'em out."

"You know I'm not talking."

"What are you going to say?"

"I'll tell them to arrest me if they got enough evidence."

"Good, baby. See, you straight."

"I'm not, Daniel. I'm scared. *Real scared.*"

"I know, baby girl, but you can't go in there looking crazy," he warned. "When you get in there, you'd better put on the performance *of your life*. I'm talking some *Oscar shit*. You can be pissed off, but not over the top. Be a little mad, but not scared."

"I know."

"You straight, baby? You gon' be alright?"

"He's gonna pick me," she said.

"Don't say that."

"I know he is. You read the paper; he remembers everything about me."

"Then we got Plan B, baby. It's still cool."

But it wasn't cool. It was far from cool. "What about Mama?"

Daniel didn't say anything.

"What abo–"

"You knew the deal," he said.

Jewell didn't have a comeback for that. She did know the deal. She chose to play anyway. "Alright," she said.

"Where y'all at now?"

"We're already downtown. On 8th."

"I'ma call the boys, baby. So we'll be ready."

"Alright."

"Girl, you okay? You're not crying?"

"No. I'm okay."

"Alright," Daniel said. "Don't worry."

"I love you."

"I love you too, baby."

"I love you," she said again and disconnected the line.

≈≈≈≈≈≈≈

They took her to one of the downtown substations rather than the actual county jail. This was the first break in Jewell's favor; it meant her alias was still above reproach. Officer O'Reilly would have run her for warrants as soon as he got back in his cruiser. If Jewell's ID was compromised, they would have taken her straight to lockup and made her wait for the lineup at their leisure.

But the *real* Vanessa Hardgraves was a thirty five year old school teacher from Midlothian. She had a spotless criminal record, a solid marriage and a boring social life. She had 2.5 children, a house with a picket fence, and good credit. On paper she was as pure as the driven snow.

In actuality, Vanessa G. Hardgraves was dead, had been since an intoxicated teenager used her Celica for an emergency brake nine months ago. Her new permanent address was at Rosemount Cemetery located in Ellis County, off HWY 287.

But since she was standing right in front of them and was clearly *not dead*, the Overbrook Meadows Police Department fast tracked what had to be an awful experience for Mrs. Hardgraves.

They took Jewell to an interrogation room on the first floor. The room was well-lit and sparsely furnished; there were two chairs, one table and nothing else. There was one window, but the mini blinds were drawn closed. There wasn't even a clock on the wall. Officer O'Reilly dropped her off there and apologized again for the inconvenience.

"Detective Morris will be right with you," he said.

"I don't want to stay here," Jewell said. "You're making me feel like a *criminal*. I don't want to be here. I want to go home."

"Ma'am, please don't take this personally. This is a routine investigation. Trust me; we would work just as hard for you if you were in need."

"But what am I supposed to do in here? How long is this supposed to take?"

"It won't be very long. If you'd like to use the phone, I can bring one in, or you can use your cell phone if you have one." He looked at her purse for the first time. "I need to search you before I go. Is that alright?"

Jewell had nothing to hide, but she didn't want to appear accustomed to such intrusions. "No, that is *not* alright."

O'Reilly nodded. "Okay. I can get a female officer to do it if you prefer."

≈ ≈ ≈ ≈ ≈ ≈

After her pat-down, Jewell waited in the small office for forty-one exhaustive minutes. She did not use the phone provided for her, and she did not use her cell phone either. From great educational programs like *The First 48*, she knew her room was wired for audio and video. If the police thought they could get her with the old *okey-doke*, they had another thing coming.

When the detective finally showed up, he wasn't nice and apologetic like his uniformed counterparts. As a matter of fact, he

99

was borderline *rude*. He asked Jewell ridiculous questions and wanted her to perform preposterous tasks. Jewell gave him as much attitude as she wanted.

"So, for the record, you have *no* knowledge of this burglary at Percy Hamilton's residence?"

"No," Jewell said, her eyebrows bunched, her lips curled.

"You did not attend a nightclub called Club Destiny on Saturday evening?"

"No." Jewell enunciated perfectly, giving the word a couple extra syllables. The more facts he came with, the more her temper rose.

"And you do not, on occasion, wear wigs?"

"*Wigs*?" Jewell stared at him like he was crazy, though she was the one close to maniacal screaming. "No *I do not wear wigs*! Is this the way you people do your police work? Drag innocent people in off the streets and make them stand in line with *hobos*?"

The burglary detective was bald on top, but he kept the back and sides of his head bushy, like George Jefferson. He had thick glasses, thick, dark lips, and a big belly. He stared at Jewell like he knew exactly who she was.

"I'ma need you to wear a wig in the lineup," he said.

≈≈≈≈≈≈≈

From the interrogation room, they led Jewell down a long hallway. There she met the other five girls who would share her very first police lineup. The women leaned against the wall, some brooding, some nonchalant. They were all short, all light-skinned, and all attractive. Jewell knew a couple of them were probably police officers. The others were most likely brought over from the jail where they faced totally unrelated charges. These women were placebos. Jewell knew she was the only one the police were suspicious about.

The other girls didn't talk to each other, so Jewell didn't talk to them. The other girls didn't complain about the matching black wigs the detective made them put on, so Jewell didn't complain about hers either. And when they got to the actual lineup, all of the women were cooperative with their instructions and their script.

When a voice came over the intercom asking *Number Four* to step forward and say her lines, Jewell did just what the other girls did: She took two steps forward, stared at the two-way glass where Percy Hamilton presumably sat on the other side, and said the lines loudly and clearly:

"So, where is that big dude gonna be? I don't get down with that freaky stuff."

She waited with her hands down to her sides, her chin up and her heart pounding.

"Um, Number Four, can you repeat the lines?"

"So, where is that big dude gonna be?" Jewell asked again with little emotion. "I don't get down with that freaky stuff."

≈≈≈≈≈≈≈

When the lineup was over, the police led the women back into the hallway and repossessed their wigs. They returned Jewell to her interrogation room, and she waited for Plan B to commence. She did not cry. She didn't bite her nails or call Daniel on her cell phone. Jewell simply sat there and stared at the walls with a dark realization of impending doom; sick doom like heartbreak, cold doom like prison bars, bloody doom like suicide by cop.

She no longer had an attitude, and she wasn't anxious either. Jewell knew she was wrong, and she knew she was caught.

The minutes ticked away slowly, and the first pangs of claustrophobia made her feel sick to the stomach. She waited for the burglary detective to come back with his accusations and confrontations, but the fat man never walked through the door. Instead a policeman Jewell hadn't seen before came with totally different news.

"Okay, Mrs. *Hardgraves*? Here's your driver's license. You're free to go. We, uh, apologize for any inconvenience this might have caused you."

Even in her state of befuddlement, Jewell played her role. "What do you mean *I'm free to go*? I've been here damned near *two hours*. Now *I'm free to go?* That's it?"

The new cop was young and less experienced than the Irishman and the detective. He was red-headed and freckle-faced and visibly embarrassed.

"Um, you didn't get picked in the lineup. It was a mistake."

"I told them it was a mistake when they brought me down here," Jewell spat. "Do you have any idea how they've been treating me?"

Opie's bottom lip hung dumbly. He blinked furiously. "Uh, if you want to file a complaint..."

Whoa, Jewell thought. *Bring it back.* "Just give me my license," she said.

He gave it to her and backed out of the room. Jewell followed quickly; still not convinced this was really happening. But when she stepped into the hallway, none of the cops seemed concerned with her at all. She walked angrily through the police station and exited through the front door.

Thirty seconds later she was in her Navigator again, hyperventilating. She gripped the steering wheel so tightly her knuckles were white. Jewell thought she might pass out, so she started the car and turned the radio up loud.

Master P's rugged voice belted through the speakers. He wondered if there was a heaven for a gangster. Jewell wondered if God listened to the prayers of a gangster*ette*. Or maybe it was the prayers of a blind old lady that caught His attention.

CHAPTER TEN
THE PRICE OF FREEDOM

She called Daniel when she made it to the freeway. He answered halfway through the first ring this time.

"Baby?"

"Yeah," Jewell said. "It's me."

"What happened? You still in the station?"

"No. They let me go."

"What do you mean *they let you go*?"

"They just, they just let me go. After the lineup. They said it was a mistake and I could go home." Jewell turned her air condition all the way up, but it was still hard to breathe. Her armpits were damp. Sweat glistened on her forehead.

"They did make you do the lineup?"

"Yes," she breathed.

"And they still let you go?"

"Yeah. I know; it's crazy."

"Where are you now?"

"On 30."

"Headed where?"

"I don't know. I'm just driving. I'm headed east, just passed Bridge. Where do you want me to go?"

"Go to Number Two," Daniel said. "How you doing? You cool? Can you talk?"

"Yeah."

"Tell me what happened when you got there."

"They took me to a room," Jewell said. "An interrogation room. I had to stay there for a while, and a detective came and talked to me."

"What he say?"

"He was talking about the job. He asked if I was at that club, if I ever went to Percy's house."

"They said his name?"

Jewell felt like crying for the last two hours. She was still too numb to break into hysterics, but a thin stream of tears flowed from each of her eyes, and her breaths hitched in her chest.

"They knew *everything*," she said. "There weren't any random questions; everything was on point. *Have I been to his house? Do I have a pink dress? Do I have a wig* – they made me put on a wig!"

"You bullshitting."

"There were six of us," Jewell recounted. "They all looked like me; short, light-skinned. They made us put on black wigs. They took us to a room, and we had to come forward one at a time and read a script."

"What script?"

"It was something I said when I was at his house. I was asking about his bodyguard before y'all showed up: *'So where is that big dude gonna be? I don't get down with that freaky stuff.'* The police made us say that *exactly*."

"Bullshit."

"Everybody did it. I'm standing there waiting my turn, knowing those were *my* words. I had that wig on, and I knew he was watching me. I felt like I was at his house again."

The full impact of her words sunk in, and Jewell suddenly felt very uncomfortable.

"I should be in jail, Daniel. I don't know why they let me go. I *know* he recognized me."

"You sure he was there?"

"He had to be. They kept me in that room for more than an hour. They were waiting for him."

"You talked to a cop or a *detective*?"

"It was a detective; plainclothes."

"Did he act like he knew you were the girl, or was he fishing?"

"He went back and forth," Jewell said. "Sometimes he'd be apologizing for holding me up, like he wanted to get through with it as fast as I did. But then when he started asking me specific questions, he acted like he didn't believe me: *'You've never been to Mr. Hamilton's house? Are you sure you haven't been there? If you were there on a different occasion, and it has nothing to do with this incident, you should tell me now. 'Cause if you've ever been there, we can find out.'"*

"He didn't ask about us," Daniel asked.

"He didn't even know how many of you there were," Jewell said. "When he said, '*three to four armed men,*' I knew he didn't have anything."

"*Damn,*" Daniel said. "Maybe fat boy didn't recognize you."

"I don't believe that," Jewell said.

"Why not?"

"I just don't."

"Well, they let you go, baby. What'd they say when they turned you lose?"

"They said they was sorry, said I was innocent."

"They said *that*?"

"Something like that. They said he didn't ID me, and it was a mistake."

"Then you're fine. What you tripping for?"

"I don't know."

"They not following you, are they?"

Jewell hadn't considered that. She checked her mirrors, but could make no assessments. "How am I supposed to know? I'm on the freeway."

"Any laws behind you?"

"No."

"Any Caprice's?"

"Um, I don't think so."

"Well take an exit and see what happens."

"Alright."

"What's coming up?"

"Cooks Lane."

"How far are you from it?"

"Hold on." Jewell turned on her blinker and merged to the right lane. "I'm exiting now... The light's red up there."

"Stay in the left lane," Daniel instructed. "Make a U-turn, like you're getting back on the freeway, going west."

"Make a left at the light?"

"*No.* You should be able to go under the bridge before you get to the light. They got that turnaround–"

"Okay, I see it."

"Did anybody get off with you?"

"Um, two cars did. A white Civic and, a, a green Buick; a Lucerne. I'm doing the U-turn now."

"Anybody following?"

"Hold on. Do you want me to get back on the freeway?"

"No. Stay on the service road. Make a right on one of those residential streets."

"The Buick's still coming," Jewell said.

"What?"

"The *Buick*, it made the U-turn behind me."

When Jewell got to the service road, she veered to the right lane without signaling. The green Buick did the same.

"I'm on the service road now. He's still behind me. *Right behind me.*"

"Who's in it?"

"I don't know. I think it's a black man."

"Where are you now?"

"Still on the service road. About to make a right on Rufe Snow."

The Buick caught up with her when she slowed for the turn. Jewell kept her eyes on the mirror until she could see the driver. What she saw made her remove her pistol from the glove compartment.

"It's *him*," she hissed. "That, that bodyguard. From the job! He's got his lights on now. He flashing them at me."

Jewell made her turn, and the Lucerne followed. Her heart thudded like a bass drum. The hair stood on every part of her body.

"Who?"

"*That big dude; from the club*," she said. "*Percy's bodyguard!*"

"How you know?"

"*I'm looking at him!*" Jewell cried. "I remember him. *This is him.*" She stared at the reflection in her mirror with little regard for the road in front of her. She cradled the .44 in her lap, gripping it with slick fingers.

"I *knew* they weren't letting me go," she said softly. "*I knew it.*"

"They *did* let you go," Daniel countered. "That nigga ain't the police."

"*I don't care what he is, Daniel!* He's following me!"

"What do you want to do, baby? You got your pistol?"

"Yeah. Right in my lap."

"Did you turn yet?"

"Yeah. I'm on Rufe Snow."

"What's he doing?'

"He still behind me," Jewell said. "He right on my bumper; flashing his headlights."

"If you get back on the freeway, I can meet you," Daniel said. "You wanna head towards Como?"

"I'm not driving that far with him behind me."

"You gon' try to lose him?"

"No," Jewell said. "I'm gon' pull over, see what he wants."

"Why you wanna do that?"

"I think Percy's in the car," Jewell said, thinking fast. "If he wanted me locked up, I would be. He obviously knows who I am, but he's not trying to run me off the road or nothing. I think he wants to talk."

"Maybe. You cool with that?"

"You think it's a bad idea?"

"Naw, I think you're right. But, *damn*, baby. I didn't think you had nuts like that."

"I just want it over with," Jewell said. She took a deep breath and stepped on the brake pedal. "I'm pulling over."

"What's he doing?"

"He's stopping, too."

"Don't hang up," Daniel said. "Keep me on the phone."

"Where are you?" she asked.

"I'm in my car, headed that way. If you want to wait for m–"

"No," Jewell said. "We're already stopped." She watched her pursuer in the rearview mirror. The green sedan pulled to a stop a good twenty feet from her bumper, and its headlights went off.

"What's happening?" Daniel asked.

"Nothing yet. Hold on." Jewell's car was eerily quiet. Her breaths and heartbeats were so loud, she thought Daniel could hear them. She studied the Buick's driver and was completely sure it was Percy's bodyguard. But the big man didn't get out of the car. The back door opened instead, just as Jewell knew it would.

"It's him," she breathed.

"Fat boy?"

"Yeah. He getting out of the car."

The furniture king wore faded blue jeans with black loafers today. He had on a blue button-down with a white tee shirt underneath. His shirt was unbuttoned, but he still looked neat. He looked like he might have been enjoying a leisurely day at the office when he got a call from the police.

Mr. Hamilton was still dark-skinned and ugly, but he wasn't the freak of nature Jewell remembered. He had short hair with a perfect edge-up. And he wore glasses today. He looked intelligent and conniving rather than hopelessly horny. He approached Jewell's Navigator with his hands to his sides. Jewell didn't see any pistol-shaped bulge around his waistline.

"What's happening?" Daniel asked.

"*Shhh*," Jewell whispered. "*He's coming.*"

"Wh–"

"*Shhh!*"

Percy Hamilton walked up to the driver's side and glared into the Lincoln. Then he smiled and waved pleasantly. Jewell checked her mirrors to make sure big Daryl was still in the Buick before she rolled down her window.

"Can I help you?"

Percy nodded. He continued to smile, but only with his mouth. His eyes made Jewell want to shoot him right then.

"How you doing, *Stacy*?" He said her name like he knew it was bullshit.

"My name's Vanessa," Jewell said. "I think you got the wrong person."

"Can you put that thing away?" Percy asked, staring into her lap. "I come over here to talk. If I wanted trouble, trust me, you'd have it by now."

Jewell was reluctant to let go of the gun. "I don't know you. I don't know what you want with me."

"Yea, you know me," he said. "You know me just like I know you. Whatever name you're going by doesn't matter. I *never* forget a face. Not one as pretty as yours."

Jewell couldn't believe he still wanted to flatter her. "Look," she said. "I don't know you, and I gotta–"

"So, you'd rather let the white man handle this?" he asked. "I already had you downtown. I coulda told them it was you. Put that thing away, so we can talk."

"I didn't do nothing to you," Jewell said. She took her hand off the pistol, but didn't remove it from her lap. "If you think I did, you should have said something at the police station."

"You can't let the police handle *everything*," Percy said, still smiling. "Some things are of a more, *sensitive* nature."

"I have no idea what you're talking about," Jewell said, telling the truth for the first time.

"Listen," Percy said. He stepped forward and put both hands on her window frame. Again Jewell thought about shooting him, but she didn't feel threatened. If he reached in and grabbed her, she had time to go for the gun.

"We're both hustlers," Percy said. His face was close to hers, and Jewell could smell his breath again. It was still rather tart. "You and your boys," Percy went on, "y'all did what you did. I ain't gonna knock your hustle, but I can't take that big of a loss either. You understand what I'm saying?"

Jewell did know what he was saying. It sounded like he wanted her to implicate herself in a crime.

"You already told the police it wasn't me," she said. "You can't go back and say you changed your mind."

Percy shook his head. "I'm not going back to the police Stacy, or *Vanessa*, or whatever the hell your real name is. You're not listening to me: I want to handle this *personally*. I don't need them folks all in my business."

Jewell finally had an idea of what he was getting at. "So what do you want?" she asked.

"You still got my eggs?" Percy asked.

"Maybe," she said.

"I want them eggs," Percy said. "I got that collection from my grandmamma. She ain't never did nothing to nobody. She doesn't deserve that; to have her heirlooms treated like that. Those things are *precious*. You really shouldn't touch them with your bare hands."

Jewell couldn't believe what she was hearing. This man had her in jail. The police were eager to put her face in the news. For all they knew, she would have rolled over on the gang. Percy gave that up for twenty thousand dollars worth of Faberge eggs?

"Alright," Jewell said. "So, that's it? That's all you want?"

"*Hell naw*," Percy said. His smile went away, and his face matched up for the first time; angry eyes with angry lips, a slight twitch in the corner of his mouth.

"I want my slab back too," he said. "Y'all came in there for the *money*. Y'all didn't know nothing about the dope."

Jewell's brain raced, but she forced her face to remain expressionless. She didn't respond because she still didn't know anything about the dope.

"Now, I ain't gon' knock your hustle," Percy said. "What you do to get paid is your business, just like what I do is my business. But I ain't gon' let you do me *any old kind of way* neither. I'm coming to you as a man. You got me fair and square, but that dope ain't got nothing to do with your lick. It wasn't supposed to be there, and you didn't know it was going to be there. Did you?"

Jewell was so shocked, she just shook her head as prompted.

"That's right," Percy said. "Y'all lucked up on that, and I want it back – them eggs too. You give me that, and I'ma let you keep the money and the rest of that shit. I'm a *businessman*, and I can tell you that's *good business*. If you wanna do it the *other way*, I got just as many niggas with guns as you do. I may not be able to find you personally, but my partner told me where they picked you up at...on *Forbes Avenue*."

Jewell didn't think she registered any alarm, but she must have. Percy's eyes flashed and his smile came back.

"*Yeah*," he said. "How you think I knew which car to follow out? My partner can tell me anything else I want to know about you."

Jewell knew Percy's connection at the police station could only tell him more about Vanessa Hardgrave's life, but Percy didn't need to know anything else. He already knew too much.

"So, I get my eggs and my slab," he said, "and y'all can keep the rest. That's a good deal, baby. I suggest you roll with it."

Jewell was speechless.

Percy's smile went away again. "If y'all wanna get *greedy*, I hope you don't give a shit about whoever lives in that house on Forbes."

Jewell felt her eyes watering but refused to show weakness. "Alright," she said. "I'll talk to them."

"Good," Percy said, and there was that salesman smirk again. He reached into his front pocket. "Here. I want to give you this so..." He stopped talking when he saw the .44 sticking out of the window. "What you doing?"

"What *you* doing?" Jewell asked.

"I was just, *ah*..." He grinned pleasantly and came up with a cell phone. "I wanted to give you this. Damn, baby. You quick with that. I like you. Maybe if we would have met at a different time and place..." He held the phone out to her. "You gonna take this or shoot me?"

Jewell wasn't sure. Daniel taught her to never pull the trigger if she wasn't sure. She took the phone from him without lowering the gun. He held his hands up and backed away from the car.

"Alright, baby. I'll give you a call later on."

Jewell rolled up her window and put the car in gear. She drove away before Percy made it back to his vehicle.

"You still there?" she asked Daniel a few seconds later.

"Yeah, baby. I'm here. You did good, girl."

"What about the dope?" Jewell asked. "Nobody said anything about drugs."

"That's what the fuck *I* wanna know," Daniel said. She could hear his nostrils flaring through the speakers.

"What about the eggs?" Jewell asked.

"Them eggs is gone," Daniel said with a tinge of regret in his voice. "They all gone, baby."

CHAPTER ELEVEN
THE HEROIN KING

Nestled deep in Overbrook Meadows' east side of town is a neighborhood known as Stop Six. When the Los Angeles gang culture migrated to Texas in the late eighties, most of the hoodlums around town picked up blue flags and banged *Crip*. On the north side, Hispanic thugs waved gold and brown panuelos and twisted their fingers for *Latin Kings, SUR XIII or VNS*.

Not to be outdone, the kids on the east side stuffed red bandanas in their back pockets. They tagged the walls with graffiti, defended their turf to the death, and recruited heavily. Soon there were more than a dozen cliques established in the small neighborhood. On one block you were in the *Stop Six Blood's* territory. Cross the street, and your ass belonged to the *Pate Street Bloods*.

The largest and most notorious Blood faction was the *Truman Street Pirus*. These goons ran everything in Stop Six from drugs to guns to prostitution. Hardly anything happened on their turf that they weren't aware of, but even the leaders of this gang didn't know what went on at 3545 Lester Granger Avenue. That two bedroom home was somewhat of an anomaly:

The residents were never there, but the lawn got mowed every week. The mail never piled up, and the trash cans never got left on the curb after a pickup. The Truman Street Pirus had a dope house right across the street from the syndicate's Safe House #2, but they had no idea who Jewell was. She parked in the driveway next to Daniel's Tahoe and let herself in the front door using one of her many, many keys. Her boyfriend waited in the living room with a look of unease marring his strong features.

"You make sure you weren't followed?" he asked, rising from the love seat.

Daniel wore a black, wool suit made by Armani. His shirt was light blue. His tie was baby blue with black stripes. He sported calfskin loafers manufactured by Bruno Magli, but Daniel liked those shoes before OJ helped make the designer famous.

Jewell stepped into her man and held on for dear life; like it might be their last embrace. She had a knot in her stomach. On one level the whole afternoon had the feeling of a dream, but she knew there would be no waking from this nightmare.

She put her head on Daniel's chest and inhaled his scents. He smelled like Marc Jacobs for men with an underlying aroma she recognized as tension.

"I wasn't followed," she said. Jewell never wondered about such things before, and it felt weird to worry about it now.

Daniel looked down at her and kissed her forehead. He put a palm on the side of her face and stroked her cheek soothingly.

"Nobody's here yet?" she asked.

"No. But they're on the way. I got everybody's ten thou'. You *know* they're coming for that."

"Do they know what happened?" Jewell asked.

"They know you went downtown with the police, and they know you got out. That's all they know. I want you to tell them the rest when they get here, so I can see how they react."

It was hard to believe there was a traitor among them, but this wasn't mind-blowing news. They were all thieves before anything else. Plus Jewell and Daniel planned to keep all the spoils from the airport job. They'd be hypocrites if they got upset about Percy's missing drugs, but still...

"Who do you think took it?" Jewell asked.

"Jesse, or Miles," Daniel said definitively. "Davis would have told me if he knew anything about it."

"What are you gonna do?" Jewell asked.

"It depends," Daniel said and left it at that.

He led her to the couch, and they sat close to each other. Jewell wrapped her arms around his torso and laid her head on his chest. Daniel draped an arm over her and stroked her shoulder. His presence and his touch took her fears away like nothing else could.

"You did good," he said after a while. "You surprised me."

Jewell looked up and saw that he was smiling. His courage gave her the strength to smile too.

"I surprised you?" she asked.

"I know you go hard," Daniel said. "But I don't get to see you work most of the time. You handled yourself like a man. I'm proud of you."

"I still think I should have shot him," Jewell said wistfully.

"What would have been your exit strategy?" Daniel asked.

"Um, *the freeway*," Jewell said sarcastically.

Daniel chuckled and nodded, but Jewell knew he was humoring her. Since the age of sixteen, Daniel made his living from illegalities. But in all of those years, he never once had to kill anyone. When it came to murder, Daniel had a philosophy that never led him astray: *If you shoot a man's daughter in the arm, he'll give you every combination he knows. But if you kill him, you leave empty handed.*

Daniel shot seven people that Jewell was aware of, but he spent a few years in South Dallas before she met him. She was sure there were a few more trauma patients she didn't know about.

"You gotta give up that Lincoln," Daniel said.

"I know," Jewell said. She liked the truck more than any vehicle she owned in the last few years, but such is the life of a career criminal. Not only did Percy know about the SUV, but the police knew about it too. Changing the plates wouldn't be enough. Just as Jewell would never use Vanessa Hardgraves as an alias again, she would never drive that Navigator either.

She and Daniel snuggled on the couch in silence and waited for the rest of gang to arrive. Daniel scheduled the meeting for four thirty, and the syndicate was always punctual. At a quarter after four, Davis entered the house through the back door. He walked into the living room wearing khaki Dockers with a lime green golf shirt. Jewell had never seen him dressed so well.

"Man, *look at you*," she said. "Got a big date tonight or did somebody die?"

Daniel chuckled.

"Well *hardee har*," Davis said. "You seem pretty chipper for somebody who was in jail an hour ago." Davis' hair was pulled back in a ponytail. His shirt was tight and tucked in, revealing a pot belly Jewell never noticed before. His skin was dark and rugged, and his smile was genuine. Daniel stood to give him a handshake and a brief hug.

"Damn, boy. What you got on?" Daniel asked, wrinkling his nose.

"Stetson," Davis said.

"You leave any in the bottle?" Daniel asked, waving a hand in front of his face.

"What's this; *Gang up on the Redneck Day*?" Davis took a seat in the recliner and leaned back with his legs crossed. "So, tell me about jail," he said to Jewell.

"I wasn't in *jail*," she said good-naturedly. "It was a line up."

"So how the hell did you get out?" Davis asked. "Is that what this meeting is for? You turning us all in?" Only Davis would take a horrible possibility like that and make light of it.

"Yeah," Jewell said. "The feds will be here in a minute. I'm wearing a wire."

"*Great!*" Davis said. He clapped loudly and rubbed his hands together. "You got my money?" he asked Daniel. "Might as well get this on tape."

Daniel had a large brown envelope on the cushion next to him. He reached inside and pulled out five bulging, letter-size envelopes. He tossed one of them to Davis and dropped the others on the coffee table.

Davis caught his package and squeezed it and smiled. "Seems a little light," he said.

"That's 'cause I didn't fill it with twenties," Daniel said. "I wish Miles would stop doing that shit."

"The whole ten's here?" Davis asked.

Daniel nodded. Davis stuffed the envelope in his back pocket without opening it.

"So I take it you got rid of those eggs," he said

Jewell gave her boyfriend a look. Daniel nodded.

"They were the easiest thing to go," he replied. "There's fools in this city who'll pay anything for those damned things. I don't get it. You can't do nothing with them but set em up somewhere and look at 'em."

"They're beautiful," Jewell countered. "I want to have a set one day."

"You coulda had *that* one," Daniel said.

"I know," Jewell said. "I wish we had kept them." Daniel gave her a look this time.

"What the hell's going on with you two?" Davis asked.

"Nothing," Jewell said. She leaned forward and selected her envelope from the pile on the table. Unlike Davis, she split hers open and fanned through the Ben Franklins. There were one hundred bills in all.

"We got something to talk about when the other two get here," Daniel said to Davis.

"The airport job?" Davis guessed. "I met up with Jesse this morning. He says he's down."

Jewell's eyes grew large.

Daniel sat up with a start. "For real?"

"Yeah," Davis said. "I told you that boy's got a spending problem. And he's not as scary as you think he is. Miles is the one who talks him out of it most of the time."

"You talked to Jesse *today*?" Daniel asked.

"Yeah," Davis said. "We had lunch at the tittie bar on Risinger – wouldn't recommend that place, by the way: Their hot wings are awful, and most of the whores have C-section scars. Good draft prices though. I guess if y–"

"Hold up," Daniel said. "Jesse said he would do the airport job with us?"

"Yes," Davis said. "You need to explain it to him again. But from what I told him, he's willing to give it a try. It has to be planned *perfectly* though."

"I know," Daniel said. "It will be." He was on the edge of his seat with a big grin on his face. Jewell rubbed the back of his neck. She loved it when her man schemed.

The front door pushed open, and Miles stepped in looking more squirrelly than usual. He scanned the smiling faces in the living room and cocked his head in confusion.

"Uh, hey. How's everyone doing?"

"Fine," Davis called. "Come on in. You look like you seen a ghost."

Miles locked the door and stared at Jewell as he made his way to the sofa. He wore a black tee shirt with blue jeans. He was always pale, but he looked extra pasty today. Daniel watched him with a cold expression.

"What happened?" Miles asked Jewell.

"They let me go," she said.

"Why?"

"We'll talk about that when Jesse gets here." Daniel said.

"He's here," Miles said. "He's in the back yard checking on something."

"Well, he needs to get his ass in..." Daniel trailed off because there was a sound at the back door. All eyes moved in that direction. Jesse sauntered in from the kitchen wearing green slacks with a white button down. His shirt wasn't tucked in and he had the sleeves rolled up to his elbows, but he always looked handsome. His eyebrows were thick, and his lips were pink. He looked around at the anxious eyes watching him.

"What?"

"Nothing, partner. Waiting on you," Davis said.

"Bring a chair in here," Daniel instructed. "We gotta talk."

Jesse dragged a chair in from the dining room and set it up backwards next to Davis. He straddled it with his arms draped over the back.

"So, what's up?"

Daniel watched him coldly. Miles stared at Jewell. Davis stared at Daniel.

"I got the rest of your money," Daniel said, nodding toward the coffee table.

"Uh, okay," Jesse said, but he didn't get up to retrieve it. He looked around suspiciously. "Uh, that's supposed to be good news, right? What's everybody mad about?"

"No ones mad," Daniel said.

Jesse looked over at Miles who was clearly on edge.

"So, how'd you get out of jail?" Miles asked Jewell.

Daniel smiled. "Damn. Sounds like you don't trust baby girl."

"I didn't say that. I just want to know what happened."

"We *all* want to know what happened," Davis said.

Daniel leaned back and gave his woman center stage. "Go ahead, baby. Tell them what happened."

"I got picked up at my mama's house," she said. "Her next door neighbor called the law on me. She saw the picture in the paper and told them it was me."

There was no shock here. Daniel already told them as much.

"They made me follow them downtown," Jewell said. "They put me in a line up with five other girls. They were all short and light-skinned, like me. The detective made us put on wigs, like the one I had on that night.”

Everyone looked worried except for Davis. It was hard to get a rise out of him.

“They made us read from a script,” Jewell went on. “It was something I said to Percy when I was at his house. I knew he was there. He remembered everything so good. I knew he recognized me too.”

“So how’d you get out?” Miles asked again.

“They just let me go,” Jewell said. “But I didn’t think it was over that easy, and it wasn’t. I called Daniel when I got on the freeway, and he asked if somebody was following me. Somebody was. It was Percy Hamilton.”

Miles’ jaw dropped. “The mark?”

“Yeah,” Jewell said. “He flagged me down, and I pulled over to see what he wanted.”

“Tell ’em what he said,” Daniel prompted.

“He said he knew I was the girl from the club,” Jewell said. “He said he didn’t turn me in because he wanted to handle things *personally*.”

Davis chuckled. Miles cleared his throat.

“He says he’ll forget about everything if he can get some of his stuff back,” Jewell reported. “He said he wants his Faberge eggs back.”

“They’re gone,” Daniel cut in.

“And he said he wants his dope back,” Jewell said. She paused then, as Daniel instructed her to. The suspense was so thick you could taste it. Jewell studied the eager faces watching her, but no one looked guilty.

“What drugs?” Davis finally asked.

“Yeah, *what drugs*?” Daniel said.

“He said he had a slab,” Jewell informed them. “He said we didn’t know it was gon’ be there, so we shouldn’t get to keep it. He said we can have everything else, but he want that slab back. And his eggs. He said those was his grandmama’s eggs.”

Miles shook his head and squinted at her. “What’s a *slab*?”

“A flat sheet of dope,” Daniel explained. “It can be crack, heroin, cocaine. It’s compressed. Somebody took it from that man’s house and didn’t say nothing about it. Somebody in *this room*.”

Everyone looked around at each other. Jewell inwardly
hoped Miles would turn out to be the rotten egg so they could be
done with him for good, but it was someone else.

"*Oh*, is *that* what that is?" Jesse said.

All eyes settled on the safecracker.

"I found it in the safe," he said. "I didn't know what it was.
I was gonna leave it, but I threw it in my bag at the last minute."

"Bullshit," Daniel growled.

"No *for real*!" Jesse looked innocent enough, but he
always did with that baby face. "*I swear, man*. I don't know
nothing about dope. Y'all know that."

That was true, but still...

"Why'd you take it then?" Daniel wanted to know.

Jesse was flustered. His face reddened like a crimson tide.
"I just *took it*," he squealed. "I figured it was *something*, but I
wasn't sure. I was gonna get it checked out later. I just dumped it
in the bag with my tools. If I found out it was worth something, *I
swear* I was gonna tell you guys."

None of the eyes watching him were convinced.

"C'mon, y'all. Don't look at me like that," Jesse pleaded.
"Daniel, you *know me*, man. You *know* I wouldn't steal from the
syndicate!"

"Why you didn't put it in the pot?"

"I chucked it in my bag, you know, as an afterthought,"
Jesse said. "I forgot it was in there. I haven't even looked at it
since that night. C'mon, man. Don't do me like that. You know
me, Daniel. I would *never* do that!"

"I believe him," Miles said.

"Yeah, *you would*," Daniel said.

"What's that supposed to mean?" Miles asked.

"What it look like?" Daniel asked Jesse.

"It's, it's flat." He looked around for a point of reference.
"Like those," he said, pointing to the envelopes on the table. "Like,
two of those, side by side."

Ten thousand dollars stacked bill on bill was a little more
than an inch tall. Jesse was describing a block of dope about the
size of a small Bible.

"What color is it?" Daniel asked.

"I don't know," Jesse said. "It's wrapped in plastic, and
tape. White, I think."

Daniel shook his head. "This fool's got *two hundred thousand dollars* worth of heroin in his fucking *tool bag.*"

Even Davis' eyes got big then.

"How do you, how do you know that?" Jesse asked.

"He wouldn't be trippin' this much if it was some fucking 'caine," Daniel said.

"I didn't know he sold drugs," Miles said.

"I think there's a lot we don't know about Mr. Percy," Daniel mused. "Maybe there's a lot we don't know about Mr. Jesse, too."

"Don't do that!" Jesse shook his head fiercely. "You *know* me, Daniel. I wouldn't even know what to do with that. You know I'd never steal from you guys."

"I don't know shit," Daniel said.

Jesse looked pained. "Come on, y'all. Y'all believe me, right?" He looked around for supporters, but no one was eager to jump on his bandwagon.

"Just drop it," Davis said. "You still got it, right?"

"Yeah," Jesse said, nodding eagerly.

"So we should just say *fuck it,*" Davis suggested. "We can't get in Jesse's head to see what he's thinking. Maybe he's telling the truth..."

"I *am* telling the truth," Jesse said.

"Maybe he *ain't,*" Davis went on. "As long as he still got it, I say we move on. No hard feelings."

Much to Jewell's surprise, her man shrugged.

"Alright," Daniel said. "Fuck it. No hard feelings."

"I'm telling the truth," Jesse said.

"Fuck it," Davis said.

"But–"

"Fuck it," Daniel said.

Miles looked around nervously. "So, so what are we gonna do?"

Daniel stared at Jesse for a second. "I think we should give it back."

Jesse's jaw dropped. "What? *Why*? You said it was worth–"

"I know what I said."

"Why do you want to give it back?" Miles asked. "We, we *need* that money. I don't think we should make any deals with that furniture asshole. We don't know him. It could be a set up."

"He knows where my mama stays," Jewell said. "He said he'd go over there if we don't give it back."

There were a few moments of silence as everyone let that morsel sink in.

"Then it's over," Miles said plainly. "If, if he knows where your mother lives, then he knows her name, which means he can get *your name.* Your *real* name. Your sister's too, and anybody else you care about. Plus Daniel doesn't have his fucking eggs, so what about that? Even if you give his heroin back, it won't be over. I say we sell the heroin, split it, and go our separate ways. Anything else is going to get us fucking caught."

Jewell couldn't believe what she was hearing.

"*Dissolve the group*?" Daniel asked. "Just like that?"

"We had a good run," Miles said. "It was going to come to an end sooner or later. Everyone knew that."

"What about my mama?" Jewell asked. "Breaking up the group won't help *her.*"

"Well, well you need to move her," Miles suggested, as if this was common sense.

"She's old," Jewell argued. "And *blind.* She can barely get around as it is."

Miles shrugged. "That's the only logical out. We *can't* give the heroin back. If you meet with that sonofabitch, you're going to end up dead or in jail."

"We don't have his eggs anyway," Davis said.

"That's right," Miles said. "What if you give him the heroin, and he still doesn't go away. You gonna look over your shoulder every time you visit your mom? The whole situation's *crazy.* We've been *compromised.* I say we pull up stakes and take that heroin money as a parting gift."

"That's not enough," Daniel said. "What we've done here, what we *have* here, together; we're not going to find anything like this again. *Ever.* You wanna throw it away for forty thou' apiece? That's *nothing.* You know it's not gonna last."

"We can't stay together anyway with the police on our ass," Miles said.

"It's not the police," Daniel said. "It's *one* motherfucker."

"One *millionaire* motherfucker," Miles corrected. "You have no idea what kind of connections he has."

"Fine," Daniel said. "If you want to call it quits, let's do my airport job first."

Miles actually smiled as he shook his head. "Dammit, Daniel, no one wants t–"

"Bullshit!" Daniel stood and put a finger in his face. "You're the only one who doesn't want to do it! You're the only coward in this bitch!"

Jewell grabbed his arm. "Sit down, baby."

Daniel did, but grudgingly. He kept a mean glare on Miles.

Miles looked around at his comrades. "Who the hell wants to do Daniel's airport job?"

Jewell was the first to stand by her man. "*I* do."

"I do, too," Davis said.

Miles glared at Jesse, but the safecracker didn't back down this time.

"I, uh, I kinda wanna do it to," Jesse said.

Miles was dumbfounded, but not defeated. "Alright," he said. "Fine. But we can't do *any* job until we get that furniture guy off our backs. And we don't have his goddamned eggs! What's your smart idea for *that*?" he asked Daniel sarcastically.

Daniel didn't have a smart idea, but Jewell did.

"We could kill him," she said softly.

Miles leaned back in his chair and grinned. "*Yeah right.*"

"I'm serious," Jewell said. The room was deathly quiet, and she felt like all of her senses were heightened. She could hear termites gnawing away at the old house. She could *feel* her eyelashes growing. "For ten million dollars, I'll kill him," she said.

"Me too," Davis said. He was the only person in the room who'd actually killed before, so no one doubted him. "If you want to kill him, I'll help."

Miles looked to Daniel. "You gonna talk some sense into your woman?"

Daniel shook his head. "She's right. I'm not letting that fat fuck mess up my airport job. If that's the only problem y'all got, then we'll take care of it."

"You're going to *kill Percy Hamilton*?" Miles asked.

"My brother can help too," Jewell said.

"Your *brother*?" Miles was hopelessly lost. "Daniel, you need to think about this. Percy Hamilton is one of the richest men in this city. You can't just kill him."

"This is our last job," Daniel said. "I'll do anything to make it work. I'll kill Percy. I'll kill a cop. It don't matter. We're all splitting after this anyway – ten million dollars richer."

"I'm not killing *anyone*," Miles said.

"You don't have to," Daniel said. "You neither, Jesse. We'll take care of Percy, so long as y'all help with the airport job afterwards."

"Cool," Jesse said. "I'll do whatever job you want, so long as I don't have to kill nobody."

"What about you, Miles," Daniel asked.

"I think it's a bad idea," Miles said. "I think you're going to mess it up. You'll probably end up getting yourself killed. And if you *do* manage to get rid of Percy, you're gonna have so much heat on you, you won't be able to steal a pack of gum for the next ten years."

"Don't worry about the killing," Daniel said. "I'm talking about the *airport job*. If we take care of Percy, are you gonna help or not?"

Miles shook his head and sighed loudly. "Alright, whatever, Daniel. If you kill Percy, and there's *no heat*, I'll help with your *fucking* job."

"Cool," Daniel said. He stood and pulled Jewell up with him. "I'm sick of arguing with y'all. I'm finna go. Don't forget your money."

They headed for the front door, but Daniel paused in the foyer. He turned back and stared long and hard at Jesse. "I'ma need that heroin."

"Yeah, it's cool," Jesse said.

"What for?" Miles asked.

"Bait."

CHAPTER TWELVE
DIRTY MINDS

Daniel made Jewell drive her Lincoln to the north side of town when they left the safe house. He followed in his forest green Tahoe. He knew of a few chop shops in the city, but only one that would give them a decent price for the Lincoln.

The blue book value for a 2009 Navigator was $48,000. Daniel walked away with only eighteen thousand, but he considered that a good deal, all things considered.

He instructed Jewell to remove all of her personal effects from the vehicle before they left the garage, but she kept the car pretty clean on a regular basis. She got her pistol out of the glove compartment and plucked her designer shades from the visor. The cell phone Percy gave her was already in her purse.

Rather than head straight home afterwards, Daniel stopped at one of the north side's honky tonks to get his woman a quick meal. Jewell hadn't eaten anything all day except for the grapefruit she nibbled on at breakfast. She planned to stop for lunch after she left her mom's house, but fate (and a couple of police officers) led her downtown instead.

The bar Daniel took her to was dark and quiet, small and smoky. Daniel ordered both of them a cheeseburger basket, and he got two mixed drinks to hold them over while they waited. Jewell knew better than to drink on an empty stomach, but her nerves were bad. She downed her glass in three gulps and sent Daniel to get her another. By the time their food arrived, she was on her third drink and already adequately laced.

"You think Miles knew about the heroin?" she asked around a curly fry.

Daniel nodded but didn't respond until he was done chewing. "I wouldn't put it past him. Them niggas are close. You see the way they always wait to see what the other one's gonna say when I ask them something?"

"I'm just glad they're finally down with us," Jewell said. She blinked slowly and saw a cache of diamonds behind her eyelids. She grinned and took a bite of her burger.

"They not down with us," Daniel said. "Don't get it twisted. Miles is a scary bitch. He won't take too many risks. And Jesse only agreed to it because he knows this is our last run. He's good, but he can't make a lot of money by himself."

"Why not?" Jewell asked. She thought of the safes she watched him break into. "He's awesome."

"Yeah, but he ain't got no heart," Daniel said. "If the safe's sitting right there, yeah; he'll get into it. But if there's somebody standing between him and the safe, he won't stick a pistol in they face. He damned sure ain't gon' shoot nobody."

Jewell smiled. "But we got him. Miles too."

"Yeah, we do. And we're gonna need them. Now all we have to do is kill the richest black man in the city. You know that's not gon' be easy."

"I know," Jewell said. "But we got Davis, and my brother too."

"You don't even know if Slim wants to get down like that."

"He will," Jewell guessed. "He'll do anything to get in on the airport job."

Daniel shook his head. "You saw him today?"

"Yeah. He looks good."

Daniel raised one eyebrow.

"Okay, he doesn't look *good*, good," Jewell said, "but he's definitely not high."

"How you know?"

"I know when he's nodding."

"What about yesterday?" Daniel asked. "What about *right now*? What about tomorrow?"

"He showed me his check stub," Jewell said. "He got paid yesterday, and he still had all of his money this morning. He only spent five dollars."

"That don't mean shit."

"What dopefiend you know goes to sleep with two hundred dollars in his pocket?"

Daniel shrugged.

"That's what I thought," Jewell said. She smiled and winked at him. "Are you gonna eat that pickle?"

Daniel only liked sliced pickles. He frowned at the spear. "Naw. You can have it."

"Feed it to me," Jewell said.

Daniel picked up the vegetable and held it out for her.

"Closer," Jewell said.

He leaned forward and Jewell wrapped her lips around the spear. Rather than bite, she sucked it, back and forth, slowly. Daniel's eyes widened.

"You drunk?" he asked.

Jewell clamped down with her incisors and removed the pickle from his fingers.

"A little," she said with a naughty grin. She chewed slowly; savoring the sourness in her mouth.

"You ready to go?" Daniel asked.

Jewell frowned. "You always wanna go home when you get horny."

He chuckled. "What do you want to do?"

"I wanna *dance*," Jewell said.

Daniel cocked his head and then rolled his eyes. "You wanna dance to *this* music?"

Jewell nodded. "You don't like Toby Keith?"

"Who?"

"Let me school you, youngster." Jewell bobbed her head to the tune until her favorite part came up: *I like talking about you, you, you, you, usually, but occasionally I wanna talk about meeee!*"

Daniel laughed.

Jewell jumped up and grabbed his arm. "Come on."

Daniel followed her booty to the dance floor, but that was as much movement as she would get out of him. Jewell was a great dancer. She could adapt to any mood, tune or locale. Daniel never even tried, but as long as his hands were on her, Jewell was happy. And Daniel *definitely* knew what to do with his hands. Unfortunately, some places don't go for all of that *touchy feely*.

"Get a room!" the fat bartender yelled halfway through their song.

Jewell felt Daniel's body grow tense against hers, so she dragged her boyfriend outside before they had an incident at the OK Corral. Daniel could get quite violent if he thought he was defending her honor.

≈ ≈ ≈ ≈ ≈ ≈ ≈

When they got home, Jewell was still a little tipsy, but not nearly enough. She fetched a bottle of Tequila and spread out on the living room floor with two shot glasses. She put in a DVD of their favorite comedian, and Daniel went shot for shot with her for more than an hour. At one point Jewell wanted to drink from Daniel's belly button, and he was eager to oblige. By the time Katt Williams finished his set, Jewell lay on the floor in her bra and panties. Daniel wore only his red, satin boxers.

"Put on some music," he suggested.

Jewell's head was spinning so much, it took her four tries to load her Jagged Edge disk in the CD player. Daniel crawled to her as she stood at the entertainment center. He put his hands on her hips and tugged on her G-string with his teeth.

"*Ooh*, what's going on back there?" Jewell asked.

Daniel kissed her right butt cheek and then the left. "*Mmm*, nothing..."

Jewell turned and cradled his bald head. Daniel pulled her panties down and kissed her pubic hairs. Jewell looked up to the ceiling and inhaled sharply.

"*No way,*" she said.

"What you mean?"

"You know you owe me one," she reminded. "Don't start something you don't plan on finishing."

"Actually," Daniel said, "I owe you *two*. You saved my airport job today."

"You would have thought about killing him yourself," Jewell said.

"Maybe. Maybe not. After going this long without killing, that's not something I think about right away." He kissed again and Jewell's leg started to tremble.

"Okay," she said. She moved away from him, heading for the bedroom, but she tripped over her discarded jeans. Daniel caught her before she fell down.

"Damn, baby. You're drunk as hell."

"I am," she admitted

He gently lowered her to the floor. Jewell lay on her back. She stared up at her man anxiously. Daniel smiled at her. He put a hand on each of her knees and parted them like the Red Sea. He got down on his elbows and ducked his head, but Jewell stopped him.

"*Wait*," she said.

"What?"

"No, I'm just kidding. Go ahead."

"Quit playing," Daniel said.

He kissed the inside of her thigh, and that was enough to get Jewell very moist. She laid her head back moaned lightly.

"You like that?" Daniel asked, sucking the other thigh.

"Lower," Jewell breathed.

"I know what you want..." He ducked down again and parted her lips with his tongue. He licked randomly at first, which was good, but Daniel knew how to please a woman when he wanted to. He found her clitoris and sucked it like a neck bone. Jewell yelped and dug her nails into their shag carpet. Daniel backed out and began to lick again. He flattened his tongue to cover more area, and he caressed her thighs rhythmically.

Jewell cried out. She put a hand on the back of his head and pulled his face closer. His tongue went deeper, pushing her to the edge of climax. Daniel felt her legs tightening, but he didn't back away. Instead he found her clitoris again and latched on with his lips. Jewell arched her back and howled. Her river became an ocean, but the festivities were spoiled *again*!

Jewell's phone called out from her purse. Only it wasn't *her* phone. She had Keyshia Cole on her ring tone. The ringing she heard was basic. It was unnerving.

Brrrring. Brrrring. Brrrring.

"What's that?" Daniel asked.

Jewell rolled onto her stomach. Her purse was on the floor three feet ahead of her. "It's him!"

"That's fat boy's phone?" Daniel asked.

"Yeah!" Jewell crawled to her purse on all fours. She didn't know Daniel was following until she felt his hands on her hips as she dug through her bag. She looked back and saw that he already had his boxers off.

"What are you doing?"

"Nothing, baby. Take your call."

He penetrated from behind just as she pulled the cellular from her purse. Jewell gasped and dropped to her elbows. She pushed the answer button on the seventh ring.

"Oh, uh, *uh*, hello?"

"Vanessa! How you doing, girl?" Percy sounded like he was in a good mood. Jewell definitely was.

"I'm, uh, I'm fine."

Daniel was digging for gold. Jewell looked back at him with a worried expression, but he smiled and kept on plowing.

"Did you talk to your friends?" Percy asked.

"Yeah."

"Do they want to play ball?"

"Yeah. They, they do."

"Good," Percy said. "So they still got my slab?"

"Yeah."

"*And* my eggs?"

"Yuh, yeah."

"*Great*," Percy said. "You're a smart girl. I knew you'd make the right decision. Can we meet tomorrow night? Just me and you; *leave your boys at home.*"

"Yeah," Jewell said. "Where?"

Percy gave her directions to a location Jewell knew very well. That was a good thing because she wouldn't have remembered anything complicated. With the liquor in her system and Daniel knocking against her walls, it was hard enough to keep from moaning into the phone.

Jewell hung up with the heroin king and looked back at her butt naked boyfriend.

"You a freak," she whispered.

He grinned and blew her a kiss. "That's what you like about me."

CHAPTER THIRTEEN
PREMEDITATED

Jewell awakened the next morning with a pulsating knot doing cartwheels in her stomach. She rolled away from the daylight peeking through her bedroom window and cradled a pillow to her belly. Her mouth felt like she had a strip of carpet stapled to her tongue. There was a mischievous pixie in her skull; stomping on her optic nerves and jabbing at her temporal lobe.

She squinted at the alarm clock glowing red on dresser. It was already eight-thirty. On a normal day, she would have been up and dressed an hour ago. But you don't have a normal day after ingesting as much alcohol as she did last night. All Jewell remembered was one tequila, two tequilas, three tequilas... floor.

Oh, and she remembered a nice session of pipe-laying too. The memory of Daniel's performance put a smile on her face, but smiling made her head hurt. Jewell moaned and pulled the sheets over her head; thinking one more hour of rest might settle things down a little.

But it wasn't to be.

Daniel came in and stood over the bed for a minute. He flipped on the lights and pulled the covers from his sickly princess. The condo still had an early morning chill, and Jewell was completely nude, but it was the lights that bothered her more than anything else. She rolled onto her stomach and buried her face.

"*Dammit, Daniel*! What are you doing?"

"What are *you* doing? It's damned near nine o'clock."

"So?"

"So, we got shit to do. You need to go holler at your crazy ass brother. If he ain't coming with us tonight, I need to know, like *right now*."

"Coming with us for what?"

"It was your idea, baby. Don't act like you don't remember. Come check this out: I got some new pistols."

Jewell rolled over stubbornly, but her boyfriend wasn't there anymore. She heard him in the kitchen fiddling with the microwave. It took her a while to sit up, but she managed. With every movement, the pressure and pain in her head relocated to a different spot and throbbed anew. Gradually memories from the previous evening trickled in.

Who the hell wants to do Daniel's airport job?
You're the only coward in this bitch!
We could kill him.
*You're going to kill **Percy Hamilton**?*
For ten million dollars, I'll kill him.
I'll help.
My brother can help too.

Jewell's heart sped up as the seriousness of her words descended upon her. The quick flow of blood cleared up some of the fog in her head, and she was able to stand with minimal stumbling. She staggered to the bathroom and ran a shower with only cold water. The spray was so frigid, she could barely force herself to stand under the stream. But the bath did the trick. Every one of her skin cells was definitely awake by the time she got out, and she didn't feel loopy in the head anymore.

She still had a headache, but that was nothing three Excedrin's and a cup of coffee couldn't tackle. Thirty minutes later she was dressed and alert and *willing*, if not ready, to begin her day. She found Daniel at the kitchen table dismantling and oiling the components of a menacing looking weapon.

There were seven more guns laid out on the floor awaiting his attention: Three were pistols. The other four were hulking automatic rifles with curving banana clips. Altogether, there was at least twenty thousand dollars worth of killing power in their kitchen.

Jewell stepped behind her man and kissed him on the side of the head.

"Good morning."

"What was you gon' do, sleep till noon?" Daniel asked.

Jewell took a seat across from him and studied the multitude of components on the table. She pushed a long spring lackadaisically with her finger. It rolled on the table, coming to a stop against her crystal pepper shaker.

"*Don't touch that!*" Daniel snapped without looking up.

"*Sorry*," she said. "You get up on the wrong side of the bed?"

"Why you oversleeping on a day like this?"

"It's not even nine-thirty yet," Jewell said. "Why you so uptight?"

He looked up at her with what she would have sworn was *malice* in his eyes, if she didn't know him better.

"You think this is a game?" he asked. "This ain't just another bullshit job, girl. This is the most important thing we've *ever* done. Since you got such a big role in it, I figured you might wanna, you know, get yo lazy ass up in the morning."

"What's the big deal?" Jewell yawned. "Am I missing something? Did I sleep through an important meeting?"

"Don't talk shit."

"You're the one talking shit. All you told me to do was go talk to my brother. He don't have to go to work until two, and I'm not gon' miss him. So unless there's something else you want me to do and you ain't said nothing about it, I don't see why you being an asshole."

For a second Daniel looked like he might respond with violence. Instead he sighed; his whole body deflating with the exhalation.

"I'm sorry."

Jewell expected a dozen responses, but that wasn't even on the radar.

"I didn't sleep good," he admitted. "I got up early and went and got you a new car. I went and got them guns too. *My nerves.* Man, I ain't never felt like this. I was in here pacing at four in the morning. Every time I went in there, you was still snoring."

Awww, Jewell thought. But she wouldn't dare emasculate him by saying that out loud. Instead she said, "I'm sorry, baby."

"It's not your fault," Daniel said. "It's me. I never been this anxious before."

Jewell saw that her man was visibly stressed. He had dark circles under his eyes. They were bloodshot too. "Do you want to call it off?" she asked.

"No," he said. "We *gotta* do this, baby – not just because of the airport job either. He know where your mom stays. And Miles is right: If he's got a connection in the police department, they can tell him a lot about that house. Even if we move her, there'll be a paper trail."

"What if Percy's cool with just getting his heroin back?" Jewell asked.

"I was thinking about that," Daniel said. "That's our only out, ain't it? If he'll forget about them damned eggs, we might be able to get through this without killing his fat ass. You the one who talked to him. What you think?"

"I don't know," Jewell said. "I think it's worth a try. Do you want me to call him?"

"Naw," Daniel said quickly. "Never set yourself up to be unprepared. What if he gets mad and says that's not what you told him last night? If he thinks you're reneging, he might do something stupid."

They both knew *something stupid* involved harm coming to Jewell's mother, so neither one of them said it.

"The only way we're gonna find out," Daniel went on, "is if you make the deal with him face to face. With the dope right in front of him, he's more likely to say '*fuck them eggs*.'"

"I hope so," Jewell said.

"Me too," Daniel said. "If we can get through this without killing that fool, that's good for everybody. But for the record, we're going in with murder on our minds. If you start getting weak in the head, just think about him hurting Miss Eveline."

"I'm not gonna get weak in the head," Jewell promised.

"You better not," Daniel warned. "We might not have to shoot a soul, but me and Davis are gonna be ready for World War III. If you know like I know, you'll be ready too."

"I am ready," Jewell said, but she could have saved that lie for another simp. Daniel knew her better than she knew herself, and he could see the hair standing on her arms from across the table.

≈ ≈ ≈ ≈ ≈ ≈

The *new* car Daniel had for Jewell was a '97 Toyota Camry. It was clean and in good repair, but she never liked the small

133

confines of a sedan. This one was tolerable however because, like the guns, it was a throwaway. Daniel may have paid three thousand or more for the decade old buggy, but they would only get sixteen hours of service from it. After the meeting with Percy, they planned to set it ablaze along with all of the guns and any article of clothing that might have blood splatter.

In the meantime, Jewell definitely felt anonymous in the small car. The driver's license she carried today identified her as Phyllis Palmer. Phyllis was a customer service representative for a small travel agency. She was single and vivacious, and she would probably roll around in something like a Camry.

Jewell stopped at a McDonald's around the corner from her brother's apartment. She got another cup of coffee for herself and a breakfast platter for Slim. She pulled into the restricted spot in front of his building at 10:06 a.m., but to her dismay she didn't have a handicapped placard to hang on the rearview mirror. With all her diligence, she left something in the Lincoln after all.

She popped open her new glove compartment, just to be sure, but the only thing in there was her trusty .44. She hefted the pistol and checked the clip and the safety before dropping it in her purse. Jewell exited the vehicle with another knot forming in her belly, but it wasn't last night's Tequila this time.

Today Jewell wore a long denim skirt and a tight, pink tee with the word *HOTTIE* sprawled across her breasts. She didn't look at all menacing as she traipsed the apartment grounds, but at least one person felt otherwise. The dopefiend who made a fool of himself yesterday was still there, strolling aimlessly; desperately seeking funds for his next crack rock. He froze and then ducked out of sight when he saw Jewell coming.

"Yeah, you'd better run!" she called after him. It was odd how much reverence you could generate from just *one* act of violence.

Jewell sauntered up the stairs leading to her brother's apartment and roused him from sleep after a full minute of knocking. Slim answered wearing only boxers. Jewell shoved the McDonald's bag into his chest and stepped into his funky apartment with a sneer on her face.

"What took you so long to answer?"

Slim wiped the sleep from his eyes and shuffled back to the couch like a zombie. Jewell sat on the loveseat and watched his every move.

"Dang, Jewell. I didn't know you were coming again – not this early. Not today. What's this?" He put the bag on the cushion next to him and put on a pair of cargo shorts he appeared to have been using for a pillow.

"I brought you breakfast," she said. "What time do you get off work, Cedric?"

"Ten o'clock."

"How you get home?"

"My supervisor bring me most of the time." Slim yawned and stretched his long arms like a tom cat. "Sometimes I walk, if he's off that night."

"Was your supervisor off last night?" Jewell asked.

"Naw. He brung me home. Why?"

"What time did you get home? Ten-thirty? Why are you still asleep?" she asked.

Slim knitted his eyebrows. "What? Damn, what are you trying to say now?"

"I'm not saying anything. I told you I was gon' check up on you. That's what I'm doing. You said you was cool with it."

"Whatever," Slim said. He stuck his nose in the McDonald's bag and apparently liked what he smelled.

"So, what'd you do last night?" Jewell asked. "How much money do you have left?"

Slim frowned and sighed loudly. He snatched a pair of jeans off the floor and dug in the pockets. He pulled out a wad of greenbacks and tossed them to his sister. She caught it and cocked an eye at him.

"You got a problem?"

"I'm *not* getting high," Slim said with unconcealed exasperation. "I walked up to the corner store and got *two beers* when I got off. That's them right there." He pointed to two empty forty-ounce bottles in the middle of the floor. "I drank them. I watched the news, then I watched the late show, then I watched the late *late* show. I pissed about eight times and made a bologna sandwich at two-thirty in the morning. I fell asleep after I ate that. Anything else you want to know?"

Jewell counted the money as he talked. There was only eight dollars missing since yesterday. "I don't see why you're getting an attitude with me," she said. "I already told you what the deal was." She folded the bills and threw the stack back at him.

"Yeah, but I didn't know you were going to start doing *this*, right off the bat. You're worse than my parole officer."

"The airport job is going to bring in fifty million dollars worth of diamonds," Jewell said. "We're going to be extra sure about *everything*."

Slim's jaw dropped. "Fuh, fifty, *diamonds*?"

"We had a complication," Jewell said. She stared into his eyes without expression. "We have to take care of something else before we can do that job. If you want in on the diamonds, you have to be in for both."

Slim nodded, his eyes bugging. "I'm in," he said. "I'll do anything. Did you talk to Daniel? He's, he said he was okay with me now?"

"He's okay with what I told him, but your actions are gonna speak louder than words, Cedric."

"Okay," Slim said, nodding eagerly. "Whatever it is you need, you can count on me. I'll never let you down again."

"You don't even know what the other job is," Jewell said. "I can tell you right now; it don't pay nothing."

His smile fell, but only a little. "What is it, Jewell? Tell me."

"Eat your food," she suggested.

Slim dug into his meal voraciously, but the Egg McMuffin grew cold in his hand as Jewell told the tale of a furniture king who turned out to be a heroin king – a heroin king who wanted his grandmama's eggs back. When she finished talking, Slim was a shell of his former self. His shoulders slumped, his head hung, and his spirits were equally low. He had that familiar look of defeat in his eyes.

"So, y'all, y'all gon' *kill him*?"

"We're doing it tonight," Jewell said, her face still without emotion. "We need one more guy. I told Daniel we could count on you."

Slim shook his head. "You, you can't kill that dude. He, he *famous*, Jewell. I saw one of his commercials – just, like, a couple days ago."

"Famous people get killed all the time."

"But, but, that, that's not even your thing. You and Daniel never – y'all don't kill nobody."

"I know that."

"He said, 'hustle *smarter*, not *harder*.' He said, 'If you shoot a man's daughter in the arm–'"

"I know what Daniel said."

"You don't wanna do that," Slim said. "You can't, you cannot kill Percy Hamilton. Just give him his dope back."

"I already told you; we don't have his eggs."

"Then give him the money you got for 'em. Or buy him some new eggs. You, you need to do *something*."

"Alright," Jewell said. She stood and pulled her purse strap over her shoulder. "So you're not interested?"

Slim stood too. "Wait. What are you doing?"

"I have to go," Jewell said. "I gotta talk to Daniel. If you're not in, we need somebody else."

"But, but, what about the airport job?"

"It's like I said," Jewell said coldly. "They come together."

"But, but..." Slim was seriously distressed. His face wrinkled up, and Jewell knew he was on the verge of tears. "But I wanna do that other job," he said. "I *need* that, Jewell. I don't want to live like this no more."

She shook her head. "I'm sorry, Cedric. It don't work like that."

"I wanna help you, but, I, I can't go back to the pen," he said. He was desperate now, and pitiful. His eyes watered, and Jewell could see real pain there; the pain of being told what to do twenty-four hours a day, the pain of living with killers and molesters and all things in between. Cedric knew what it was like to be behind those bars when they closed on you for years. That was a woe Jewell was fortunate to be unaware of.

"I can't go back there," he said.

"No one's going to the pen," Jewell promised. "We might get killed, but we're not getting arrested."

That troubled Slim even more. "Why, why you wanna do this? There's *got* to be another way."

"Listen," Jewell said. "I don't want to talk you into it. This is a bad deal. I already know. It's the worst thing I've ever even *thought about* doing. But we went over it already. We'll lose everything if we don't kill that man. If you wanna help, that's good, 'cause we need you. But if you don't, that's fine too, Cedric. I still love you. Nothing's gonna change."

"But what about the other job?"

She shook her head. "You're out."

"*That's not fair!*" Slim bawled, and he could hold his tears no longer.

Jewell hated to see her brother cry, but this wasn't a new experience for her. Back when Slim first started shooting up, she would track him down and drag him out of the dope houses. When she got him to a safer environment, he would always break down and cry. He would tell her he wanted to stop but couldn't. He would tell her he hated himself for being so weak, and maybe he'd be better off dead. He'd thank her for saving him and go right back to the dope man as soon as he had enough money for another fix. After a couple years, Jewell stopped dragging him out of those dope houses.

"Slim, we're doing our last job in a couple weeks. I'm not letting *anyone* mess that up – I don't care how rich he is. Plus he threatened Mama – right to my face. I know he looks honest and clean-cut on TV, but he's not. Trust me; I know him a lot better than you do. So, as bad as this is gonna be, it's worth it to me."

Slim nodded. "Alright then. Me too."

"Slim–"

"Naw," he said, wiping his face. "I'm serious. If you gon' do it either way, then I'll help you. You're the only one in the family who ever cared anything about me, Jewell. I love you, and I don't want nothing to happen to you. If something goes wrong, it might as well happen to both of us."

This is what she wanted to hear, but Jewell played reluctant now. "Slim, you *just said* you didn't want to do it."

"I know. I know, but I do now. I'll help."

"Why?"

"'Cause, 'cause I can't keep living like this, sis. I don't wanna mop floors for the rest of my life. I'm 44 years old. Out here, I'm just gon' get depressed, and, and desperate, and I'll probably end up doing something stupid that's gon' send me back anyway. I trust you. And I trust Daniel. If y'all think it's a good idea, then I'm in."

He took a deep breath and stuck his chest out. "I'm ready."

Slim looked anything *but* ready, but beggars can't be choosers. So far no one thought it was a good idea to kill Percy. Jewell doubted if Daniel could find another warm body in the nine hours of daylight they had left.

She told Slim everything she knew about Daniel's plan and said she'd be back around six to pick him up.

"*Six*? I'll still be at work," Slim said.

"You might have to call in tonight," Jewell suggested.

Again Slim looked doubtful, but he said he would.

≈ ≈ ≈ ≈ ≈ ≈ ≈

Jewell made it back to her car with no regrets. She knew her brother's hesitance would lead to his certain death if he got cagey in the middle of a firefight, but Slim was a grown man. He had a choice, and he chose to murder a man. You should never get involved in such plots unless you're willing to die yourself.

She called Daniel as she exited the complex.

"Hello?"

"I talked to Slim. He's in."

"He still looking good?"

"Yeah. He's scared. He really don't want to do it, but it's like I told you; he'll do anything to get in on the airport job."

"Hope he ain't too scared to pull the trigger," Daniel said.

Jewell didn't say anything.

"If he gets himself killed, that's on *you*," Daniel said.

"I know."

"Did you get his sizes?"

"Yeah," Jewell said. "His pants are 34X36, 11 ½ in shoes. He could probably fit a medium shirt, but he has long arms."

"Cool. What are you doing now?"

"I'm on my way to Mama's."

"What are you, *crazy*? *You can't go over there.*"

"Why not?"

"'Cause you got arrested at that house yesterday! *Damn, girl.* What are you thinking about?"

"The police let me go. They're not looking for me anymore."

"You don't know that! You have no idea what kind of connections fat boy has. You need to lay low until after the airport

139

job. That bitch might call the law on you again. And didn't you already get rid of that other ID. What license are you going to pull out if they pick you up again?"

"He's getting his stuff back tonight," Jewell said. "Why would Percy do anything to get me in trouble?"

"I don't know," Daniel said. "But I don't like the idea of you being over there. Bring yo ass home."

Jewell sighed. "Fine."

"Alright," Daniel said. "Bye."

He disconnected, and Jewell continued the drive to her mother's house. They were going to kill a man tonight. They might all die in the process. If Daniel thought she wasn't going to see Miss Eveline at a time like this, *he* was the crazy one.

≈≈≈≈≈≈

Jewell saw her mother's neighbor as she turned from Miller onto Forbes Avenue. Mrs. Gaffney was standing on the curb; painting her wooden mailbox a nifty yellow to match the trim on her white house. Daniel believed this woman should be avoided at all costs, but Jewell always preferred a more confrontational approach.

The older woman didn't recognize the new car or its driver, so Jewell made it all the way to her mother's driveway before Mrs. Gaffney saw her. The color in the woman's face went from carnation pink to skim milk white. Jewell jumped from the Camry quickly before the skittish do-gooder could run inside.

"You wanna tell me why you called the police on me?" Jewell asked as she closed the distance between them with long strides.

"I, I was..." Mrs. Gaffney held a small can of number five yellow in one hand and a ¼ inch paintbrush in the other. She held out her arms, putting these items between herself and Jewell, but her expression told the whole story: She knew these *weapons* would not be enough.

"I'm just looking out for my community," she said. "I don't want any trouble with you."

Mrs. Gaffney wore denim overalls with a lavender blouse. She wore flip flops and had her pants rolled up to the knees. She planted her feet for a quick take off, and Jewell could see blue veins standing out on her chubby legs.

"How are you looking out for the community?" Jewell asked. She stopped, less than five feet away. "All you're doing is harassing people. You know I'm not a *fugitive*! Why would you do that?"

"You, you looked a lot like the drawing they had in the paper," Mrs. Gaffney said, the bucket shaking in her hand. "That's *all* I told them. I didn't say it *was* you."

"I saw that drawing," Jewell said. "It looks like a lot of people. Am I the only black woman you know?"

"You're, I..."

Playing the race card always caught white people off guard.

"I just come over here to see my mama," Jewell said. "I never bothered you. None of the people you call the police on have done anything to you. You're not even on the *neighborhood watch*. What do you want, attention?"

Mrs. Gaffney's complexion changed again, this time settling into a nice tomato red. "I *am so* on the neighborhood watch."

"You're supposed to be helping the people *in* the neighborhood," Jewell lectured. "Not calling the police on us." She put a hand on her hip and stared the older woman right in the eyes; totally oblivious to the irony of her rant. "Do you honestly think I did those things – what they had in the paper? You really think I'm that type of person?"

Seeing there was no violence coming, Mrs. Gaffney lowered her paint and raised her nose a little. "Well, I really don't know you. I have no idea what you may or may not do in your private life. I assumed things would get straightened out. If it wasn't you, they would come to that realization and let you go. I take it that's what happened."

Jewell shook her head. "You have no idea what you're doing to people, do you? Do you know what it's like to have the police accuse you of something you didn't do? Yeah they figured it out, but I was down there for *two hours*. Because of *you*."

"Well, well then I apologize," Mrs. Gaffney said. "I suppose I never really thought about it, like that, from your side of things. But honestly, nothing I ever did was out of spite. I only want to make this world a better place."

Jewell couldn't believe she said something so corny. Even worse, Mrs. Gaffney truly believed in her cause. Jewell couldn't help but feel sorry for the woman. The world was an ugly place, getting uglier by the day. A whole legion of nosey neighbors couldn't fix it. Unless God called a redo, everyone was destined for misery.

"My mother's old and sick," Jewell said. "Seeing me is about the only thing she has to look forward to. I would appreciate it if you don't try to get me arrested when I come over here."

Mrs. Gaffney nodded. "Okay. And, again I apologize."

Jewell turned and left her standing at the mailbox. Remarkably, she actually learned something from the encounter: Sometimes it *is* possible to make peace without going to war. Jewell stored that fun fact in her memory bank for future reference.

Inside she found the new nursing giving her mother a gentle scrubbing in the bathroom. Given Miss Eveline's level of dependence, it was quite acceptable to perform her sponge baths in the bedroom, but Priscilla was on a mission to impress. She had Jewell's mother in the bathtub sitting up in a shower chair. She supported Miss Eveline with a sturdy hand on her chest and rinsed her back with a detachable shower nozzle.

"Is that you, Clarissa?" Miss Eveline asked when Jewell got to the doorway.

"Yeah, Mama. How you doing today?'

"Oh, I'm fine."

"How's everything going?" Jewell asked the nurse.

"We're getting along just *dandy*!" Priscilla replied. "She didn't have much of an appetite this morning, but I think we'll make up for it at lunch. I'm about to get her food ready when we get through in here."

"Go ahead," Jewell said. "I'll finish up."

Priscilla smiled and she and Jewell switched places.

"You've got a great daughter, Ms. Hunt," the nurse said on the way out. "If my daughter cared half as much about me, I'd consider myself very fortunate."

Miss Eveline smiled. The twinkle in her eyes faded long ago, but Jewell could still see heaven in her countenance. She smiled too.

"Thank you," Miss Eveline told the nurse. "She is a sweet girl."

"How you been doing?" Jewell asked when they were alone.

"I've been better," Miss Eveline admitted.

"How come you didn't eat breakfast?"

Jewell rinsed the remaining suds from her mother's flesh and dried her off.

"My pressure was up again," Eveline admitted. "I felt a little weird when I went to bed last night. This morning I couldn't, it was hard to get my senses."

"How you feeling now?"

"I'm better. I think I'll be able to get something down. What happened to you when you left from here yesterday?"

"What are you talking about?" Jewell asked.

"It was some police out there," Eveline said. "I heard you talking to them."

Jewell shook her head. "Mama you were dead asleep when I left. How'd you hear that?"

Miss Eveline lowered her head sheepishly. "You not gonna fire *another one*, are you?"

Jewell sighed. "Priscilla told you about the police?"

"She didn't mean no harm, Clarissa. You let that lady be."

Jewell smiled. "Alright, Mama. I won't say anything to her."

"So, what happened?"

"You *know* what happened," Jewell said. "Your dumb neighbor called the police on me!"

Miss Eveline laughed, but laughter is an action better suited for fools and babies. The old woman's shoulders hitched. Her chest rose and fell erratically.

"That's not funny," Jewell said, hoping to calm her down.

"What'd you do?" Miss Eveline asked, "walk across her lawn?"

"Even worse," Jewell said. "She thought I looked like one of *America's Most Wanted*."

Again Eveline had heard nothing funnier.

"That's not funny, Mama. I had to go to the police station and everything."

"Are you *serious*?"

"Yes, now stop laughing at me so I can get you dressed. Do you want me to do your hair today?"

"Yes," the old woman said, fighting back a chuckle. "That'd be nice."

≈≈≈≈≈≈≈

Thirty minutes later they were in the older woman's bedroom. Miss Eveline sat on the corner of her bed with Jewell standing on her knees behind her. Jewell had her sandals off so she wouldn't soil her mother's sheets. She brushed Miss Eveline's hair slowly, marveling at the strength and volume of her locks.

"I need to talk to you about something," Jewell said. It pained her to initiate the conversation, but she knew it had to be done.

"What is it?" Eveline asked.

"Do you remember when I told you me and Daniel might move out of town?" Jewell asked. Daniel introduced Plan B as a possibility a few years ago. Jewell had been warning her mom about the possibility ever since.

"Did you get that promotion?" Miss Eveline asked.

"It's not totally decided yet," Jewell said. "But, yeah. So far it looks like I'm going to get it."

"Well, that's good," Eveline said. Jewell's *promotion* would increase her wages to six figures a year, but her mom didn't sound excited at all. "So, are you leaving, with Daniel?"

"If I get the job, I have to," Jewell said. "But you don't need to worry about anything. I've already set it up with my bank: I'm going to send Yolanda money every month so she can take care of your bills."

Miss Eveline nodded.

"And I'll still talk to you," Jewell said, "Everyday if you want."

Again the old woman nodded.

"And I'll still come to see you," Jewell said, *Unless the heat's on my ass.* "Maybe once a month..."

"What about Cedric?" Miss Eveline asked. "Are you going to be able to help him before you go?"

"I talked to some people," Jewell said.

"I sure would feel better if you could get him a job before you go..."

"What about *you*, Mama? Are you going to be okay?"

"I'm *old*, child," Miss Eveline said. "You go right on ahead and live your life. You and Daniel. Don't worry about me. I'll be dead here any day now."

"Mama don't say that."

"Oh, now don't you start getting all *sappy* on me. I get enough of that with Yolanda. You're the only one I can talk to about everything."

Jewell didn't know if her mother was serious or being melodramatic. But losing *the only one* of anything seemed like a terrible predicament.

A very sad thing indeed.

CHAPTER FOURTEEN
A MEETING AT
SYCAMORE CREEK

Jewell made it back to the condo at three p.m. Daniel wasn't there, and that was good. Jewell didn't feel like explaining why she visited her mom against his wishes. She didn't keep many secrets from her man, but when she did, she kept them well. Daniel still thought they lost his little bronze Buddha during one of many moves. In reality Jewell couldn't stand the sculpture. She donated it to Slim, who probably donated it to *bling* fund of one of his dope dealers at the time.

Jewell went to the kitchen and threw a DiGiorno pizza in the oven. Priscilla made her mom grits for lunch, and Jewell ate a little bit, but she wasn't very hungry at the time. She still wasn't hungry now, but she knew she should eat something. She found a few dishes to wash while she waited for her meal. After a while, the smell of garlic and cheese had her salivating. But Jewell could only eat one slice when her pizza was done. She left the kitchen feeling gassy and bloated.

She went to the living room and tried to get lost in one of the daytime dramas on television, but it was hard to stay focused on the plot. Her mind kept wandering. Jewell had daydreams about Percy. She saw diamonds and blood, and blood covered Faberge eggs glistening in a pile of blood covered diamonds.

She went to the bathroom and busied herself with cleaning. The little room wasn't soiled to begin with, but she dumped *Comet* in the tub and scrubbed until she couldn't see blood anymore. When she was done, Jewell got on her hands and knees and wiped behind the toilet. She polished the mirrors and basin too. Daniel still wasn't home at four, so she set about reorganizing their closet. Halfway through the task, she heard a sound at the front door.

Jewell went to the living room to greet her man. She had a lump in her throat and a dull pressure in her chest. Daniel stepped in wearing khaki slacks with a short-sleeved button down. He sported a straw hat, straight from Havana. He brought the smell of ozone and gasoline in with him.

Jewell studied his face, hoping for a smile or slight grin that would let her know things weren't so bad anymore. Daniel gave her a strange look and then walked past her without a hug or a kiss. His face was hard and indecipherable. He headed for the restroom unbuttoning his pants along the way.

"You can't wear that," he called over his shoulder. "Go put on another dress. Something *short*."

Jewell went back to the closet and changed. For her second date with Percy Hamilton, she put on a black leather skirt with a white camisole. The blouse had spaghetti straps, so she went braless. Her breasts were perky, and her dark nipples were almost visible through the thin fabric. Her skirt was tight and short, extending only midway down her thighs. A slit on the side exposed even more flesh.

Jewell slipped on her favorite Manolo sandals. She had three rings on her left hand and two on the right. She draped a 17 inch herringbone over her neck and spritzed Safari perfume behind her ears. She checked herself in the full-length mirror before leaving and thought she never looked uglier.

≈ ≈ ≈ ≈ ≈ ≈

Slim's apartment complex was an entirely different beast at sunset. Jewell was used to seeing a few junkies scattered here and there, but they were out in force now. The dealers were too. Young hoodlums with baggy britches and bad tempers congregated in the parking lot; sitting in their cars, listening to music, serving their clientele. Jewell had to park further away than usual, but she made it to Slim's apartment with no problems. There was something in her eyes that let everyone know this bitch was not to be tested today.

Slim answered after only one knock. He was dressed in blue jeans and a blue tee shirt. His Reeboks were well worn, but his shirt was clean. He had a new haircut and was clean shaven as well. He was wide-eyed and alert; a possible side-effect of *crack*, but definitely not heroin.

"You ready?" Jewell asked.

Slim took a deep breath and nodded. "Y'all still gon' kill him?"

Jewell nodded. "Come on."

≈≈≈≈≈≈≈

The drive to Safe House #3 was long and tedious. Jewell kept her eyes on the road. She breathed slowly and spoke little. She kept her mouth closed so her brother wouldn't see her teeth chattering.

Slim was worse for wear. His voice quavered every time he spoke. He fiddled with his seatbelt often; loosening it each time it retracted. He bounced his knee and cracked his knuckles. He stared at his sister like she was a stranger.

"You, you look good," he said.

"Thanks," Jewell said without looking over at him.

"Did Daniel say exactly what I'm supposed to do?"

"Just make sure I don't get killed," Jewell said. "That's all I know. He'll be at the house we're going to. You can talk to him then."

"I know. I'm just saying; we not gonna shoot him right off, right? Y'all gonna try to work it out?"

"We'll try."

"But if–"

"Cedric." She gave him eye contact while they waited at a light. "We don't want to kill this man. That's a *last resort*. But if we do, trust me, you'll know what to do. If Daniel starts shooting at somebody, then you shoot at them too. If somebody's shooting at you, you shoot back at them. That's not too much to remember."

Slim didn't like those terms of agreement. He changed the subject to something even more bizarre to him. "Y'all really got a house nobody lives in?"

"We have four," Jewell said.

Slim closed his eyes and shook his head slowly. "After the airport job, I'm gonna have a bunch of houses like that too. All over the city."

"We still have to do this job first," Jewell reminded. "Don't get ahead of yourself."

Slim kept his mouth closed for a while, seeing as how nothing he said was appreciated anyway.

He didn't get lively again until they stopped at Jesse's house. The safecracker rented an apartment building not far from the chop shop where Daniel sold Jewell's Navigator. Jewell made Slim wait in the car when she went inside to retrieve Percy's slab. Jesse gave it up easily enough, but Jewell saw plenty of reluctance in his eyes. She made a mental note to remind Daniel about that reluctance.

When she got back to the car, Slim was overly interested in what she had in her purse.

"Did you get it?" he asked before they exited of the parking lot.

"Yeah, I got it," Jewell said.

"Can I, can I see it?" Slim asked.

"Why?"

"I just wanna see it."

"Why?"

"'Cause I ain't never seen nothing like that before."

"You're a *heroin addict*, Slim. You think it's a good idea for you to be messing around with heroin?"

"Damn, sis. What do you think I'ma do; tear it open and eat it right in front of you?"

He'd get shot if he tried that, so Jewell let him examine the dope. "Go ahead."

Slim removed the brick from her purse and stared at it in awe. The slab was just as Jesse described it; a nice-sized block of dope, securely taped over in all directions, about the size of a box of Kleenex. It weighed almost as much as two canned sodas.

And even though it would take a lot more than Slim's scraggily fingernails to get at the heroin, Jewell didn't feel comfortable with him touching it. It might trigger some buried *yearnings* for all she knew.

"Put it back," she said after five seconds.

Slim gave her a look before complying.

≈≈≈≈≈≈≈

Jewell and Slim were completely quiet when they reached the gang's north side hideaway. She parked in the driveway because Daniel already had two cars in the garage. Jewell would drive to the meet point alone in her Camry. Davis would go by himself, and Slim would ride with Daniel. The meeting with Percy was set up for eight p.m., but Jewell was the only one scheduled to arrive on time: Daniel wanted to have his crew in position no later than six thirty.

"We're here," Jewell said.

"Oh, okay," Slim said. It took him longer than normal to get out of his seat belt. Jewell watched him struggle with the buckle, knowing this behavior was exactly the opposite of what she wanted in a trigger man. Or maybe it didn't matter. When someone's shooting, you don't care if the bullets are coming from a coward.

All you care about are those bullets.

Davis met them in the living room wearing an outfit similar to the one he donned for the original Percy job. But his black sweatshirt, black Dickeys and black Nikes were all brand new. Daniel never allowed them to get lazy in these regards. He watched Forensic Files diligently, like there might be an exam afterwards.

"Well, what d'ya know?" Davis said to Jewell. "Is this our guy?"

"This is my brother, Slim," Jewell said. "Slim, that's Davis."

"Huh, hi," Slim said. He offered a hand and Davis shook it. Davis stared long and hard at him before letting go.

"Where's Daniel?" Jewell asked.

"In the kitchen."

"Does he have Slim's clothes?"

"Naw. They're over there." Davis pointed to a bag on the living room sofa.

"Those are your clothes," Jewell said to Slim. "You need to put them on now. There's a restroom down that hall; on the right."

Slim hesitated only slightly before doing what he was told.

"What's wrong with him?" Davis asked when he was out of sight.

Jewell bit the inside of her jaw. "He just nervous, I guess."

"That's the *secret weapon* you promised us?" Davis asked.

Jewell couldn't immediately respond.

Davis' face cracked into a smile. "Nah! I'm just kidding!" He slapped her on the shoulder as hard as he would a man. "A warm body's better than *nobody*! You shoulda seen some of the boys they had me with in Iraq: Sonsofbitches couldn't even fire off a *flare*! But we still won!" He grinned, and crow's feet grew in the corner of his eyes.

Jewell smiled too. "Check it out," she said, reaching into her purse.

Davis' eyes bulged when he saw Percy's brick. "Good*night*!" He took it from her and flipped it around in his big hands. "I see why Jesse wanted to keep this."

"Huh?"

"Come on." He grabbed her shoulder and turned her towards the kitchen. "Check out what we got."

What they had in there was an arsenal right out of Terminator 2. Spread across the kitchen table and counters were pistols, shotguns and automatic rifles. They had night vision goggles and binoculars, infrared scopes and lasers. The sight of it made Jewell feel better about her fate, but it also gave her a sense of foreboding. It was not lost on her that she was the one who set this terrible train in motion.

Daniel stood in the midst of the armaments, adjusting the straps on his shoulder holster. He wore all black, like Davis, but Jewell's man always looked better, bigger and badder. His chest bulged in the sweatshirt. His shoulder muscles stood out, too. His traps were like small hills. With his bald head and fiery eyes, he reminded Jewell of Laurence Fishburne in The Matrix.

Daniel stepped to his woman and enveloped her like her mom used to do when she was a child. He kissed above her ear and buried his face in her neck. He made her feel so good, Jewell thought she was going to cry.

He backed away and stared into her eyes. "Your brother here?"

"Yeah. He's getting dressed."

"What he look like?"

Jewell shrugged.

"Looks like he's about to shit his drawers," Davis offered.

Daniel grinned and nodded. "Good. I want him to have that nervous energy."

"He's more'n nervous," Davis said with a chuckle.

Daniel didn't laugh. "What about you, baby?" he asked Jewell. "How you holding up?"

"I'm alright," she lied.

"You wanna go over what you're supposed to do?"

"No. I got it."

"Let me hear it."

They already went over her role three times, but Daniel never believed you had it until you said it back to him. He always did this, so Jewell didn't resist.

"I show up at the meet by myself, in the Camry."

Daniel nodded.

"I wait in my car and try to get him to come to me."

"What if he won't?"

"Then I get in the car with him." Jewell normally wouldn't go for that, but Daniel assured her she'd be safe. He never led her astray before.

"What do you say to him?" Daniel asked.

"I tell him we had a problem with the eggs. We thought we were going to get them back, but we couldn't. I give him the heroin and tell him we want to squash it with that."

"What if he ain't cool with that?"

"I tell him I can make a few more calls and try to get the eggs back. I tell him to call me tomorrow, and then I get out of the car."

"What if he ain't cool with you getting out of the car?"

Jewell didn't want there to be anything after that. "I guess I'll start rubbing my ear," she said.

Daniel stared long and hard at her. "Don't do it unless you're sure," he said.

Jewell nodded. No way would she order a man's execution unless she was sure.

"Let me see that," Daniel said to Davis.

Davis tossed him the dope, and Daniel examined it carefully. He sniffed it and shook his head. "Jesse's a goddamned fool."

Slim walked into the kitchen a moment later looking a little pitiful in his ebony outfit. Compared to Daniel, he looked like The

Little Ninja That Could. He scanned the arsenal on display and seemed to whimper silently.

"What's up, Slim," Daniel called to him. Daniel had no warmth in his countenance or in his voice.

The last time they saw each other, Slim was facedown on the carpet at a west side shooting gallery, suffering the effects of a mild overdose. The proprietors wanted to let him die right there, but Jewell talked Daniel into paying her brother's debt. They dropped Slim off at the hospital, and four weeks later he was in prison.

No matter how much he changed, Daniel would forever see Slim as that foul and twisted scarecrow on the floor of the dope house. In a way, so would Jewell.

"Hell, hello, Daniel. How are you, sir?"

They met halfway and shook hands. Jewell looked on; inwardly hoping Daniel would reject him.

"You been doing alright?" Daniel asked.

"Yes. Yes, sir." Slim was eight years Daniel's senior, but he submitted effortlessly.

"You off that shit?" Daniel asked. The deep bass in his voice reverberated through the house.

"Yes," Slim said quickly. "Yes sir. I quit *before* I got out this time. Been sober eleven months."

Daniel nodded. "You sure you want in on this? You think you ready?"

Slim nodded. "Yes, yes sir. I'll do anything to help my sister."

"If you fuck up, she's dead. You know that, right?"

"Yes, yes sir."

Daniel gave him a long once-over. "Come on then," he said after a while. "Come get your shit."

Slim followed Daniel to the counter to try on his shoulder holster. He looked over his shoulder and gave his sister a weird look and an even odder smile. If she didn't know any better, she'd think he was shitting his pants right then.

≈≈≈≈≈≈

The men left at six o'clock. That gave Jewell more than an hour and a half to wait by herself. She paced and cursed and prayed more than a few times. She knew God wouldn't listen to a sinner like her – mainly because she hadn't repented yet and she was headed towards more sin rather than turning away from it – but she prayed anyway.

It didn't help. She never felt so restless. She grabbed the remote as a last resort, and television proved to be her savior once again. Even in the midst of her mental anguish, Jewell was still able to get lost in the ignorance of a *Flavor of Love* rerun. That show was wrong on so many levels, you almost *had* to watch.

Before she knew it, Flavor Flav had two new butt cheeks in his hands, and it was 7:32 p.m. Jewell left Safe House #3 with rocks in her stomach. She headed for a neighborhood called Poly, where Sycamore Creek ran adjacent to a large community center.

She wondered if you automatically cursed yourself by praying before doing something bad.

≈≈≈≈≈≈≈

In the late eighties Dennis Hopper directed a bullet-riddled blood fest depicting the life and times of East Los Angeles' 70,000 gang members. When *Colors* first hit theatres, Overbrook Meadows was a sprawling metropolis with a population nearing one million, but it was still considered a sleepy town. There was crime, but it was by no means rampant. There were 24 murders in Overbrook Meadows in 1987 and only 22 in 1988.

Jewell was 14 years old when she and her girlfriends went to see Dennis Hopper's flick at the dollar cinema. At the time, she thought it was cool how the young men on the screen banded together to protect their *turf* to the death. She thought the slang was exotic, and the guns were awesome. The killings were definitely captivating.

When she went back to school the following Monday, Jewell thought it was cute how some of the upperclassmen had colored bandanas hanging from their back pockets all of a sudden. It was innocent. Those guys didn't know the difference between the *Five Deuce Hoovas* and the *West Avenue Pirus*. All they knew was they got a lot of attention when they twisted up their fingers and represented a clique. Jewell even found herself attracted to these new gangbangers.

But things changed.

Soon there were fights in school over the colored rags. The fights spilled into the streets, and gradually gangbanging wasn't just a kid thing anymore. The drug dealers became gang members. The thieves, the jackers, the hoodlums and losers did too. By 1992 every part of town was run by a different gang. By 1993 every part of town had several separate gangs. By 1994, there was a different gang on damned near every street, and Overbrook Meadows' homicide rate jumped to 256 bodies a year.

The local parks and playgrounds became hosts for some of the most vicious slayings in recent history, and no piece of land got hit harder than Overbrook Meadows' famed Sycamore Creek.

Running from the north side of town all the way to southern parts of the city, this tributary flowed through the territory of fifty different gangs. In it's hey day, the playgrounds and community centers built around the creek were bustling with family reunions, daycare facilities and lazy Sunday afternoon cookouts.

At its low point, the city's rescue team fished bloated gangbanger bodies from the waterway almost every weekend. Six boys from Jewell's graduating class were killed at Sycamore Creek. One of them was her high school sweetheart.

Eventually the police created a gang taskforce to help ebb the violence. That, coupled with new RICO laws and longer drug sentences, helped transform Overbrook Meadows once again. In 2005 the annual homicide rate was down to fifty. Most of the knuckleheads who kicked up so much dust a decade ago were now serving twenty years or more in Texas penitentiaries. Those not in jail were most likely dead or in wheelchairs. Some bangers left the lifestyle and got jobs, but they were few and far between.

The police gave Sycamore Creek back to the community, but after what they experienced in the nineties, no one wanted it anymore. The playgrounds became gloomy and dilapidated, the merry-go-rounds rusted. Delinquents stole the swings and trashed the community centers. The actual waterway was no longer fit for human or animals. There were broken bottles, full trash bags, tires, car batteries, and the occasional drowned dog floating in the stagnant pools.

There hadn't been a murder at Sycamore Creek in years, but it was still a terrible place to be.

Jewell turned down her radio and listened to the sounds of nature as she veered off the main road onto one of the side streets that ran through the park. At one point this road attracted bumper to bumper traffic jams on Sunday afternoons. Now Jewell barely had enough light to see where she was going. The street lamps had been shot out or broken with rocks some time ago. No city crew had been assigned to the park in at least two years.

Jewell drove slowly and cringed at the sight of so much degradation. Grass was overgrown in all directions. Metal trash cans set up for picnickers were now the site of rampant illegal dumping. Small brick buildings erected to house restroom facilities were similarly decimated. Old graffiti still stood out on the walls, but vegetation had most of it covered up by now.

The Camry's headlights cut into the vast darkness before her, but headlights aren't meant to be the end all in illumination. Jewell never realized how much street lights helped.

She rounded the last corner to the meeting place and saw Percy Hamilton's green sedan squatting on the side of the road with its parking lights on.

There was no sign of Daniel and his crew, but there wasn't supposed to be. Jewell knew her man was out there *somewhere,* concealed in the thick foliage like a Navy Seal. That knowledge, more than anything else, gave her the courage to pull to a stop behind the Lucerne.

Jewell put her car in park and left the engine running. She waited and breathed and listened, but nothing happened. Her brain raced. Her palms were sweaty. She wanted to pull out her gun. She felt like a fool for not having it out already. She stared at the back of the green sedan for a couple of minutes and then beeped her horn to persuade Percy to come to her.

It didn't work.

The back passenger window of the Buick lowered, and a black hand protruded from the opening. The hand had no ring or bracelet. The hand gestured for Jewell to come to it. That wasn't totally unexpected, but it put her at an immediate disadvantage. There were at least two people in that Buick, and they were both men. Jewell had the .44 in her purse, but there was no telling what they had waiting for her.

She got out anyway with a million terrible scenarios running through her mind: *What if the boys weren't in position* *yet? What if they were staking out the **wrong** position? What if their equipment malfunctioned and they couldn't see inside the dark sedan?*

Jewell stepped slowly on the gravely road, her legs moving with a confidence that belied her inner turmoil. She wanted to look right and left for any sign of her saviors, but she forced her eyes to stay focused on the green sedan. She walked to the side opposite of where the hand came out and opened the back door. She peered inside, not at all surprised by what she saw.

Percy Hamilton sat in the back seat wearing a black suit with a white button-down. He had no tie, and his shirt was unbuttoned halfway down his chest. He had his glasses on, and his hands were empty. Big Daryl looked back at her from the front seat. She couldn't see much of him, but she saw his eyes. They were focused and angry. Jewell had to assume he had *some kind* of weapon up there.

"How you doing, little lady?" Percy asked. He smiled at her, much like he did when she first met him at the club. That shit-eating grin made the hairs stand on the back of Jewell's neck. Her heart knocked hard, like the police. It was hard to get air. She felt herself growing light-headed.

"I'm fine," she said. "How about you, Mr. Percy?"

"'Bout to get better," he said. "Come on in here." He patted the leather seat. "Sit your fine ass *right here.*"

Jewell had time to contemplate life and death and the senselessness of it all as she got into the car. When she closed the door behind herself, the interior lights went off, and she felt like they were closing the lid on her coffin.

She grinned weakly at the furniture king as her eyes adjusted to the darkness. They were close enough to touch, and it was hard to see in there. Jewell wondered how the hell Daniel would be able to tell their heads apart from so far away. She looked around nervously. Percy watched her quietly, still smiling.

"You scared?" he asked. He pronounced *scared* to rhyme with the word *said.*

"A little," Jewell admitted.

"Tell me something," Percy said. "This gang of yours, y'all do jobs like that all the time?"

"Like what?"

"Like *jacking niggas,* home invasions, *setting a nigga up with the pussy.*"

"I, um, I don't think we should talk about that."

"Why not?"

"'Cause it has nothing to do with what we're here for."

"How you know?" Percy asked. "Maybe I want to hire y'all to do a couple jobs for me."

Hire us or get us all together so you can kill us? Jewell wondered. "We don't do that," she said. "We only work for ourselves."

"You sure?" Percy asked. "I don't know how much y'all making with that nickel and dime shit you got going on, but I can set you up with some *high-dollar* licks, a hundred thousand apiece *easy.*"

Jewell shook her head. "No. They wouldn't be interested."

Percy shrugged. "Oh well."

Jewell reached into her purse to get things moving along. "Here's your stuff," she said, producing the heroin.

Percy took his slab and examined it briefly. He sat it down on the seat between them. He didn't turn on the dome light to inspect it. Jewell was hoping for that move so Daniel or Davis could line up their shot.

"Don't look like my eggs can fit in that bag of yours," Percy said.

Jewell thought her heart might stop beating altogether. "I don't have your eggs," she said. "We tried to get them back, but they're gone."

Percy stopped smiling, but he didn't seem too upset. "That wasn't our deal."

"I know. And I want you to know we did everything we could to get them back. Maybe if you give us a couple more days, we can come up with some of them. I could call you, and let you know."

Percy shook his head. "I don't give a fuck about them eggs."

Relief washed over Jewell like a cool breeze, but it was short lived.

"Tell me something," Percy said. "Who that nigga that hit me in the head?"

At that moment, Jewell knew someone was going to die.

"What are you talking about?"

"When you was in my house," Percy said. "That dude came in my bedroom and knocked me upside the head with his shotgun. Who was that?"

"Wh, why do you want to know?"

"I was in the privacy of *my own home*," Percy said. "A man comes into your house and hits you like that, trust me, you'd want to know who he was."

"That's just gonna cause trouble," Jewell said. "I think we should let it go right here. You got your stuff back."

"But I didn't get my eggs," Percy said. "I was thinking; maybe we could have a little *switch-out*. You gimme that nigga who hit me, and I let y'all keep the eggs."

Jewell couldn't believe what she was hearing. "Don't do that, Mr. Percy. Don't even talk like that."

The furniture king pursed his lips and nodded. He reached behind his back and came up with a small, black revolver. It looked like a .38. He drew it slowly. Jewell could've drawn her .44 faster, but she let him make his move. He pointed the piece at her chest, and the smile came back.

"Now what you think?" he asked.

Jewell sighed and shook her head, more disappointed than afraid. "Percy, what are you doing?"

"I want you to take me to that nigga who hit me," he said. "Don't *nobody* put their hands on *Percy Hamilton. Nobody.* I don't know who the fuck y'all think y'all dealing with."

Jewell closed her eyes. A lone tear snaked down her cheek. "It's not worth it," she said. "Put that thing up."

Percy chuckled. "You see this shit, Daryl? Bitch don't know when she lost the upper hand. You know where you fucked up at?" he asked Jewell.

She didn't answer.

"You fucked up coming up here by yourself. What kind of ignorance is that?"

Jewell lowered her head, both eyes leaking now. "I didn't come by myself," she said softly.

"Huh? You say you *didn't*?"

"No," Jewell said. She looked up and met his eyes. "Just let me go, man. It don't have to go no further."

Percy laughed. "You hear this shit, Daryl?"

Daryl chuckled, his big shoulders rising and falling.

"So, where's your crew?" Percy asked. He looked around, scanning the darkness. "Where the fuck they at? Out in the fucking *woods*?"

Jewell nodded. "They'll kill you, if you don't let me go."

Percy shook his head, still laughing. "Daryl, *this bitch is crazy*! You hear this shit?"

Daryl nodded, but he wasn't smiling. He was looking around for the crew Jewell said was out there.

Jewell turned away from him and reached for the door handle. "I'm going to get out," she said slowly.

"Get yo hand off that fucking door," Percy said.

She turned to face him again. In addition to her eyes, her nose was running. Her chest rose and fell sporadically. Percy had the pistol pointed at her face now.

"You ready to start talking?" he asked.

Jewell reached up slowly and rubbed her left ear. She didn't know where Daniel was, didn't know if he could see her left hand from his vantage point or if he knew which head was hers and which was Percy's. She didn't know if their equipment could see through the dark tint on Percy's windows.

With a faith that sat somewhere between spiritual and *blind*, Jewell stared into the heroin king's eyes and kept rubbing. After five seconds Percy Hamilton's head simply exploded.

Jewell flinched and let out a sharp squeal as blood and brain matter splashed her face like she got hit with a water balloon. She didn't know where the shot came from, both the front and back windshields were shattered. She never even heard a gunshot.

But she heard the second one.

BOOM!

Daryl barely had time to turn in his seat before his head was similarly cracked like a fat kid's piñata. Jewell stared in awe. It looked like someone took a sledgehammer to a watermelon. The top of his skull detached and flipped once in the air. It landed on Jewell's forehead and stuck there like a Yakama.

Percy's limp body slumped forward. What was left of his head landed in Jewell's lap and bled between her legs.

Jewell began to scream. Her eyes were as big as quarters. Covered in blood, she looked like the pig scene in Carrie. It never struck her to get out of the car. She might have stayed there forever; screaming and crying until her screams became maniacal laughter, but a dark figure appeared in the sedan's window. He opened the door and grabbed her roughly. Her savior was completely clad in black. He had a ski mask and goggles on. If not for his lips, Jewell wouldn't have known it was Davis.

"Come on!" he barked.

He yanked her from the vehicle and they stumbled towards Jewell's Camry. She couldn't see at all. The whole world looked like she was staring through red stained glass. Davis had a hand around her waist, pushing her in the right direction. If not for him she wouldn't have made it.

"*My purse!*" she screamed. She tried to turn back to Percy's sedan, but Davis dragged her the other way.

"*No! Stop! My purse!*"

"*I'll get it!*"

Jewell didn't know where that voice came from, but she knew it was Slim. She was glad to hear that he had her back, but what Jewell heard next would forever rank among her worst experiences. Davis shoved her behind the wheel of the Camry just as all hell broke loose.

POP! POP!
POP!
BRRRRRRATTT!
BRRRRRRATTT!
CRACK!
CRACK!
BOOM!

Jewell didn't know where the bullets were coming from, but she knew where they were headed. From inside the Camry, it sounded like she was in a hailstorm.

PINK! PINK! PINK!
SHWOOP!
TINK! TINK!
TINK!TINK!TINK!TINK!

The back windshield shattered and something like a bee whizzed by her ear.

"*It's a set up! Get outta here!*"

Jewell knew that voice was Daniel's, but she couldn't see where he was. Everywhere was red. Everything was *blood*. She wiped at her face furiously.

Davis pushed her legs in the car and slammed the door closed. He ran to the passenger side and screamed, ***"Let's go*!"** before he was all the way inside.

"*What about Daniel*?" Jewell wailed.

"*He's alright! **Go***!"

The bullets kept coming, but Jewell still couldn't see who was shooting at them. She shoved the gear shift into DRIVE with slippery fingers.

TINK!TINK!TINK!

"*Sgeeakawush!*"

That last noise came from Davis, but that didn't make sense.

"What?" Jewell turned and saw him leaning hard against the passenger door. He gripped his neck like it was a snake he was trying to catch, but the blood still squirted freely past his fingers. It skeeted from his neck like pinched water hose, splashing on the windshield and dashboard.

***"Davis*!"**

"*Fucking go!*" he squealed, and there was a new quality to his voice. He sounded like he was underwater.

Jewell couldn't move.

Davis slid over and threw his leg over hers. He slammed his foot on top of her foot, indirectly punching the gas pedal. The Camry lurched forward, and Jewell had to look away from him because her lights weren't on and she still had blood in her eyes. She flipped the switch in time to see that they were headed right for the creek. She veered hard to the right and pealed out into a doughnut. The bullets were still coming, and she heard voices now.

She jerked the wheel the other way and managed to straighten up, and all she saw before her was grass. There should have been a road, but there wasn't. Jewell floored it anyway, knowing she was about to plow into a picnic bench or one of those useless light poles, but such a demise was not to be.

A gravel surface suddenly appeared beneath her wheels, and Jewell followed it, doing 60 miles per hour on a road meant for 20.

She cried fiercely, loud and crazy. Mucus spilled from her nose and hung like icicles from her open mouth.

"*Davis, Davis are you okay*?" she blubbered.

"*Uhn, I'm okay*," he said, but that was a lie. Jewell knew it as well as she knew the furniture king was dead.

CHAPTER FIFTEEN
FALLEN SOLDIER

Jewell made it back to the north side hideaway, but her memory of how she got there was spotty, like those of a black-out drunk. One minute she was in the park, ducking bullets and plowing down shrubs. She had a vague recollection of being on the freeway, but most of that was a blur. When she looked up again, she was in the driveway of Safe House #3. She clicked the remote transmitter on her visor, and the garage door opened slowly.

Jesse's Camaro was already in there. Jewell didn't know the safecracker was meeting with them after the hit, but she was glad to see his vehicle. Daniel's car wasn't there, and Davis hadn't made any sounds in the last five minutes. Jewell was starting to feel like she was the only one who would make it back alive, and that's a predicament you don't want to endure alone.

Jewell pulled in and slowed to a squeaky stop. She peered over at Davis. It was hard to get a good look at him while she was driving, but the lights in the garage were bright. *Too bright*. Davis slumped against the passenger door almost like he was taking a nap. His legs were bent comfortably. His left hand rested peacefully on his lap. His right hand was still clamped down over his wound. From Jewell's perspective, Davis looked just fine.

Except for all of the blood.

The whole passenger side was drenched and speckled. Davis' face was ashen. Blood beaded in his hair and leaked from his mouth and nose. His sweatshirt was completely saturated from collar to waistband. His leather holster and pistols were similarly drenched in maroon. His eyes were closed, and there was no rise and fall of the chest or stomach.

The last thing Davis said to her was, *"I'm okay."* That was almost twenty minutes ago.

Jewell got out of the car and staggered to the back door like an old woman. She was uninjured, but her adrenaline rush had faded; leaving her muscles tight and weak. She felt blood all over, in her panties, between her toes.

The back door opened before she reached it. Jesse stepped out wearing blue jeans and a white tee shirt. He had a smile on his face, but it fell quickly, almost comically. He stared at Jewell like she was missing both arms.

"*Oh shit*! What the fuck?"

Jewell swayed side to side with both hands at her sides. Her face was a mess of tears and mucus. Her hair was completely matted with gore. Some of it was already drying. Some was still dark black and sticky. She had pink clumps of tissue and bits of brain matter sprinkled on her like the devil's confetti.

In the middle of her chest, a sharp skull fragment stuck to her skin like a pendant. Her camisole was fully soaked, as was her skirt. Blood ran down her legs like she had a miscarriage.

In the middle of all the gunk and goo, Jewell's big, brown eyes stared out with more pain than Emmett Till's mother. She wiped her nose with the back of her hand, leaving an ugly smear on the side of her face.

"Duh, *Davis*," she said. "*Daniel? Davis...*"

"Man, what the fuck?" Jesse cringed and took a step back. "Are you okay? You hurt?"

Jewell shook her head. "Is, is Dan–"

Jesse turned back towards the house. "*Miles!*" he screamed. "*Miles! Get out here, man!* Something went wrong!"

"Are you hurt?" Jesse asked again. He scanned her body looking for a wound.

Jewell shook her head. "Not me. *Davis...*"

She heard quick footsteps on the kitchen floor. Miles appeared in the doorway eating a Snickers. He dropped the candy bar and put a hand over his mouth when he saw Jewell. His body stiffened like he got tazed.

"What, what the hell, man? What the, what the fuck *is* this?"

"*It was a set up*," Jewell bawled. "*They was* **everywhere**! I didn't see them."

"Did you get shot?" Miles reached for her and then withdrew his hand like she might have Ebola. "Are you, are you alright?"

Jewell nodded. *"I'm fine."* Her lips curled in another interminable grimace. *"Davis.* They got—"

"Who, who's that?" Jesse asked, staring at the slumped figure in the Camry's passenger seat.

Jewell tried to answer but her chest hitched too badly. *"Da, Duh, Da..."*

Miles stepped past her to inspect that tragedy that was once a Toyota: The back windshield was completely shattered and caved in. There were bullet holes in the hood, the trunk, and all places in between. The tires were caked with mud and grass. One of the side mirrors was missing altogether. The radiator hissed and dripped.

And there was blood, everywhere, most of it on the passenger side. It was starting to leak from the door.

Miles approached the car like something might jump out and attack him. He peered through the windows, his jaw dropping by degrees.

"Is that, is that, *Davis?"*

"Nuh uhn!" Jesse rushed to his friend's side and they stood there like two squeamish girls.

"Aw fuck, man! It is!" Jesse cried.

Miles leaned in closer but was definitely not touching anything. He turned back to Jewell, his face ashen, his jaw working but not articulating.

Jewell didn't know how she would explain all of this by herself, and thankfully she didn't have to. A grumbling motor approached the house at a quick pace. It came to a stop in the driveway and went quiet.

All eyes turned in that direction.

The garage door began to open, and Jewell's heart jumped up her throat. Was it the police on the other side? She was standing next to a bullet-riddled Camry with a dead guy still in it. She was covered in someone else's blood, and Jesse and Miles looked like they'd roll over on anyone to get out of this mess.

But it wasn't the police.

As the door rose, Jewell saw that it was two men there, both clad in black. One of them toted her ensanguined purse.

Jewell rushed forward before the door was fully retracted. She ducked under and ran to her man hard enough to knock him over. Daniel wasn't disgusted at all by her appearance. He wrapped her up like a blanket, lifting her feet from the ground. He carried her back into the garage with hardly any effort.

Slim stepped in with them, and Jewell heard the door grinding closed behind them.

"Baby, you alright?" Daniel asked, his lips brushing her ear. "I thought I lost you." He sniffled, and she could hear the moisture in his nose.

Being in Daniel's arms again was a release like no other. Jewell allowed her body to go limp. She sobbed and gripped his sweater. She shivered like a wet kitten.

"Are you okay, baby? Tell me. *Are you hurt?*"

"*No,*" she said. "But *Davis!*"

"It's okay, baby. It's alright."

"*No!*" she screamed. "*He's dead, Daniel! He's dead!*"

Daniel put his woman down and pushed her away. He held her shoulders tightly, staring into her eyes like they were foreign to him.

"What'd you say?"

She put a bloody hand to her mouth and shook her head.

Daniel's eyes burned like coals. He released her and hurried to the passenger side of the Camry.

Jewell turned to her brother, happy to see him only as an afterthought. Slim looked more spooked than ever before, but at least he was alive, and apparently uninjured. He put an arm around her and pulled her close.

"It's okay, lil sis."

Daniel opened the passenger door with all eyes on him. He stared and then leaned into the bloody vehicle. He reached inside and stayed there for what Jewell thought was a long time. When he backed out, his face was without expression. He looked from Jesse to Miles and then back to his woman.

"Bring her in here," Daniel said to Slim, and then he turned and went inside the house.

≈ ≈ ≈ ≈ ≈ ≈

167

Safe House #3 was unoccupied most of the time, but the gang always kept it stocked with the necessities: There was food in the refrigerator, clean linens for the beds, and a few changes of clothes for each member of the syndicate.

Jewell never used the shower there before, but it was just as warm and comforting as the one she had at home, even more so.

She stood under the hot spray and watched the blood run towards the drain. Her hair didn't stop producing a red discharge until the third time she shampooed it. She never realized how complicated and disgusting brain matter was. The stuff was everywhere. She had to cut her shower short when it started to clog up the drain.

It was either that or get down on her knees and scoop it out with her fingers.

When she stepped out of the tub, Jewell realized there was blood splatter everywhere, on the curtains, the tiles, and even on the ceiling. She knew she should clean it, but she barely had the strength to get dressed.

Jewell exited the bathroom wearing gray jogging pants and a tight blue tee shirt. She had brand new socks and a new pair of Keds, but she still felt filthy. Slim was waiting for her in the hallway.

"They fighting," he said.

Jewell already knew that. She could hear the argument the whole time she was in the bathroom.

"I made a mess in there," she said. "There's blood on the shower curtains, the wall, and the ceiling too. Can you clean it for me?"

Slim nodded.

"There's bleach already in there," Jewell said. "Actually you don't have to clean the shower curtain. We're throwing it away after you and Daniel bathe."

Slim nodded, regarding her oddly. "You okay?"

Jewell shrugged. "I've known Davis for six years. He was the bravest man I know. He saved my life. I wouldn't have made it out of there if not for him."

Slim gave her a hug. "He probably looking down on you right now from heaven."

But Jewell knew that wasn't true. Everyone in their group was on a slow train destined for hell. She wouldn't even insult God by asking for a pardon.

"You gonna go in there and calm them down?" Slim asked.

Jewell shook her head. "Davis was the only one who could do that."

She left Slim to clean up her mess while she checked out the battle raging in the dining room. Miles and Daniel had a history of bad blood, but she never heard them go at it like this.

"They were coming out the fucking *trees*, Miles! How the hell am I supposed to check every *goddamned tree*?" Daniel's voice boomed like an 808.

"You *can't*," Miles agreed, "when you've got *bad planning*! You can't just come up with a plan like that, like out of the fucking air, and just run with it! I told you to leave that asshole alone. *I told you*! But you wouldn't fucking listen, Daniel! You think you know everything!"

"You say a lot of *bullshit*, Miles! If I listened to you every time you opened your goddamned mouth, we wouldn't have shit right now!"

"We *don't* have shit right now!" Miles screamed. His face was beet red. Spittle glistened on his bottom lip.

Jewell rounded the corner and saw both men on opposite sides of the dining table. They were both standing and they both had a hand in the other's face. Jesse sat between them with his hands in his lap. He gnawed at his bottom lip viciously, like he wanted a meal from it.

"What the fuck you mean *we don't have shit*? We got just what we wanted. *That motherfucker is dead!*"

"Fucking Davis is dead too!"

"He's a *grown man!*" Daniel bellowed. "What do you think we carry guns for, Miles? All these jobs we did, you think nobody would ever get hurt? He knew what he was getting into."

"*What*? What the hell is that, Daniel? Is that how you're gonna act when another one of us gets killed because of your stupid ass jobs?"

Jewell watched her man from behind. She saw Daniel's shoulder muscles flex on his *back-slapping* arm, but Dapper Dan didn't attack his friend.

"Everything you got, you got 'cause of *me*!" Daniel growled. "I *never* had a plan that didn't go through. You got paid *every time*."

Miles was incredulous. "What the, what the hell do you think just happened? You call this a *success*?"

"We wanted a man dead, and he's dead!"

"Yeah, and *Davis is too!* You don't even care!"

"*Don't tell me what the fuck I care about!* **You don't know me**! You weren't even around when I met Davis. Don't tell me I don't cuh–" His voice hitched, and there was a twitch in the corner of his eyes. "Don't tell me I don't care about Davis," he breathed in a lower tone, his voice coated with pain and aggravation. "Don't you ever say that again."

Jewell sat at the table next to Jesse. They watched the argument like a ping pong match.

"Alright," Miles said. "Alright. Whatever."

"So we're still doing the airport job," Daniel said calmly. He looked from Miles to Jesse, then back to Miles.

Miles shook his head, almost on the verge of tears himself. "Man, *what the hell, man*? I mean, dude, you just got one of us killed, Daniel. *Seriously*."

Daniel stared him down, a deep sneer rising in the corner of his face. "You said you would help me if we took care of that fat motherfucker. We took care of him."

"Yeah, but it didn't go like you said. Your airport job's probably the same."

"That was an *ambush*, Miles! There's no way you can plan for that."

"But–"

"*Ain't no fucking **buts**!*" Daniel barked. "We did what we said we was gon' do. Now *you're* gonna do what you said you would. Don't tell me I went through all of this for nothing."

Miles opened his mouth, but Daniel cut him off.

"I swear, Miles, you'd better not tell me Davis got killed for *nothing*."

Miles looked like he wanted to tell him just that, but he wouldn't dare. He sighed and took his seat slowly. Daniel did the same. Miles held his hands up in defeat.

"You're still doing the airport job, right?" Daniel asked Jesse.

Jesse shrugged. "Yeah. I guess."

"Ain't no '*I guess*,' nigga. You down or you not?"

"I'm down," Jesse said. "I'm down. Calm down, man."

"What about you, Miles?" Daniel asked across the table.

"I'm not going inside that airport," Miles said. "I already told you that. And now you don't have Davis. I don't know what you're going to do about your other guy."

"I only need two people to go in with me," Daniel said. "I got Jesse, and..."

He trailed off as Slim walked into the room rubbing his hands on his pants legs. The room grew quiet, and all eyes moved to Jewell's big brother.

"What?" he asked. "What's everybody looking at me for?"

≈≈≈≈≈≈

Jewell put her soiled camisole and leather skirt in a heavy duty trash bag. She had to give up her panties and her Manolo sandals as well. Slim thought she should soak her jewelry in bleach so she could keep it, but Daniel vetoed that. He said *everything* with Percy Hamilton's blood on it had to go.

In one of Daniel's favorite Forensic Files episodes, New Hampshire detectives found a knife that had been left in the snow for four years. They couldn't get any DNA off the blade but thought there might be hope under the wooden handle. Sure enough there was a small rust-colored stain there. Some poor sap got 25 years to life because he was sloppy.

Daniel was never sloppy.

Jewell dropped five rings in the trash bag along with her 17 inch herringbone. All in all, she would throw away six thousand dollars worth of jewelry and clothing, but the airport job was in a few weeks, so that loss was pretty insignificant.

≈≈≈≈≈≈

Later there was another big argument about who should move Davis' body to the trunk of the Camry. Daniel thought Jesse and Miles should do it since they were at the safe house *chilling* when all the evil went down. Miles thought Daniel and Slim should do it since they still hadn't changed out of their ninja suits.

Miles' suggestion made more sense logistically, so Daniel gritted his teeth and headed for the garage.

"Come on, Slim," he called over his shoulder.

Jewell stayed right where she was. No way did she want to see that.

≈ ≈ ≈ ≈ ≈ ≈ ≈

After they got Davis folded in the trunk, Daniel and Slim wiped down the windows and dashboard briefly. It was dark, so no passing motorist would be able to see those stains anyway. They draped a blanket over the front bucket seats, and the Camry looked somewhat presentable again – except for the bullet holes and smashed windshield. That still left them at risk, but Daniel said they'd be alright. They were in the hood where ugly, bullet-riddled cars were not that uncommon. Plus they only had to travel half a mile.

Daniel placed their one murder weapon, a 50 caliber Barrett M107 long range sniper, in the trunk with Davis. Daniel took the $3,000 scope off of it, and they kept all of their unused handguns as well.

Daniel and Slim finally took their showers at 11:00 p.m. Jewell gathered their clothes, but Daniel didn't want them in the same bag as hers. He knew that if the police found her jewelry with Davis' body, they'd know Percy's murder was linked to the previous burglary. If a bright detective got hold of the file, he'd probably want to check out Vanessa Hardgraves again.

Daniel was like a mad scientist when it came to out-thinking the police.

≈ ≈ ≈ ≈ ≈ ≈ ≈

At a quarter after midnight the gang was finally ready to roll out. Jesse and Miles had kept their hands clean thus far, so there was no need for them to help dispose of the Camry. Miles caught a ride with Jesse, and the Camaro was the first vehicle to leave the safe house.

"Them two is getting off too easy," Slim told Daniel when they were out of sight.

Daniel said it was okay because they were going to get theirs in the end. He didn't elaborate when Slim asked what that meant.

Jewell and Slim road together in the Cutlass Daniel bought for the job. Daniel rode by himself in the Camry, and Jewell followed. They drove slowly, more carefully than they needed to. Jewell had a small heart attack every time they stopped at a light, but the convoy made it to Rockwood without incident. Daniel chose this location because, like Sycamore, this park had long since been abandoned by the community. The four miles of winding trails and dirt roads were completely deserted at this hour, and there were no street lights once you turned off Rockwood Drive.

Jewell tailgated the Camry through the trees for what felt like an awfully long time before Daniel pulled over at a spot of his liking. Jewell parked twenty feet behind him. She left her headlights on and exited the Cutlass with a new chill running down her spine. She brought the bottle of champagne Daniel gave her at the safe house. Slim popped the trunk and grabbed two five gallon gas cans.

"What are you thinking?" Daniel asked as his woman approached him.

She snaked an arm around his waist and laid her head on his chest. Daniel put a big hand on her shoulder and watched her eyes.

"It's fine, I guess," she said.

"I'ma miss my nigga," Daniel said. He stared up at the bright moon, and she saw a tear glint in his eye. It didn't fall, but this was still a lot of emotion for him.

"I am too," she said. "He saved my life."

Slim walked to the back of the Camry and dropped one of the heavy cans. "You want it all over, right?" he asked Daniel.

"Don't worry about the outside," Daniel said. "Use a whole can on the inside. Mainly on that passenger seat. Use the other can in the trunk, and make sure your pour some *directly* in that trash bag."

Slim nodded. He popped the top on one of the jugs and got to work.

"I wished I'd looked around more," Daniel said. "I don't know why I didn't think to check them damned trees."

"Nobody thinks to check trees," Jewell said.

"*I* should have," Daniel said. "It was my plan. I wasn't thorough. It should have been me instead of him."

"Davis didn't even think to check the trees," Jewell said, hoping to curtail her man's survivor's guilt. "And he was in the Army."

Daniel nodded.

"Did you see them?" Jewell asked. "I never even saw who was shooting."

"There were about five of 'em," Daniel reported. "They were in camouflage, green and black. When Davis went to get you out of the car, they started coming. They had on masks, like us, but they were sloppy. We should all be dead. They only got one person."

"How'd you and Slim get away?"

Daniel smiled a little for the first time that day. "Your fool-ass brother probably saved my life," he said. "Once you and Davis got in the car, I was about to let lose on them fools, but Slim grabbed my arm and pulled me away. You and Davis were already moving by then, and all of Percy's guys were chasing *you*. Me and Slim ran back to the car like it was nothing. They either didn't see us, or didn't care about us."

"I'm glad," Jewell said.

"I wasn't, not at first" Daniel said. "I didn't know if y'all were okay or not. I didn't even know if you made it out of the park. That was a hard drive for me, all the way back to the safe house. If I would have got there and you still weren't back, I think I would have gone crazy right then."

Jewell threw her other arm around his waist and gave him a big squeeze. Daniel kissed her on the top of the head and then walked away.

"Let me go help this boy out," he said.

≈ ≈ ≈ ≈ ≈ ≈ ≈

After they got the Camry thoroughly soaked, the three of them gathered in the Cutlass' headlights for Davis' eulogy. Daniel wasn't too good with speeches, and Slim didn't know the man at all, so Jewell had to do the honors. She stood in the middle with her man on her right and her brother on her left. She grabbed both of their hands, and they lowered their heads in reverence.

Jewell took a deep breath and sighed. "Alright, well, um… We are all gathered here, in this park, to pay our last respects for Davis. He was, uh, he was a veteran of the Gulf War. He served his country proudly, in a winning effort, and he was, *honorably*…?" She looked to Daniel and he nodded. "Honorably discharged," Jewell went on. "I, uh, I can't say too much about Davis' personal life. I only knew him for what he did for the syndicate. But I can say this…"

Jewell began to cry. Daniel let go of her hand so she could wipe her face.

"Davis never let me down," Jewell said. "Whenever, whenever he was with us," she sniffled loudly. "Whenever Davis was with us, I knew I was safe. And even tonight…" She stopped to take another deep breath.

"It's alright," Daniel said. "You doing good, baby."

"Tonight," Jewell said, "I wouldn't be here right now if it wasn't for Davis. Davis was the best white man I know. He was better than most black men too. *I'ma miss him!*"

She broke up again. Daniel pulled her in for a full body hug. "You did good," he whispered into the top of her head. "You did good baby. You through?"

"No," Jewell said. She pushed away and stared up at the full moon. "God, I know you don't like what we do, but Davis is a *good man*. You hear? When he gets up there, *you let him in*."

Slim grabbed hold of her this time. Jewell cried on her brother's shoulder, and Daniel bent and grabbed the champagne bottle standing between her legs. He broke the neck off on the bumper of the Camry and poured the bubbly out slowly.

"This is for you, Davis."

When the last drop was gone, Daniel tossed the bottle in the open trunk and patted his pockets for the matches.

"Get in the car," he told Slim and Jewell.

They did, and she was glad for it. There was so much gasoline, the car burst into flames with a small explosion.

WHOOOMPH!

A huge fireball lifted into the air, dissipating only after surpassing the height of the tallest trees. Daniel jumped into the Cutlass, and Jewell pealed off like they were being chased.

≈≈≈≈≈≈

She never asked who *specifically* fired the two shots at Percy and Big Daryl's heads. Davis had the most training, so she assumed it was him. But that was one thing Jewell never needed to be sure about. In the eyes of the law, they were all guilty of murder anyway.

CHAPTER SIXTEEN
TIT FOR TAT

They didn't talk much on the way to Slim's apartment. When they got there, Jewell pulled into her usual spot. Daniel had never seen the complex before, and he was taken aback by all the freaks on display at one in the morning.

"*Damn, boy*. You live with all these crackheads?" he called to the back seat.

"Yes. Yessir," Slim said, nodding.

Jewell looked in her rear view mirror, and she could only see his eyes and teeth.

"How you manage to stay clean with all these dopefiends around?" Daniel wanted to know.

"I, uh, I just don't wanna use no more, sir," Slim said. "I made up my mind, and that was it. Never again."

Daniel nodded. "What kind of work they got you doing?"

"I, uh, I mop floors, sir. I'm a janitor. Today was the first day I missed in four months."

"You get in trouble for that?"

"I don't know. Prolly. They can get anybody to do what I do, so, um, they don't put up with too much."

Daniel reached into his pocket and pulled out a fat roll of bills. He counted off ten Franklins but hesitated.

"You did good tonight," he told Slim. "I won't lie to you: I didn't think you'd ever be useful. But you handled your business. You didn't freak out or nothing."

"If you only knew what I've been through..." Slim reminisced. "I done had niggas point guns in my face, put them in my mouth. Some of my homeboys got killed right in front of me. I ain't hardly scared of nothing no more."

"That's good," Daniel said. "You gon' need those balls when we do the airport job. That's gon' be the scariest shit you ever did, trust me."

"Uh, if you don't mind, sir, I *still* don't know what this job is all about. My sister won't even tell me what you want me to do." He chuckled nervously.

"This job is the most important thing we've ever done," Daniel said. "I told baby not to tell you about it 'cause I wasn't sure about you. If you went running your mouth, I would, I... It would have been bad, Slim. *Real bad.*"

"I wouldn't *never* talk about your jobs to nobody else." Slim sat up in his seat, leaning forward. "Even back in the day, I ain't never talked about your jobs."

"I know," Daniel said. "But this one, I have to be more careful with it."

"So, you can, you can tell me about it now?" Slim asked.

Daniel chuckled. "It's gon' be a lot easier than what we did tonight."

Slim nodded, listening intently.

"You ever heard of Herzberg Diamonds?" Daniel asked.

"Yes. Yes sir. They got them stores everywhere."

"That's a German-owned company," Daniel said. "I'm sure these local stores get some of their merchandise from other places, but mainly every diamond they sell comes straight from their headquarters in Germany. You with me?"

Slim nodded quickly.

"In a couple weeks a plane's coming in," Daniel said. "This plane is gonna have enough diamonds to stock all the Herzberg stores in the metroplex. There's eight of 'em, so you know that's a lot of diamonds."

Slim nodded, his mouth open.

"My plan," Daniel said, "is to take those diamonds off the truck before they make it to the first store. I wanna take them off the truck before the truck even leaves the airport." He waited, but Slim didn't seem spooked.

"We're going in the airport to jack the truck," Daniel clarified. "You understand me?"

Slim nodded again. "What else?"

Daniel grinned. "Damn, boy. *That's it.* That ain't enough to scare you?"

Slim shook his head. "No, sir. I trust you. If you say it can be done, I believe you. Everything you touch turns to gold."

Jewell shuddered inwardly. The last person to have such blind faith in Daniel was currently broiling in the trunk of a shot-up Camry.

"So you down?" Daniel asked.

Slim nodded. "Yes sir. I'm with you. Whatever you want to do, I'm with you."

Daniel handed the thousand dollars over his shoulder.

Slim took it with a confused look. "What's this for?"

"In case you get fired," Daniel said. "That should hold you till it's time for our job."

"Alright. Thank, thank you, sir."

Daniel turned in his seat so he could look Slim in the eyes. "You ain't gon' get high with that there money, is you?"

"*Oh no!*" Slims eyes grew wide. He shook his head furiously. "*No way*, sir. *I guarantee it!*"

"Baby's gonna be checking on you," Daniel said. "We got a couple things we need to do before we go in that airport. I might need you for something else. I don't know yet. Use some of that money to get a fifty dollar cell phone so we can stay in touch. It don't have to be nothing fancy."

"Okay." Slim nodded. "Yessir."

Daniel gave him another long look and then reached back to shake his hand. "Alright, boy. You in now. Don't fuck up, Slim. *Please,* don't fuck up."

"I won't. *I'm not.* I'm just thankful you believe in me. I won't let y'all down, I promise!" He opened the back door and wished his sister a good night before slipping into the darkness.

Jewell backed out of her parking spot with another knot forming in her stomach. She had no idea what she felt uneasy about this time, but the feeling was there, and it was strong.

≈ ≈ ≈ ≈ ≈ ≈

Daniel made a call on the way home. When he hung up, he asked Jewell to drop him off at a local titty bar.

"Why, baby?" she whined. "I thought we was going home."

"I had this meeting set up already," Daniel said. "Trust me, I didn't know Davis was gon' get killed. I thought we'd have a smooth night. But what happened, happened. It's over. We still gotta move on with things."

"Who are you meeting?"

"It's my guy from the airport," Daniel said.

Jewell was eager to meet this mystery contact, but more than that she didn't want to be home alone. Not tonight.

"How long are you gonna be with him?"

"The club closes at two," Daniel said. "I'll be in there thirty minutes, top."

"Can I go?"

"Yeah, baby. It'll probably be good for you to be there anyway. We gon' talk about the part I need your help with."

"What's my assignment?" she asked.

"Same old, same old," Daniel said with a grin. "*Same old, same old.*"

≈≈≈≈≈≈≈

Harlem Nights was one of only three black-owned strip clubs in Overbrook Meadows. They specialized in a body-type you couldn't find at Classy Lady or New Orleans Moon. To get a job at Harlem Nights, you needed but one attribute; an ass big enough to set a drink on. Stretch marks? *Fine.* Bullet wounds? *That's alright.* Missing teeth? *Who cares?* At Harlem Nights, your *assets* are your only asset.

Daniel paid ten dollars apiece to get them in. He found his contact at the main stage, chunking five dollar bills at a butt so big Jewell suspected implants. Daniel walked up behind him and tapped his shoulder.

"*Harvey!*"

The man turned around with an angry expression, but he smiled when he saw who it was. "*Danny Boy!*" He grabbed Daniel's hand and pulled him in for a brief hug.

Even without an introduction, Jewell knew this was the *inside man.* Harvey still had his work uniform on. He was a security guard at the airport, a sergeant according to the stripes on his shoulder. He wasn't an unattractive man, but he wasn't good looking either. He was light-skinned and chubby, with chipmunk cheeks and fat lips. He wore thick glasses, and his gut hung over his belt.

"*Dizamn!*" Daniel said, staring at the stripper's gyrating glutes. "What you got going on over *here*?"

"That's *Divine*," Harvey said. He rubbed one of the stripper's well-rounded butt cheeks affectionately and then smacked it like they were in the bedroom. Divine didn't mind at all.

"*Uhn, uhn, uhn*," Daniel said. He shook his head and then looked back at Jewell with no guilt at all. "This is my baby," he told Harvey. "She's the one I told you about, gonna get that card from old boy."

Harvey looked away from the booty and looked Jewell up and down. "Yeah. She'll *definitely* be able to get it," he observed. He stuck out a hand for her to shake. "How you doing? I'm Harvey."

Jewell didn't want to shake that hand. She had no idea where it had been – actually she had a pretty good idea where it had been, and that was the problem. But business is business. She took his hand and smiled pleasantly. "I'm Jewell."

"Can we go over there and sit down?" Daniel suggested. "Baby girl's tired. I need to get her home pretty soon."

"Yeah, cool," Harvey said, but he didn't want to get too far away from Divine. He looked back at her three times before he finally took a seat and gave Daniel his attention.

"So, what's up?" Harvey asked. "It's a go? You take care of what you had to take care of?"

"Yeah," Daniel said. "It's done. My boys are ready. Two of 'em are coming in with me."

"You got their sizes?" Harvey asked.

"Yeah," Daniel said. "You gon' remember, or you want me to write it down?"

"*No paper*," Harvey said. "They gonna look at everything I threw away in the last ten years when this goes down. Just tell me. I'll remember."

The security guard didn't look like he had that type of memory, but he paid attention when Daniel rattled off his, Jesse's, and Slim's sizes.

Harvey closed his eyes for a second and then nodded. "Okay. Got em."

"Harvey works at the airport," Daniel said to Jewell. "He works in security."

"I *run* security," Harvey said.

Daniel smiled. "He's gonna get our uniforms. We'll be able to walk in there looking like everyone else once we get those."

"Not till you get your IDs," Harvey reminded. "And that access card." He looked at Jewell when he said *access card.* Jewell looked at Daniel.

"That's what your job's gonna be, baby," Daniel said.

Jewell was getting confused. Harvey offered to clear things up.

"These are our badges," he said pointing to a stack of cards affixed to his chest. "I can get Daniel the uniforms, but these cards are harder to come by. I've been looking for a way to steal them, but it's impossible. Unless you work in Human Resources, you're not gonna get hold of one of our access cards. Same with the ID cards."

"I'm gonna get Miles to make the IDs," Daniel said. "But the access cards are different. That's the card that lets you in all of the doors down there."

"You need three cards?" Jewell asked. "One for everybody going in?"

Daniel shook his head. "No. We only need *one.* Slim and Jesse can wear fake cards. We're staying together, so they can follow me through all the doors."

"So, how do I get an access card?" Jewell asked, but she already had a pretty good idea.

"The only way to get one," Daniel said, "is to take it right off a security guard, like him." Daniel nodded at Harvey. "If you walked into this club by yourself, you think you could get that card off of his neck?"

Jewell smiled, remembering the way Harvey was captivated by Divine's ass.

"I'm pretty sure I could get his card."

"It's not gonna be that easy," Daniel said. "'Cause all of the guards have to notify Harvey *immediately* if they lose their card. So not only do you have to take his card, but you have to replace it with a dummy card."

Jewell still thought she could do it.

"*And,*" Daniel said, "he can't realize it's a dummy card until *after* we do our shit. If he goes to work and finds out his card is fake, the gig is up. They'll cancel our card right then."

Now Jewell was worried. "So, how do we keep him from knowing?"

Daniel smiled. "You're fucking with a genius. You know that right?"

Jewell grinned. "Okay."

"No, say it," Daniel said. "You're fucking with a genius. Say it."

"*I'm fucking with a genius*," Jewell said. "So how's it gonna work?"

Daniel smiled. "The only way to get the card *and* make sure it isn't reported until after we do our job is to take a card from somebody who won't be there when we do the job. Mr. Harvey ran through the schedules, looking for that somebody."

"There are a few who'll be off on that day," Harvey explained. "But only one of them is also a little weak when it comes to women. The other two are married. And the guy we're looking at goes on vacation the day before those diamonds come in."

"One guy," Daniel said. "That means we get one shot to get it right. I mean, *you* get one shot to get it right."

Jewell lived for this kind of pressure. She grinned devilishly. "Well, I guess I'd better not fuck up."

"You won't," Daniel said. He looked at Harvey and grinned. "Baby girl never let us down."

≈ ≈ ≈ ≈ ≈ ≈

When they got home Jewell had a dozen messages on her answering machine. The majority of them were unimportant, but three were from her sister. Yolanda never called to chit chat.

The first message left Jewell a little curious: "Hey, this is Yolanda. Give me a call when you get home. It's important."

The second one had her a little worried: "Hey. It's me again. I need to talk to you, Jewell. Call me as soon as you can. No one's answering your cell."

And as bad as Jewell's day had already gone, the last message made things much worse: "Hey, it's Yolanda again. Jewell, it's after midnight. I was trying to wait up for you, but I can't stay up no more. I'm sorry to have to say this over the phone,

183

but Mama passed last night. Give me a call as soon as you get this, if you wanna talk. Otherwise I'll call you tomorrow."

Jewell backed away from the answering machine and sat on the couch with a blank expression.

"It's my fault," she said.

"How the hell is that your fault?" Daniel asked.

Jewell didn't say anything because Daniel didn't understand how God and karma work together sometimes: She killed two people. They lost Davis, but that was not enough to balance the scales. The Lord required one more soul.

Tit for tat.

CHAPTER SEVENTEEN
LOCKDOWN

Percy Hamilton's murder was as big a bombshell as everyone expected it to be, especially with the violent circumstances surrounding his death. Jewell woke up early the next morning, but Daniel was already out of bed. She found him in the living room watching the local news. The early morning massacre was being sensationalized by a local reporter.

Jewell sat on the floor between Daniel's legs. He put a hand on her cheek and then rubbed her shoulder.

"I'm here at the scene," the reporter said. The sound of low-flying helicopters almost drowned him out.

Seeing the park again brought Jewell a myriad of emotions. Pain, fright, disgust from all the blood.

The reporter was young and cocoa-colored. His hair was short, his eyebrows bushy. He wore a dark trench coat over his suit for what had to be the biggest story of his budding career.

"As you can see behind me," he went on, "the police have this whole area sealed off. But that car over there, I'm told, is the sedan Mr. Hamilton's body was removed from – as well as his bodyguard.

"The police, at this time, have not been specific about how many shots were fired at the Buick, but as you can see the front and back windshields appear to have been shot out. That would corroborate statements from some of the nearby neighbors who described '*a really long shoot out.*'"

"Shaun," the anchorwoman back in the studio interrupted, "are the police giving *any* word on the shooter or *shooters* and their possible motive?"

"No, Diane," Shaun said. "At this point the police are being very sketchy with the information they're releasing. Here's what they've confirmed: Two units responded to several calls of shots fired at approximately 8:12 p.m. When they arrived at this location, they found the Buick with two deceased males inside. They did not encounter anyone fleeing the scene. They have not made any arrests, and so far no witness has come forward who actually saw what happened.

"This park, as you know, has been the scene of a number of murders in the past, Diane. The people who live in this area say they're used to hearing gunfire. They were, however, surprised by the amount of shooting that went on last night. One woman said, *'It sounded like Vietnam down there.'* Another reported hearing at least *one hundred* separate gunshots."

"That's a lot of bullets, Shaun," Diane said. "I'm sure, with that many shots, the police will be able to find evidence of more than one weapon being involved..."

"That's right, Diane," Shaun said. "If you'll look behind me, you can see all of those numbered, yellow cards on the ground back there. I'm told each one of those cards represents a different bullet or bullet casings that might have been used in this crime.

"And those yellow cards are pretty much everywhere, Diane. Some of them are near the car where they removed Mr. Hamilton's body. Some are further down along that trail. About half of them are next to that tree there, a good twenty yards away from Mr. Hamilton's car."

"That's where they were," Daniel said, studying the screen intently.

"Where were y'all?" Jewell asked.

"We were on the ground, directly in front of the sedan. They haven't showed that spot."

"Did y'all leave any shells?" Jewell asked.

Daniel shook his head.

"What's interesting," the young reporter continued, "are these *tire tracks*. If you'll look to my right, you can see where a vehicle performed what looks like a doughnut in the middle of that road. Those tracks are fresh, Diane, and you can actually see which direction that car left in."

"Is that going to be the getaway vehicle, Shaun?"

"Why the hell these niggas playing detective?" Daniel wondered.

"They shouldn't even be that close," Jewell noticed.

"They're not saying right now," Shaun said, "but you can see the care they're giving those tracks, Diane. They've already made plastic molds since I've been here, so those tracks are *definitely* important to the detectives working this case.

"I'd also like to remind viewers about the burglary that took place at Percy Hamilton's residence just a few days ago, Diane."

"You don't need to remind them *shit*," Daniel muttered. He talked to movie screens as well as small screens.

"Just three nights ago," Shaun went on, "Mr. Hamilton was awakened from sleep by three to four masked gunmen–"

"*Sleep my ass*," Daniel said.

"–who tied him up at gunpoint, along with his bodyguard. They made it out of there with quite a bit of cash and valuables. The police still haven't made any arrests in that case."

"Have they said yet whether these two incidents are connected?" Diane wanted to know.

"Not yet," Shaun said. "But from what I'm hearing, everyone believes this is not a coincidence. I'm Shaun Mast with Fox Six, news."

"Alright, thank you, Shaun," Diane said. The scene cut back to the studio. Diane was a brunette with short hair and a nice smile. "If you're just joining us," she said, "we are reporting on the *horrible, horrible* shooting death of Percy Hamilton, a business mogul whose furniture stores have been a mainstay in this city since his grandfather opened the first warehouse in 1941.

"As Shaun was mentioning, Mr. Hamilton's home was burglarized just three nights ago by armed men who still have not been apprehended. According to police documents, nearly one hundred thousand dollars in cash and valuables was stolen during that crime.

"The body of Percy Hamilton was found in the back seat of his sedan last night at approximately 8:28 p.m. by police officers who responded to a call of shots fired at Sycamore Creek Park. The body of Mr. Hamilton's bodyguard was also found in that sedan, but the police have not released his name yet pending notification of his relatives."

Someone handed Diane a stack of papers. She looked down at them and then back up at the camera.

"Okay, *this just in...* Were getting word that there was *another body* found at *another* park! This one is on the north side of town. For more on that, we'll go to Jason Owens in Chopper Six. Jason, are you there?"

The scene cut to an aerial view of Rockwood Park. Jewell leaned forward and gasped when she saw the decimated Toyota. It was hard to believe that Camry was operable one day ago. The car was still smoking. There were police and firemen all around it.

"Yes, Diane. I hear you." Jason had to speak loudly over the helicopter noise. "What you're seeing now is *what's left* of a vehicle the fire department found fully engulfed in flames at 3:30 this morning."

"Good," Daniel said.

"Why is that good?" Jewell asked.

"We left that car at one o'clock," Daniel said. "After two hours of burning, ain't nothing left."

"In the trunk of that vehicle," Jason went on, "the police found the remains of a still unidentified individual. At this point they don't know if this is a male or female. The body is still in the trunk now, Diane. They plan to tow the entire vehicle back to the crime lab before they touch anything."

The view was jerky, and you couldn't see the body, but Jewell still got chills.

"Are they saying what the cause of death was," Diane asked.

"Not yet, Diane. Apparently the fire was started at least an hour before the first unit arrived at the scene. As you can see, this area is pretty isolated. Thankfully the fire didn't spread to any nearby trees.

"I'm told it was reported by a nearby resident who said she saw smoke rising in front of the full moon we had last night. But even then, she didn't know exactly where the fire was. The fire department said they had a difficult time locating this vehicle."

"As you know, Jason," Diane said, "Percy Hamilton's body was found in his car at another park about twenty miles away from you. Have the police said whether this new victim has any connection to Mr. Hamilton's murder?"

"At this time, *no*," Jason said. "But they're still pretty early in the investigation. And, as I mentioned, the police haven't begun a thorough search of this vehicle. Th–"

"Were there any weapons found in that car?"

"If they have found anything," Jason said, "They're not telling us yet. I'm sure once they get it to the lab and can go through..."

Jason's voice was lost in static. The view went back to Diane in the studio.

"Okay, we've apparently lost our chopper feed. If you're just joining us–"

The screen went blank. Jewell looked up and saw that Daniel had the remote in his hand.

"Why'd you turn it off?" she asked.

"I already heard all of this," he said. "I been up since four. All the channels are saying the same thing: so far no one knows shit."

"They didn't say anything about the heroin?"

"Naw." Daniel rubbed his chin. "They may be keeping that from the newspapers. Or one of Percy's gunmen might have picked it up."

"What about my picture?" Jewell asked fretfully. "None of them are going back to that?"

"A couple," Daniel admitted, "but they said the police had no idea who that woman is. And now that Percy's dead, they don't know if they'll ever make a positive ID."

"They said that?"

"Yeah. But that don't mean you can go crazy. You still need to lay low for awhile. We don't need somebody else calling the police on you."

"I wanted to go to Mama's house," Jewell said.

"Why?"

"I just want to get some things."

"Can't you send your sister to go get it?"

"She's the one I'm worried about," Jewell said. "She gon' take the stuff I want."

"What do you want?"

Jewell turned and laid her head on his thigh. Daniel wore flannel pajama bottoms with a tank top. His arm muscles bulged like he'd been doing push ups.

"I want to get her photo album and some of the jewelry."

"Why don't you just tell Yolanda what you want?"

Jewell smirked. "Then she'll take it for sure."

Daniel shook his head. "Well, I don't know what to tell you about that. But I know you'd better keep your ass in the house today."

Jewell rolled her eyes. "For how long?"

"*All day*," Daniel said. "Probably tomorrow too. Depends on what kind of blowback we get. I think we'll be alright though. They still don't know nothing about the burglary, and I damned sure didn't leave anything at the park."

He stood and stretched.

"Where you going?" Jewell asked.

"I gotta get rid of that Cutlass. I need to take care of some other shit."

"Like what?"

"Why?"

"I don't wanna be here all day if you get to leave."

Daniel grinned. "You gon' miss me?"

"Sure," Jewell said. "Take me with you."

"Not right now. Your bloody jewelry's still in that Cutlass. Plus we left tire tracks at Rockwood. I don't want you in that car. I'll come get you when I get another ride."

"You better," Jewell said. She stood and put a hand on his broad chest. "Don't say you're coming back if you not. I don't even have a car. I'm stuck here *for real*."

"You're on *lock down*," Daniel confirmed. "I know you went to your mama's house yesterday after I told you not to."

Jewell tried not to look surprised. He was probably bluffing, but there was a chance he knew for sure. She chose the path of least resistance.

"Can you take me to lunch when you get back?"

"Where you wanna go?"

"Somewhere nice. I wanna dress up and get away from all this."

"Alright," Daniel said. "But you can't wear no jewelry."

"That's fine."

"I'll be back around one."

He gave her a kiss on the mouth and then went to the bedroom to change. It was only six a.m. Jewell had no idea what she would do until he got back. She hated all of this heat, but anything that got her closer to those diamonds was worth it – or at least tolerable.

She went out to the front porch and scooped the newspaper from the sidewalk. Of course Percy's murder made the front page. That wasn't a big surprise, but Jewell's police sketch was on the front page with him. Seeing that made her heart do a little flip.

Jewell looked around nervously and felt relieved when she ducked back into the safety of her home.

≈≈≈≈≈≈≈

She waited until seven o'clock to call the nursing agency. They apologized for her loss and said they would get Priscilla to call her as soon as they could get in touch with her. Jewell called her sister while she waited to hear from her mom's nurse. Mr. Chauncey answered after only one ring.

"Hello?"

"How are you doing, Chauncey? This is Jewell."

"Hey, baby. You doing okay this morning?"

"I'm okay."

"I'm real sorry about your mother. You know the church has been praying for you, in this, your time of suffering. We're having a prayer service tonight for Miss Eveline. She was a faithful woman, very devoted to God. Sure would be nice if you and Daniel could make it down..."

Miss Eveline might have been at the church every time the doors swung open, but her oldest daughter only took in five to six sermons a year.

"I don't know," Jewell said. "We'll see. I'll ask Daniel when he gets back."

"This service tonight is especially for your mother," Chauncey went on. "It really is important to have the entire family there."

"Why?" Jewell asked. "My mama *died*. What are y'all praying for?"

"Well, uh, it's more of a memorial. We would like to honor your mother's life. She was a special woman, very good to our church."

For the last ten years Miss Eveline was unable to volunteer for any of the church's activities due to her declining health. Other than simply showing up, the only thing Miss Eveline did for the church was put one hundred dollars of Jewell's money in the offering basket every week.

Jewell wondered if they would really miss her mom or the pastor's car payment she gave them each month.

"Alright," Jewell said. "I'll talk to Daniel when he gets back."

"Okay, child. God bless you."

After a rather long wait Yolanda came to the phone as flustered as ever.

"Huh, hello?"

"Hey, girl. What you doing?"

"Getting the boys something to eat."

"You want to call me back?"

"Uh, no. I wanna ask you something anyway."

"What?" Jewell asked.

"Uh, I can't say right now. Hold on..."

Jewell listened to her sister's heavy breathing.

"Are you there?" she asked.

"Yeah. I'm here."

"What do you want to ask me?"

"I have to go to another room. Gimme a minute."

"When did Mama pass?" Jewell asked.

"About eight-thirty," Yolanda said.

It didn't take too much figuring for Jewell to remember where she was at that fateful hour: Eight-thirty was pretty close to Davis' time of death.

"Did you see her?" Jewell asked.

"No. The nurse called me though, right after she called the funeral home."

"You go over there?" Jewell asked.

"No. I had the boys," Yolanda said. "Chauncey was at the church. I didn't have nobody to watch them for me."

"Girl, you stay right around the corner. You could have gone over there for a second."

"I would've had to take them, and I didn't want them to see their grandmama like, you know, like that."

"So you left the nurse over there by herself?"

"She's used to that," Yolanda said. "She sees that kind of stuff all the time."

Jewell felt her temper rising. She changed the subject.

"What's this thing going on at your church tonight?"

"Prayer," Yolanda said. "We have a prayer service every Tuesday."

"Oh. Chauncey made it sound like they were doing something for Mama."

"We *will* pray for her," Yolanda said. "Whenever any of the church members are going through something, if they bring it up, the whole congregation will pray for them."

That's not the same thing, Jewell thought.

"Okay. I'm in the bathroom," Yolanda said.

"*Ewww*. I don't need to know all that."

"I'm not *using it*. I told you I want to ask you something."

"Alright," Jewell said. "What?"

"You know your picture's in the paper, right?"

Jewell thought she might pass out. She took a rough seat at the dining table.

"Wh, what are you talking about?"

"Girl, you don't have to lie to me," Yolanda said. "I *know* what you do."

That was true, but still...

"I don't know what you're talking about," Jewell said. The phone was slick in her hand. Her breaths came quick and hot.

"You haven't been reading the paper? *Watching the news*? You gon' tell me you have no idea who Percy Hamilton is?"

Jewell's head spun so fast she could barely respond. "Yeah I know who he is. I saw the news this morning."

"Did you see the paper?" Yolanda asked.

"Yeah," Jewell said. "Why do you think that lady is me?"

"Why you *lying*?" Yolanda asked. "I *know* you, Jewell. You my sister. I know how you look, I know what you like to wear, and I know you and Daniel do stuff like that. I'm not the police. You ain't gotta lie to me about it."

Jewell didn't say anything.

"I just wanna know..." Yolanda sighed into the phone. "I need to know y'all didn't have nothing to do with that man's murder."

Jewell didn't like the way her sister said the word *need*. She didn't think Yolanda would call the police on her, but there's no telling what a religious zealot might do.

Jewell forced a chuckle. "Yolanda, you know me and Daniel don't get down like that. We did some bad stuff, but we never killed *nobody*. You know that."

"Well, why he get killed?" Yolanda asked. "He was a business man. They did a biography on him this morning. He never did nothing to nobody. I can't understand why this happened."

Jewell thought fast but spoke slowly. "Yolanda, if you think me and Daniel had something to do with that burglary, why would we kill him afterwards? I mean, we wouldn't never kill nobody to begin with, but why would we mess with him if we already had the money? Ain't no sense in it."

"I know," Yolanda said. "I just, I guess I been watching too much of this stuff on TV. Everybody got their own little scenarios about what happened, but mostly everybody think that girl in the paper had something to do with it."

"They just saying that 'cause that's the only lead they got from the first case," Jewell said. "They can't catch the killers, so they're gonna wave that picture as much as they can. You didn't tell Chauncey any of this, did you?"

"No," Yolanda said.

"You're not going to, are you?"

There was a pause, but Yolanda finally said, "No."

"Alright," Jewell said, her heart still thudding. "I gotta go. Have you talked to the people at the funeral home?"

"No," Yolanda said. "Hey, I guess you made it."

"Made what?" Jewell asked.

"Made it all the way to Mama's death without her finding out what you do."

If not for the conversation they just had, Jewell would've cursed her little sister out for that one. "Alright, I'll talk to you later," she said instead, and hung up.

≈≈≈≈≈≈≈

Jewell called Spencer's Funeral Home when she got off the phone with Yolanda. Unlike most deceased African Americans in the city, Miss Eveline would not have to wait a week or more for burial while her finances were straightened out. Jewell paid for everything, sight unseen, with a credit card over the phone.

She would have liked to examine the casket she was buying. It would have been nice to smell the floral arrangements or at least meet the man who would give Miss Eveline's eulogy, but Jewell was on lockdown. She had to assume everything would be as beautiful as they said it was. If not, she had no problem with raising hell at her mother's funeral.

They scheduled Miss Eveline's wake for Friday and her funeral for Saturday afternoon. That gave Jewell three days. She hoped her police sketch would slip to the back of the papers by then and to the back of everyone's mind. If not, she knew Daniel wouldn't let her see her mother one last time before Miss Eveline became one with the earth.

≈ ≈ ≈ ≈ ≈ ≈ ≈

Priscilla called back at nine thirty, and she sounded more upset than Jewell.

"I'm so, *so* sorry," she said. "Your mother was a *great woman*. I wish I had met her sooner. I would have loved to be with her longer."

"That's sweet," Jewell said. "But she was already pretty sick when you got there. The doctors were surprised she made it this long."

"I know," Priscilla said. She blew her nose loudly and sniffled. "But your mother was so *different*. She was a strong woman, you could tell. Even though she didn't have the strength to do a lot of things, she was still strong; in her heart and mind. We talked a lot. She would tell me stories about when she was younger. She was so frail, but she wanted to be independent..."

Jewell began to cry too. "Thank you," she said. "Can you tell me about, the end? Were you with her when she passed?"

"No," the nurse said. "I think I missed it by thirty minutes. We had dinner at six o'clock, but she wouldn't eat much. I told her, '*You didn't eat your breakfast either. I think you should try to get more down.*' And she tried, but she didn't have an appetite.

"I put the dishes away and gave her a bath at six-thirty. When I put her back in bed, she was tired. She said she was going to take a nap. I checked on her at eight, and she was asleep. I checked on her again at nine, and she was, she was gone... Oh I wish I'd gone in there at eight-thirty!"

The nurse began to sob again, which made Jewell do the same.

"It's okay," she said. "It's not your fault."

"I know," Priscilla said. "But if I was in there, I keep thinking—"

"You couldn't have done anything to stop it," Jewell assured. She wiped her eyes with the back of her hand. "My mom was ready to go. It was her time. She's better now, trust me. She's happy."

"I know," Priscilla said. "I know. You're a great daughter. She loved you more than anything else."

"Really?" Jewell asked, her face twisted in despair.

"Really," Priscilla said. "She told me so everyday."

≈≈≈≈≈≈≈

When Jewell got off the phone, she called a flower shop and arranged for a gift basket to be delivered to Priscilla at the nursing agency.

Anything can be done from home, she told herself. *Lockdown's not so bad...*

But it was.

With no more tasks to occupy her time, Jewell found her condo to be a very small and boring place. Television was usually her most faithful escape, but today even the boob tube turned against her. No matter what channel she put it on, a news bulletin cut in with more information about Percy Hamilton's murder.

Jewell finally stopped trying to avoid it. She turned to Channel Six and stared at the screen for hour after wide-eyed hour. Whenever things started getting repetitive, a different reporter would pop up with another *brand new* development.

At eleven o'clock the police finally issued a statement regarding the crispy Camry. They decided the dead guy in the trunk *probably did* have something to do with Percy's murder. They confirmed there was a weapon found with the body, and they were pretty sure that weapon was fired at Percy's sedan at some point.

At a quarter till twelve, the detective's working the original crime scene confirmed there was a massive shootout prior to or immediately following Percy's murder. They knew there were two groups involved, and they believed one group was trying to protect Mr. Hamilton.

At noon the Overbrook Meadows police chief held a press conference for a roomful of rowdy reporters. He said his detectives had a lot of evidence bagged up, but so far none of it pointed them in any definite direction. He said they had no suspects at this time, but they were tracking every lead religiously. He said he was sure there would be a break in the case soon because there were too many individuals involved. He did not believe everyone who participated would be able to keep such a big secret.

Again he did not say anything about the heroin.

≈≈≈≈≈≈≈

At twelve-thirty Jewell got in the shower. She anticipated Daniel's return and looked forward to their lunch together. As she washed her hair, a shadow moved on the other side of the shower curtain, as if someone walked by, heading for the toilet.

"Daniel?" she called, but there was no answer.

Jewell strained to hear over the noise of the water. The only sounds in the house came from the television still on in the living room. She reached for the curtain, poised to throw it aside and catch Daniel trying to sneak up on her, but a horrible thought struck her when she touched the plastic: Whoever walked by wasn't tall enough to be Daniel. They were short and chubby.

Jewell backed away from the curtain, her heart fluttering like a caged bird. She kept her eyes on the area where she saw the shadow, and *there it was again*! With no doubts, she knew she was no longer in the bathroom alone. Even worse, she knew who was in there with her.

"Daniel?"

He didn't answer because that wasn't his name. And without seeing, Jewell knew what her stalker was doing: He was standing next to the toilet, waiting for her to step out so he could grab her arm and drag her into the bedroom to finish what they started. He was short and fat and black like the dark waters at Sycamore Creek.

He was grinning and drooling with his arms outstretched and his fingers bent into claws, claws that would hold her still and not let go no matter how hard she struggled. Most of his head was gone, but he still had one good eye. It hung from the socket, but it worked just fine. It would drip down and roll against Jewell's cheek as he had his way with her.

Jewell knew that what she was thinking was irrational, but the shadow she saw was *real*. She saw it twice, as a matter of fact. Who else could find out where she lived so easily? Who could get into her home with no key? Who would breathe like that – and yes, she heard breathing now. It was low, and guttural, and close – *very close*.

Jewell put a hand over mouth to trap her scream. She was nude and defenseless, but she'd be damned if she would die like this. She would fight until there was no fight left in her. If he wanted sex, he would have to take it from her lifeless corpse.

She took a deep breath and then grabbed a handful of the shower curtain. Jewell leapt from the tub, tearing the plastic from the rings as she moved. She exited the bathroom and made a mad dash for the bedroom – giving her back to the creature who thought she would go the other way.

The bedroom door was open. Jewell darted inside and made a quick left into the walk-in closet. She did not close the door behind her because she wanted to know when Percy was coming. She ran all the way to the back wall and spun quickly. Her eyes were wide, her nostrils flared.

He wasn't there yet.

Jewell slid down and sat on her haunches with the shower curtain wrapped around her like a safety blanket. She could still hear the water running in the bathroom but nothing else.

Jewell shivered in the darkness and waited. She didn't know what she would do when Percy poked his tattered head inside the closet, but she'd be dammed if he'd catch her off guard.

CHAPTER EIGHTEEN
I KNOW FEAR

Jewell was still in the closet thirty minutes later. Daniel found her there when he returned to take her to lunch. He helped her up and held her for a long time, as long as she wanted. He didn't press her when she couldn't tell him what was wrong.

≈≈≈≈≈≈≈

Daniel mopped the bathroom while Jewell got dressed for their date. She put on a flowing black gown with a V-neckline and a satin waist band. The dress was long and beautiful. It brushed the floor when she walked, totally concealing her sexy legs and her square-toed pumps.

She put on pearl earrings, but Daniel drew the line when she tried to wear the matching necklace. He stepped out of the bathroom with his sleeves rolled up to his elbows. His hands were wet. Water stained his shirt and pants as well.

"I thought I told you don't put on no jewelry," he said.

"I'm not wearing any diamonds."

"Jewelry's jewelry."

Jewell took the necklace off and left her neck bare, say a couple sprits of Safari perfume. She went into the bathroom to do her hair, and she was pleased with the work Daniel did in there. The floor was completely dry, and they had a new shower curtain. It was a gold-colored drape Jewell bought a few months ago but never found time to put up. Daniel grabbed his mop and stepped out of the room, still not asking why she ripped the old shower curtain.

When she was done with her hair, Jewell went back to the bedroom to watch her man dress.

Daniel put on a black, wool suit with a white shirt and a red tie. He selected a black derby with a red feather in the band and stepped into a pair of crocodile loafers. Jewell sat on the bed and followed his every move. Daniel turned and smiled at her as he slipped on the Movado watch she bought him for Christmas last year.

"You ready to go?"

"Where you taking me?" Jewell asked.

He walked around the bed and took her hand gently. Jewell stood, and Daniel put his hands on her waist. He pulled her closer and kissed her upper lip once, and then the bottom.

"Where you wanna go?"

"Italian," she said.

"I got you a new car."

"What kind?"

"Come see."

≈≈≈≈≈≈≈

Jewell's new car really was new this time. It was a 2012 Chrysler 200. She would have preferred an SUV, but this bad boy was candy-apple red with a convertible top. And it was a *stick*!

"Can I drive?" Jewell asked, beaming like a much younger girl.

Daniel handed her the keys and headed to the passenger side.

"Don't let down the top," he advised. "You already got enough people looking for you."

That was exactly what Jewell planned to do, but she enjoyed her new ride anyway. The seats were leather, the 18 inch wheels were chrome and shiny. And the system was *banging*.

There was only one CD in the car and it was from Daniel's collection; *The Best of the Isley Brothers*. Jewell popped in the disc, and let Ron Isley groove them all the way to Maggiano's.

Set sail with me

Mystic lady set my spirit free

≈≈≈≈≈≈≈

The restaurant was large but cozy. Daniel pulled Jewell's chair out for her, and he looked better in his suit than their waiter did. For dinner Jewell had basil and saffron pasta filled with fresh lobster meat. Daniel enjoyed slow-cooked chicken smothered in red wine with tomato gravy, mushrooms, roasted peppers and onions.

They ordered a bottle of champagne and pretended they weren't the most wanted couple in the city. Everything was delicious.

Towards the end of their meal, Daniel started looking at her with an odd expression.

"What?" Jewell asked.

He smiled, but it wasn't genuine. "Do you wanna tell me what happened today, when I was gone?"

Jewell was still embarrassed about her little episode, but there was nothing she couldn't talk to Daniel about.

"I heard this poem once," she said. "I don't remember the poet's name, but he used to read at The Embargo. You remember when we used to go there?"

The Embargo was one of the nicer bars in Overbrook Meadows' downtown area. It was dimly lit and always packed. On Tuesday nights, the city's best spoken word artists gathered for open mic and slam events.

"I remember," Daniel said.

"There was this guy," Jewell went on. "I liked all of his poems, but one of 'em creeped me out. It was called, '*I Know Fear*.' You remember that?"

Daniel shook his head.

Jewell stole a mushroom from his plate. "It was about this man who killed somebody, and he started having a hard time with it, whenever he went to sleep or when it was dark. The poem was about how he knew what fear was, for the first time ever – 'cause of all this stuff that was happening. It was a good poem. You said you liked it."

"So, that what's happening with you?" Daniel asked.

Jewell nodded. "I never thought nothing like that would happen to me. I don't *see things*, like some people say they do. I never been scary before. But today, in the shower, I thought he was in there with me. I knew he wasn't, but at the time, I don't know what came over me. You couldn't convince me he wasn't standing *right there*, by the toilet. I was home by myself, and I knew it wasn't you, so I just ran." She looked away and sighed. "I'm stupid. I know."

Daniel reached across the table and held her hand. "You not stupid."

Jewell rolled her eyes. "You just saying that 'cause you want some."

Daniel grinned. "I *do* want some, but I'm serious. See, what you got going on is what white people call a *conscious*."

Jewell giggled.

"If you didn't feel bad," Daniel said, "You'd be a *monster*. I love you for who you are: You strong, but you also weak. You smart, but sometimes you silly. You brave, but sometimes you scared, too."

"You forgot *crazy*," Jewell said. "I really thought somebody was in the bathroom with me."

"Was you watching the news a lot?" Daniel asked.

Jewell looked away innocently.

Daniel shook his head. "You'll be alright," he promised. "Long as you not scared to go to the bathroom again."

Jewell giggled. "No. I'm not." She put her napkin down. "I gotta go to the bathroom right now, as a matter of fact."

"Can I go?" Daniel asked.

"Go where?"

"With you."

"Yeah right," Jewell said. But when she got up, Daniel did too.

"Where you going?" she asked.

"I thought we was going to the bathroom."

"Are you serious?"

He nodded. "Yeah, pretty much..."

"Alright, come on," Jewell said, thinking they were going to use the facilities separately. But when they got to the washrooms, Daniel grabbed her wrist and yanked her into the men's lavatory with him. Before Jewell could scream or resist, he led her into one of the stalls and locked it behind them.

"*What are you-*"

He put a finger to her lips and put his other hand on her back. He pulled her to him until their bodies touched.

"You can't talk. You're in the boy's bathroom," he whispered.

Jewell's eyes were wide. Her heart raced.

"What are you doing?" she whispered.

"Shhh." Daniel shook his head. "You still too loud. You got stockings on?"

She nodded.

Daniel dropped to his knees. He lifted her dress and ducked his head underneath. Jewell stood stiffly, on trembling legs. The restroom was empty, and it was clean, but still...

She felt Daniel's hands on her hips. He groped around until he found the waistband, and then he pulled her panties and stockings down together. Jewell was obliged to slip off her shoes. Daniel put the pumps on the toilet's tank behind her and then rolled the stockings off her feet. He balled them up with the panties and reached between her legs to drop them in the toilet.

He stood and faced her again. Jewell's chest rose and fell. Daniel's did too. He kissed her as he unbuttoned his pants. Jewell reached between his legs to see if he was serious. He was *serious*. He let his pants fall around his ankles.

"Switch with me," he said.

Jewell was too shocked to argue. He put his hands on her waist, and they turned in the small space with short steps. When Daniel had his back to the toilet, he let the seat down and sat on top of it. His slid his hands up Jewell's legs and gave her ass a nice squeeze. He pulled her closer. His penis poked up at her, big, brown, and inviting. Jewell couldn't resist. She hiked up her dress and eased down onto him.

She put her hands on his shoulders and stared into his eyes. Daniel kept his hands on her hips, caressing and directing her movements. Jewell gasped as she took him in deeper. She leaned forward with her mouth ajar. She whispered in his ear.

"Why are we in *here*?"

"Cause *bitches* are *snitches*," Daniel replied. "Boys don't care."

And once again Dapper Dan was right. Just a few minutes into their escapade, the door opened and an unseen customer walked into the bathroom with them. Jewell froze, but Daniel was just getting started. He put his hands under her armpits and was strong enough to raise and lower her, so the stroking never stopped. Finally Jewell threw caution to the wind and worked it out herself.

She stared into Daniel's eyes, and he watched hers. Her breaths quickened. The friction from their hips sounded thunderous. Jewell shook her head in disbelief, but she kept getting wetter. Daniel grinned.

On the way out, their visitor let it be known he was aware of their activities but was not condemning them. "Right on," he said, and exited with a chuckle.

"Right on," Daniel whispered.

Jewell laughed. *"Ooh, right on,"* she cooed.

≈ ≈ ≈ ≈ ≈ ≈ ≈

When they left the restroom, Daniel dropped two Ben Franklins on the table to pay for their meal. He grabbed his jacket from the chair, and they scooted out of the restaurant post-haste.

Half a mile down the road, Jewell pulled into a McDonalds' parking lot.

"Damn, girl. You still hungry?" Daniel asked.

"I still gotta *pee,*" Jewell said. "You didn't let me go to the bathroom!"

≈ ≈ ≈ ≈ ≈ ≈ ≈

On the way home they met with Daniel's inside man at the airport again. Harvey had three brand new security guard uniforms for them, shoes included. They were perfect, only missing the badges and access cards. Harvey also had a photograph of the mark Jewell was supposed to seduce. He was big and black and ugly, but still better looking than Percy Hamilton.

Jewell had no qualms about the role she had to play in the airport job.

≈ ≈ ≈ ≈ ≈ ≈ ≈

On Friday evening they attended Miss Eveline Cynthia Hunt's wake.

On Saturday afternoon they went to her funeral. Jewell thought her mother never looked more peaceful.

CHAPTER NINETEEN
SLIM'S NEW FRIENDS

Five days before the airport job, Jewell awakened one morning to an odd sense of *airiness*. She never slept without a sheet or blanket, but her feet were definitely exposed to the morning cold. Her legs were too, now that she thought about it. And what the hell was – *oh*.

Jewell was lying on her stomach, but she didn't need to roll over to know what was going on. She felt Daniel on top of her. He had her panties pulled down to her knees and was attempting a crude penetration from behind.

Jewell opened her eyes and smiled. She kept her face in the pillow and pretended to be asleep – just to see how far it would go. Without her participation, Daniel was at a dead *end*, literally, but he kept trying (*bless his heart*).

Just when Jewell was about to roll over and tell him how busted and silly he was, an awful thought flashed in her mind.

What if it's not Daniel?

But that was ignorant. Jewell reminded herself of how she was wrong when she had her little episode in the shower a week ago. But that reminder did very little ease her mind.

And now that she was thinking about Percy again, she could imagine the whole scene: The creep hovered over her, straddling her with a butt cheek in one hand and his penis in the other. His face was still split like a spent fire cracker. His lip hung dumbly. His drool was like the juice on a butcher's cutting board.

Jewell closed her eyes hard and tried to force the thoughts from her mind, but they wouldn't go away.

What's wrong with me? she wondered. Deep down she knew Percy was not in her house. He was dead, buried a few days ago according to the papers. And Jewell was a realist. She believed in facts and numbers, evolution over creationism. Dead people simply *do not* come back to haunt the living. Every psychic who has ever said he could communicate with ghosts was a *goddamned liar.*

But still...

Sick thoughts filled her head like a cerebral bleed.

It is him! Maybe the first time was a false alarm, but it's him for sure now. Daniel wouldn't violate you in your sleep like this, and you know those aren't Daniel's hands! They're **different***. He's going to rape you, and when you get pregnant, your baby will be dead because the father was dead too...*

Stop it! Jewell pleaded with herself. She knew arguing with her inner voice was the first step towards insanity, but she was going crazy either way.

Please, just stop.

Her eyes were wide open now, close to tears. She felt like a child again, struggling to come to terms with the monster who lived under her bed and sometimes took furloughs in the closet. As she got older, Jewell came to understand that she would never find the boogeyman in her bedroom, but even during her middle school years she still had to check some nights – just to be sure. Jewell tried to remember when she finally stopped checking her closet. Right now it felt like she never really did.

She gathered her nerves and rolled over quickly, sweat glistening on her face and chest. She propped herself up on her elbows and stared at Daniel like she never met him. Even seeing his face didn't calm her down because Percy's features were superimposed over his. It took a few seconds for this illusion to fade away.

Daniel cocked his head and watched her with a confused expression. Jewell backed away from him, pulling the sheets over her body.

"What's wrong with you?" he asked.

She shook her head.

"You had a bad dream?"

She nodded.

"Well, what's wrong, baby? Can't you talk?"

She shivered. "I can talk."

"Was it fat boy again?"

Jewell almost told him Percy wasn't *fat*. As a matter of fact, he was on the *super deluxe* weight loss plan thanks to her:

No eating, no drinking and *no breathing* until you're down to skin and bones! Call now! Snipers are standing by.

She nodded.

Daniel pulled up his pants and scooted up on the mattress. He sat next to her with his back against the headboard. He put an arm around her, and Jewell laid her head on his bare chest. Daniel wore only pajama bottoms. His erection was still fierce.

"I'm going crazy," Jewell said.

Daniel shook his head. "When you think about that dude, is it *sexual*?"

Jewell was taken aback. She and Daniel were often on the same page, but as far as she knew, he wasn't a mind-reader. She nodded nervously.

Daniel nodded too. "I took some classes at the community college," he said.

This was news to his girlfriend. "When did you go to college?"

"When I was eighteen," Daniel said. "Right after high school."

"You never told me about that."

"I only went for one semester. Actually I didn't even finish that. I don't go around announcing my short-comings."

"*Short-comings*? *Please*." Jewell smirked. "Going to college ain't a short-coming, no matter how long you stayed there. What was your major?"

Daniel grinned. "I didn't have a major."

"What'd you take?"

"I studied psychology," he said.

"You wanted to be a *psychiatrist*?"

"Naw," Daniel said. "I wanted to be a *pimp*."

"Oh my God."

"Naw, seriously. I didn't know any pimps when I was coming up. I knew what pimping *was*, and I knew I wanted to be one, but all of my pimping knowledge came from TV. I kept hearing it was, like, ninety percent mental, so I went to school."

There was no end to Daniel's oddities.

"Okay," Jewell said with a frown. "Hurry up and tell me what this has to do with my dream."

"Oh yeah," Daniel said. "I think what you're going through was triggered by that killing."

Duh, Jewell thought.

"But more than that," Daniel went on, "you got a lot of underlying issues with men and sex because of your line of work. You get through all of your jobs pretty good, and it don't seem like it's any harm done, but deep inside it hurts you when you play around with your sexuality like that."

Jewell was stunned.

"I think all of that buried stress and pain is coming out," Daniel went on. "See, when that guy comes in your dreams, he doesn't want to kill you, does he?"

Jewell shook her head.

"He wants to have sex with you, right?"

She nodded, listening intently.

"All this time you been setting men up, you never felt guilty," Daniel deduced. "But that killing was different. You *knew* that was wrong. This is probably the first time you ever accepted the fact that what you did was wrong. Your conscious is manifesting your guilt sexually because deep inside you know all of that other stuff was wrong too."

Jewell shook her head. "What the hell, man? Who are you? What are you doing in my bed?"

Daniel laughed. "I told you, you're fucking with a genius."

Jewell stared into his eyes, still lost in his explanation. "So, how do I make it stop?"

"It's hard," Daniel warned. "First you have to accept that you're an evil person."

"I'm not *evil*."

"Told you it was hard."

"But I'm *not* evil."

He shook his head.

"Don't look at me like that," Jewell said. "You're the one who's evil."

He smiled. "I *know* I'm evil. That's why I can sleep at night."

"I'm serious."

"I'm serious too, baby. If you wanna stop having bad dreams, you need to come to terms with who you are."

"But I don't wanna be evil."

"That's the *second* step," Daniel said. "You have to repent and turn away from your sins."

"But you didn't repent. And you *damned sure* haven't turned away from any sins."

"That's 'cause I'm cool with who I am," Daniel said and grinned. "See, we both evil, but you just said you don't wanna be evil. That's called *inner turmoil*."

Jewell sighed. "You didn't learn all of that in one semester."

"I read a few books on my own."

"I'm for real, baby, I need help."

He gave her a straight face. "You don't plan on stealing nothing else after we do this last job, right?"

"Naw. Why would I?"

"You won't have to," Daniel agreed. "You won't have to set up no more tricks, you won't have to steal, and you won't have to hurt nobody else. When you not doing bad shit no more, you'll be able to live life as the good person you are, on the inside."

"And no more bad dreams?"

"Not like the ones you having now."

Jewell smiled, and then she remembered she had one more trick to set up. "This job I do tonight is definitely my last one."

Daniel lifted her shirt and bent to kiss her belly button. "You pregnant yet?" he asked.

"I don't know," Jewell said with a smile.

He lifted the sheets and pulled her panties the rest of the way off. "If you help me this time, we might be able to get our little boy started."

Jewell grinned and licked her lips. "You the crazy one trying to have sex with an unconscious body. And at that restaurant last week... *You a freak*."

"That's what you like about me," Daniel said, and he mounted like he wanted his baby right then.

Forty minutes later Jewell would swear he wanted *twins*.

≈≈≈≈≈≈≈

Daniel left at ten o'clock. Jewell wouldn't see him again until four p.m., when the gang had their first formal meeting since Davis' untimely departure. Jewell was instructed to pick up Slim and bring him with her so Miles could take the picture for his airport ID card.

JEWELL AND THE DAPPER DAN

After the meeting, Jewell would embark on her solo mission: *Operation Access Card.* The plan was already set. When Harvey got off work this evening, he would take the mark to a west side bar for drinks at happy hour. They usually went to a strip club, but Daniel thought a more formal setting would make Jewell's job easier.

She would walk through the doors alone at approximately 6:15, looking more delectable than anything the Coco Lounge had to offer. Jewell planned to get the mark's attention and make him come to her. If he was reluctant, Harvey would steer him in Jewell's direction.

Jewell was prepared to go wherever she had to go and do whatever she had to do to get the access card off the mark's lapel. She expected to call Daniel with a *Mission accomplished* announcement no later than nine p.m.

≈ ≈ ≈ ≈ ≈ ≈

To pass the time alone, Jewell read her favorite Donald Goines' novel, *Daddy Cool.* Technically she could have left the house if she wanted to. Her picture wasn't in the paper anymore, and so far none of Percy's hired guns had come forward. But Daniel didn't think her anonymity would last much longer. Sooner or later one of Percy's goons would get arrested for something unrelated. To lessen his charges, he'd offer information on one of the city's most notorious slayings.

The police would go looking for Vanessa Hardgraves again, but by then Jewell expected to be out of the state with her dapper boyfriend. They would be fifty million dollars richer and hopefully raising a child like *normal* parents. And it wouldn't be easy, but Jewell was prepared to never wear another diamond.

≈ ≈ ≈ ≈ ≈ ≈

At two-thirty she put on her most flattering cocktail dress. It was black with spaghetti straps, stretchy fabric and a low neckline. From her vast wig collection, Jewell selected a mop that made her look like Christina Milian. It was long and wavy, fiery like the sunset over the Santa Monica Pier.

She wore no jewelry, say a silver ankle bracelet that brought attention to her second favorite pair of Monolo sandals. Jewell didn't normally wear makeup, but tonight she was *Tasha Murphy*, and Tasha liked red lipstick with a little blush and eye shadow.

Before she left the house, Jewell checked her purse to make sure she had everything she needed. Her coach bag contained a fake access card, a pair of wire cutters, two GHB pills and a mouse gun (a .32 ACP Derringer – in case things went *terribly* wrong).

She left the house feeling confident, but still a little on edge. Every mark she set up was different, but so far she never had a problem getting them in position for manipulation. According to Murphy's Law, an upset was long overdue.

≈ ≈ ≈ ≈ ≈ ≈ ≈

She made it to Slim's apartment at a quarter after three. Jewell's first moment of apprehension came when Slim didn't answer the door himself. A Mexican guy opened it for her. He was about thirty-five years old, dark-skinned and long-haired. He didn't look positively *high*, but *addict* was the first impression he gave Jewell.

He stared at her with uncertainty, and Jewell returned the look.

"Who the hell are you?" she asked.

"I'm, I'm Marcos," he said. "I was on my way out."

Jewell stood with her hands on her hips, her head cocked and a sneer on her face. She didn't move out of the way, so Marcos slipped by her, heading down the stairs she just climbed. Jewell watched until he was out of sight and then pushed the apartment door open. Slim stood in the living room wearing jeans with no shirt or shoes. He smiled at his sister and stepped around the couch to greet her.

"Hey, Jewell! What's going on?"

She stepped in without responding. Jewell's look of scorn grew deeper when she saw that he had *another* visitor, this one was a blonde female with dirty hair and gaunt features. In her peripheral, Jewell saw that Slim's apartment had changed in other ways: He had an entertainment center now, a couple pictures on the walls and a used dining table with four mediocre chairs.

But more than anything else, Jewell saw the skank. She couldn't take her eyes off her.

"Uh, Jewell?" Slim approached her hesitantly. Jewell turned and burned holes in him with her eyes.

"We're supposed to be leaving," she said as calmly as possible.

"Uh, okay," Slim said. "I was getting ready right now." He looked innocent and curious about what might be bothering her, but Jewell knew that routine well.

"Well go get ready," she said.

Slim looked from his sister to his female friend. "I'll be back," he told them both and took off in the direction of the bedroom.

Jewell walked round the couch and sat down – never taking her eyes off the girl in the loveseat. The stranger sat up straighter and looked around anxiously. When her eyes came back to Jewell, she saw that Slim's sister was still watching her. Jewell's expression was far from friendly.

"Hi. I'm Amy," the stranger said. Amy was petite; her black jeans no more than a size two. She wore white sneakers with no socks and a black tee shirt that was too big. She didn't have on any makeup. Her skin was pasty white. Jewell had never seen anything so disgusting.

"What the fuck you doing over here, *Amy*?" she asked. "Bitch, you getting high with Slim?"

Amy shook her head, her mouth working faster than her brain. "No, I, we don't, I..."

"*Get the fuck out of here*," Jewell growled.

Amy hesitated, looking from Jewell to Slim's room and then back again.

Jewell stood with the quickness of a panther. "Bitch you better..."

Amy jumped up like there was a fire and made it out of the front door in 2.2 seconds flat. Jewell sat her purse on the couch before going to her brother's room. Her derringer only held four shots, and she didn't want to waste one on Slim's sorry ass. She stomped down the hallway, already in full tantrum mode.

"You ain't got the sense God gave a flea! What the hells is wrong with you?"

Slim turned, slipping a tee shirt over his head. He had more furniture in the bedroom too; a queen-sized bed, a dresser, and another small television.

"What? What I do?"

"You couldn't wait *two weeks*?" Jewell asked. "*Two weeks*, Slim? Damn, why do you have to do this *every time*? Can't you ever do right?"

"Do what, Jewell? What I do?"

"Let me see your arms." She grabbed one, and Slim snatched it back roughly.

"What are you doing? *Why you tripping?* What I do?"

"You're in here getting high!"

"No I'm not!" he spat. "Why do you keep accusing me of stuff?" He was mad, but Jewell was hot lava.

"Don't give me that shit. You got a house full of dopefiends!"

"What *dopefiends*, Jewell? Everybody I hang around is not a *dopefiend*. Shit, I can't have regular friends?"

"Those weren't *regular friends*!" Jewell barked. "You can't tell me that ho's not on drugs."

"Why?" Slim asked. "'Cause she not all pretty, with nice clothes and stuff? Maybe I can't get a girl who looks good and smells good. You ever think of that?"

"Don't try to play me."

"I get lonely too, Jewell! I know she don't look like somebody you'd hang out with, but I take what I can get sometimes. She likes me, and that's enough."

"She's twenty years old, Slim. You're fucking *forty*! You can't tell me that bitch wants anything to do with you if drugs aren't involved."

"She stay around here," Slim said. "She poor, like everybody else. I got some money. I got a job, my own place. I ain't doing that bad. I know I'm ugly, but I can take care of a broad."

"Is that what you're doing with the money Daniel gave you, tricking with these ho's?"

"*Daniel* gave me that money, not *you*! And he didn't tell me what I can and can't spend it on. I bought some shit for the apartment, and I'm *not* getting high! I done been in the penitentiary damned near all my life, Jewell. Done lost everything! I'm forty-four years old, and my heart will prolly give out when I'm fifty. If I wanna be with a female, *so what?* I don't have nothing else, can't I at least get some head? I ain't hurting nobody."

Jewell thought he sounded more pitiful than Mike Tyson, but she was still not convinced. "Let me see your arms."

He flashed them with a lot of attitude, but Jewell took her time inspecting them. There was nothing. There was no sign of heroin in his eyes either. She let him go, and Slim breathed down on her angrily with his lip curled.

"I don't care if you're mad," Jewell said. "You fucked up a lot in your lifetime. You got a track record, and you just have to live with that."

Slim didn't say anything.

Jewell didn't like being on the receiving end of his aggression. "If you don't like it, you can bail out right now. We can find somebody else."

That was a lie, but Slim didn't know that. He backed down. His posture wilted like a flower. "I still wanna be in."

"Don't be getting an attitude when I ask you questions then," Jewell said. "'Cause I'm *not gon' stop*. This is too much money to have you fuck it up."

"Alright," Slim said.

"Who was that man?" Jewell asked.

"That's Marcos. He's my homeboy."

"He get high?"

"He just smoke weed."

Jewell stared into his eyes but didn't think he was lying. "Come on," she said. "Everybody waiting on us."

She left his bedroom, and Slim followed with his head hanging.

When they got in the car, he tried to smooth things over with a technique that always worked on his little sister.

"You look real pretty," he said.

"Thank you," Jewell said with a slight smile. "I do look good, don't I?"

≈≈≈≈≈≈≈

Located on the southwest side of town, close to the intersection of Alta Mesa and McCart, was a large complex called the Polo Fields Apartments. Back when Jewell and Daniel's relationship was blossoming, and the syndicate was just a twinkle in Dapper Dan's eye, the lovers rented a one bedroom unit there. They signed the lease as Mr. and Mrs. Finney; newlyweds fresh off their honeymoon.

Some five years later, Daniel still paid the rent for apartment 112 every month. At just $4,200 a year, this was the gang's cheapest hideaway by far. It was also the easiest to maintain. There was no trash to take out, no lawn to mow and no nosey mailman to worry about because Daniel had a secured box set up at the post office around the corner.

And because of the Finney's odd work hours, Daniel gave the landlord permission to enter their apartment any time he pleased for exterminations and other maintenance needs. The last time Daniel renewed the lease, they said he and his wife were the best tenants they ever had: The Finneys never had a complaint from the neighbors, were never late with the rent, and their carpet still looked showroom fresh.

Jewell pulled into a parking spot next to Jesse's Camaro and scanned the scene.

"Who stay here?" Slim asked.

"We do," Jewell said, staring out at a distant memory. "This is Safe House number *1*."

≈≈≈≈≈≈

When they got upstairs, Miles answered the door with his digital camera in hand. He wore a blue golf shift with canvas shorts and flip flops. He smiled at Jewell and offered Slim a hand to shake.

"Hey guys! You look really nice, Jewell."

She was surprised by his cheery attitude, but fifty million dollars will do that to people.

"Hey, Miles."

Slim shook his hand respectfully. "Hello, sir."

Daniel stood in the living room with his back against a blank wall. He wore his new security uniform complete with jacket, slacks, and shoes. With his bald head and military stripes on his shoulder, Jewell's first impression was that he looked like a Navy man. But since his badge clearly read SECURITY, the military mystique faded, leaving her man looking a bit *square*. Jewell stepped to him and put her arms around his waist.

"You look handsome."

"I look like a lame," he said and kissed her on the mouth. "What's up, Slim?" he called over her shoulder.

Slim closed the door behind himself and swayed on uncertain legs. "Hello. How you doing, sir?"

"I got your uniform," Daniel said, pointing to a stuffed paper bag on the couch. "Why don't you go try that on?..."

"Jesse's in there," Miles said.

"No, I'm out," Jesse said. He stepped into the living room still tucking in his shirt. "What's up, everybody," he said. His eyes got stuck on Jewell for a second. "Damn, you look *good*!"

She smiled. "This is my *fifty-million dollar* dress."

Daniel held her arm up while she did a little twirl.

Jesse liked that a lot. "I'd give up anything you wanted," he teased.

When they first met, Jesse had a serious crush on Jewell. But before he made any moves, Daniel let it be known that Jewell was not just another female he was bringing along for the job. She was his *woman*, which meant messing with her was just as bad as messing with Daniel's money. Jesse quit his advances, but every now and then he got caught up in her beauty.

"Is this it right here?" Slim asked, picking up his bag.

"Yeah," Daniel said. "That's all you."

Slim took his garments and headed for the restroom.

"What was he up to?" Daniel asked when he was out of the room.

"He bought some furniture," Jewell reported. "He had some friends over there when I picked him up, but everything looked cool."

Daniel nodded. Miles watched them with obvious dread in his eyes.

Daniel sighed. "What's wrong *now*, Miles?"

Miles shook his head and spoke quietly. "So no one else is going to say anything?" He looked around and found no support.

"Say what?" Jewell asked.

Miles shrugged. "Fine. I'll be the one. I know you're all thinking it, but I'll be the one to say it."

"Say *what*?" Daniel asked.

"I don't know or trust that guy," Miles said, throwing a thumb in the direction Slim had gone.

"*Goddammit*," Daniel said, speaking softly like Miles. "We're doing this job in less than a week, and you want to come with thi–"

"I didn't say I was backing out," Miles said. "I'm just telling you I don't trust him. The last time we used him, he got high and almost messed us up."

"We're watching him," Daniel assured. "He's not getting high. I gave him a thousand dollars last week, and he's still straight."

"Yeah but, if you have to *watch him*," Miles noted, "that means you don't trust him either. Why are we using someone like that on our most important job?"

"You didn't want to help kill that boy," Daniel reminded. "Neither did you, Jesse."

"I'm not saying anything," Jesse said quickly.

"I told Slim if he helped with that killing, he could get in on the big job," Daniel said. "I aims to keep my word."

"He's your responsibility then," Miles said. "I don't trust him. I'm saying that right now. If you keep him, anything he does is on you."

Daniel nodded. "Cool."

"Alright," Miles said. "Then we're through with it." He smiled and brought the camera to his face again. "You ready for your picture?" he asked Jesse.

≈≈≈≈≈≈≈

Miles had his laptop, digital printer and laminating machine set up at the apartment already. He loaded Jesse's, Slim's and Daniel's pictures onto the computer and used a Photoshop program to duplicate the blank ID card Harvey provided them. Jewell watched his every move, growing more and more awed by his technical prowess. In twenty minutes he had the cards ready for lamination. Ten minutes after that, the new badges were complete.

Miles put a hole in them with a slot punch and affixed three reels he got from Wal-Mart. When he was done, the finished product was above reproach. Even under close examination, Daniel could find no flaws.

"Now all we need is that access card," Miles said.

Everyone looked at Jewell, and she looked at her watch. It was a quarter till six.

"I guess I'd better go," she said.

Slim gave her a worried look. Jesse did too.

Daniel took his security jacket off and laid it on the couch. "Come on," he said. "I'll walk you out." He grabbed her hand, and they exited the apartment like the regular couple she longed to be.

"Be careful," Slim called after them.

"Yeah," Jesse said. "Be careful, Jewell. We're counting on you."

Once outside, Jewell wrapped both arms around her man, and they walked down the stairs awkwardly, like he was going off to war.

"You got everything?" he asked when they reached her car.

"Yeah."

"Let me see."

Jewell handed over her purse, and Daniel pawed through it like a bear digging in a picnic basket.

"What are these for?" he asked, holding up the wire cutters.

"I was gonna use those if it was hard to get off."

He shook his head and put the tool in his back pocket. "Uhn, uhn. You can't *cut* it off. Think about it, baby."

Jewell sighed.

"You can't *shoot him* either," Daniel said.

"That's just for an emergency," Jewell said.

"Emergency like what?"

"Like if he catches me."

"If he catches you, you need to apologize and give his card back," Daniel lectured. "We can wait awhile and find another mark if you don't get it. But if you shoot him, the card's no good and everybody'll be more careful next time." He didn't take the gun from her though, and Jewell was glad for that.

"You got those pills?" he asked.

"Yeah."

Daniel nodded. "Put his ass to sleep, baby. That's yo best bet."

"Okay."

Daniel wrapped his arms around her and squeezed hard.

"I wish I could do it for you," he said.

"Just don't forget your call," Jewell reminded.

Daniel said he wouldn't, and Jewell got in the Chrysler by herself. Daniel watched her back up, and he didn't head back upstairs until she rounded the corner out of sight.

Jewell never felt so alone.

CHAPTER TWENTY
JEWELL'S SOLO MISSION

The Coco Lounge was a combination night club and sports bar located on the west side of town. The patrons were generally white collar/middle class types, but it wasn't uncommon to see a few soiled and exhausted construction workers throwing a few back before heading home to their nagging wives and needy children. On Saturday evenings the manager brought in a band and packed the establishment to near capacity.

But this was a Thursday night, and the place was half empty. Jewell spotted the mark as soon as she walked through the doors. He sat at the bar with his back to the main entrance. Daniel's contact sat next to him, but Harvey was half-turned on his stool so he could watch the whole place. That was an amateur move. Jewell was definitely going to make her presence known. She didn't need that idiot making it so obvious, but such is life.

Harvey saw her when she walked in, so Jewell didn't get her first drink from the bar as she planned. Instead she took a seat at one of the far tables and waited for a waitress to come to her.

Harvey watched her for a second, and then he turned away without nodding or winking. Jewell was glad for that. Maybe he wasn't so stupid after all.

She checked her watch, and it was exactly 6:15 p.m. Jewell looked around as if waiting for someone, but she kept her eye on the mark at all times. He was a big guy, about Daniel's height and build with a little extra fat. He was dark-skinned with short hair and broad shoulders. Whenever he threw his head back in laughter, a fold of fat formed on the back of his neck. Jewell thought it looked like a plump sausage.

There were approximately forty people in the club. Most were white and most were men. Jewell was the *only* black female, and this worked to her advantage. According to Harvey, the mark never had eyes for blondes or red-heads.

Jewell leaned back in her seat and crossed her long legs. She checked her watch again and shook her head as if frustrated.

At 6:17 a waitress came to take her drink order. Jewell asked if a man named Tony had come by or called. The waitress said he hadn't, but she'd look out for him.

At 6:25 Jewell finished her first drink. She checked her watch again and sighed loudly. She crossed her arms over her chest and looked seriously annoyed. Harvey pointed her out to the mark for the first time, and they made a few vulgar remarks while admiring her physique. Jewell looked the other way, pretending not to notice, but she lowered her arms so her breasts remained in full view.

She heard the mark say something like, *Got-damn!*

Without looking *right at him*, Jewell studied his features intently. The mark had a slightly protruding brow, bushy eyebrows, and a flat nose. His lips were big, and his teeth were too. When he smiled, it looked like he had someone else's dentures in his mouth.

At exactly six thirty Jewell heard a phone ringing behind the bar. She waited forty seconds, and the bartender began to look around the room.

"Is there a Tasha here?" he asked loudly. "I got a call for Tasha!"

"That's me," Jewell shouted. She stood and all eyes swam in her direction. She walked up to the bar and stood on the mark's left side. He watched her like she was in a pageant.

"I'm Tasha," she said.

"I got a call for you," the bartender said. "Are you expecting someone?"

"Yeah, and he'd better not be standing me up."

The bartender shrugged and handed her the telephone. The cord was long enough, but Jewell leaned fully on the bar, giving the mark a nice look at her breasts and an even better look at her ass. Her skirt rose almost to her panty line.

The mark's jaw dropped. He gave Harvey an elbow without looking away. Harvey leaned back and chuckled.

Jewell put the phone to her ear. "Hello?"

"What you doing?" Daniel asked.

"I'm doing great," Jewell said. That meant the mark was there, and she was in position. "What are you calling for when you supposed to be here?" she asked. That was for the mark.

"Is Harvey there too?" Daniel asked.

"Of course I was here on time," Jewell said. That meant *yes*. "Why can't *you* ever be on time?"

"Is he watching you now?" Daniel asked.

"*Yes!*" Jewell said. "I'm not going through this with you anymore, Tony. I'm sick of giving you chances!"

The bartender backed away shaking his head.

The mark couldn't take his eyes off Jewell's butt. He didn't care if he got caught staring, but Jewell continued to ignore him. She saw Harvey grinning in her peripheral.

"You feeling good about it?" Daniel asked.

"What do you think?" Jewell said. That meant *yes*. "You know what, *fuck you*, Tony. You're wasting my goddamned time!"

"I love you, baby," Daniel said.

"*Fuck you*," Jewell said. She put the phone down and slid it across the bar. "I'm through with that."

The barkeep had long, blonde hair and a scraggily goatee. He tried to hide a smile as he hung it up. "You alright?" he asked.

"Nothing a couple of shots won't fix," Jewell said. She reached into her purse but knew she wouldn't have to pull out any money.

"What you drinking?" the mark asked.

Jewell gave him her full attention for the first time. He had a nice haircut and his teeth weren't as big as they looked from across the room. He had smooth hands with clean fingernails, but the only thing Jewell *really* saw was his ID card. It was an exact replica of the ones Miles made a couple hours ago. Behind his picture was another card Jewell recognized. The access card twinkled like white gold.

"Tequila," she said. "My name's Tasha."

The mark took her hand and held it softly. "I'm Winston."

"I'm going to the bathroom," Harvey said. Jewell didn't acknowledge him. From all outward signs, she was totally lost in Winston's eyes.

≈ ≈ ≈ ≈ ≈ ≈

Operation Access Card got off to a smashing start. Winton bought the *jilted lover* act fish line and sinker. By the time Harvey got out of the bathroom, his co-worker was overwhelming Jewell with condolences. Harvey took his beer to the pool tables and started up a game with a crowd of rowdy college students. Winston didn't even notice he was gone. When Jewell wanted to play pool (get away from the nosey bartender), Harvey switched places with them and went back to the bar.

All in all, Winston bought her four tequila shots and two Long Island iced teas. With the liquor in her system, Jewell wanted to dance. The mark did too. Winston was hesitant at first, but after a few songs he had his hands all over her like Daniel liked to do. Jewell wanted to cry. She wanted to scream and vomit, but every time his badge brushed her skin she got a renewed boost of motivation.

She almost lost it when he kissed her on the mouth, but Jewell was a trooper. She hitched up her britches and took one for the team. He didn't get his tongue in, and that had to be considered a *minor* victory.

At 8:45 Harvey came to their table to say he was leaving. Winston didn't give a damn. Harvey wished him a happy vacation and nodded at Jewell behind the mark's back. Jewell gritted her teeth and cursed his immaturity, but it was all good. His job was done, and it was all up to her now.

At 9:00 Jewell got her first shock when she told Winston she wanted to leave. He was a big time freak on the dance floor, but now he wanted to go back to being a gentleman.

"Is it alright if I get your number, Tasha? I sure would like to see you again."

She batted her eyes. "You can see me again *right now*."

"I, uh." He blinked quickly. "I don't want you to think–"

Jewell put a finger to his lips. "We both grown. If you want me, you don't have to be shy. We ain't nothing but animals."

Winston liked that. He smiled and she could see his canines. "You wanna get a room?" he asked.

"See. That wasn't so hard, was it?"

≈ ≈ ≈ ≈ ≈ ≈

But it was.

They got a suite at the Ramada, and Winston immediately began to show Jewell just what an *animal* he was. As soon as she sat her purse on the bed, he grabbed her arms from behind and shoved her forward. The mattress was soft, but Jewell was pissed. She rolled onto her back, and he was already coming, unbuckling his pants on the way.

"*Wait!*" She sat up and shoved him in the chest. He didn't budge one inch. Her size was hardly ever a hindrance, but Jewell was suddenly aware of the hundred plus pounds she gave up to this guy.

"Calm down, man! *What the fuck?*" she shrieked.

Winston laughed. "My bad. But haven't you ever wanted to do it like that? Like *Fatal Attraction*; just tearing off clothes and shit?"

"*No!*" Jewell said. "Not with *you.* I don't know you like that. You scared me."

"I'm sorry," Winston said. He rubbed his hands together like he was staring at a Lobster platter. "I just want you, *bad.* We can take it slow, though." He dropped to his knees and reached under her skirt. "You want me to eat you?"

"*No!*" Jewell blocked his hands and scooted back quickly. She kicked a leg over his head and jumped out of the bed.

Winston's smile fell as he watched her. His eyes narrowed by degrees.

"Dude, *take it easy*," Jewell said. "We got the room all night. What are you in such a rush for?"

He stood. "I'm sorry, baby. I thought you wanted it like that."

"No. I don't. I want to listen to some music, drink a little." She smiled. "I ain't going nowhere."

Winston didn't smile back at her. "I got a woman," he said. "I can't be in here all night."

Jewell cursed Harvey's very existence. Finding a *single* mark was ninety percent of the deal. How could he get that wrong?

"How long can you stay?" she asked.

"About thirty minutes."

Jewell's face fell. She tried not to let it show, but it did. Winston saw the disappointment in her eyes, and he didn't like it. Not one bit.

"What kind of games are you playing?" he asked.

"I'm not playing games, baby. I just thought we'd have more time together."

"Alright, well, we don't. So we need to get down to it." He unbuttoned his pants and let them fall. His penis was big. *Porno* big. It pointed at her, like *Ah, ha. You're finally gonna get it this time!*

Jewell swallowed hard. He was closer to her purse than she was, but she had the date-rape pills in her bra. "Can we have a couple drinks first?"

Winston shook his head. "I don't want no more to drink. If you was bullshitting, tell me now. I ain't got time for games."

Jewell was scared, but she kept her eyes on the prize. "I'm not bullshitting. Are you gonna take your clothes off?"

"You take *your* clothes off," Winston said. His eyes were cold and unyielding.

"Why are you acting like this? What you mad at me for?"

His features softened a bit. "I just don't like being played with," he said. "You making me think you're full of games. You said you wanted to fuck. We get here, and you don't wanna fuck."

"I didn't say that."

"Then take off your clothes."

Jewell bent and removed her sandals.

Winston sat on the bed and took off his shoes.

Jewell pulled the cocktail dress over her head and Winston's smile came back in full flair. He unbuttoned his shirt and threw it on the bed behind him with the ID badge still attached. He sat there in only a tee shirt and socks, still closer to her gun than she was. Her phone was in that purse. As if to verify this, the damned thing started ringing.

Winston looked slowly to his right and then back at Jewell.

I remember when my heart broke, Keyshia Cole belted on the ringtone. *I remember when I gave up loving you...*

Jewell hesitated, as if she needed permission to answer it.

Winston looked at the purse again, and Jewell rushed to it, afraid he'd dig in it and find her gun and fake access card. She picked up her bag and removed her cellular. It was Yolanda. Jewell turned her back on Winston and took the call.

"Hello?"

"Hey, girl. What you doing?"

"I'm busy right now. Let me call you back."

"I just w–"

Jewell hung up and dropped the phone back inside her purse. Before she could turn back to Winston, she felt his hand on her arm. It was a hard hand, squeezing tight enough to break the skin, Jewell thought.

"What are you–"

He jerked her hard, spinning her in his direction. The purse flew from Jewell's hands and landed close to the front door. Winston was standing over her. He breathed roughly, his big chest rising and falling.

"I thought you didn't have no phone," he said.

"I didn't say I didn't have a phone! *Let me go! What are you doing?*" She tried to jerk away, but his grip was true. He grabbed her other arm just to be sure.

"*Let me go!*"

Jewell was trapped, but not defenseless. She knew a swift knee to his testicles would free her, but there would be no chance to get the card after that. She wouldn't abandon the job unless she absolutely had to.

"Your boyfriend called you at the bar," Winston recalled. "Why didn't he call your cell phone?"

"I don't know!" Jewell said. "*You're hurting me! Let go!*"

"I coulda got me some ass," the mark said. "I'm fucking around with you all night, spending all my money. You playing games, bitch."

"No, I'm not!"

"Then what the hell is it?"

"You're too big!" Jewell shrieked. It was the first thing that came to her mind, but she ran with it. "I can't take you in me. It won't fit."

Her adlib turned out to be a stroke of genius. It was something Winston had heard before, Jewell could see it in his eyes.

"Well, you gonna give me some head or *something.*"

Jewell noticed that wasn't a question. "Alright," she said. "Sit down."

Winston's smile came back again. He let go of her and took a few steps back. "I'm sorry," he said. "Bitches be running game so much. I didn't mean to hurt you."

Jewell rubbed her arms and sighed. "Sit down."

He did.

Jewell stepped between his legs and dropped to her knees. Winston lay back, but he propped himself up on his elbows so he could see her face.

"Why you looking at me?" she asked.

"I like to watch."

"I'm embarrassed," Jewell said. "Don't watch me."

She reached up and grabbed his pulsating erection. It was vile and disgusting and *huge*. A bit of vomit made it to the back of her throat, but Jewell swallowed it down without expression. She stroked him, squeezing gently. Winston moaned, and she could see the tension ooze from his body. Jewell opened her mouth and went for gold, but she stopped with her lips less than an inch away. She looked up and saw that he was still staring at her.

"For real," she said. "I can't do it if you watch me."

Winston sighed and lay flat on his back. He stared down his nose at her, but Jewell had him exactly where she wanted him. A long time ago, a prostitute named Bird told her it was possible to give a man a *hand job* and make him think he was getting bonafide fellatio. Jewell never thought she'd have to pull the move, but now was her time to shine.

She put her mouth over her hand and generated as much saliva as possible. Her nausea helped a lot. She spit into her hand quietly and started stroking when she had enough lubrication. She bobbed her head up and down with her fist, but her lips never went past her own thumb. She spat and stroked, spat and stroked. Winston didn't know the difference. He looked up once and was satisfied the rest of the way out.

Jewell started to cry halfway through. She wiped the tears with her free hand and tried to convince herself that it wasn't that bad since it wasn't really sex. And even if it was sex, it was still okay because her boyfriend condoned it.

But deep down she knew what she was. Whether it was for fifty dollars or fifty million, she was prostituting, and that made her a dirty whore. She didn't need the mark's hot semen on her chin to know that, but she got it anyway.

When she was done, Winston wanted to take a shower. He further humiliated Jewell by taking his wallet and car keys with him, but she could care less about his measly pocket change.

Jewell switched the access cards as soon as she heard the water start. She left the room before the mark made it out of the tub.

≈≈≈≈≈≈

When she got home, Daniel was near panic.
"What happened? Why didn't you call?"
Jewell handed him the plastic card and headed for the shower. He followed.
"Girl, what's wrong with you?"
He could see her arms better under the bathroom light. The bruises stood out like hickeys.
"What happened, baby? Tell me what happened!"
Jewell reached and turned the water on. "He wouldn't let me go till he got a nut."
"What happened? Y'all fucked? He *raped* you?"
"I just had to play with him," Jewell said numbly, "make him think I had it in my mouth."
Daniel grinned. "Is that it? Damn, girl, you made me think he *hurt* you." He shook his head, laughing. "This thing here is worth *fifty million dollars!*" he said, waving the card in her face. "You ain't happy?"
Jewell forced a smiled and nodded.
Daniel pulled a cell phone from his pocket and left the restroom dialing numbers.
"This is fifty million dollars, baby," he called over his shoulder. "You tripping."

≈≈≈≈≈≈

Jewell went to bed that night with doubts about her man for the first time since, *ever*.

CHAPTER TWENTY-ONE
REGARDING AMY

Jewell woke up early the next morning. Daniel found her in the living room watching Creflo Dollar on a Christian network. He sat next to her and plucked the remote from her lap. A moment later they were watching Stuart Scott on ESPN. Jewell got up, heading for the kitchen where she had a grapefruit waiting. Daniel grabbed her arm and pulled her back to the sofa.

"*What*?" she said, yanking her arm away from him.

Daniel cocked his head and stared at her. He wore only boxers this morning. His chest looked massive. His arms were equally formidable.

"What's wrong with you?" he asked after a few seconds.

"Nothing."

"Why you up so early?"

Jewell shrugged. "I just am."

"You had a bad dream?"

She shook her head.

He reached up and slapped her playfully. "Why you looking like that, all mad and stuff?"

Jewell knocked his hand away with much more force than was necessary. "Get your hand off of me."

Daniel grinned, but he didn't like being hit. You could see it in his eyes.

"You better keep your hands to yourself," he said patiently.

"You keep *your* hands to yourself," Jewell said. She got up again, and he pulled her down again, more roughly this time. He didn't hurt her, but the gesture reminded Jewell of Winston's strong hands last night. It reminded her that no matter how tough she thought she was, she was no more than a 123 pound female, pretty frail when it came down to it. Jewell felt she would always be victimized by stronger men.

When Daniel saw the tears leaking from her eyes, he put an arm around her and drew her to his chest. Jewell allowed it. It felt good to be held, even if this was another brutish, forceful and manipulating *man*.

"You wanna play twenty questions, or you wanna tell me what's wrong with you?" he asked.

Jewell lowered her head and cried on his shoulder. It was easier to talk now that she didn't have to look at him. "You don't love me," she said.

"Yes I do, baby. Why you say some shit like that?"

"You, you didn't care. I told you what happened, and all you cared about was that *card*."

"Baby, I *did* care. You said you was alright."

She shook her head. "One day you know everything. The next day you don't know shit."

"Then tell me, girl. Tell me what I don't know."

"I was scared," Jewell said. Thinking about it now brought all of the fear back. Jewell quivered as she cried. "He grabbed me, and I thought he was gonna hurt me. He could have *killed* me."

"You're being melodramatic, baby. You said all he wanted was a nut."

"That don't mean nothing to you?" she asked. She looked up at him, and Daniel cringed a little from the sight. "I'm stuck in a room with a man who'll do anything to get off. That don't scare you at all?"

"Baby, *you tripping*. He didn't want to kill you. He just wanted to *fuck*. And you didn't even have to do nothing."

"I *did* do something."

"Yeah, but you didn't have to fuck or nothing."

"What if I did?" Jewell asked. She didn't want to hear the answer, but a part of her wouldn't be at peace until she knew.

"If you would have fucked, then you would have fucked," Daniel said bluntly. "It's just sex, baby. I wouldn't have treated you no different."

"I thought you stopped pimping," Jewell said.

"What? Girl I'm not *pimping* you. You my woman. You know that."

"It would have been worth it?" she asked.

"Baby, why you doing this? You knew the deal – you *know* the deal. You starting to sound like a lame."

"I just—"

"This is the same thing that happened to Davis," Daniel interrupted. "We go to every job strapped to the teeth, and Miles is acting like a bitch when somebody gets shot. Somebody was gonna get shot *sooner or later*. And you wear those wigs and high heels with your dress all up your ass—"

"So I was gonna get fucked sooner or later?" Jewell asked.

"No, baby. That's like a *worst case scenario*. But you can't go in thinking it's never gonna happen. This is business, baby. We in this together. Davis died for this job. You're worried about giving up a little ass."

"So it would have been worth it?" she asked again.

Daniel sighed. "*Yes, girl*. Why you even asking me that? You know what I'm gonna say. You was sitting right next to me when I saw that *Indecent Proposal* movie, and what did I turn and say to you? Huh? I said that boy was a goddamned fool if he wasn't gonna let his girl fuck for a million dollars. Didn't I say that? Don't try to act like you don't know who I am! I been the same since *day one*. You the one trying to flip the script."

Jewell had no comeback for that because Daniel was right. She was the one who changed, not him.

"I don't want to keep all the money from the diamonds," she said instead.

Daniel was stupefied. "*What the hell is wrong with you?*"

"It's not right," Jewell said, shaking her head. "I been thinking about it, and I know it's wrong. I won't feel right if you do that."

"What you mean you won't feel right? What the hell is that? Miles and Jesse didn't do *shit* to get this job going! We killed a man for this! They're sitting at home watching the fucking *TV!* Eating doughnuts and shit!*"

"But they're helping *now*," Jewell said. "Miles made those cards and Jesse's going in with you."

"Baby, this is my motherfucking job, I'm the only one who can sell those *motherfucking diamonds*, and I can do whatever the fuck I want with *my motherfucking money*! I can't stand Miles! And Jesse ain't nothing but a *yes man*. You know that."

"But they're still our friends," Jewell said. "They been with us for years. They helped us a lot! Miles is scary, but he's loyal. He would never screw us like that, Daniel. *Never*."

Daniel got up and tossed the remote in her lap. "Gone and watch your church show, girl. I don't know who the fuck you is no more."

Jewell wondered how they could be at odds but still be on the same page; she didn't know who his crazy ass was either.

≈≈≈≈≈≈≈

In order to intercept an armored truck in the cargo area of the Dallas/Overbrook Meadows Airport, you must first obtain one of the airport's security vehicles. The security personnel drove white Impalas with yellow beacon lights on top. And while it was totally possible to steal the car *and* rob the truck on the same day, Daniel thought they should do these tasks separately.

If you try to steal a car the day of the heist, you'll have to rely on an Impala being exactly where you want it when you want it. You'll have to steal it before the armored truck loaded the diamonds, and you'll have to get in position before the truck got moving again.

Daniel suggested they take the Impala a few days before the heist, and everyone agreed this worked better logistically: They'd be able to take their time down there and get a car at their leisure. Jesse was an expert when it came to grand theft auto, but he didn't like to be rushed. After they got the car, they could look around and map out their interception point as well as their plan of escape.

So three days before the Herzberg plane was expected, Daniel and Jesse made plans to go to the airport for a *test run*. If they could make it out of there with the Impala and no attention came their way, the diamond heist would get a bright green light. If they got caught, then the heist was no good to begin with. They would bail out of jail, lick their wounds, and aim for more realistic goals in the future.

≈≈≈≈≈≈≈

Jewell and Slim had no roles in the test run, but as a show of unity all five gangsters agreed to meet at Safe House #2. Daniel planned to have his Bluetooth on during the entire mission so those left behind could keep in touch with him when he got to the airport.

Slim had his own cell phone now, but Jewell showed up at his apartment unannounced. She got out of her Chrysler wearing denim Capri's with a white tank top.

When she got to her brother's building, Jewell saw the dopefiend who tried to rob her a few weeks ago. He was standing at the foot of Slim's stairs with his back to her, but Jewell didn't have the heart or energy to harass with him today.

"How you doing?" she asked when she got closer.

The junkie turned around and jumped when he saw who it was. "How ya, I'm, I'ma…"

"Chill," Jewell said. "I don't want no trouble. I come to see my brother."

The older man stepped aside to allow her access to the stairs. Halfway up, Jewell stopped. She turned and eyed the derelict suspiciously. She reached into her purse, and his hands shot up in the hair.

"I, I, I, I didn't do nothing, Ma'am. I'm just, I'm just minding my business – ain't messing with *nobody*!"

"Put your hands down, fool," Jewell said. Instead of a pistol, she came out with a ten dollar bill, and the junkie's expression changed again. He might have been hungry or tired or even in need of medical care, but when he saw Alexander Hamilton, his brain immediately prepared itself for crack cocaine. Jewell felt guilty for contributing to his madness, but she handed him the money anyway.

"Tell me what you know about Slim."

The fiend balled the bill in his fist and nodded eagerly. "Everybody know Slim. He a good dude."

Jewell found that odd. A few weeks ago the junkie said *no one* knew her brother. "How come everybody knows him," she asked. "Y'all get high with him?"

"*Oh, no*. No ma'am. Slim don't smoke crack. He never be where we be at."

"So why does everybody know him?"

"He popular," the crackhead said. "He got a lot of money, a lot of friends."

"He get high with his friends?"

"Uh, I don't know, ma'am. I don't know them people. I can't say."

"Do any of his friends get high?"

"I, uh, I don't know, ma'am. I don't know them people. I don't like to speak on stuff I don't know."

Jewell's temper started to get the best of her. "Nigga, I just gave you ten dollars. You better know *something!*"

"*Amy,*" he said quickly. "That white girl that be up there. She use needles."

Jewell nodded, not really surprised. "Alright, old school. Go on now, move around."

The addict disappeared, in search of that awfully elusive dragon. Jewell marched up the stairs and tried to open Slim's door without knocking, but it was locked. She balled a fist and banged hard, like the police.

"Open this door, boy!"

Amy opened it instead. Before Jewell could stop herself, she had a handful of the girl's hair. She yanked her out of the apartment and commenced to swinging. In the back of her mind Jewell wondered what Creflo Dollar would think of her savage behavior. But in the front of her mind, Jewell wanted *blood.* She would have got it too if someone didn't wrap her up from behind and pull her off the whore. Jewell kicked and struggled like a trapped fox.

"Let go of me! *Let me go!*"

"What the hell you doing?" The voice came from right above her ear, and it was Slim. Amy was on the ground, balled in a fetal position. She looked up at them fretfully and then wobbled to her feet when she saw Jewell was restrained. Her hair was messed, her face was stop sign red, and her tee shirt was torn. Other than that she was unharmed.

"*What the hell, lady?*" she said to Jewell.

"This bitch is shooting *heroin!*" Jewell yelled. "*Let me go, Slim!*"

"*Go on, Amy,*" Slim said. "I'll come get you later."

"What I do?" Amy asked.

"Gone!" Slim warned. She took his advice and skipped quickly down the stairs.

"Let me go, Slim!"

Jewell didn't remember her brother being so strong, but she couldn't break his hold. He lifted her and carried her into his apartment with almost no effort. He slammed the door closed and leaned against it to keep Jewell from going back out. He crossed his arms, breathing hard. Jewell did the same. They sneered at each other and breathed and considered their next move. Slim spoke first.

"You ain't got *no* right to mess with my company like that. This is *my* house!"

"*You lied,*" Jewell said. "You said she wasn't getting high!"

"*I didn't know she was getting high!*"

"You're full of shit!"

"I just found out yesterday. *I swear!*"

"Well, why she still over here?"

"'Cause I like her, Jewell. What's it to you?"

"You know what it is to me, Slim! I need your ass to stay *clean.* Just for three more days–"

"I *am* clean!"

"Your girlfriend's a *fucking addict,* dumbass! That's the stupidest thing you could do!"

"She don't do it around me," Slim said. "And she don't come here high. I've never seen her high. What she does at her own house is her business. You still ain't got no right to put your hands on my friends!"

"I can do what I want!"

"I can't wait till this shit is over," Slim said, shaking his head.

"Me too," Jewell said. "Let me see your arms."

Slim held them out and gave her the ugliest look possible while she examined them. Still nothing. Jewell completed her inspection with a big "*Hmph!*"

"Come on," she said. "We got a meeting today."

"I know," Slim said. "And I got my own ride."

"You can't bring nobody to our safe house."

"I'm not," Slim said. "I got *my own ride*; a car."

"You don't have a car."

"Yes I do. I got it the day before yesterday."

"How can you afford a car?'

"It's a hooptie," Slim said. "I paid six hundred for it. It looks like shit, but it runs real good."

Jewell shook her head and rubbed her temples with the heels of her hands. "Oh my God, Slim. You not gonna be happy till you fuck it all up."

"How am I gonna fuck it up? 'Cause I got a car? I got my driver's license, and it's registered. Inspected too. You just don't want me to have shit, no car, no pussy, no *nothing*! You not happy unless you got me under your thumb."

"I don't want that, Slim."

"Look how you be acting when you come over here. You're mad every time I get something nice."

Jewell was pretty sure his six hundred dollar car wasn't *nice*, and she knew for a fact Amy wasn't either, but she could see his point.

"Alright," she said. "You can follow me in your car if you want. What kind is it?"

Slim smiled. "It's a Taurus."

When they got downstairs Jewell got a chance to smile too. His Taurus had been in an accident at some point. The previous owner attempted to fix it with used parts, but somewhere along the line he got lazy and eventually said *Fuck it*. Most of the car was champagne colored, but the hood was blue. The right front fender was white, and the left front fender was gray. It looked like a patchwork quilt.

"Don't laugh at my car," Slim said. "It still runs."

And it did. He started it up for her, and Jewell could tell the engine was good, probably rebuilt. The inspection and registration stickers were valid also, so she let go of her reservations and told him to follow her.

≈≈≈≈≈≈≈

When they got to Stop Six, Jewell pulled into the driveway at Safe House #2 with Slim right on her bumper. He parked quickly and ran to open the door for her.

"Thank you," Jewell said. She got out of her car and stretched in the sunlight.

Slim studied her for a second and then said, "I'm sorry."

Jewell yawned. "Sorry for what?"

"For having that girl over my place. I should've stopped messing with her when I found out she gets high."

236

"Slim, you've been in and out of rehab more times than I can count. You know better than anyone what bitches like that lead to. You might be sober now, but you'll be high right along with her if you keep playing.

"I know." Slim lowered his head. "I know."

"I'm just looking out for you."

"Thank you, lil sis." He gave her a hug, and they entered the house with much better moods than they had thirty minutes ago.

Daniel and Jesse were already dressed and ready to go.

"What took you so long?" Daniel asked when Jewell walked in. His uniform was complete now with the badge, access card, and a charcoal-colored .45 holstered on his hip. He had a solid blue baseball cap on too, to cover his shiny dome.

"I thought y'all weren't leaving till one," she said.

"It's past one."

Jewell checked her watch and saw that it was. Rather than tell him she was in a fight, she said, "Slim was showing me his new car."

Daniel's eyes brightened. "*Slim*! You got you a new ride?"

Slim smiled and looked down nervously. "It's, it's not *new* new."

"But still!" Daniel slapped him hard on the back. "You doing *good*, boy! I just knew you was gon' get high by now."

Slim chuckled. "No sir. Not this time."

Miles came in from the kitchen with a sandwich and bag of chips in hand. "Oh, hey, Jewell. What's going on Slim? You guys ready?" he asked Daniel and Jesse.

"Man, how can you eat right now?" Jesse asked. "My stomach's doing flips."

"'Cause he ain't gotta do nothing but drop us off," Daniel said. "Can't go to jail for that."

"Give it a rest," Miles said.

Jewell went to the dining room where they had an office phone on the table.

"Have you tried it?" she asked. "You sure it works?"

"It works," Daniel said.

"Try it, baby."

He pushed a button on the device hooked over his ear and said, "Call Peter." Everyone waited. A few seconds later the phone in front of Jewell began to ring. She pushed a button and put him on the speaker.

"Alright. So it works," Daniel said.

Jewell smiled. The reception was flawless.

"Come on, y'all," Daniel said. "Let's go."

Jewell rushed to the door before he left. "Are you going to give me a hug?"

He put his arms around her waist and looked down at her. "I thought you was mad at me."

"It's not you," she said. "It's me."

He kissed her briefly on the lips and then on the forehead. "Alright, baby. I'll see you later." He let go and followed Jesse and Miles to the car.

"I love you," Jewell said.

Daniel stopped in the front yard and turned to look at her. He smiled and gave her a wink. "I'll be right back, baby. You won't even know I'm gone."

CHAPTER TWENTY-TWO
THE TEST RUN

But Daniel was wrong.

Jewell waited *forty* horrific minutes before the phone rang on the dining table. She ran from the living room and caught it on the first ring. She fumbled to find the speaker button. Slim abandoned the cartoon he was watching and came to the dining room with her.

"Huh, hello?"

"Hey, baby. What's going on?" Daniel's voice was loud and clear.

"What happened?" Jewell asked. "What's wrong?"

"What you mean?"

"What happened? Why are you just now calling?"

"We just got here, baby." He chuckled. "Did you want me to call you while we were driving?"

"Maybe once or twice."

"Everything's alright, *baby*!" That was Jesse's voice.

"Get off me, man!" That was Daniel. "Miles just dropped us off," he said. "We haven't even went in yet."

"Where do you have to go?" Jewell asked.

"We're at Terminal D," Daniel said. "There's supposed to be a security checkpoint at gate D17."

"What gate are you at now?"

"I don't know. This place is *huge*. You won't believe this, baby; they've got the cargo bay *right off* the freeway. Soon as you leave it, you hit 114 and you're gone."

"They just have one cargo area?"

"Naw, they have four, the north, south, east and west. Our diamonds are gonna be in the East Cargo Area. That's where we're going now. They got a gate for vehicles to enter, and they got a secured door next to it. *Supposedly* our access cards will let us in that door and out that gate."

Jewell bit her pinkie nail and gave Slim a look. He took a seat across from her, but Jewell was too jittery to sit down.

"Are there a lot of people around you?" she asked.

"It's some," Daniel said, "but not a lot. Not too much foot traffic over here."

"Have you seen any other security guards?"

"From a distance," Daniel said. "None of them have been close enough to really look at us yet."

"Are you still walking?"

"Yeah. What's that over there?"

"Huh?"

"I was talking to Jesse. Is that it?"

"You're already there?" Jewell asked.

"Naw. But I think we see it. There's a gate up here, with a guard station. I can't read what it – oh you can see it? Yeah. That's it, baby. I'm looking at the cargo area right now. I don't see a door though. It's supposed to be... Okay. I see it now, baby, about fifty yards out."

"Are there a lot of guards?" Jewell asked. Her heart thumped like she'd been exercising. Her forehead was slick with sweat.

"I see *one* guard at the gate," Daniel said. "No, *two*. There's two of 'em in there. It's..."

Jesse said something Jewell couldn't hear.

"What?"

"There *are* a lot of guards," Daniel said.

"How many?"

"Like six of them, but I think we can... Naw, baby. We have to go through at least two of 'em."

Jewell thought she might pass out. "Are they looking at you?"

"Naw, baby. We look just like them."

"But what–"

"Hold on. I gotta quit talking for a minute."

"I love you," Jewell said, but he didn't respond. She and Slim listened to the sound of wind and footsteps for what felt like hours, but according to the clock on the phone only three minutes passed.

Suddenly a strange voice came over the speaker, a *Caucasian* voice.

"How you guys doing?"

Jewell put a hand over her mouth. Her eyes were big like saucers.

"Ah, we're okay sir." That voice was Daniel's, but it had a thick southern twang to it. "Rather be fishing," he said with a hearty laugh.

"You ain't never lying," the new voice said, and that was it.

"You still there?" Daniel asked a few seconds later.

Jewell had to sit down then. Her legs were weak like blades of grass. "I'm here," she said. "What happened?"

"Our uniforms just passed the test," Daniel said. He laughed. "You should see this nigga over here. He's whiter than a sheet of paper!"

"Jesse?"

"Yeah. This fool's a trip."

"What are you doing now?" Jewell asked.

"We're here," Daniel said. "I'm about to slide my card right now. If it don't work, we're fucked. There's a couple people looking at us – they're not *looking*, looking, but they can see us. We'll look suspicious if we don't go in."

Jewell crossed her fingers and held her hands together in prayer. She heard a very small *beep* that barely got picked up by the Bluetooth. Then she heard chuckling.

"What's happening?" she asked.

Daniel laughed softly. "Baby, you ain't gonna believe this."

"*What*?"

"This motherfucker *opened*," he said. "We about to go in."

Jewell let out a sigh of relief, but it was short-lived.

"This is it," Daniel said. "This right here…" His voice faded out. A second later a flurry of static blasted through Jewell's speaker phone. A moment after that, they lost the connection altogether.

Jewell shot to her feet. She looked at Slim without expression, and then her face crumpled in on itself. Slim jumped from his seat and rushed to console her.

"It's alright, girl."

Jewell held her brother, and Slim rubbed the back of her head.

"Why you acting like this?" he asked. "You trust your man, don't you? He never got caught before."

"This is different," Jewell moaned.

"No it's not," Slim said. "If he made it before, then he'll make it now."

That was the dumbest reasoning Jewell ever heard, but she clung to her brother's words. She held on to hope like it was her last breath.

≈ ≈ ≈ ≈ ≈ ≈

The phone didn't ring again for another twenty minutes. During that time Jewell paced, shivered, and bit every nail off her fingers. She went over all possible scenarios and decided her man was in handcuffs by now. It only took a few minutes to find a car. Jesse could start it in ninety seconds. What the hell could be happening for the other fifteen minutes?

Handcuffs, that's what.

When the phone did ring, Jewell didn't want to answer it. She knew it was Miles, and she knew what he would say:

Have you heard from Daniel yet?

No, Jewell would respond. *I was talking to him, but the phone went off when he went in the building.*

I haven't heard from him, either, Miles would reply. *He should have called by now.*

Slim put the phone on speaker and rolled his eyes at his little sister.

"Hello?"

"Hey," Daniel said. "Where baby at?"

Jewell felt like she won a Grammy. "I'm right here!" she squealed.

"You believed in your man?" Daniel asked.

"*Yes!*" Jewell lied. "You got it?"

"We got it."

Jewell threw her arms around Slim's neck and jumped up and down, almost strangling him in the process. He peeled her off and laughed.

"What took you so long?!" Jewell asked. "You had me scared to death!"

"Your man's *crazy!*" That was Jesse.

"I was just looking around," Daniel said. "Baby, that place is huge. We drove around over there where they got the safes. I know exactly where that truck is going to pull up, and I know which way it's going when it leaves. It has to take this turn, just like Harvey said. Wasn't nobody over there. It's gonna be easy."

"I'm so happy!" Jewell said. "How'd you get the car out?"

"We went right through the gate," Daniel said. "I waved my card over the reader they had, and the gate opened. The guard waved at us and everything."

"That's crazy," Jewell said. "Where are you now? You on your way?"

"We're meeting Miles at a garage," Daniel said. "I told you we weren't taking this car all the way back to the city, right?"

Jewell couldn't remember. So many thoughts were in her head.

"This garage we got is about five miles away from the airport," Daniel said. "It's perfect."

"Alright," Jewell said. She was smiling ear to ear, bouncing on the balls of her feet.

"Hey Slim!" Daniel called.

Slim leaned his ugly mug forward. "I'm here."

"We're going out to celebrate," Daniel said. "All of us. Miles too. It's on me."

Slim looked at Jewell. "I, I can't go," he said. "I already got something to do. That's why I brought my car."

There was a pause. "Alright," Daniel said. "You straight. We'll get you some other time. Hey, baby, I gotta call Miles. I'll call you back when we're on our way."

"Alright," Jewell said. "I love you, baby."

"Love you too."

"I'm fucking with a genius," Jewell said with a grin.

Daniel laughed and disconnected the line.

≈≈≈≈≈≈≈

By the time the guys returned, Slim was already gone. Daniel said that was fine, more food for him. He and Jesse changed out of their security uniforms while Jewell and Miles watched Jeopardy in the living room. Miles was happy and talkative. He got damned near every trivia question right, even the thousand dollar ones. Jewell found herself feeling more and more sorry for him, but she couldn't think of any way to stop Daniel from stiffing his comrades.

Jesse emerged from the bathroom wearing black slacks with patent leather shoes and a lime green button-down. Daniel stepped out of the bedroom a few minutes later sporting a black zoot suit with a red vest and red tie. His fedora was black with a black band and no feather.

"You always gotta out-shine us," Miles noticed.

"I don't mean to," Daniel said with a grin. "I can't help it if *sensational* runs through my veins."

≈≈≈≈≈≈≈

They went to Benihana's for an early dinner and had a pretty good time, all things considered. Jewell was happy about the success of the job, but she couldn't get Daniel's betrayal off her mind. They still had three days to go before the heist, and she planned to nag him relentlessly during this time. It was bad enough they were all *criminals*, at least they should be able to trust each other.

They ordered three bottles of wine and ate like this was their last meal. They toasted everything from Jewell getting the access card to Jesse getting the Impala. Most of the praise went to Daniel for coming up with the whole scheme, but Dapper Dan got a little emotional when they tried to toast to him.

"Let's not forget *Davis*," he said. "He did more to get this shit rolling than any of us. He paid the *ultimate price* for everybody at this table."

Daniel poured a glass of wine on the floor in remembrance. Their waiter cleaned it up with no complaints.

≈≈≈≈≈≈≈

When they got back to the car, Daniel turned and stared at his woman. She smiled, but he didn't seem happy at all anymore.

"Take me to Slim's house," he said.

"Why?" Jewell asked. "What's wrong?"

"I got a feeling," Daniel said. "Him wanting to leave like that, that don't seem weird to you?"

Jewell shrugged. "I don't know. I guess."

"What kind of nigga will pass up a free meal?" Daniel asked.

"The kind that's got something better to do." Jewell guessed.

"Something better like getting high?" Daniel offered.

Jewell told him what the dopefiend said about Slim being *newly popular*. She told him about Slim's new girlfriend too.

Dapper Dan rubbed his chin and was quiet as they drove.

≈≈≈≈≈≈≈

When they arrived at her brother's apartment, Daniel told Jewell to play it cool. She knocked on the door and wasn't surprised when Slim's Hispanic friend answered. Marcos looked from Jewell to Daniel and didn't like what he saw.

"Where Slim?" Jewell asked.

"He, he in there," Marcos said.

"Well, you gonna let us in or not?" Daniel asked.

Marcos stepped aside and held the door open for them. "Slim! Your sister's here! Some guy too!"

Jewell walked inside and didn't know whether to laugh or cry. Amy was back. The tramp jumped up out of the love seat and ran to the bedroom when she saw Jewell. Jewell started after her, but Daniel grabbed her arm.

"Sit down," he said.

"I gotta go," Marcos said and slipped out the front door. Daniel closed it behind him.

Slim emerged from the hallway with no shirt or shoes on. Jewell studied his face intently. His eyes were big, but now *low*. Either he really wasn't using anymore, or he switched to crack. Jewell couldn't figure him out.

"Hey, uh, what y'all doing here?" he asked.

Jewell took a seat on the couch. Daniel came and stood next to her.

"We just come to visit," he said. "Where your girlfriend at?"

Slim scratched his head. "She, she's in there. I'm finna break up with her though. *I swear!*"

Daniel shook his head. "Boy, you can be with whoever you want. That ain't my concern. Ain't Jewell's neither. Tell her to come out here."

Slim looked from Daniel to his sister.

"I ain't gon' touch her," Jewell said and rolled her eyes.

Slim looked over shoulder his hesitantly. "Y'all, y'all come on out," he said.

Jewell cocked her head. *Y'all?*

Amy stepped out of the bedroom with another slut close behind. The new one was a brunette, but just as scroungy. She wore only boxer shorts and a tee shirt. They both stood next to Slim and looked around fretfully. Jewell thought she was going to throw up.

Daniel laughed. "These yo girls, Slim? Big Slim! *Big Slim!* You got *two* of em?"

Slim cracked a smile. "This Amy, and this Bridgette."

"This is *disgusting*," Jewell said. "I'm going to the bathroom." She got up, and the girls flinched like she was Mike Tyson. Slim moved them out of the way, and Jewell stepped right by.

"How you do it?" Daniel asked with a big grin. "Tell me *how you do it, Slim!*"

Jewell didn't go to the restroom. She went straight to the bedroom as instructed. It was a mess, but she knew where to search for things that are precious to people. She found what she was looking for in the first place she looked, only it wasn't exactly what she was looking for.

Right under Slim's mattress was an object Jewell had seen before. The tape was familiar, and the blood stains definitely struck a chord: Even though a nice-sized chunk was missing, Jewell recognized Percy's missing slab immediately.

CHAPTER TWENTY-THREE
THE BIG H

Jewell returned to the living room with the brick of heroin in her hand. Slim was sitting on his loveseat with a girl standing on either side. He was chuckling about something Daniel said, but all laughter stopped when he saw Jewell.

"I think I know why Slim's so popular all of a sudden," she said. Jewell tossed the slab to her boyfriend. Daniel caught it, but a few crumbs spilled from the wrapping, one of them was about the size of a crouton. Jewell saw it roll under the couch. Slim's girls watched too. Jewell knew they'd get on their hands and knees to find it once she and Daniel left.

Daniel didn't seem surprised at all by Jewell's find. But then again, he was a pretty good actor, especially in the heat of the moment. He flipped the package over a couple of times, scrutinizing it thoroughly.

Slim sat as stiff as a board. He watched Daniel like he was watching an abortion. Amy coughed roughly and started scratching her arm. It took all of Jewell's composure to stay put. She wanted so badly to snatch that heifer bald-headed.

Daniel put the dope down on the couch and stared at Slim with a slight smile. He shook his head and the smile faded.

"This how you do it, Slim? This how you get all the honeys?"

Slim was literally scared speechless. One of his girls tried to bail him out.

"I don–"

"*YOU SHUT YOUR GODDAMNED MOUTH!*" Daniel's voice boomed like Barry White with a megaphone. Everyone flinched, Jewell included.

Daniel sucked his teeth and rubbed his chin. He turned and stuck his hand out to Jewell.

"Gimme that thang."

Jewell reached into her purse and pulled out the .44 magnum he told her to bring in. She handed it to him, and, just as Daniel wanted, all attention went to the weapon. The gun was huge, the barrel was almost twice as long as the rest of it. It was the same model Clint Eastwood toted in the old Dirty Harry movies. Daniel flashed this gun when he wanted to *intimidate* rather than kill people, but it was effective either way. Nothing got your point across like a fist-size exit wound.

Daniel pointed the pistol at the squirming group in front of him. The girls hit the floor quickly and crawled behind Slim's loveseat, screaming like grade-schoolers at recess. Slim sunk into the cushions as far as he could, bringing up his arms and legs for cover.

"*Please, Daniel!*" he wailed. "*Please don't shoot me, man!*"

Jewell watched the scene, standing stiffly some twenty feet away. On one level she didn't want to see her brother die, especially at the hands of her boyfriend. But on the other hand, she knew Slim was a fool. He dug a deep grave for himself at least once a year. Sooner or later he was bound to get dumped in one of them.

"GET OUT FROM BEHIND THAT GODDAMNED COUCH!" Daniel barked.

The girls crawled out together, shivering and crying. They stood on their knees, holding on to each other like twin sisters at Auschwitz.

Daniel turned the gun on them and waited a few heartbeats, long enough for their senseless lives to pass before their eyes.

"Which one you want me to kill first?" he asked Jewell.

"The blonde," Jewell said immediately. She didn't know if he'd do it or not, but if she had a say in it, that was her choice.

"What you know about old Slim here?" Daniel asked Amy.

"*Please, mister. We don't know him. We don't know* **nothing!**" Amy pleaded.

"*We don't,*" her friend agreed. Their faces were so close, Daniel could get them with one shot.

"Y'all over his house everyday," Daniel said. "Don't tell me you don't know *nothing.*"

"I just met him," Amy cried. "He real nice. He lets me stay over sometimes. He gives me some, you now... some *shit.*"

"Where he get his *shit* from?" Daniel asked.

Amy looked at her friend and they both shook their heads. Daniel looked back to Jewell. "What you think, baby?"

"They're lying," she said coldly.

"*We're not!*"

"*We're not, mister!*"

"They don't know nothing," Slim said meekly. The room went quiet. He put his legs down slowly and lowered his arms. Slim was crying too. His bottom lip quivered rhythmically. His face hung like the sad clown's makeup. He was the epitome of sorrow. If he broke into a tearful rendition of *Old Man River*, Jewell wouldn't have been surprised.

"What you say, boy?" Daniel pointed the .44 at Slim again. He was like a conductor with that thing, wherever he pointed he got a reaction. Slim flinched and threw his hands up again. He peered at Daniel through his parted fingers.

"They don't know nothing," he repeated. "This ain't got nothing to do with them, Mister Daniel."

If not for such dire straights, Jewell might have commended her brother for finally talking responsibility for his foolishness.

Daniel nodded. "Alright," he said. "Y'all bitches gone and get out of here."

The girls looked from Daniel to Slim and crawled hesitantly towards the door.

"Hurry up now, for I change my mind!"

They shot to their feet. Jewell opened the door and glared at them as they flew by. The brunette was still barefoot with a pair of men's drawers on. Her feet clapped like a seal on the cold cement. Jewell locked the door behind them and leaned heavily on the frame. No way could there be more drama packed into one day.

Daniel stepped forward and stood between Slim's legs. He put the barrel of the pistol on his temple, and Slim lowered his head and took a deep breath. He let it out with shudders. Jewell put a hand to her face, but she didn't have any nails left to nibble. She bit alongside her cuticle until she found a layer of skin to peel up.

"You took it out that car?" Daniel asked. He was calm and cool.

Slim nodded. He kept his eyes closed, resigned to whatever fate awaited him.

Daniel pushed the gun hard enough to make Slim's skin bunch around the barrel.

"Open your eyes, boy."

Slim looked up at him. Sweat glistened on his black face like oil.

"You *answer me* when I talk to you," Daniel instructed.

"Yessir," Slim said. His hands trembled in his lap.

"How many people saw that dope?" Daniel asked.

"*Nobody*," Slim said. "*I swear, sir. Nobody saw it.*"

Daniel cocked the hammer back slowly. It was loud from where Jewell was standing. She couldn't imagine what it must sound like so close to her brother's head.

"*Don't lie to me!*"

"*I ain't lying, Daniel. I swear!* I'd break off a little at a time, and they'd see *that* – what I was giving them – but I never showed nobody where I was getting it from."

"Why you take it, Slim?

"I, I didn't mean no harm, sir. I saw it when I went to get my sister's purse. It was just laying there."

Daniel's lips curled into a sneer. "*Why you take it?*"

"I, I, I was *greedy*, man! Ain't nothing good I can say about it. I was wrong. I knew I was doing wrong, and I figured I'd prolly get caught. But it was just, it was just..."

Slim groped for words, and Jewell felt his pain. This was like asking a snake *Why do you slither on your belly*? It was in Slim's nature to be sneaky and underhanded. How could he explain a basic instinct?

"At first I was gon' tell you," Slim said. He was still crying, growing more pathetic by the second. "*I swear I was gon' tell you!* But then, but then I kept thinking, what if your job don't go through? Or what if you don't use me? What was gon' happen to me then? I was, I was supposed to go back to mopping floors?" He shook his head. "Naw. That, that, that dope, that was my *ace*." Slim swallowed hard. His eyes darted. "That was my ace in the hole, Mister Daniel. I didn't mean no harm."

"You *stole* from me," Daniel said.

"*No! No, sir! No I didn't.* I wouldn't *never* take from you, Daniel. I stole that from a *dead man*."

Daniel looked back at Jewell and chuckled. She didn't see the humor in it.

"So what you been doing with it?" Daniel asked. "Passing that shit out like candy? It's a lot of dope missing, Slim."

"I, I been giving most of it away, yes sir," Slim confirmed. "I sells a little bit too. I gave some of it for my car."

"And where does everybody think you're getting it from, Slim?"

"I told them I robbed a dealer."

Daniel shook his head. "You a *janitor*, boy! Who the fuck believe you robbed somebody?"

"They, they do," Slim said. "They wanna get high. They don't ask too many questions."

Daniel took the gun away from his head but kept it pointed at him. He looked back at Jewell. "Come here," he said.

Jewell stepped slowly and stood at her man's side. If he was calling her up there so she could witness her brother's death up close, Jewell would never forgive him. But Daniel didn't appear to be in the killing mood anymore.

"This, this nigga here..." He held the gun loosely, waving it in Slim's face. "What you think about this?" Daniel asked.

"I think he *sorry*," Jewell said.

Slim gave her a look like, *Et tu, Brutus?*

"I should kill you," Daniel said. "You know that, don't you?"

Slim nodded. "Yes, yessir. I know."

Daniel un-cocked the pistol and gave it back to Jewell. She put it in her purse with an uncertain sigh of relief.

"You *still* doing the job," Daniel commanded with a finger in Slim's face. "You gon' have your ass at the safe house *on time*, and you gon' have your *head right*. I *counted on you*, Slim. I put money in your pocket. I can't see why you do me like this."

"I didn't mean to hurt nobody," Slim cried. "I didn't think nobody would care about it since he, he was dead."

"That's cause you *selfish*," Daniel explained. "You sitting up in here thinking you not hurting nobody, but everything you do affects me. Until we do this job, I don't even want you to get stopped for *jaywalking*."

Daniel's face softened a bit. "I don't like to treat you like this, Slim, but you *hard-headed*, boy. Seem like that's the only kind of talk you understand."

Slim nodded. "Yes, yes sir."

"And I hate to tell you this, Slim," Daniel went on, "but just so you we're clear: If I hear *anything* about you getting heat from that damned heroin, I'm gon' take you out in the woods and burn your silly ass *alive*. You hear me, boy? You'll be wishing I'd put a bullet in your head."

Slim nodded. His chest looked more concave than ever. His potbelly rose and fell with his halting breaths.

Daniel turned and scooped up Percy's slab on the way out. Jewell gave her brother a long, hard stare before following.

≈≈≈≈≈≈≈

When they got to the car, she asked Daniel why he didn't kill him.

He sighed. "You want me to kill yo brother?"

"No, I don't *want* you to kill him," Jewell said. "I'm just asking."

"I need his dumb ass," Daniel said earnestly. "If he don't do nothing but stand there and look stupid, I still need his ass there. It's too late in the game to get somebody else. I already got Slim's uniform ready and everything."

"You think you can trust him?" Jewell asked.

"Trust him as far as what?" Daniel pondered. "I trust Slim to be *Slim*. He's dumb as hell, but I can't fault a man for hustling. He did what any other sneaky-ass nigga would do in those circumstances: He saw a chance to make a little extra on the side, and he took it."

Jewell nodded.

"If he would've took it from *me*," Daniel went on, "I'd be singing a different song right now. But I can't be mad him for stealing from a dead man. I'm mad 'cause he didn't tell me, but truth be told, I woulda did the same thing."

Jewell didn't want to be the one to say this, but she couldn't live with the guilt if she kept her mouth closed: "I don't think we should use him."

"We through talking about that," Daniel said without looking at her. "This shit's going down in *three days*. No matter what, it's going down."

≈ ≈ ≈ ≈ ≈ ≈ ≈

The Herzberg plane was scheduled to arrive on Thursday night. The heist was to take place the following Friday morning. The few days leading up to the job crept by like time on death row. Jewell thought she'd be excited about the prospect of becoming a *millionaire*, but Slim's antics coupled with Daniel's plan to double-cross the gang left her with a dull pain in her stomach most of the time.

She tried to talk him out of the scheme twice, but Daniel grew more and more irritable as the heist drew closer. Reasoning with him was like trying to take a bone from a pit bull dog. Once he got angry and asked if she was going to tell Miles about his plans.

"No," Jewell said. "I would *never* do that. You should know that."

He looked at her, judging her really, like she might be a potential rat.

"You sure are concerned about them niggas," Daniel said. "You and Jesse been fucking around?"

Jewell's whole face fell. "I can't believe you asked me that."

"I can't believe you want to give away money I already told you we're keeping. *You and me,* that's all for *us*. How come you don't want it?"

"We don't need that much," Jewell reasoned. "If we live a regular life, we could make it with just two, three million. If we split it with the crew, we'll all have ten apiece. I don't want to get greedy. It's bad luck."

Jewell knew she had trouble as soon as the words left her mouth. Referring to a job as *bad luck* was Daniel's only superstition. She might as well say *Macbeth* while inside a theatre.

Her boyfriend's eyes became wide, and then they narrowed and filled with rage. Daniel jumped from his seat and grabbed Jewell by the shoulders, lifting her to a standing position. Jewell had never seen him so angry. The lines in his face were hard, his eyes and lips were set in a deep sneer. He inched his nose very close to hers.

"You trying to jinx my motherfucking job?"

"No," Jewell said quickly. "I didn't mean it." She spoke softly. She didn't know if he would crush her or throw her to the floor. Daniel hit her a few times early in their relationship, but there had been no violence for the last four years.

"*Don't you ever say nothing bad about my job,*" Daniel growled. "*You understand what the fuck I'm saying?*"

"Yes," Jewell said. She swallowed hard. Her eyes filled with tears. Daniel saw the pain he was causing and let her go. Jewell's arms pulsated from where he held her, like his hands were still there.

Daniel pushed her out of the way, headed for the bedroom.

"I can't stand no ungrateful ass woman!" he said on the way out. "You *make* a nigga wanna hit you."

After that, Jewell didn't ask him to split the loot anymore.

And things got a little better.

On Wednesday afternoon she went to her mother's house and packed up the keepsakes she wanted. The photo albums were still there, as well as Miss Eveline's jewelry boxes. Before leaving, Jewell went to the backyard and watered her rosebush one last time. The house was paid for, but Jewell knew she'd never see those struggling buds again. After the job, she planned to call her sister and tell her she could have the place. If there was too much heat, she would deliver this news by postcard.

At 11:42 p.m. on Thursday evening, Daniel received a call from his inside guy at the airport: Harvey said the plane was on the runway. At 01:04 a.m. on Friday morning, Daniel got another call. The diamonds were in the safe.

Jewell and Daniel made love that night. It was good, and they were excited. Jewell found that if she simply went along with Daniel's will, things could be like they used to be. They would be rich. She wouldn't have to use her body to manipulate men anymore, and they wouldn't have to hurt anyone else.

Just one more lie, she told herself, thinking about Jesse and Miles.

One more lie.

≈≈≈≈≈≈≈

They did not sleep at all that night.

At 4:30 a.m. Daniel and Jewell took a shower and ate a light breakfast. They left at six and made it to Safe House #3 before sunup. They hadn't been there since Davis died, and the garage was filled with sick memories. It also brought back the feeling of warmth and love Jewell felt that night when Daniel and Slim got back from the park. She remembered how Jesse and Miles were disgusted by her, but Daniel wrapped her up in his strong arms without pause, brain matter and all.

But there were no warm hugs this morning. They walked in together and immediately went in different directions.

Daniel changed into his security uniform while Jewell made breakfast for the gang. She was still cooking when Daniel came back from the bedroom. He was fully dressed, carrying the pistols he, Jesse, and Slim would tote in their holsters. He sat at the dining table with a small bag of tools and began to disassemble and then clean the guns one at a time.

There were no sounds in the house other than the small noises Jewell made with her dishes and Daniel made with his tools. They worked within six feet of each other, but neither said a word. Daniel was in his zone, and Jewell was in one as well.

She knew it was senseless to ask God for anything at this point, but she talked to Him anyway. Jewell prayed no one would get hurt, and she prayed they wouldn't have to hurt anyone either.

She hoped Daniel would see the folly of his ways before it was too late, but at this point Jewell was content with whatever decision he made. She wanted to travel and see waters so pristine they looked like a painting.

She wanted to see hills and canyons, mountains and volcanoes. Every member of the syndicate deserved these things, but Jewell learned not to speak on their behalf anymore. *Right is right*, but an ass-whooping is something totally different. Things were okay between her and Daniel now, and she aimed to keep it that way.

≈≈≈≈≈≈≈

Miles showed up at 7:15 wearing jeans and a tee shirt. He came in from the garage, sniffing the air like a rat.

255

"*Mmm, mmm!* What's that you're cooking?" he asked Jewell.

"Eggs and sausage."

He went to the stove and looked over her shoulder. "Is that for you guys or can I have some?"

"It's for y'all," Jewell said. "Me and Daniel already ate."

"How you doing, Daniel?" Miles asked. He was as chipper as he was last week when they went out to eat. He went to the table and clapped Jewell's man on the back.

Daniel grunted and rolled his eyes, still consumed with his gun parts. "What's up, Miles," he said without looking up.

"It's the *big day!*" Miles announced with a grin. "You excited?"

Daniel nodded.

"Man, *grum-pee!*" Miles said. He went back over to the stove where conversation was a little easier. "You said I could have some?" he said to Jewell.

She smiled at him. "Sure, Miles. Get you a plate."

≈≈≈≈≈≈≈

Jesse arrived at the safe house twelve minutes later. He looked sleepy and nervous at the same time, it was an odd mix of emotions. He walked into the dining room carrying his world famous burglary bag.

"'Sup everybody."

Daniel stood and grabbed a bundle of clothes from the seat to his right. He walked across the room and shoved the garments in Jesse's chest.

"You late."

"No, I'm not," Jesse said. "We're not leaving till eight."

"You show up here at *seven-thirty* and think you got enough time?"

"I *do* got enough time," Jesse said. He looked around the kitchen. "Where's Slim?"

"He late, too," Daniel said with obvious annoyance.

"Well, what are you worried about *me* for?" Jesse asked. He turned, headed for the bedroom.

Daniel glared at the back of his head for a second but didn't say anything.

≈≈≈≈≈≈

At 7:40 Daniel asked Jewell to call her brother's new cell phone. She did, but there was no answer.

At 7:45 Daniel told her to call Slim again. She did, and there was still no answer.

At 7:50 the whole gang moved to the living room. They stared at each other in silence until Miles finally said what everyone was thinking.

"I knew we shouldn't have used him. He's always been a fuck up – excuse me, Jewell. I know that's your brother, but y'all know I'm right. But you guys depended on him, *again*. And now we're screwed, *again*. How are we supposed to do your job now, Daniel? I already told you, I'm not going in."

Daniel didn't say anything, so no one else did either.

At 7:55 Daniel asked Jewell to call Slim one more time. She got the same result.

At 8:00 Miles stood and began to pace the room. No one wanted to argue with him, so he argued with himself. "I told you, don't let her brother in this. This is too important. I said *we can't count on that dude*, but *noooooo*. No one wanted to believe me. Now look at us. *All this planning! All these risks we took.* We fucking killed a man for God's sake. *And for what? Huh?* We got *nothing*, man! We got *nothing!*"

"Miles, shut the fuck up!" Daniel called from the couch. Jewell sat next to her man, but they weren't touching. She leaned back with her legs crossed. Daniel sat on the edge of his seat with his elbows on his knees. He stared at Miles, his brow furrowed. A fat vein stood out on his neck.

"Why are you getting mad at *me*?" Miles asked. He stood by the front door with his arms crossed.

Jesse sat on the loveseat looking like he either had to throw up or take a dump, it could go either way.

"Just shut up," Daniel said.

"No!" Miles shouted. "You tell me where your big plan is now, Daniel! You only got *two guys*. How you gonna work it out? I already told you, *I'm not going in.*"

"We don't need you to go in!" Daniel yelled.

"*Then what are you gonna do?!*" Miles shouted back. "It's *eight o'clock*, Daniel! We're supposed to be leaving at *eight o'clock*! Remember?"

"We don't have to leave till eight-fifteen," Daniel said calmly.

"You said *eight.*"

"I lied."

"You, you..." Miles shook his head. "Why would you lie to us?"

"I wanted to make sure y'all was here on time."

"We're not your *children*," Miles said. "You don't have to lie to us! If we're leaving at *eight-fifteen*, you should have said fucking *eight-fifteen*!" He put his hand on the front door and opened it.

"Where are you going?" Daniel asked.

"*Outside!*" Miles hollered. "Get away from your crazy ass." He exited and closed the door behind himself.

Jewell looked at Jesse. The safecracker shrugged. Jewell looked at Daniel, but he just stared at his balled fists. Jewell was about to apologize on her brother's behalf when the front door opened again. All eyes moved in that direction. It was Miles. He didn't look upset anymore. Jewell wondered what could have happened in only two seconds.

"Well," he said. "I've got some *good* news and some *bad* news." No one prompted him, so he kept talking. "The good news is Slim's here."

Daniel jumped to his feet, but Miles held his hand out. "The *bad* news is," he went on, "Slim's asleep in the driveway. I'm no doper, but I'm pretty sure he's high."

Jewell felt like she got kicked in the stomach. Daniel turned to glare at her, but she glared right back at him, refusing to let him blame this on her. Daniel looked back at Miles and shook his head.

"Bring him in here," Daniel said. "You help him," he told Jewell.

≈≈≈≈≈≈≈

The sun was out now; shining bright on the Overbrook Meadows neighborhood. There were two vehicles in the driveway

258

of Safe House #3. One was a forest green Isuzu Trooper Miles bought just yesterday for this job. His role was to drop Daniel, Jesse and Slim off at the garage where they stashed the security vehicle and meet them an hour and a half later after they commandeered the armored truck.

The other vehicle in the driveway was Slim's three-toned Ford Taurus. The bucket looked especially *ugly* this morning, but nothing was as ugly as what Jewell found slumped behind the steering wheel. Two years had passed since the last time she saw her brother like this, but the flood of emotions she felt was immediately familiar.

Slim wore a white tee shirt with black jeans. He was completely out of it. His head rested on his left shoulder. His eyes were half-open, but Jewell could only see the whites. His neck was bent at an angle that looked terribly uncomfortable, but Slim was feeling no pain. His mouth was open, and his tongue protruded through the orifice. He was drooling, breathing steadily.

Slim's shirt was soiled, his hair was nappy, and there was no need to speculate as to what might be the cause of this dilemma. His right arm lay open in his lap. In the crook, Jewell saw fresh track marks. One was still bleeding slightly.

Jewell didn't cry because this wasn't something totally unexpected, especially after worrying about him for the last thirty minutes. But a deep sorrow enveloped Jewell nonetheless. She had half a mind to push Slim to the passenger seat, jump in his car, and drive far, far away from there. Everything would be much easier that way, but Jewell was not one to run from her problems. With Miles' help, she got her big brother out of the car and took him inside the house instead.

Daniel was waiting when they got back inside. He closed the door behind them and grabbed the arm Jewell was holding. Slim was awake now, but *awake* is such a relative term. They sat him on the couch, and Slim tried to lie down. Daniel sat him up forcefully. He slapped him across the cheek, but Slim was way past the effectiveness of such physical stimulants.

He rolled his eyes and nodded, his head swaying like a bobble-head doll. "I'm sorry," he said weakly. "I tried, but... I can... Can't do right..."

Daniel bent over him with a grip on both of his shoulders, much like he held Jewell a couple days ago. Jesse stood on

Daniel's right side with Miles on his left. Jewell stood further
back, not wanting to see what might happen next.

"*Slim!*" Daniel shook him. Slim flopped around like a
black scarecrow.

"He's out of it," Jesse said.

"*Fucking wasted,*" Miles agreed.

Daniel's nostrils flared. "*Slim!* Wake up, nigga!" He shook
him again. Slim's head flopped back and fourth. Jewell started
crying and Miles started yelling.

"*Stop it, Daniel!* He's fucked up! You can't shake him out
of that!"

Daniel turned and scowled at Miles, but he knew he was
hearing right.

"I can't believe this shit," he said. He let go of Slim's
shoulders and grabbed his shirt collar with his left hand. Before
anyone could react, Daniel balled his right hand into a fist and
started pummeling Slim's slack face.

WHAP!

WHAP!

"Dumb ass nigga! *How the fuck you gonna get high
today? Huh?*"

WHAP!

WHAP!

"You wanna make a fool out of me, nigga? Huh? You
wanna make me look *stupid*?"

WHAP!

"**STOP!**" Jewell wailed. Knowing Daniel might kill her
brother was one thing, but standing there and watching him do it
was something totally different.

She rushed forward and jumped on his back, but Daniel
was hard and unmoving. Jesse grabbed his punching arm, and
Miles managed to free Slim's shirt from Daniel's vice-like grip.
With all three of them holding him, Daniel gave up his assault.
Slim fell sideways with blood spilling from his mouth and nose.
He had a deep cut on his bottom lip that would require stitches. A
mouse was already forming under his right eye.

Slim tried to sit up, but he couldn't. He looked around the
room with glassy eyes that never managed to focus on anything.
But on some level he understood what was going on.

"*I'm sorry*," he said. Sweat poured from his brow and mingled with the blood on his face.

Daniel pushed everyone away and stood with his fists balled, his chest rose and fell like a silverback's. Jewell wondered what he would do next, as did everyone else in the room. Daniel only had two choices, and they were all surprised by the one he picked.

"We *still* doing the job."

"*How are we going to do the job*?" Miles whined. "You said you need three guys to go in!"

"Baby can go." Daniel spoke calmly without looking at her.

Jewell was shocked. Miles was floored.

"*How the hell can* **she** *go? She doesn't have a uniform!* We didn't get her an ID!"

"She can wear Slim's uniform," Daniel said. "And she don't need no ID. She can stay in the car the whole time. All we need her to do is drive out."

"You said all three of you were getting out," Miles reminded.

"Me and Jesse can do it by ourselves," Daniel said. He turned to face his woman, but he didn't have the words of comfort she needed right then. "Go put on Slim's uniform," he ordered.

Jewell heard him clearly, but she hesitated. Miles came to her defense again.

"She can't fit his uniform! *It's too big!*"

"She can roll up the pants and the sleeves," Daniel said. "If she don't get out the car, no one will notice."

He seemed poised and sure of himself, but Jewell never doubted him more.

"It's not gonna work!" Miles said. "We're calling it off."

Daniel spun on him. "We ain't calling shit off! You don't have to do nothing but pick us up! Quit crying like a *bitch*!"

Miles' mouth snapped shut like he'd been slapped.

Daniel turned to Jesse. "We can do it by ourselves, right? Just me and you."

Jesse shook his head. "I don't know. I thought we needed him."

"We don't," Daniel said. "It's *two* of us and *three* of them. We'll get the drop on them. It'll still work."

Jesse shrugged. "Alright, man."

Mile's mouth fell open again.

"We need this," Jesse said, but he sounded unsure.

Daniel didn't give Miles a chance to talk Jesse out of it. "I told you to go put that uniform on!" he said to Jewell. She took a deep breath and then went to the kitchen to retrieve it.

"Well, what about him?" she heard Miles ask when she left the room.

"We'll leave him here," Daniel said. "Deal with that when we get back."

"He's *high*," Miles said. "He could run down the street saying *anything* – to *anybody*."

"We'll tie him up," Daniel said as if this was common sense.

Jewell didn't hear a response to that. She collected Slim's uniform from the dining table, still in a daze. When she got back to the living room, they were moving her brother to the loveseat.

≈≈≈≈≈≈≈

Jewell went into the bedroom and dressed quietly. Slim's uniform was too big and way too long. She rolled up the pants and sleeves and still looked ridiculous. And she couldn't wear Slim's shoes at all, so she kept on her white Keds. She hoped they'd call an end to this travesty once they saw how silly she looked. But when she got back to the living room, Slim was tied down to the sofa with nylon ropes.

The men all stopped what they were doing and waited to see Jewell's reaction, but she didn't have one. So much was already wrong with this job and this day. *Why not* tie her brother up? Why not make her go in his place? Hell, why not stop by the cemetery and dig up her old mammy's bones on the way?

"See. She look fine," Daniel said. "Let's go."

CHAPTER TWENTY-FOUR
THE FINAL CHAPTER
THE AIRPORT JOB

Everyone left the safe house, except for Slim of course. Jewell stopped and kissed his sweaty forehead on the way out. He didn't look at her, but he seemed to smile a little when she rubbed his cheek.

"I love you," Jewell said.

Slim batted his eyes and began to snore lightly. Jewell's eyes filled with tears. She wiped them away and steeled her heart to feel no pain. She held her head high and marched out of the safe house like a soldier.

Slim's gun was heavy, and his belt didn't have enough holes in it for Jewell's small waistline. She had to hold her pants up as she walked to keep them from falling to her ankles.

≈ ≈ ≈ ≈ ≈ ≈

Slim was high, the plan was shot, and Miles was a nervous wreck, but Daniel was as confident as ever. He, Jesse, and Jewell huddled in the back seats of the Trooper while Miles drove. Daniel went over the game plan with them one last time, and Jewell listened like her life depended on it.

With Slim out of the picture, Jewell would have to drive the security car out of the airport after Jesse and Daniel subdued the guards and took possession of their armored truck. Daniel assured Jewell she would be able to drive right past the security gate with no problem.

"How?" she asked. "Won't they see this isn't my ID card?"

"Naw," Daniel said. He put a solid blue baseball cap on her head and pushed the bib down. "Just keep this hat on, and don't look up at him too much. You got the car, and you'll have the good access card. You can swipe it and let yourself out."

He made it sound so easy, but Jewell had no idea *where* she would swipe the card. She didn't know what the gate looked like, and she was pretty sure they wouldn't let her drive out without looking at her. But Daniel wasn't doubtful at all, and Jesse didn't object either. Jewell agreed to everything, and when Daniel asked if she was ready she lied and said she was.

"It's gonna work," Daniel promised.

Easy for you to say, Jewell thought. *You can make your getaway in an armored truck if the shit hits the fan.*

She felt like jumping from the moving vehicle and running – all the way to Mexico, but she smiled and said, "You're right. It's gonna work."

"You fucking with a genius," Daniel reminded her.

I'm fucking with **something**, Jewell thought.

≈ ≈ ≈ ≈ ≈ ≈ ≈

They stayed on the freeway for a long time. Miles drove in silence, and a prickly hush fell upon the Isuzu. Jesse tried to spark a couple of awkward conversations, but his voice shook too much when he talked. He finally had to stop himself after struggling through a particularly ragged sentence.

"I, I'm not scared," he said.

"It's alright," Daniel said. "Just quit talking."

That was good advice, so everyone took it.

When the freeway signs started directing them to the airport, the knot in Jewell's stomach became a kicking, grumbling thing. She balled her fists and applied pressure to her belly as if she was performing the Heimlich on herself.

"You alright?" Jesse asked her.

Jewell looked to Daniel before responding. He stared at her without emotion, but Jewell knew what he wanted to hear.

"I'm fine," she said. "It's just my nerves."

On the outskirts of the airport district, Miles pulled into the driveway of a concrete building Jewell had never seen before. He parked in front of a large bay door and got of out the car. Jewell leaned forward and watched him through the front windshield.

Miles unfastened a padlock with a single key not connected to his ring and pulled the door up with much a clank and rattle of chains. It was dark in there, but Jewell could see there was only one vehicle in the garage. It was a white Impala with a yellow beacon light on top.

Miles got back in the Trooper and pulled in next to the security car. He got out again and shook everyone's hands individually as they transferred to the other vehicle. Jewell was the last to go. Standing there, she looked like a young soldier who lied about his age to make the draft. Miles pulled her in for a big hug before she climbed into the Impala.

"Good luck," he whispered close to her ear.

"Thank you," Jewell said. "You'd better be there when we get out."

"I wouldn't miss it for the world," Miles assured her.

He kissed her on the cheek and let go. Jewell got into the backseat of the Impala and sat behind her man. Jesse was on the passenger side. Jewell nervously fastened her safety belt.

Daniel started the car and put it in drive.

Three minutes later they were on the freeway again. Jewell still felt like jumping from the vehicle, but she knew it was too late to bail out now. In his current state of mind, Daniel would probably make a U-turn so he could run her down. And he would *still* do the job after that, even while her blood bubbled on the Impala's exhaust pipes.

≈ ≈ ≈ ≈ ≈ ≈

The Dallas/Overbrook Meadows Airport was an immense, towering structure no matter what angle you approached it from. Jewell sat stiffly in the back seat and tried not to look around too much once they made it onto the property. There was so much that caught her attention and *begged* for a long stare. It was in her nature to pay attention to her surroundings, but a security guard wouldn't be concerned with such things if he worked there everyday.

They drove by the main terminal and passed gate after gate. Ten minutes went by and they were still driving. Each time Daniel slowed to a stop, Jewell's heart started to hammer again.

But when she looked up, he was just at a pedestrian crosswalk or a stop sign.

She almost asked if he was lost a few times, but Daniel was being so quiet, she didn't want to disturb whatever thought process he had going. Plus Jesse never said anything, so she figured they were still on the right track.

After five more minutes of what had to be Jewell's most mind-numbing ride, Daniel made a turn into an area that was definitely not part of the general airport. The population changed from tourists and businessmen to security guards dressed like them. There were a lot of other airport employees too, and each crew wore different colored uniforms. A guy on a forklift drove by on Jewell's left.

Straight ahead of them was a large gate with a security tower in the center. There were two guards at the station: One looked to be running the booth, and the other appeared to be talking casually. Jewell was about to ask if this was where they were going in, but Daniel spoke before she got the question out.

"This is it," he said, heading right for the tower. "Jesse, just look normal. Baby, keep your head down, so he can't see your face."

What about my clothes? Jewell wondered, but it was too late for that. Daniel pulled to a smooth stop next to the guard tower and unclipped the badge from his lapel. He waved it in front of a black scanner as if he had every right to be there.

But nothing happened.

The guard at the station was still talking to his coworker. He was a white man with a thick, handlebar moustache and a large gut. He looked over at the stolen Impala, but his friend kept talking. He held up a finger to Daniel, but Dapper Dan wasn't waiting for help or closer scrutiny. He waved the card again, and it beeped this time.

"I got it," Daniel called.

The gate rolled open slowly on metal wheels, and the guard turned back to his conversation. He never gave Daniel a second look. Jewell didn't think he saw her at all. She let out a pent-up breath and sat up in her seat as they entered the cargo area. Her palms were wet on the leather seat. She wiped them on her pants, but they were slick again a few seconds later.

"We in here," Daniel said with a grin. "What I tell you, baby."

Jewell sighed, and her fear was replaced by a mild exhilaration. Rather than suppress it, she allowed the excitement to build. If they got this far, they were going to make it. She never believed in the job one hundred percent, but she had to believe now. It was either make it or die at this point – because given his mood, she knew Daniel would rather shoot it out than surrender and worry about the penitentiary.

≈ ≈ ≈ ≈ ≈ ≈

The cargo area reminded Jewell of an underground parking lot, except there wasn't a lot of room for parking. It was the colors that made her think that. The building they were in was gray. The whole structure was made of concrete, and no one ever thought a coat of paint might liven things up.

To their immediate right was a row of forklifts like the one Jewell saw outside. There were a few guys over there wearing bright orange hardhats and yellow vests with a reflective stripe around their bellies. There were a dozen or so security vehicles lined up behind the forklifts.

To their left was a large wall with orange numbers and directional arrows painted on it. According to a sign posted near the ceiling, the East Cargo Bay had gone 241 days without an accident.

A hundred yards ahead of them was a row of bay doors stretching from right to left. Some of them were open, and beyond these doors Jewell could see blue skies, a runway scarred with circular, crisscrossing tire tracks and even a few airplanes parked in the distance. There were security guards everywhere, at least ten of them in their immediate vicinity. Jewell saw white Impalas moving in all directions.

It was hard to believe, but she really did feel anonymous in there. Daniel said they'd be able to roll around with immunity, and she was starting to think he was right.

Daniel headed towards the bay doors, going no more than five miles per hour.

"Our truck's coming from that way," he said, pointing to his left.

Jewell didn't see anything significant in that direction, but the place was huge. He could have been referring to a point fifty feet or fifty yards away.

He made a right down one of the long aisles and had to slow for a forklift attempting a U-turn in the tight space. They came to a complete stop and waited, and the driver gave them a courtesy wave before heading off in the opposite direction.

"See," Daniel said. "We're all one big, happy family down here."

Jewell grinned like a child at Christmas. She couldn't help it. This whole thing was fantastic. Outlandish even. But they were really doing it! And so far everything was proceeding perfectly.

Daniel made two more lefts and pulled to a stop next to an empty security car. He was facing the gate they came in through, but they were so far away Jewell could barely see it in the distance.

"Is this where the truck's coming by?" she asked. She hoped it wasn't, because this spot was not isolated at all. If someone pulled a gun, there would be at least twenty eyes on them.

"Naw," Daniel said. "I'm waiting..." He checked his watch. "I want to see the truck when it comes in."

Jesse looked at his watch too. "We're late," he said. "The truck's probably already here."

"Not yet," Daniel said.

"Let's go see," Jesse suggested.

Daniel shook his head. "I don't wanna go over there. I don't want nobody to see us anywhere near those safes."

Jesse gnawed on his nails. "So what are you gonna do if the truck's already here? We won't have time to get in position."

Daniel looked at his watch again. "I don't think it's here."

Jewell had no idea who was right, but Jesse's idea sounded better. "I think we should go check," she said.

Daniel shot her a look in the rear-view mirror and sighed. He put the car in reverse and backed out of his spot. He drove west this time, with the bay doors on their right. At nine o'clock in the morning, the building was already bustling. It got even more congested as they neared the safes.

After few minutes of slow driving, Daniel said, "Alright, the safes are coming up. But *don't look*." He nodded to his left.

Jewell watched out of the corner of her eyes. She didn't see an actual *safe*, but she knew this was an area of high security. The guards over there looked more militaristic. They stood at attention, some wore helmets, and a few were decked out in camouflage. These men had bigger guns too, the kinds you have to hold with two hands.

What Jewell was looking at was like another building within the building. This new structure was concrete also, divided into a dozen or so garage-size cells. Each cell had its own metal doors, and each cell had its own iron gate.

Jewell knew Daniel was right about the impossibility of robbing one of those safes. Even if you got past the guard posted outside, there were dozens more within earshot.

Most of the safes were idle, but two of them were open. Jewell couldn't tell if they were removing or depositing valuables, but the activity around them peaked her interest, especially the one with the Brinks truck backed up to it.

"That's it!" Jesse hissed.

Daniel kept his neck stiff and his eyes forward. "I told you we were late," he mumbled under his breath.

Jewell couldn't help *but* look at the truck. All of her dreams were in that thing, her whole life. She watched it openly as Daniel made his approach.

"It's okay," Jesse said. "They're not done loading yet."

And that was true. Jewell saw that the back of the truck was still open, and two Brinks guards were standing on the loading dock. But the truck drivers were wearing *black* uniforms. This was the first Jewell knew of that.

"I thought you were going to drive their truck out," she said to Daniel.

"I am."

"But they got different color uniforms."

"Ain't nobody gon' be worried about our uniforms," Daniel said. "Long as we don't have on tee-shirts, I think we okay."

Jewell thought it was a little late in the game to still be assuming things. But Jesse didn't seem worried, so she kept her mouth closed.

She sat back and studied the scenery as Daniel maneuvered the Impala around pillars and parked cars like he worked there all his life. He pulled to a stop around the corner from the safes and

left the car running. If this was their interception spot, Jewell
wasn't pleased.

"There's a camera *right there*," she said, pointing towards
the ceiling.

"It's alright," Daniel said without looking. "No one's
watching it right now."

"Harvey pulled them away from the monitors?" Jewell
asked.

"Naw," Daniel said. "Harvey ain't here. He took off today,
on purpose."

"How you know nobody's watching it?" Jewell asked.

"'Cause he told me nobody was gon' be watching it right
now," Daniel said. "I don't know how he arranged it or if he even
had anything to do with it, but he was *positive*."

Jewell accepted that, but she still had a million other
questions, especially after ten minutes passed and they still didn't
have an armored truck headed their way. Instead of asking Daniel
if he was sure a dozen more times, she asked Jesse, "What are you
going to do with your money?"

"I'm moving to Brazil," he said quickly.

Jewell liked the way his tongue rolled with the word.
"*Oooh*, I wanna go to Brazil," she said.

"Shhh," Daniel said.

"Quit being a grouch," Jewell said, but Daniel didn't
respond. His eyes were stuck on the rearview mirror. Jewell
turned and looked behind them, and there it was; their future
rolled towards them in a big white truck.

"Is that it?' she whispered.

Daniel nodded. He looked over at Jesse. "You ready, boy?"

Jesse nodded, but it was clear that he wasn't.

"What about you, baby?" Daniel asked.

"Yeah," Jewell said. "Get in the front seat and follow you
out."

"*No!*" Daniel grunted. "We're following *you* out! *You're*
the one who can open the gate!" He snatched the good access card
off his badge and handed it to her over his shoulder. "Don't forget,
baby: Get in front of us after we get the truck."

"And go *where*?" Jewell asked.

"*Out the gate,* girl!"

Jewell paid attention to where they were going, but not the kind of attention she would have paid if she knew she was leading the charge to freedom, *precious freedom*.

But it was too late to get directions now. The Brinks truck passed slowly on their left, and Daniel immediately swooped into position behind it.

Jewell thought he'd give them a few yards, but Daniel pulled up fast and got right on the truck's bumper. He pushed one of the buttons on his dash, and the beacon light atop their car began to spin, flashing yellow lights in all directions.

Rather than pull over, the truck stopped in its tracks. Daniel slowed to a stop behind it and pulled up the Impala's emergency break.

He took a deep breath and looked over at Jesse again. "You ready?"

Jesse nodded. He was as white as a sheet.

Daniel turned and looked at Jewell. "Don't get in the front seat until *after* we got 'em tied up," he said. "If it goes bad, we're jumping back in this car."

"I love you, baby," Jewell said. She leaned forward and gave him a deep kiss. His lips were cold, but his breath was hot. Daniel turned back around and pulled his cap down over his eyes. He and Jesse exited the Impala at the same time. Jesse took his lucky tool bag with him.

≈ ≈ ≈ ≈ ≈ ≈ ≈

The next few hours of Jewell's life took the form of horrifying, fast-paced dream. Her heart started to kick like a donkey when Daniel got out of the car. She watched from the backseat, knowing full well this shit wasn't going to work. The drivers of armored cars are trained not to leave their vehicles for any reason once they're en route. If there's an exception to this rule, they have to radio it in to their superiors and get permission first.

But Dapper Dan walked up to the driver's side and smiled confidently. He looked up at the window and started talking and pointing to the back of their truck. The Impala's windows were up, so Jewell couldn't hear what he was saying, but she knew he wasn't going to pull it off. There was no way. And Jesse stood a few feet back looking seriously out of place, Jewell thought. He looked towards the ground and back at her for some reason, and he wouldn't look up at the truck at all.

But Daniel was different. He kept laughing and talking, and then he gestured towards the back of their truck again. At one point he looked directly at Jewell and winked. She gasped, thinking that was the most ridiculous thing he could do, but damned if the Brink's front door didn't swing open. A big guy dressed in all black stepped out, and Daniel put a hand on his back and turned him towards the Impala.

Jewell ducked out of sight. She scooted as far back in her seat as she could go, but it wasn't far enough. She would squeeze between the leather and get in the *trunk* if she could.

After a few seconds, Jewell mustered the courage to peer around the front seat. She couldn't believe what her boyfriend was doing: Not only did Daniel have the driver out, but the passenger door was open too. Daniel stood at the back of the truck with a guard on either side of him. One was undoing the lock.

As soon as they rolled the door up, Daniel took a step back towards the Impala and drew his gun. Jewell saw a third guard in the back of the truck. He had two weapons close by, one looked like a Mossberg pump, but he didn't have time to reach for either. Daniel had the drop on all of them from his position, and once Jesse decided to help out a little, the guards had no chance.

Daniel spoke softly. Jewell barely heard murmurs from her vantage point. He instructed the two men nearest him to put their hands behind their heads and climb into the truck with their comrade. Both were totally surprised, expecting anything but this. The driver looked back at the Impala and locked eyes with Jewell for a second. Daniel bumped him on the head with the butt of his .45 and repeated his order.

The guards climbed into the truck as instructed with Jesse quick on their heels. The safecracker holstered his weapon and dug in his tool bag for the zip ties Miles gave him. Daniel stayed outside the truck with his pistol pointed. Jewell didn't understand how or why, but no traffic was coming towards them in either direction. Even Daniel's beacon light attracted no attention.

One full minute passed. Jewell sat up and leaned on the front seats. She had a perfect view of the truck. She saw Jesse working like a mad man in there. He had all three guards on their bellies with their hands tied behind their backs already. He moved to their legs, jerking them roughly like he was calf-roping. When he got down to the last guard, Daniel holstered his pistol and pulled the back door closed.

He looked at Jewell and motioned for her to turn the light off on the Impala. She scrambled to the front seat and toggled the switch she saw him hit earlier. She released the emergency break with fingers that were cold and shaky.

Daniel climbed into the front seat of the armored truck, and Jewell pulled along side him. He smiled at her and pointed to the left. Jewell made the turn with her man rolling right behind her. The whole robbery took no more than two minutes.

Jewell didn't think she'd know which way to go, but everything became familiar to her once she started looking around. The bay doors were to her left, so she knew she had to make a right to get out of the cargo area. She drove slowly with Daniel right on her bumper. She squeezed the steering wheel so hard her knuckles were white. Sweat dampened her armpits and beaded on her forehead.

When she got to a large intersection, Jewell looked right and saw the guard station some twenty yards away. She expected there to be a roadblock set up, or at least a long line of vehicles that would delay them long enough for someone to figure out what happened, but as far as she could tell her ride to riches was completely uninhibited. Jewell made the turn and had to fight off a strong urge to floor it and plow through the gate.

There was only one guard at the station when she approached, and he was looking right at her this time. Jewell slowed to a stop and fumbled with the access card Daniel gave her. It wasn't even connected to her badge like it should be. She was stupid not to think of that, but it was too late to affix it now.

Jewell lowered her window and held her breath as she waved the access card in front of the sensor pad. Less than three feet away, the guard with the handlebar moustache watched her every move, it seemed. Jewell knew he was studying Slim's uniform, how it was bunched up on her arm.

But the sensor beeped, and the gate began to roll open. Jewell snatched her arm in quickly and raised her window. She faced forward, not even looking at the guard in her peripheral, and he didn't do anything to halt her progress. She rolled out as smooth as silk. Daniel made it out right behind her before the gate had a chance to close again.

Five minutes later they were on the freeway. Jewell slowed and let Daniel get in front of her then, because she had no idea where Miles was supposed to pick them up.

≈≈≈≈≈≈

Riding behind a stolen armored truck filled with stolen diamonds that would soon be all yours was almost as nerve-racking as being in the airport. Jewell kept checking her mirrors, expecting a few black and whites to swoop behind her with their berries flashing. But the cops never came. As soon as they left the airport district, Daniel merged to the right lane and took a county road exit Jewell had never been on before.

He made a right and stayed on CR 113 for only a few minutes before turning on his signal lights again. This time he made a left turn. Jewell followed, and she saw Miles' Isuzu parked on the side of the road fifty feet ahead of them. She would have preferred a better switch point, preferably one with a *roof* overhead, but this road was deserted. It was also right off the freeway.

Daniel pulled to a dusty stop next to the green Trooper and jumped out like the truck was on fire. Jewell parked behind him with the whole world spinning around her. She shook her arms furiously, like she was trying to fly or escape from a straight-jacket, and the sleeves on Slim's uniform came free, leaving her with six inches of fabric hanging past her hands. Jewell used this material to wipe off the steering wheel and gear shift and everything else she thought they might have touched. She worked recklessly, breaking a knob off the air conditioner with little regard.

Daniel pulled his gun before opening the back of the truck, but there was no need. The guards were still on their stomachs, and they weren't struggling at all anymore. Miles stepped forward sweating like he was in a sauna. His arms and face were totally slick, and there was a dark stain on his chest.

"I got em out!" he screamed. "But they're heavy!"

Daniel re-holstered his weapon and jumped in the truck like an Olympic hurdler. Miles got out of the Trooper as pale as ever, but he didn't hesitate at all. He ran to the back of the truck just as Daniel slid a huge, metal box towards the edge. Miles tried to lift it by himself, but he couldn't. Daniel jumped out again, and together they hauled it to the Isuzu. The box was three feet long, four feet wide and two feet deep. Jewell watched them with wide eyes, and then she hustled to the backseat to wipe down everything she touched back there.

In her peripheral, she saw Jesse scramble out of the armored truck with his tool bag in one hand, and a large deposit bag in the other. He ran towards the Impala, but Daniel steered him the other way.

"Get in the other one!"

Jesse reunited with Miles, and Daniel went to help Jewell instead. He opened the passenger door with a large towel and started wiping like he was at a carwash.

Jewell looked over the seat at him. Daniel was sweating, and he looked panicked, but he was smiling too.

"You got it?" she asked.

"Oh, baby, we got it. It's *everything*, girl. Everything we ever wanted. Hurry up. Go get in the car."

Jewell took another second to wipe the back of the bucket seats, and then she used her sleeve to let herself out. Her pants got tangled around her ankles, and she took a tumble on the hard grass, but that was just fine. The air was fresh out there, and the breeze felt good on her face. She made it to her feet and hobbled to the Isuzu like a battered soldier escaping the Hanoi Hilton.

Jesse grabbed her arm when she got to the side door. He pulled her up like she weighed nothing at all. Daniel dove in behind her a half a second later, and Miles floored it before the door was closed behind him.

≈≈≈≈≈≈

They waited until they got back on the freeway before declaring the job a victory, but once the declaration was made, all hell broke lose. They were like a rowdy soccer team heading home after a road win.

"Didn't I tell y'all? *Didn't I tell y'all?!*" Daniel stood in the SUV and tore his uniform shirt off. He wore only a wife-beater underneath. His arms and chest were huge.

"You the man!" Miles called from the front seat.

"You did it," Jesse agreed.

"I'm the *motherfucking man!*" Daniel yelled. He pounded his chest like a gorilla. "I'm the *motherfucking man!*"

Jewell took off her cap and shirt as well. She leaned over the seat to monitor the progress Jesse was making with the metal box. There was only one lock on it. And since it didn't matter if he left evidence of tampering, he abandoned all of his trademarked finesse. He went at it with a hammer and chisel. No one cared how much noise he made.

"Check this out, baby," Daniel said. He handed her the bank bag Jesse brought out with him, and Jewell almost choked when she peered inside. There were twelve stacks of bills. Each stack had nothing but hundreds. According to the bank tape binding them, each stack contained ten thousand dollars.

"How much is it?" Miles asked.

Jewell looked up and saw him watching her in the rearview mirror.

"A hundred thousand," she said. "A hundred and *twenty*!"

Miles whistled.

"*My God*," Jesse said.

"*Goddamn!*" Daniel agreed, but the last two remarks weren't for what was in that bank bag. Jesse had the strong box open, and the sparkle that emanated from it had his face aglow.

Jewell leaned forward and she nearly passed out. There was a flat bed of black felt with small indentions in it. In each hole was a large diamond, each one more beautiful than the next. All of the rocks were huge, about the size of a marble, and there were at least fifty of them.

With just what she was looking at, Jewell knew they were set for life, but this was only the first layer. Jesse dug around the corners and lifted it up, and underneath it was another bed of felt with more diamonds embedded. Some were set in rings and bracelets already, but most were loose. Jewell saw yellows and blues, greens and pinks. And Jesse was still at the very top! They would have to dig down two feet to get to the last of them.

Noticing the quiet, Miles looked up in the mirror again. "You got it open?"

Jesse nodded. He returned the first pad carefully and lowered the metal lid.

"Yeah," he said to Miles. "It's, it's everything he said it would be." He leaned back and nodded at Daniel.

Jewell looked into her man's eyes, and he met her stare. He grinned and wiped the sweat from his forehead. He winked at her, and she blew him a kiss.

Miles was smiling too, but Jewell watched him in the mirror and saw that it was only *half a smile*. It didn't reach his eyes at all.

"What's wrong?" she called to the front.

Miles sighed and cleared his throat. His grin went away entirely. "I, I went back to the house after I dropped you guys off."

Jewell's face fell. She knew he had bad news, and she knew her brother was involved. "Is Slim alright?"

Miles nodded. "He is. He was coming around a little bit."

That was a relief, but it left everyone even more curious.

"Why you go back over there?" Daniel asked.

"I didn't have anything else to do," Miles said. He shrugged. "I was antsy."

"So what you looking all ugly for?" Daniel asked.

"He, uh, Slim says he got that brick of heroin out of Percy's car," Miles announced.

Jesse looked from Jewell to Daniel, but neither of them said anything.

"He said you guys knew about it," Miles went on.

Jewell felt a tightening in her chest. She looked at Daniel, and his strong features were already forming a vicious sneer.

"So what?" he shouted. "We just found out a couple days ago. What about it?"

Miles shrugged. "Nothing, I guess. I'm just wondering why you didn't tell *us* about it. Did you know about it, Jesse?"

Jesse shook his head, and Jewell didn't like the way he was looking at her and her boyfriend.

"It wasn't that big a deal," Daniel said.

"What do you mean it wasn't that big of a deal?" Miles asked. "You knew a heroin addict had a boatload of heroin, and you still kept him on the job? Plus you said that thing was worth two-hundred thousand dollars. I thought we always split everything."

"What are you trying to say?" Daniel growled.

"I'm just, I'm just wondering," Miles said. "Were you and Jewell going to keep that heroin for yourself, or what?"

Daniel shook his head. "Man, I don't believe this shit."

"What?" Miles asked.

"We got all these diamonds here, and you're worried about a fucking brick of dope. Do you know how much this shit here is worth?"

"It's not the value," Miles clarified. "It's the *principle*. If we're together, then we're *together*. Everything gets disclosed."

"Alright," Daniel said. He grinned, and the tension wafted from him. "Fuck it. My bad, nigga. *I'm sorry.*"

His apology was weak, and Miles took it as such. He rolled his eyes and kept his attention on the road.

Daniel looked around at Jesse and Jewell and chuckled. "Can you believe this shit?" he asked. "We got fifty million dollars here, and this nigga's worried about some *goddamned dope*!"

Jesse grinned a little, but he didn't seem to think it was so insignificant either.

Fresh off a clean getaway from the largest diamond heist Overbrook Meadows had ever known, and the syndicate drove home in a brooding silence.

≈ ≈ ≈ ≈ ≈ ≈ ≈

Things didn't get any better when they got back to Safe House #3.

Miles pulled into the garage, and the gang piled out like anxious strangers. They left the strong box in the back because Jewell and Daniel were supposed to leave together in the Trooper after they changed clothes and divided up the cash from the bank bag. But when they got inside, it was immediately clear there would be no calm division of funds.

Jewell went in first because she was worried about her brother. For the rest of her life she would regret not letting Daniel go in ahead of her.

Slim was still tied down in the same position she last saw him in, but even from halfway across the room, Jewell could see he was dead.

His head lay awkwardly on his shoulder. His face was dry and ashen. Slim's eyes were wide open, but they didn't follow

278

Jewell as she approached him. They stared past her, *through her*, to the very ends of time she supposed. His mouth was open too, but his lips and tongue were dry. The drool in the corner of his mouth had long since crusted over.

With all the ropes on him, Slim looked like he got lynched.

Jewell stood over him, and her body began to convulse uncontrollably. Everything grew dark around her. She knew it was wrong to blame herself for this, but how could she not? *She* brought Cedric into this. She gave him access to Percy's heroin, and she didn't kick him out when she knew the pressure was too much for him.

Instead of her brother's life passing before her eyes, Jewell saw her feeble old mother. Miss Eveline was speaking to her, and her words cut like a knife:

Could you try? If he messes up, then that'll be on him. But he says he's doing right this time. I talk to him sometimes, and I believe him, Clarissa. He say he don't wanna go to jail no more. He wants to get a regular job, but no one will hire him. I know you can help him, baby. This'll just be one less thing I have to worry about when I go home. I pray for that boy all the time.

Rather than accept this huge burden of guilt, Jewell turned on the first person she saw. When Miles came and stood next to her, she vented *just because*.

"Oh my God, Jewell. What's wrong with him?"

"What did you do to him?"

Miles reached to put an arm around her, and he backed away when he saw her expression.

"Jewell? *I* didn't do anything to him. I would never…"

Deep inside Jewell knew she was wrong, but it was much easier to attack him than herself. She started swinging and crying simultaneously.

"Why'd you kill him? Why'd you do it? He never hurt nobody! I hate you! I hate you!"

Miles backed away and blocked her blows easily. "Jewell! *Stop!* I didn't do anything! You know I could never hurt anyone!"

Someone grabbed her from behind. She could tell by the size and strength it was Daniel. He spun her around until she was facing the kitchen again, and then he shoved her in that direction.

"Go get in the car!"

Jewell stumbled forward. Tears streamed down her face like blood. She reached out blindly and ran into the dining table. Daniel grabbed her again and pushed her out the back door.

"Get in the car!"

Jewell staggered on wet noodle legs. From what felt like miles behind her, she heard a commotion. Jewell listened, but her soul was detached.

"What's wrong with her? She knows I would never do that!"

"It's alright," Daniel said. "She'll be alright."

"What happened to him?"

"Fucker probably overdosed. Man, what the fuck?"

"But she knows I didn't do that, right?"

"Don't worry about it. She's just in shock."

"Goddamn. Man, this is *screwy."*

"Well, what's gonna happen now?"

"I'm gon' take her home. I'll come back and help you get rid of this."

"Wait! I wanna talk to her."

"We'll be *right back."*

"Hold on, man. What, what about the diamonds?"

"I'm going to take care of those like we planned. Nothing's changing."

"But, but hold on."

"I gotta go, man! I said I'll be back!"

"Wait, Daniel. Just, just, you know, I've been thinking, and, and I, I want my diamonds now."

"What the fuck, man? We had a deal! You can't even get rid of them."

"I might take a loss, but I'd really feel better if I had them *now."*

"Why, Miles? Why? What the fuck is wrong with you?"

"Dude, she thinks I killed her brother. There's no telling what's gonna happen when you leave."

"I said I'm coming back!"

"Well, that's fine, man. If you do, you do. But I *really* want to get my diamonds before you go."

"Me too."

"Man, get away from me! We're doing it like we said!"

Jewell stumbled down the back porch and fell into the front end of the Trooper. The hood was hot. She backed away from it like she got shocked. She moaned like an old slave and teetered to the driver's side. Her legs threatened to collapse any second.

When she got behind the wheel, Jewell saw Daniel storm out the back door with Jesse and Miles right behind him. Daniel punched the button to make the garage open and kept moving.

"Start the car, baby!"

The keys were still in the ignition, but it took Jewell a couple of tries because her head was so muddled. Her fingers were slick. The engine roared to life, and the garage opened slowly behind her.

Daniel marched to the passenger side, and Miles grabbed his arm. Daniel turned and shoved him to the ground easily.

"*Get the fuck off me, nigga!*"

"*Wait, Daniel! Stop!*" Jesse yelled.

"*He's trying to steal the diamonds!*" Miles squealed. "*Just like he stole the heroin!*"

Daniel turned back to the SUV, and Jesse pulled the .45 from his holster with all the finesse of Barney Fife.

"*Stop!*" he screamed. "For real, man!" His face was a twisted mess of fear and confusion. He pointed the gun at Daniel. "Please, man. Just, just, let's talk about this."

Daniel turned and smiled at him. "Nigga, put that shit down."

"Give us our diamonds, man. Just, we want our diamonds."

Daniel put his hands in the air playfully. "You gon' shoot me, Jesse? You ain't have the nuts to pull the trigger the whole time I've known you, but you ready now? You ready to kill somebody?"

Jesse started crying. Miles made it to his feet and headed for the Trooper's side door. "We just want our–"

Daniel hit him in the mouth before he could finish the sentence. He turned towards Jewell one last time and screamed *"GO, GIRL! DRIVE OFF!"*

Jewell was so dazed, she might not have done it, but the gunfire brought everything back into focus.

BAP!

BAP! BAP!
Jewell slammed her foot on the gas pedal and shot out of the garage like a crocodile lunging from a river. She jerked the wheel hard to the left when she hit the street and somehow avoided plowing into the curb on the opposite side.

She punched the brake and threw the Isuzu into drive again. She panted furiously. Her heart was on fire. The gunfire rang in her ear.

Before she pealed off again, Jewell looked back at the safe house, still not believing any of this was happening. Through her tears, she saw a scene she wouldn't have expected in a million years: Jesse and Miles were running after her. They both had guns now, and they were pointing them at her.

POP!
POP!
POP!POP!
TINK!
TINK!TINK!TINK!
Jewell screamed and stomped the gas just like Davis would have wanted her to. With blood rushing in her ears and gun smoke in her nose, she navigated the Trooper through the quiet neighborhood like Jeff Gordon on crack.

But she didn't wreck.

Five minutes later she got on the freeway, headed west.

≈≈≈≈≈≈≈

Jewell drove until the sun set, and she was still driving when it rose again.

Thirteen hours after embarking on her journey, she stopped and got a room for one at an Albuquerque Motel 6. She was dehydrated and half-starved, but her body still had enough moisture to pump out what had to be a years worth of tears.

Sleep finally fell upon her, like the sweet release of death. And in her dreams, Jewell saw Slim's dead eyes, Percy's hanging eye, and her mother's foggy eyes. She saw the feds searching her Trooper, and she saw them towing it out of the motel's parking lot.

But when she woke up the next morning, everything was just as she left it.

EPILOGUE
FIVE YEARS LATER
LA JOLLA, CALIFORNIA

"Alright folks, I'm sitting here with Detective *Randy Miller* who worked the case originally. This guy's a real live *Texas State Trooper*! Detective, what's your take on the bandits?"

The man asking the questions was young, blue-eyed and bushy-haired. He wore no tie or sports coat because his show was *new*, *fresh*, *cutting-edge* and *cool*; all things needed when delving into old, dusty capers like the Glasgow Train Robbery and the Laughlin Casino Heist.

The interviewee sported a gray seersucker suit with a white shirt and black tie. He was about fifty years old and completely bald on top. He wore coke-bottle glasses. He had the look of a serious man. He looked slightly put-off by his host's casual nature.

"They were cunning," the detective said.

"*Sophisticated*?" the interviewer asked.

The detective frowned. "I wouldn't say *sophisticated*. There, there really wasn't any sophistication involved in this crime. No intricate technology, no high-tech gadgets – nothing like that at all."

The host of the program leaned in conspiratorially. "So, how'd they do it?"

"A bunch of luck," the detective said flatly. "And inside help. They definitely had an inside guy."

Clarissa Hunt, who was no longer known as Jewell, watched the broadcast intently, although she already saw it when it premiered two months ago. She sat on a fiberglass chair that was as uncomfortable as it was ugly. She had to crane her neck because the television was mounted on a bracket that extended from the ceiling.

It hadn't been a decade yet, but already their robbery was a thing of folklore.

"This *inside guy*," the interviewer said. "Who was that?"

This television program didn't get very high ratings, but it was one of Clarissa's favorites. She liked how the host made each clue feel like *breaking news*. If you didn't already know the story of Jack the Ripper, this man would have you thinking the killer was still at large.

"We had a really strong suspect," the detective said.

The interviewer faced the camera. "And that suspect is *this man!*" The screen went black and a creepy baseline ensued.

Thun Thun Thun...

"Harvey Brumley!"

Harvey's picture suddenly filled the screen. It was a mug shot, so he looked guilty of *whatever* they wanted to say about him, but Clarissa knew this was just another industry trick. Harvey only got arrested once in his whole life, and that was for a DUI back when he was in college. Rather than use a more recent photo, the producers of this program picked the most unflattering one they could find.

The scene cut back to the detective and the young host. "Harvey Brumley was a security guard at the airport at the time of the robbery," the policeman said. "At one point, he was our prime suspect in this case."

"Well, why didn't you arrest him?" the interviewer asked.

The detective sighed, more upset with the line of questioning than the results of his investigation. "He had a solid alibi. We were never able to prove beyond a reasonable doubt that he had anything to do with it."

"Tell us why you suspected him," the host prompted. "Why do you think there even was an inside man?"

Clarissa grinned. This guy was cool. She'd like to meet him one day.

The cop rolled his eyes. "The suspects had uniforms just like the ones the other security guards wore. They had one of the airport security access cards. They had one of the airport's security vehicles, and they knew exactly when the truck was coming in and going out. There's no way they got all of that without help from someone inside."

"But why *this guy*?" the host asked. He reached under the table like a magician and pulled up an 8x10 of Harvey's mug shot.

"We did, extensive research on *all* of the cargo employees," the detective said. "And Mr. Brumley was the only one to raise any red flags."

"What were those red flags?"

"He was in charge of security, first of all. He had access to the uniforms. He didn't report the security vehicle stolen until after the heist, and we have reason to believe he set up a co-worker and facilitated the theft of the access card."

The interviewer tossed Harvey's photo over his shoulder. "But couldn't all of that have been, merely coincidental?"

The detective nodded. "Of course it could've. Which is why Mr. Brumley is a free man today."

The host nodded. He reached under the table and came up with another picture. This one was a facial composite of a female. It was similar to the one that graced the papers when Percy Hamilton got robbed, but this portrayal of Clarissa had a different hairstyle. Some of the facial features were off as well.

"Who's this?"

"That's the female accomplice," the detective said. "We believe she stole the access card later used by the thieves to gain entry into the cargo bay."

The host held the picture at arm's length and examined it, as if for the first time.

"She's kinda hot," he observed.

The cop looked around awkwardly. "Um, okay."

The camera zoomed in for a close-up of the host. "Okay! When we get back, we're going to find out who this sexy lady is, and maybe *you* can help us break this case! I'm Lance England, and you're watching *World Famous Heists and Robberies!*"

They went to a Luvs commercial, and Clarissa stretched out her arms and yawned.

"They ain't never gon' catch them people," the man next to her said.

"How you know that?" the guy sitting across from him asked.

"'Cause ain't nobody even stole nothing," the first one replied. "Them white folks got that money! They do it all the time; say somebody stole it so they can steal it theyself, and get the *insurance!*"

Clarissa chuckled. Both men were aged, at least seventy years old. The first guy was dark-skinned with totally white hair. His friend had a fair complexion, and he was bald. They were dressed like a 1970 Sears catalogue.

"What's your take on this?" the first one asked Clarissa.

"Shut up, you old fool!" the second one blurted. "She look like the kind of girl who got something to say to you?"

Clarissa wore a long black skirt with a white blouse. Her hair was a bit longer these days, but she still preferred short hairstyles. Her bob was jet black with auburn highlights. She wore no make up, but she was still a beautiful woman, stunning really. She wore knee-high leather boots that made her look like a sexy school teacher. Her diamond studded earrings were the only jewelry she had on.

"Y'all a trip," she said.

The first one chuckled. "So, what you think about that there heist?"

Clarissa shrugged. "Sounds like somebody got away with a lot of money."

"Wish I had money like that," the old-timer replied.

Clarissa grinned at him. "Why? What would you do with it?"

He grinned back. "I'd get me *two* gals, just like you! Take 'em wherever they wanted to go. Get me some of them Venetras..."

Venetra was the newest version of the outdated Viagra drug. It was supposed to be twice as potent and long-lasting.

Clarissa laughed, but the second guy chastised his friend.

"Boy, you can't be talking 'bout no Venetra to a young gal like that! You trying to get your crazy-ass locked up?"

"Young gal?" Clarissa said, still smiling. "I'm almost forty years old."

The first one turned and gave her his full attention then. "*Forty*? You sho' don't look it."

"Thanks," Clarissa said. She looked at her watch and curiously eyed the one-person restroom on the other side of the room. She stood and crossed the small waiting area. "This girl's been in here too long," she said to herself.

"My *goodness*!" the first geezer said when she walked by him. "I hate to see you leave, but I *love to watch you go*!"

Clarissa looked back at him and raised an eyebrow. "Oooh, I'm gonna have to watch you!"

He leaned back and patted his belly. "*Watch me, baby*!"

"Leave that woman alone!" his friend warned.

"Shut up! I ain't said nothing to you."

Clarissa shook her head and knocked softly on the restroom door. "You doing alright in there?" she asked.

"Yes," a small voice called from inside.

"What's taking so long?" Clarissa asked.

"My stocking got a hole."

"Open up," Clarissa said. After a couple seconds, she heard the lock un-latch. She went inside the bathroom and closed the door.

Danielle stood in front of the toilet with the front of her dress pinned under her chin. She had her panties up, but her stockings were twisted and soiled. They bound her ankles like leg irons. She looked up at her mother with the cutest expression of innocence. Clarissa wondered if she taught her that or if it was genetic.

Danielle certainly didn't get those locks from her mom: The little girl had a head full of hair. It was dark, thick and bushy. Clarissa puffed it all out once, and her little girl looked like a Jackson Five reject.

Danielle was four years old and as cute as a button. She had big, Bambi eyes and skin the color of a manila folder. Today she had wore her hair in two thick ponytails that hung down to her shoulders. Her dress was denim, with pink buttons down the front.

"How did this happen?" Clarissa asked, staring at the stockings.

"They fell off," the pint-sized cutie said. "I tried to put them back on, but I messed up."

"How did your stockings fall off? You'd have to take your shoes off first."

The girl looked down at her feet. "I took them off."

"You took your stockings off and got them on the floor?"

Danielle looked up at her mother. She was so adorable, you just wanted to squeeze her, no matter what she did wrong. "I don't like them," she finally admitted.

"I should make you wear 'em anyway," Clarissa said. She kneeled and took her daughter's shoes off so she could remove the offensive stockings. "You can't be taking off your clothes and letting them get on the floor. Especially in a *public restroom*! You have no idea who's been in here."

"I'm sorry," Danielle said.

"No you're not. You think money grows on trees."

The little girl had reason to believe such things. She never wanted for anything, and neither did her mother, as far as she could tell.

Clarissa got the stockings off and the shoes back on. She straightened her daughter's dress and stood again with her hands on her hips. Danielle looked up at her and smiled. "Can we get ice cream when we leave here?"

"The first thing you're getting is a new pair of stockings," Clarissa said. "After that, we'll see."

They exited the restroom hand-in-hand. The older fellows were still in the waiting room when they got out.

"I see you got her straightened out," the dark-skinned one remarked.

"Shut up messing with people!" his friend warned. "You don't know that lady, to be all up in her personal business!"

"You shut up!"

Clarissa smiled. "Yeah, I think we got it," she said. She took a seat in the same fiberglass chair. Danielle preferred to play with the gumball machines standing in the corner.

"That's your daughter?" the darker fellow asked.

Clarissa nodded.

"She sure is pretty," he said. "You still married to her daddy?"

"If she ain't, she don't want you," his friend said.

"Man, why don't you stay out my business?"

"Are y'all brothers?" Clarissa asked giggling.

"Hell naw he ain't my brother!" the light-skinned one said.

"I woulda strangled him in his sleep a long time ago," the other replied.

"That's my neighbor," the bald one clarified. "Been staying across from him for, *damn*, it's been thirty something years now, huh?"

"Yep," the other agreed. "Thirty years of *hell*!"

"Least my car runs," the other said to Clarissa. "I got to carry him up here at least twice a month to get his bucket fixed."

"We don't come up here no twice a month!"

Clarissa laughed. "No," she said to the flirty one, "Danielle's father died before she was born."

The little girl looked over at them when she heard her name, but the pretty toys in the machine quickly had her attention again. She already knew her father died in a car accident. There was nothing exciting about that.

"I'm sorry to hear that," the old man said and got quiet for a second.

"See what happens when you ask personal questions?" his friend said.

"Shut up."

Clarissa returned her gaze to the television. World Famous Heists and Robberies was about to conclude, and the host was as excited as ever.

"So if you see *any* of these people in your neighborhood, call the police immediately! They are considered *armed and dangerous*."

The screen went black, and then the pictures appeared again one by one, with Lance England narrating in the background.

"This one is the presumed ringleader," he said.

Clarissa studied the screen just as she did when she first saw this episode, and she still didn't think that drawing looked like Daniel: The face was too pudgy, the eyes were too close together, and they drew him with the baseball cap on rather than guess at what his bald head might look like.

"This guy's dangerous too," Lance said as Jesse's composite replaced Daniel's.

Clarissa thought they did a little better with the safecracker's sketch, but with the baseball cap on, they lost out on his luscious mane – which was always Jesse's best feature. Without the hair, you could find three Latinos on any baseball field who looked like that picture.

"And let's not forget this little guy," the host went on.

Clarissa had to laugh then, because this was her all-time favorite composite. Apparently the guard at the front gate thought she was a *boy*, and they drew the sketch accordingly. The result was a very young-looking kid with smooth features and oversized clothing. Clarissa had seen a few sketches of her in her lifetime, but this one was by far the most inaccurate.

"And last but not least, we've go this beautiful lady here," Lance said.

They showed the composite of the girl who supposedly stole the access card, but these days Clarissa Hunt felt no apprehension. If no one recognized her five years ago, she doubted if they'd get a breakthrough now.

"Alright," Lance said. "Now, take a look at them all together, because there's a good chance they're still working *side by side*."

The bastard filled the screen with all four drawings, and Clarissa did start to feel weird then. It was like the syndicate was together again. Daniel's drawing gave her no problems by itself, but now she could barely look at it.

The last time she saw her man, Clarissa was in a state of shock. But she fully understood what was going on. And though she knew Daniel was dead wrong – he referred to himself as *evil* as a matter of fact – Clarissa still didn't want it to go down like that.

≈≈≈≈≈≈≈

When she first left Overbrook Meadows, Clarissa prayed for a miracle. She heard the gunshots, but she never saw her man's body fall, so she dared to hope... But when Daniel didn't show up at their predetermined meeting spot after a few days, she knew he was dead. And she knew Jesse was the one who shot him.

That was a hard pill to swallow. But Clarissa also knew she had to move on. Especially after a pregnancy test revealed Daniel's child was on the way.

She rented a condo overlooking the beach and thought long and hard about what she wanted to do with her life and the diamonds. She figured she could sell them herself, but that meant going back to Texas. Either that, or establish new contacts in California. She would have preferred the latter, but the heist was front page news in all fifty states. The last thing she wanted was to confide in someone who might later backstab her for the reward, or even worse, kill her for the strongbox.

Daniel was always the one to handle things like this, and it was hard to accept that he would never be there for her again. Clarissa fell into a deep depression, and the oddest person came to her rescue. Flipping through the channels one evening, she saw Creflo Dollar giving a sermon on forgiveness and the importance of friends. Clarissa watched the whole program, and when it went off she knew exactly what she had to do.

If she had any hopes of becoming the new woman she needed to be for her daughter, then she would have to right the wrongs still lingering in her past. She knew she had to call Miles. Not only did some of that money rightfully belong to him, but he also had connections who could help move the diamonds. And although that meant reaching out to the very people who killed her soul mate, Clarissa swallowed her pride and forgave them for what they did.

It helped when she looked at things logistically: Those diamonds belonged to the whole gang, and Daniel was, without a doubt, trying to steal them. Even in the eyes of the law, you have the right to defend your property, with violence if necessary.

When she called him, Miles was very happy to hear from her, to say the least.

He apologized for what happened with Daniel first and foremost. He went on incessantly about how it was the heat of the moment, and they got scared and panicked. But that was the one thing Clarissa didn't want to talk about.

Miles apologized for shooting at her car also. He *swore* they were only aiming at the tires, so Clarissa didn't inform him of the two bullet holes she found in the driver's door. That would have only served to complicate things.

When Miles was done apologizing, Clarissa asked him about her brother. She cried like an infant as he told her about a twilight drive he and Jesse took to Alvarado with Daniel and Slim's bodies in the truck of an old school Cadillac. They buried them both in the same shallow grave. Miles said it was near a wheat field, and he could take her to see it if she wanted, but Clarissa had no interest in that. Not now at least.

When they were done discussing the dead, Clarissa and Miles talked money. Miles said he could still get rid of the diamonds if she wanted, and they agreed on a three-way split. Clarissa knew she was risking her life by giving Miles her address, but she was sure he wouldn't try to hurt her – Jesse wouldn't either.

The last two members of the syndicate arrived in San Bernardino on a Saturday morning. Things were tense for the first couple of days, but they eventually started to loosen up. And it turned out Daniel was right about Miles' inability to fence the goods effectively. They had fifty million dollars worth of diamonds, but he only managed to bring back half that much in cash.

No one complained though. They got more than eight million apiece. It didn't seem like enough, considering how many people died over those diamonds, but Clarissa knew she could never spend it all in her lifetime.

Miles taught her how to buy a dozen or so carwashes so she could launder the money slowly, and he gave her the low down on a few foreign banks in the Cayman Islands. Then he and Jesse booked it back to Texas, never to see her again.

≈ ≈ ≈ ≈ ≈ ≈

Clarissa went through another bout of depression and loneliness when they left, but a child was growing inside her, and she knew she had to move on with her life. She started taking GED classes so her baby wouldn't have a dropout for a mom, and Clarissa found that she actually enjoyed learning. With no gossip, cutting class, or bad boys to distract her, Clarissa discovered that not only could she do well in school, but she could excel if she gave it her all.

By the time Danielle was born, her mother was a freshman in community college. Clarissa was doing great, and she had plenty of money, so she transferred to Maric College at the start of her sophomore year. She made a lot of friends there, and her tale of being the daughter of a Texas oil tycoon never got second guessed.

It was hard being a first time mother, but Clarissa learned that if you simply loved your child more than anything else, all of the little things sort of fall into place. She raised Danielle to be different than her parents. Danielle would never steal or fight, and Clarissa would die before her little girl ever had to be with a man she didn't want to be with. Danielle was the most precious thing in the whole wide world.

And over time, Clarissa even started to date again; men with minds and ideas that didn't involve sticking up the local check cashing store. She was expected to graduate in the spring with a degree in finance. She planned to open one, maybe two restaurants that specialized in down south cooking. She never had dreams like that before, but Daniel was right about what it meant to have money in America: She could literally do anything she wanted to.

Clarissa used the clean money she laundered through her carwashes to buy a house. It was on a hill, and there were palm trees in the front and back yard. She had a pool, a spa, and a park-sized playground set up for Danielle. Clarissa hosted sleepovers for her daughter's pre-school friends, and she was known for the legendary buffalo wings she brought to the neighborhood block parties every summer.

The police never linked Percy's killing to the airport job, and Yolanda never blabbed to anyone about her suspicions. Once she found out she was inheriting their mother's house, Yolanda didn't care about anything her sister might have been involved in. She didn't seem to notice Slim went missing either.

On occasion, Clarissa still found herself daydreaming about Daniel. But time does heal wounds. Plus Dapper Dan lived on through his daughter. Already Danielle was starting to show some of his ornery characteristics.

≈ ≈ ≈ ≈ ≈ ≈ ≈

"HUNT! YOUR VEHICLE IS READY."
Clarissa looked up with a start. She got up and grabbed her daughter's hand on the way out of the waiting room.

"You take it easy!" one of the guys called after her.

She turned and smiled at him. "Alright. You too, mister."

"It's okay if you wanna leave me your number," he said, but the door was already closing on them.

"Shut up, you old fool!" his friend chided.

293

When Clarissa got to the lobby, one of the mechanics was waiting on her. He was tall, light-skinned, and handsome. He wore the same work uniform as everyone else, but he had his shirt tucked in (which brought attention to his butt), and his sleeves rolled up (to show off his nice biceps). Clarissa smiled pleasantly as he recapped her services.

"Your oil was one quart low," he said. "I checked all of your other fluids, changed your wipers. And we got you four new tires." He smiled. Had a nice smile, good teeth and pink lips. "I already brought your car around for you."

Clarissa looked out of the front window, and there was her silver Escalade, sitting pretty with blue skies and rolling hills in the background. She loved driving that thing. There was never any place she absolutely *had* to be, but she loved driving just the same. California was the best place for cruising aimlessly.

She paid her bill with a credit card and thanked the hunky mechanic.

He held out her keys but didn't let go when she reached for them.

"Hey," he said. "You think a woman like you would ever go out with a guy like me?"

Danielle rolled her eyes.

Clarissa smiled. "What kind of guy *are* you?" she asked.

"I'm a hard worker," he said. "I been to jail before – I might as well tell you that right now. I got two kids. I play ball. I try not to get into too much trouble."

"You *try*?"

He grinned. "Yeah. *I try*. So, what's up? Can I get your number, or you don't get involved with people like me? You look like you only date goody-goodies."

Clarissa had to laugh at that. "Actually," she said with a grin. "I've gone out with a couple of bad boys in my lifetime..."

THE END

BY KEITH THOMAS WALKER

ABOUT THE AUTHOR

Keith Thomas Walker, known as the Master of Romantic Suspense and Urban Fiction, is the author of a dozen novels, including *Fixin' Tyrone*, *Dripping Chocolate* and *The Realest Ever*. Keith enjoys reading, poetry and music of all genres. Originally from Fort Worth, Keith is a graduate of Texas Wesleyan University. Visit him at www.keithwalkerbooks.com.